EXTRAORDINARY ACCLAIM
FOR CAMERON JUDD

"An impressive performance . . . a classically simple, fast-paced tale . . . Marks Judd as a keen observer of the human heart as well as a fine action writer."
—*Publishers Weekly* on *Timber Creek*

"Abundance of historical detail . . . a heartfelt attempt to glimpse the soul of an American hero. By any standard, Judd succeeds."
—*Booklist* on *Crockett of Tennessee*

"Gripping and entertaining."
—*Virginia Tennessean* on *The Overmountain Men*

"Judd writes a mean story."
—*Zane Grey's West*

"Truly interesting Western writing . . . Judd does his usual, exquisite job of character development . . . This book will restore your faith in Westerns."
—*El Paso Herald Post* on *Jerusalem Camp*

THE GLORY RIVER

THE UNDERHILL SERIES

CAMERON JUDD

St. Martin's Paperbacks

THE GLORY RIVER

Copyright © 1998 by Cameron Judd.

All rights reserved. No part of this book may be used or reproduced in any manner whatsoever without written permission except in the case of brief quotations embodied in critical articles or reviews. For information address St. Martin's Press, 175 Fifth Avenue, New York, N.Y. 10010.

ISBN: 0-312-96499-4

Printed in the United States of America

St. Martin's Paperbacks edition/April 1998

10 9 8 7 6 5 4 3 2 1

To Richard Curtis

PROLOGUE

*Kentucky, just south of the Ohio River, near the
close of the 18th century*

A heavy storm, this one. Lightning flashed to the north, over
the river. Clouds whipped and churned like restless souls.
Thunder masked the sound of the young frontiersman's pick
digging into ash-blackened dirt that had once been a cabin
floor. Nothing remained of the structure now but crumbled
logs charred into skeletal black things. It was a dead place,
dark and empty.

There are ghosts here, the man who had guided him had
said. *No one goes to that place since it happened . . . No one
dares to disturb them.*

If ghosts there were, the frontiersman ignored them just as
he ignored the storm. His lean form bent to its labor, his dripping face concentrating on the muddy ground beneath him. He
picked away burned soil, then scooped it off to the side with
a small wooden shovel. Water gathered around his feet, making him work faster.

The pick came back into service, tearing up ground that had
been below the reach of the fire. He was closer now. The storm
abated momentarily, the clouds thinner, a bit of golden western
light from the setting sun providing a haze of illumination in
the overall gloom.

The pick descended one more time, turned dirt, and this
time something else besides. The frontiersman paused and
stared at what he'd uncovered.

Throwing aside the pick, he dropped to his knees with the
wooden shovel and began scraping away sodden dirt, uncovering more and more. His breath came faster; he worked hard-

er. The shovel, not made for this use, finally cracked and broke. He threw it aside and continued working with his bare hands, scooping mud and water away . . .

Until he stopped, and stared silently, a long time, the thunder grumbling off in the west. He reached down, touched what he'd found.

Slowly he rose. He stood in the hole, which was gradually filling with water, his shoulders slumped, tears beginning to mix with the rain on his face.

A shrill cry from the forest nearby made him turn. He heard the sound of fast-moving hooves on wet ground. A rider burst from the edge of the woods and angled across the ragged clearing, face white and drawn in fear. The horse nickered, frightened by something, bucked and threw the rider to the ground. He came to his feet, covered now in mud, and turned a ghastly expression upon the frontiersman.

"Something comes . . . hurry, hurry! You must go from here! Something comes . . ." Without bothering to remount, he ran on past, entering the woods on the opposite side and vanishing.

The frontiersman did not run. He climbed slowly out of the hole, the spirit gone from him now, as from the forest a new sound came. He stood and watched, waiting. The rain hammered down harder all at once, and a fresh bolt of lightning seared across the sky, bathing the clearing with light just as the barren brush moved, and the frontiersman saw what had frightened the running man, emerging now from the forest, and coming his way.

PART I

SON OF THE WILDERNESS

CHAPTER ONE

Forty miles from the French Lick of the Cumberland River;
Spring 1781

Jean-Yves Freneau lay flat on his belly with his Pennsylvania-made flintlock rifle at his side, inspecting the cabin at the base of the ridge and wondering how long it had been since that baying, half-crazed hound tied in front of it had eaten.

Freneau was wary in any circumstance, but this lonely, isolated cabin in a substantially unsettled wilderness made him more cautious than usual. Something was amiss here. He could feel it in the atmosphere, hear it in the mad bark of the hound, sense it from the way the beast lunged and pulled against the rope around its neck.

Another thing intrigued him: Just what was that odd something barely visible inside the cabin's open door? Freneau strained his eyes—and strong eyes they were—but couldn't quite tell, though he had a notion. If the wind would only shift a bit, maybe his nose could inform him of what his eyes could not.

He hadn't known a cabin stood in this spot, and certainly not one several years old, as this one appeared to be. This was no Indian dwelling. The tiny log-walled habitation and its surrounding outbuildings bore the marks of white man's work. But what white man? Substantial settlement of this area had begun only months ago. But Freneau remembered stories, ones he'd only half-believed, that a handful of Carolina Tories had fled into this wilderness around the time of the war's outbreak a few years back, making an attempt at a settlement somewhere in the vicinity. As he had heard it, those Tories had been driven out soon by the Indians. Maybe one hadn't been driven out. Maybe this cabin had belonged to him.

Freneau would have already slipped down to the cabin if not for that madly barking dog. The beast was frantic, yanking on its tie so hard it had worn a raw, bright crimson circle around its neck, hair and even flesh rubbed away. Yet still it barked and struggled, torturing itself in its fervor to break free. Freneau didn't fear the dog; what concerned him was the fact that it was tied, indicating a fairly recent human presence here, possibly a continuing one.

Or perhaps not. The dog looked to be nearly starved. No one had fed it for a long time. And it seemed to Freneau that it was desperately trying to get into the cabin, maybe to reach that hard-to-see something barely visible inside its shadowed doorway. Something edible, maybe?

Freneau had watched the place for the better part of an hour, and was reasonably certain that no one was in the cabin at the moment. No one living, at least. But still he was slow to move. Only a fool took at face value what he saw in the wilderness. Freneau had run across the bones of several such fools in the decade or more since he and his brother, Michel, had first come to this wilderness in the company of Jacques-Timothe De Montbrun.

Eventually, Freneau put his hand around his rifle stock and rose slowly, looking about through gray eyes shaded by a reddish flop hat. His clothing made him seem to blend into the very landscape around him. His dark deerskin rifleman's coat, fringed and sashed about his waist and hanging to his thighs, covered a pale, well-worn linsey-woolsey hunting shirt made in much the same pattern as the coat. Thrust into the broad sash belt were a sheathed long knife, a much shorter patch knife, and a belt ax; hanging over his shoulder were a plain deerskin pouch filled with parched corn and jerked meat, an ornamented bullet pouch, and over that, his priming and powder horns, the latter shaved fingernail-thin so that the very powder grains inside showed through the tough and translucent membrane when the light struck just right.

A soft rain had dampened the forest that morning, and his moccasins, tall and strongly made, with flaps tied leggin-style around his calves and over the legs of his woolen French-fly trousers, merely whispered over the sodden leaves as he began his descent toward the cabin. The dog, seeing him, ceased its barking, then began again, more frantic and fierce than before. Freneau's eyes shifted subtly as he moved, and his nostrils, trained to a nearly animal sensitivity by years as a woodsman, sniffed the air carefully. Though he thought himself a rationalist and did not wish to admit that anything superstitious could touch his mind, the truth was that something about this spot and this cabin made him want to turn away and flee, as if he had stumbled upon some devil's den. Too much time among the superstitious natives, he figured.

He caught something, a whiff on the breeze, undeniable and instantly identifiable. Pausing halfway down the slope, he looked again through the cabin door. Eyes narrowing, he studied what had been impossible to fully make out from higher up, and smell and sight together confirmed to him what he had expected.

The dog barked wildly, pulling vainly on its rope. Frantic with hunger, mad from confinement while a source of food lay barely out of reach, just inside the cabin.

Freneau dug beneath his rifleman's coat and pulled out a folded kerchief, which he shook loose and tied around his face, covering nose and mouth. It didn't help much. The death-stench he had caught carried right through the fabric.

Advancing, he circled away from the big-boned but emaciated dog, which snarled and pulled and tried hard to reach him, and edged along the cabin front toward the door. The cabin had no windows and was well-chinked; he could not examine any of the interior before entering.

The space allowed him between snapping beast and open door was small indeed, and the dog grew particularly berserk as Freneau backed inside, keeping his face toward the just-out-of-reach animal. Once inside, he turned and looked upon what was there.

Freneau jerked the kerchief from his face, turned back to the door, leaned out, and was instantly sick.

* * *

Freneau's first thought was one of gratitude that no companion had been around to observe what he had just done. He'd seen many a gruesome sight in his time, and had always been proud that he'd never heaved his belly empty at the mere sight of gore. He could no longer make that claim.

Really, though, it was shock, more than gore, that caused the reaction. He'd already known he'd find a dead man inside—it was, as he had thought, a man's legs and bare feet that he'd seen through the doorway from up on the ridge—but for some reason the possibility of encountering a second corpse farther inside the cabin hadn't crossed his mind.

So he'd been thoroughly appalled when he saw her: A dead woman flat on her back, eyes open but with the orbs shriveled away, forehead destroyed, evidently by a rifle ball that had entered the back of her head and blown the contents of her skull down her face. Her wounds were badly infested with flies and maggots. The woman was, overall, the most repellent bit of formerly human flesh that Freneau had ever run across. The stench alone was almost more than he could bear.

Along with repulsion, he felt pity for her, and anger at the one who had done this to her. The details of the scene itself, the posture of the bodies, the location of the rifle, all told the story: This woman had been shot to death by the man now lying in the doorway, shot through the back of her head with the same rifle that lay at his side. After he'd killed her, he'd reloaded, stepped to the doorway, closed his mouth over the end of the muzzle, and blasted away his own life with the hooking of a toe against a trigger.

Freneau didn't much care that the man had decided to end his existence. A man's life was his own, to do with as he would. But to kill a woman, to shoot her from behind—this infuriated the Frenchman. A man did not do such a thing. Had this woman been given the same choice of life or death that the man in the doorway reserved for himself? Freneau doubted it.

He abruptly spat upon the man's corpse, and cursed at him. The dog outside barked violently.

Another sound, barely heard beneath the dog's clamor,

made Freneau freeze in place and hold his breath for several moments.

Stepping across the woman's corpse, he found a square wooden box in the corner, hewed out and pieced together with obvious care. Freneau looked inside and experienced a second shock.

Slowly he reached into the box and pulled the child he found up in his arms. The little one was weak, listless, limp like a bundled rag, foul with wastes. A girl. Freneau pulled the pitiful creature close, cradling her.

Merciful Father, he thought, how could a man be so cruel as to do what was done here? How could a man kill his woman, then himself, and leave a child to die slowly and alone? He turned and glared at the man's corpse. His first thought was: *If a hell there is, murderer, then you are surely there, and there you deserve to be!*

His second thought was to get the girl out of this poisoned atmosphere at once, into the open air and healing light.

Freneau tucked her weak body close to his and was about to step toward the door when a bundle of rags in the farthest corner of the cabin moved abruptly. He sucked in his breath as the rags reared up and fell away, revealing a nearly naked boy, thin and crusted in dirt, who had apparently been sleeping beneath the rags. He was perhaps five years old, hollow-eyed, unshorn, pale. But his eyes met those of Freneau and did not falter, and something in them flashed and snapped, lightning-like, as he lunged forward with a surprisingly loud yell, a broken knife in his hand aimed directly at Freneau's leg.

Freneau howled, dodged, and missed a cutting. The unsteady boy was knocked over by his own motion. But he did not lose the knife. Yelling again, noise without words, he swished the broken, rusty blade at Freneau and made him dance back, almost stepping onto the corpse of the dead woman.

"*Dieu!*" Freneau exclaimed, balancing the baby, which now began to cry feebly. He edged away from the miniature madman, eyes flicking back and forth between the boy's face and the broken knife. Reflexively speaking in his native

French, Freneau demanded that the boy leave him alone. The boy instead came after him, jabbing with the knife, beginning to cry now.

English! Freneau thought. *Speak English to this wild child!*

"Stop this, please!" he demanded. "I'm not here to hurt you—I want to help."

The boy reacted now, understanding. "My sister," he said, pointing at the baby. "My sister . . ."

Freneau looked down at the child he held. "Ah, yes. I see. I see. She is weak, and sick."

"My sister . . . don't hurt her," the boy pleaded. His voice was thin, reedy.

"I want to save her, not hurt her. She is nearly starved." Freneau looked up and down the boy's slight frame. "And you. You are hungry?"

"If you hurt her, I'll kill you!"

"I believe you would, young warrior. But I'll give you no reason. Come with me to the outside. I have meat you can eat."

"Meat . . ."

"*Oui*, yes. Dried meat, but good and hearty. Venison."

The boy lowered the knife. He was trembling all at once. "Venison . . ."

"Yes. Come, young warrior. You look hungry. Come outside with me and—"

Freneau cut off as the boy gave a shudder and collapsed in a heap. He fell beside the body of the woman who was surely his mother, his breath making a loud, hissing sound as he passed out. The rusted knife remained in his hand. Freneau smiled sadly. "Ah, what a little warrior! Nearly starved, and yet you go to the last of your strength to protect your sister. And even now you cling to your knife!"

Wrinkling his nose against the stench that filled the cabin, Freneau went to the unconscious boy, reached down, and swept him up under his arm. The knife fell from thin fingers to the dirt floor.

With an infant balanced on one arm and the boy dangling

under the other, Freneau left the cabin, stepped widely around to avoid the dog, and went on to the hillside.

He laid the boy down gently and turned his attention to the tiny girl. She seemed agonizingly small. Her eyes blinked repeatedly, sensitive to light. Her flesh was translucent—a wax creature, come to life—her body brittle in his big hands. Yet her face was perfectly formed, destined to be beautiful, if only she lived to grow. He saw only one flaw, that being a dark brown birthmark, like an oversized mole, on the lower left side of her neck.

The boy moved on the cool woodland floor, rustling the wintered leaves of a summer long past. But he did not open his eyes.

Freneau stripped away the baby's soiled rags. Afterward he simply sat, staring at the girl in his arms, wondering what he could do. This child was nearly starved. Freneau struggled to think rationally. Freneau rarely encountered problems that seemed to have no solution, but this time, perhaps he had.

He had to try . . . something. Anything. Improvising as he went along, Freneau made a bed of soft leaves and placed the naked baby on it, heaping other leaves over the lower portion of the body. Nearby, the boy moaned and moved again. Freneau ignored him. From his pouch he dug jerked venison. He selected a narrow, long strip and chewed the end of it until it was soft and pulpy. Picking up the baby, he held the sodden meat to the little mouth.

"Eat, child!" he whispered in French. "Come, now—eat!"

The baby recoiled at the first touch of the meat against her mouth, then thrust a dried tongue over her lips. They parted. Freneau put the chewed tip of the jerky between them.

The tiny girl sucked at the pulpy venison, tentatively, then vigorously.

Over on the leafy ground, the boy opened his eyes. He sat up slowly, looking around, focusing on Freneau and his sister. Weakly, he stood, and hobbled over on spindly legs.

Freneau looked up at him. "She is eating. She'll grow stronger now, I think." He smiled gently at the boy.

The boy smiled back, uncertainly. But still a smile.

"There is meat there for you, too," Freneau said, nodding down at his pouch. "Eat some of it. Slowly, slowly, until you are accustomed to it."

The boy, hungry as he was, did not immediately accept the invitation. He stared at his tiny sister. "Will she live?"

"I think she will," Freneau said. Pausing, he added, "If there is anything I can do . . . *we* can do about it, she will."

The boy nodded. Bending, he took up a piece of jerky and began to eat, never taking his eyes off his sister.

"What is her name?" Freneau asked.

"Marie," said the boy.

"And yours?"

"Bushrod."

"Bushrod. I once knew a man named Bushrod. A fine Englishman, he was. Was your father an Englishman?"

The boy did not answer, maybe not understanding the question.

"The man and woman in the cabin . . . they were your parents?"

"Yes."

"My last name is Freneau. A French name. What is your last name?"

"Underhill," the boy said, and took another bite of jerky.

CHAPTER
TWO

Freneau spent the night holding the tiny girl, chewing jerked meat until its juices were restored, letting the baby draw them out. The boy, though cold and tired, refused to wander more than a few feet away from his sister. Eventually he lay down on the ground and slept. The dog, meanwhile, ceased barking sometime after dark. Freneau wondered if it had died.

He sang to the little girl, who soon slept. When morning came she awakened and cried, hungry, like before, but now strong enough to make it known. Freneau nodded, relieved.

"You are strong, little one. You will live."

The boy awakened, silent, and sat in the same heap of leaves in which he'd slept. Freneau's supply of jerky was growing scant, but he gave the boy more of it, and from another pouch, a handful of parched corn.

"Don't eat much of the corn," he instructed. "It swells in the belly. Now, watch your sister for me a moment."

He left the child on its bed of leaves, picked up his rifle, and started to walk down to the cabin again. The dog snarled and barked, but less energetically than the day before. Freneau paused, thinking, then turned to the boy.

"Do you love the dog?"

Bushrod Underhill shook his head. "No. He bit me twice."

Freneau nodded, and proceeded down the slope, where he faced the snarling dog.

"You have suffered here, my friend," Freneau said, speaking French, though he could have addressed the animal in any of several languages. "I pity you, *chien de meute*—mad with hunger and thirst.'' He looked around and found a hollowed section of log that apparently had been used to water the dog in the past, but now was dry. He took it to a nearby brook, filled it, and brought it back to the dog. Setting it down, he scooted it with his foot into range of the dog. It drank for a long time, drank the container dry.

"You feel better now, I hope? Still hungry, I know, and there is a part of me that would gladly let you feast on the *meurtrier* in the cabin, but I have other use for you. Far more important. A noble sacrifice for you to make." He raised the rifle and shot the dog between its eyes. Glancing up the hillside, he gauged the boy's reaction, but saw nothing change in the impassive young face.

There was little meat on the dog's bones, but what there was, when stewed, rendered a brownish broth that the boy accepted with ease. But Freneau, eager to strengthen tiny Marie, overfed her, and the meal was lost. Waiting a while, Freneau tried again, more carefully. This time the broth stayed down.

Freneau and Bushrod dined on jerky and parched corn, plus a few stringy pieces of dog. Letting his stomach settle, Freneau dug flint and punk from his bag, left the children on the hill again, and went back to the cabin.

Later, with Bushrod at his side, he sat on the ridge with the baby in his arms, letting her suck water from a piece of patchcloth as he watched flames devour the cabin and its corpses. When the structure was substantially gone, he looked down at Bushrod. "It's a good thing, maybe, that they are gone?"

"Yes. I think it is."

"They were hard people? Cruel to you?"

"My father was cruel. My mother was soft. She was a good mother."

"I'm glad you had a good mother, Bushrod. Your sister here, she is still small enough to need a mother, too. One who can give her milk, not just broth and the juice of chewed venison."

"But my mother is gone."

"Then we must find her another, eh? But I fear you aren't strong enough for a journey, Bushrod."

"I am strong enough. If it will help Marie, I'm strong enough."

Freneau looked into the determined, thin face, and nodded. "I believe you are. So come, Bushrod. Let's be on our way."

Renfroe Settlement, the Red River

She was drowsy; nursing her child always seemed to make her so, particularly now that the cabin was complete. Its chinked poplar walls were thick and strong and made her feel safe, relaxed. Her daughter slept in her arms, content with a belly full of warm milk. The woman sang to her and gently stroked her downy hair.

In the distance she heard the steady chop of her husband's ax. A reassuring noise, telling her that he was free from harm. She lived in fear of Indians, but her husband assured her that there was no real threat. The settlement was not near any established Indian towns. The wilderness was vast. Game was abundant, plenty for any Indians who hunted here, and for the whites as well. No reason to worry.

She rose and placed the baby in its crib, then sat down again, wiping her breast clean with a scrap of cloth and putting her linen chemise and bodice back into place. She closed her eyes and relaxed. A few moments of sleep would not hurt. There was much to do in a new settlement, and idleness was of the devil, but the days when even such a brief respite was possible would soon be gone. Her daughter would grow and become more demanding. There would be other children, other labors. For now she would rest and listen to the distant music of her husband's busy ax.

When she opened her eyes next, she gazed first in numb disbelief at what she saw before her, then in panic-stricken fear. She came up from the chair and lunged for the corner and the rifle that stood there—but it was gone. The man who had just intruded her house had moved it. She turned and faced him, eyes wild, and saw that he had a baby in his arms. He had taken her daughter! But no. Another glance revealed that her own child still slept in her crib.

"Ma'am, I beg your pardon for this intrusion," he said. His voice was odd, accented. French, she thought. He spoke his English quite well. "I have not come to hurt you, but to ask your help."

"My husband will shoot you when he finds you here!"

"If your husband is the man with the ax, he is still far away. And he would have no cause to shoot me. I've come only to help this tiny little girl." He held out the thin and sickly looking child. "Please . . . I have come here to ask if you would give this poor little one milk. If she has milk, she will grow strong much faster. Maybe she will live . . . if she has milk."

"Who are you?"

"My name is Jean-Yves Freneau. I have been in this wilderness for many years. I am a *coureur des bois*, a woods runner."

"The child is yours?"

"I found her in a cabin. Her parents are dead, and she was nearly so. I've given her broth, enough nourishment to keep her alive, but a woman's milk would strengthen her like nothing I can provide. And so I came to this settlement, to find someone like you."

She gazed at the emaciated baby, then cut her eyes to where he had moved her rifle—the opposite corner. She would have to go past him to reach it, something she did not dare try. She felt helpless and violated. He had entered her home while she slept! And he had obviously watched long enough to know that she had a nursing child, and that her husband was far away. Suddenly the thick cabin walls didn't seem so protective after all.

She feared the stranger, but also pitied the sad-looking child he held. She had lost a baby of her own a year before, one who looked much like this little girl.

She held out her arms. "I will feed her."

Freneau stood near the door, back circumspectly turned, while she gave her milk to the baby. "What is her name?"

"Her parents were named Underhill. I found them dead. Her Christian name is Marie."

"How can you know her name, if her parents are dead?"

Freneau smiled. A clever woman, this one. "Her brother told me."

"Brother?"

"Quite a little man. Ready to fight me tooth and nail until he knew I was a friend, though he was nearly starved. A brave fellow . . . but not brave enough to come in here with me. He's outside, in the woods, waiting."

"How old?"

"Maybe five, six. It's hard to tell. These children have been without enough to eat for a long time."

"How did their parents die?"

"The father shot his mother, then shot himself. And left the children to starve."

"Mercy!"

"It was a wicked thing, the act of a *monstre*, a beast. But the boy was braver than the parents. He stayed by his sister, protecting her. He is hungry and fragile, but I think that he is strong, too. Do you understand what I mean?"

"Yes. I think I do. Will he come in? I can offer him food."

"If I could take food to him, better food than the jerky and parched corn I carry, I would be grateful indeed."

As a minute passed and the silence between herself and this stranger grew uncomfortable, she asked, "What is a woods runner?"

"A *coureur des bois* roams the wilderness. He traps, hunts, deals with the Indians, and lives among them."

She recoiled. "You live with Indians?"

"I do."

"But . . . not near? There are no Indian towns near here. My husband told me."

"Not near. But this is Indian land, as much as if many towns were here. Hunting ground. The presence of white men here will be resented. There will be bad times for you all, if you stay."

"But there was an agreement. A sale of the land. We have the right to be here."

Freneau shrugged. "What are sales? What are agreements? They hold no force for those who don't make them. And what are rights to those who don't recognize the law that gives the rights?"

The woman did not desire to continue this line of conversation, which threatened to distress her. She looked down at the nursing girl and asked, "What will you do with this child?"

"I will take her to my home. Raise her as my own."

"You would raise her among heathens—among Indians?"

"Yes."

"Why must a white man live among Indians?"

"I live among them not because I must, but because I choose to do so. I am happy to do so."

"You say you are French, but you speak English."

"Can a man speak only one language? I speak French and English. And German. And Latin. And the Cherokee language as well." He shrugged again. "And a few other Indian tongues, though not so well as Cherokee."

"How did you learn so many languages?"

"The Indian languages I learned by living among the Indians. The other languages I learned in university. Paris."

"But a man like you are . . . living among Indians, away from your own kind . . . I don't understand. Why?"

"You ask many questions."

"I'm sorry."

"I am what I am, and where I am, because I choose it. I can give you no better answer than that."

The distant chopping was still going on when little Marie Underhill finally ceased her nursing. When the woman had covered herself, Freneau turned and took the child from her.

"I will keep her, sir, if you will let me have her. I'll raise her as my own daughter."

He actually considered it a moment, but shook his head. "No. I will keep her."

"But she needs a mother."

"And she will have one. A fine mother indeed."

"You have a wife?"

"Yes."

"An Indian?"

"Yes. Her name is Waninahi."

"But this child is not an Indian. She should be among her own kind."

"Maybe this child will have more than one kind among whom she will live, eh? Maybe all the people of this land will be this girl's people, and her brother's people."

"I wish you would leave her with me, sir."

"No. She would not be safe here. Nor are you safe. There will be trouble for all of you here. This is not your land."

"It *is*, sir. There was an agreement, and a sale. And the Indian towns are far away."

He smiled lightly and touched the brim of his red-hued hat. "Perhaps you are right, madam. And whatever may be, may God keep you in His hand for the kindness you have done today to a poor and weak child."

"It was only my duty, sir. And my privilege."

She gave him bread, meat, and dried vegetables. He thanked her, smiled at her with his thin lips, turned and was gone, loping across the meadow to the woods with the child in his arms. She had wanted to ask him if he believed the little girl could survive without further nourishment during the time it would take him to reach the Indian towns—they were, after all, quite far away, she again reminded herself—but he was too swift and there was no time. She watched him go out of sight, caught a glimpse of the small-framed boy who in the woods awaited him and the baby girl. They vanished together.

She listened again for the reassuring sound of her husband's ax. Hearing it, she whispered a prayer of thanks.

The *coureur des bois* was surely wrong. All was well. This was their rightful land. They would find no trouble here.

Even so, she closed and barred the door, and pulled her chair closer to her daughter's crib. She sat silently for a long time watching her child very closely, as if at any moment she might vanish from sight.

CHAPTER THREE

Just outside Coldwater, near the Muscle Shoals of the Tennessee River, Spring 1787

"Move carefully and slowly, Skiuga," the gray-haired Cherokee, speaking in his native tongue, said to the boy at his side. "Many a man has been laughed at for falling into a stream like a clumsy bear, simply because he didn't take the time to be careful on rocks that are slick and wet."

"I've never fallen into the water, Tuckaseh," the young one bragged. "And see those rocks across the water? I've run over them many times, from one bank to the other, and never even wet my feet."

The man looked in the direction the boy pointed, and nodded, but the boy was unsure whether Tuckaseh really saw the rocks he had indicated. The aging man's eyes were growing glassy with the years, clouding over, and vision that had once been keen was now fast dimming into a kind of perpetual twilight. Yet Tuckaseh was so confident in his movements, so adept at the skills of life in the forest and on the river, that the boy often forgot the man's creeping blindness until such moments as this.

"If you've run those rocks, then you are certainly fortunate, just as you are certainly headed for a broken bone or two, and laughter from your friends. Now, go down to the bank, Skiuga, and see how we have done for fish."

The boy's light, thin frame danced lithely down to the riverside. He knelt and reached into the water, pulling up a kind of loosely woven reed basket held beneath the surface by the weight of rocks. The cleverly designed contraption, made by Tuckaseh, was enclosed and rounded at one end, open at the other. But the reeds at the opening were not cut off and bound down as on a normal basket; instead they were left long, sharpened, and curved back into the interior of the basket, which was in fact a fish trap. Fish could easily swim into the basket through the mouth, but once inside, could not easily find their way out again past the sharp reeds they found pointing at them and trapping them inside.

"Eight fish!" the boy called up to the man. "Eight fat ones!"

Tuckaseh smiled and nodded. "Very good. A good trap we've made there."

The boy, bearing the trap with the fish flopping inside it, returned to his companion. "We didn't make it. *You* made it."

"That is true. So you'll make the next one. And why not do it now? You should be well prepared for it. You watched me closely as I put this one together?"

"I did." Just now the boy was wishing he'd watched a little more closely than he had. Tuckaseh's deft fingers moved fast when he made his baskets and traps, skills that he'd practiced increasingly since his vision began to fade some years ago. It was hard even to trace, much less recall, the movements of those swift fingers when Tuckaseh was working at full speed.

Tuckaseh, it was said by some, had never been a great warrior. He'd been a peace chief in earlier days, never a war chief. He'd fought many battles, nonetheless, and had done many a brave act and earned war titles, but he'd never seemed to glory much in them. It was in more peaceful and gentle pursuits that Tuckaseh revealed his true and deeper self, the version of the man that young Bushrod Underhill—whom Tuckaseh and most of the Indians of Coldwater called Skiuga, or "ground squirrel"—had come to cherish and admire.

"I don't see why I should make another fish trap when this one is still in good condition," Bushrod said. "Besides," he added, bluffing, "making fish traps is easy. I can do it when need be without taking time out for it now."

"When I was your age," Tuckaseh said, "my mother's brother told me it was time I learned to chip arrow flints. I watched him do it many times, thought it looked easy. But when I sat down to try, I could do nothing right. So he made me do it again and again and again until at last I could do more than break worthless pieces of flint into smaller worthless pieces of flint.''

Bushrod nodded, knowing that an afternoon of fish trap manufacturing lay in his immediate future.

But a shout from the edge of the nearby village changed that. ''Bushrod! Bush!''

It was Freneau, yelling for him. Bush glanced at the sun and realized he was late again for Freneau's daily schooling, which he usually called, rather formally, *L'Instruction*. Bush learned much from Freneau's tutoring, but the time was always much more like work and less like pleasure than the time he spent with Tuckaseh.

One good thing, though: Freneau never scolded him for his lateness when Tuckaseh was responsible for it. Freneau admired Tuckaseh, spoke often of the man's insight, his *sagesse*, and considered the time Bush spent with him almost as much a part of Bush's *instruction* as his own daily contribution.

''I must go,'' Bush said to Tuckaseh, glad for once to be called away. He was in no humor to make fish traps this afternoon.

''Go,'' Tuckaseh said. ''I'll see to these fish, and when you are done with your white-man's learning, you may replace the trap.''

Bush darted away toward the town. It was a beautiful day, one best spent out of doors, and for a moment he considered asking his adoptive father and tutor if they might take their lessons outside. But he wouldn't. He'd asked before, and Freneau's answer was always the same: A young man learns best when there are no distractions about him. And they would stay indoors.

Bush liked Tuckaseh's way of teaching better. Instead of hiding from ''distractions,'' Tuckaseh used them as the tools and even the objects of his teaching. The woods, the streams, the rivers, the barren mountaintop knobs—these were Tuckaseh's classroom. And what he taught seemed to Bush to have far more value than the English and French and mathematics and history that Freneau forced upon him. Certainly it was much more fun.

But Freneau's schooling, useless as it seemed to Bush, was not optional. The Frenchman had immersed Bush in his academics virtually from the moment he'd found Bush and his sister six years before. There was no sign yet that *L'Instruction* was anywhere close to ending.

Except for the tiny, dark-haired, white-skinned girl riding his shoulders, the singing man looked like any of the Cherokee or Creek warriors who populated this town. He wore moccasins, leather leggins reaching halfway up his thighs, a breechclout that covered his buttocks and groin but left the sides of his hips exposed. A long linen shirt covered what the breechclout did not, and a woolen, silver-trimmed headband held long dark hair back and away from his clean-shaven face. Only his relatively light skin and the boisterous French drinking song he belted out in an off-key voice identified him as a Frenchman rather than an Indian. This was Michel Freneau, brother of Jean-Yves and a long-time trader among the Indians of the region, and at the moment he was hungry and heading for food, carrying with him the petite Marie Underhill, now about six years old.

His spirits were high—the usual state for Michel Freneau. Unlike his older brother, who had been a serious scholar in younger days and tended to be somber about most of life, Michel had never taken much anything seriously, and was certainly no scholar. His impression of scholars had been shaped by his observances of Jean-Yves and his academic peers in a life long past for both of them: Scholars were a breed of men who didn't laugh as readily as a man should. Michel Freneau would have none of that. He loved laughter far too much. Just as he loved little Marie, who in his mind was his niece.

Michel greeted those he passed in the village, drawing smiles and kind words from the women, who idolized him, and notably less enthusiastic responses from the men. But if the warriors and fighting men of Coldwater didn't consider Michel Freneau a friend, all did trust him. He had been a trader among them for many years and had never cheated anyone, nor betrayed the interests of any Indian to a white man. Michel Freneau, Frenchman, was several cuts above the dishonest English traders many of the Cherokees of Coldwater had been forced to endure back in the Overhill towns farther east.

Finishing his song with a loud crescendo warbling with clumsy vibrato, and giving Marie a shake that made her laugh and dig her fingers into his thick hair, Michel let his nose lead him off the main pathway through Coldwater and ducked into the open door of a particular cabin.

"Ah, Jean!" he said in French, blinking in the darker interior and deftly setting Marie to her feet on the floor. "What is this delicious food I've been smelling all the way across town?" Not awaiting an answer, he made for the fire, where a turkey roasted on a spit, sizzling and sending out a wonderful odor. Michel turned the bird until he found a portion that was substantially cooked, and began picking off strips of hot, roasted meat, cramming them into his mouth at great risk of a burned tongue.

Jean-Yves, seated cross-legged on the dirt floor beside Bushrod, lifted his eyes from the homemade slate he held, and looked at his brother with mild displeasure. "Please," he said in French, with heavy sarcasm, "feel free to help yourself to our supper, Michel."

"Ah, thank you, Jean. You are indeed kind." He put another hunk of turkey into his mouth, wincing at the heat.

Jean-Yves glanced woefully at the boy at his side. "Intemperate," he said in English. "Always intemperate. It will be the death of him someday."

"I don't know what it means, 'intemperate,' " the boy said, also in English, concentrating on every word. He spoke French and Cherokee with ease, but English, though the language of his earliest days, had begun to slip away from him after he came to Coldwater. So Jean-Yves, ever the scholar and teacher, had taken on the task some months ago of bringing Bushrod back to his original language.

"It means, Bushrod, that my brother doesn't know how to

control his own passions. He eats too much, drinks too much, romances too much—''

Michel, who spoke English even more haltingly than little Bushrod, frowned as he tried to interpret what his brother was saying about him. "No, no, Bushrod," he said in French. "It means that unlike dear Jean, I believe life is not a mystery, not a challenge, not a thing to be taken apart and studied like some pretty toy. No, life is an *adventure*! If there is food, eat it! If there is liquor, drink it deep! If there are women . . . well, someday, when you're not so young, then we'll talk about that, eh?"

"You are interrupting us, Michel," Jean-Yves said. "Why is it that you do that each time we sit down for our lessons?"

"Lessons! Bah! It's foolishness! What need does the boy have of your lessons?" Michel peeled off more meat and ate it.

Jean-Yves sighed and surrendered. "Bushrod, you may go. We've done enough for today, I believe . . . and all we'll be allowed to do, in any case, now that Michel has come."

Bushrod didn't have to be told twice. He bounded to his feet and raced out the door, embracing the gift of freedom with enthusiasm, wondering where Tuckaseh might have gone.

Michel licked his fingers clean, walked over to his brother, and squatted near him. He nodded toward the slate. "Why do you teach the boy English, Jean? What need does the boy have of it?"

"He comes from English-speaking stock. He should know his native tongue. It is his heritage."

"Heritage? His heritage is *here*, Jean. And what do you care of heritage, anyway, you, who turned your back on your own years ago?"

"I've turned my back on nothing . . . merely added to what I was born with. A man can choose to embrace new ways of life without forsaking his heritage, can he not? I was born a Frenchman and will die a Frenchman."

"Nonsense! We are more Indian than French, you and I. And that boy is more Indian than we are. Life among the

Creek and Cherokee is all he has known from the day you brought him here.''

''No. He's known far more than that, thanks to my teaching. He knows about the world around us, the world we came from, which he may never see. And he knows about the world of the white men, the settlers, where he himself came from and to which he will one day return.''

''Why should he return? I for one never will. I enjoy the life I lead here.''

''He'll return because this life will not last. Oh, for you and me, maybe it will, because we have fewer years ahead of us. But it will not last for one so young as Bushrod. He'll remain long after Coldwater and towns like it, and the Indian people, are gone far away and forgotten.''

''So I have heard you say too many times. Why do you think this way? Why are you such a fatalist?''

Jean-Yves quirked one brow. ''Fatalist! I'm surprised you even know so deep a word, brother. I congratulate you! I am a fatalist because *they*—,'' he thumbed northward,''—have superior numbers, an endless supply of themselves ready to spill over the mountains and fill the wilderness and drive the Indians away. I am a fatalist because *they* were exploding gunpowder and fighting wars with rifles while the Indians knew of no greater weapons than blowguns and arrows and spears. Because *they* are more prone than the Indians to make unions and fight together, rather than among each other. Because *they* are not so burdened with superstition that they starve themselves before battle, or turn back from a fight they would have won because some supposed 'sign' presents itself. And most of all, I am a fatalist because I know how badly *they* need this land. It is their hope and chance, the difference between poverty and success. They will fight until it is their own. The Indians may struggle and die with honor and glory . . . but they will be swept away with history, and you and I with them, I do not doubt. But I won't see Bushrod and Marie swept away. I want them prepared to live in the world as it will be.''

Michel shook his head disgustedly. ''I have no intention of being swept away by history or anything else. I believe in survival. If you are so enamored of the *gitlu-ale-tsaqwali*, and see such great victories coming to their people, why don't you go live among them? Add yet another heritage to your list!'' *Gitlu-ale-tsaqwali*. "Hair and horses.'' It was a common way in Coldwater to refer to the Cumberland settlements to the north, frequent targets for bands raiding out of the hidden town, bands that almost always returned with fresh horses and fresh scalps.

"I am where I want to be,'' Jean-Yves said. "I have no desire to leave here. But Bushrod, I believe, will someday do so.''

Michel stood, looking down his handsome nose at his older brother. "Jean, I do fear for you. You claim to be wise, a man of reason, and yet you believe only foolish things. The whites to the north will not prevail. Don't you realize they don't even know this town exists? The raiders that strike them are like phantoms in their eyes, coming from nowhere, vanishing like fog to the south.''

"It won't be that way forever, Michel. It can't be. They will find us one day, and they will come.''

"By that time the town will have moved elsewhere.''

"How can you be so sure? Do you really believe this life of ours will go on unchanged forever?''

Michel glowered at him and turned, silent. He went to the fire and tore off another strip of turkey meat. He glanced down and smiled at Marie, who had been listening to the conversation but understanding none of it. An infant when her parents died, she knew no English at all but the smattering that Jean-Yves was beginning to teach her.

Chewing on the turkey, Michel left the cabin. A few moments later, Jean-Yves heard Michel's voice ring out again. Another noisy, jolly song, another celebration of his seeming eternal optimism and good spirits. Jean-Yves envied him. It must be grand to be so confident that all the good in life would remain as it was, like a spring that never ran dry.

He looked down at the slate and the word he had been teaching to Bushrod when Michel had come in. He chuckled at the irony.

The word was "destruction.''

CHAPTER FOUR

Bushrod was outside town, setting rabbit snares with Tuckaseh, the day two Chickasaw hunters came into Coldwater. They found the town purely by accident while ranging along the river. When Bushrod and Tuckaseh came back from the woods, they found the predominately Cherokee population of Coldwater welcoming the two roamers, feeding them, telling them with satisfaction of the many raids their warriors had launched against the Cumberland settlements. The Chickasaws listened with remarkable interest, and Tuckaseh, Bush noticed, looked on with obvious displeasure.

"It's unwise to trust a Chickasaw," he said to Bush when the latter inquired about his grim manner. "There will be trouble because of this, Skiuga. The Chickasaw are too closely aligned with the *unakas*. There will destruction to come of this."

"Destruction? Why do you say such a thing as that?" Bush couldn't see anything in the friendly scene with the Chickasaws that suggested anything so extreme.

But Tuckaseh had no more to say at the moment. After watching the Chickasaws leave, bearing gifts, he turned away, a dark expression on his face, and spat on the ground.

Minor as the incident with Tuckaseh seemed, Bush couldn't shake from his mind a sense of deep and impending doom that had settled over him in its wake.

For days, Bush shunned his typical habits of roaming, hunting, and horseplay with the other boys of Coldwater. He shunned even Tuckaseh, and was atypically silent during his daily round of schooling under Freneau. He stayed close to Marie. Protecting her, he thought. Yet her nearness also served to comfort him. She was all that remained of his true family. The only other person in the world, as far as he knew, through whose veins flowed the same blood that flowed in his own.

A few days after the visit of the Chickasaws, Waninahi, who sat beneath the shade of a maple, chewing leather to soften it, watched her adopted son lingering near his sister, and pondered the pair. Though the sun had tanned both of the young ones to a deep nut brown, and both dressed like any Indian children in the town (Marie was young enough yet that she often didn't dress at all when the weather was warm) the *unaka* heritage of both remained as evident as the indelible birthmark on the neck of Marie.

Waninahi was unaccustomed to seeing Bushrod in such an obvious state of worry, and wondered what was wrong with him. Something Tuckaseh said, probably. She knew Tuckaseh to be a wise man, but Bush listened too closely to him sometimes. Waninahi remembered well a time, from the old Overhill Town days, when Tuckaseh, interpreting one of his own dreams, had predicted a storm that would destroy the town with lightning. Several families believed him and took to the woods. When the night of the predicted storm passed with nothing more than a mild, dry wind, the believers came slinking back to town, unwilling to talk, and ready to send Tuckaseh across the mountains for good. For months he was bitterly called "The Prophet" behind his back, sometimes to his face. The incident sparked a decline of Tuckaseh's influence among the people. He never fully recovered it.

Waninahi chewed the leather, ignoring the unpleasant taste, evaluating its changing texture with her tongue. It was softening nicely.

Tuckaseh. Yes, she decided, Bush's somber manner was almost certainly the old man's fault. Tuckaseh had always been prone to see the worst of things. Perhaps such an attitude was natural in a man who was slowly losing his vision, and who had long ago lost his prestige, and his wife. Tuckaseh was a declining man living in the house of his unloving daughter. He had reason to be a pessimist, Waninahi decided.

But he didn't have a right to force his dark attitude on a growing young man such as Bushrod. Nor, for that matter, did Jean-Yves, whose attitude lately was as bad as Tuckaseh's, maybe worse. Lately Jean-Yves talked to her by night of coming decline and the end of the life they knew. She was sure he said the same to Bush during their daily tutorials. Thus Bushrod, so deeply under the sway of both Tuckaseh and his adoptive father, was being bombarded with foreboding from two sides. No wonder he was glum!

Waninahi chewed harder on the leather, beginning to feel angry. She would not have Bushrod made unhappy without good cause. He was her son, as much as if he had been born of her own loins. She had not been gifted with children of her own flesh.

Not yet, anyway. She touched her belly, wondering . . . almost sure. There were signs, feelings. She would know soon.

She wondered how Jean-Yves would react when he learned that he was to be a father. Perhaps the news would cure him of some of his pessimism.

She hoped so. No mother desired to bring a child into a world that was unhappy and grim. If there really was a child in her womb, she wanted it to live in a way that was bright as sunshine, happy, and destined to go on for a long, long time.

Bushrod squatted in the middle of his uncle's trade house at the edge of Coldwater, surrounded by the goods by which Michel Freneau made his living: knives, tomahawks, guns, ammunition, blankets, beads, paints, sugar, coffee, clothing, casks of rum. Marie was somewhere amid the clutter, off in a corner, playing. She was here more frequently than was Bush; Marie had won the heart of Michel from the moment he first saw her as an infant, and he spent at least as much time with her, maybe more, as did Jean-Yves.

"So it's fear of destruction that has you so glum, is it?"

Michel was saying to Bush. "You've been listening to Jean-Yves, I take it."

"Mostly to Tuckaseh."

"Tuckaseh! Hah! 'The Prophet.' Don't give him heed, Bush. He's an old, blind fool. I know you admire him, but truth is truth."

"Tuckaseh says a mistake was made when the Chickasaws were welcomed. He says they are friends with the *unakas*, and that they'll bring destruction to us."

"He's like Jean-Yves, full of fear and pessimism. I have no love of the Chickasaws, but there will be no trouble."

Bush played with a round stone he'd found, rolling it about like a marble, and said nothing. Marie was singing quietly to herself, an old children's song taught to her by Waninahi. "*Ua'nu une'guhi' tsana'seha'; E'ti une'guhi' tsana'seha' . . .*" Her voice was high but pleasant.

Bush asked, "Why are you so different than my father, Michel?"

Before he answered, Michel paused to fill a clay pipe and light it from a twig taken from the small fire that burned in the center of the cabin, the smoke pouring out a hole in the roof.

"Jean is an unusual man, Bushrod. He spent his earliest years filling his mind with knowledge, then fell in love with a woman who died the day before they were to be married. Me, I had problems of my own at the time, with the law, and we joined together, fled our troubles and sorrows and found a new life in this wilderness, me as a trader, Jean as . . . well, just what Jean is. A man of the woods. A content man, especially after he found Waninahi. But you know all that already, eh? What I am saying to you here, Bushrod, is that your father is maybe too much a thinker for his own good. He has too much learning, I think. Too much thinking draws lines on a man's brow, and makes him full of darkness and dread. One can study life so deeply that he forgets that life was made to be lived, not picked to pieces. I think maybe that Tuckaseh is much like Jean-Yves, in his own way. What do you think?"

"Well . . . I think that Tuckaseh is very wise. And so is my father."

"Then you, too, will have some deep wrinkles on your brow, my young friend. Don't think too much or too hard, Bush. Better to be like me, eh? Happy, full of joy all the time!" He playfully punched at Bushrod's shoulder, trying to cheer him. "That's what life is for, the pleasure of it."

"Tuckaseh says that life is greater than pleasure. Father says the same."

"And who is happier, those two, or me? Hmm? Forget all this worrying, Bush. It's inappropriate in one so young."

Several days later

The army of frontiersmen moved with remarkable swiftness, considering the winding, twisting route they were obliged to follow. They traveled by the mouth of the Little Harpeth River, along Turnbull's Creek and Lick Creek, on to Swan Creek and to Blue Water Creek, whose course led directly to the Tennessee River at a place nearly opposite to Coldwater.

Boats that were supposed to meet the marchers near the Muscle Shoals, to ferry them and their supplies across, failed to arrive. A leather boat was quickly made, and little by little, as a driving rain set in, the goods and men were shipped across a few at a time. Drenched by the rain, the soldiers took refuge in abandoned Indian cabins south of the river, building fires and drying their clothes and footwear, eating from their supply packs.

Scouts, meanwhile, forged ahead, deeper into the dark land, keeping an eye out for any Indians who might see their advance. When the throng was dried out and fed, the march began again along a six-mile-long path.

The army at length divided, one division heading for the mouth of Coldwater Creek. The rest advanced farther until cornfields appeared. There they paused, checking and rechecking weapons.

Coldwater was just ahead, beyond the corn and across the

creek. Open, unprepared, and utterly unaware of what was about to come.

Bushrod, visiting his uncle again in the trade house, was asleep amid the clutter when the attack came.

Howling frontiersmen charged across the creek and into the very town itself. Sitting up, Bushrod blinked in confusion and looked around for his uncle.

"Michel?" No reply. He stood. "Michel? What is happening?" But Michel was not there.

Shots popped outside; there were yells, the sound of children crying, women screaming, men running.

Hot panic gripped Bushrod. Inside the trade house, he could see nothing but unidentifiable flashes of movement through the doorway. Michel was nowhere around, and no one else was in the trade house.

Bushrod stood still as a tree, scared and confused. Should he hide somewhere among the trade goods? Should he slip out and run? He looked around for an escape route other than the single front door, though he well knew this cabin had no windows. He was terrified by the idea of leaving here, going out into that hellish uproar outside.

Where was Michel? Where was his father? His mother . . . and Marie? *Where was Marie?*

A rifle fired just outside the door; someone screamed in pain. Bushrod dived behind a stack of blankets.

A shadow moved in the room; someone had stuck his head in the door. Bushrod heard words half-shouted in English, something about damned French traders. Bushrod hugged the floor, fearing that the man would come in and find him, then surely kill him. But a moment later he realized that the man hadn't come in at all.

They'll burn this house, he thought. He'd heard about how white men would burn Indian towns, burn every building to the ground and leave the residents homeless. *Maybe he's setting fire to the logs right now! Maybe he's already set them afire!*

Bushrod rose slowly, looking over the heap of blankets. The

door was open. Figures in buckskin and linsey-woolsey moved and fired, and swore, and fired some more in the heart of the town. Bushrod ducked again, huddling, hiding.

I can't hide here forever. They'll come back because of all that's in here. Things they'll want. I must run.

He came to his feet and lunged for the door. He paused a moment in the doorway, then ducked out to the right, heading for his house.

Through the roiling smoke he caught a glimpse of Marie, being carried along beneath someone's arm. Panic hit again. She'd been captured! Then he saw that it was Waninahi who carried Marie. She ran with her around the back of a flaming cabin. Three or four of the raiders circled around after them, the smoke closed in, and Bush could see them no more.

Bushrod saw flames leaping, people running everywhere. The shooting would not stop, and he wondered how there could be so much gunfire from weapons that required painstaking reloading after every shot. He ran in the direction he'd seen Waninahi go with Marie.

He came into view of his own house and halted, gaping.

His house was ablaze. Thoroughly engulfed with fire.

Father!

He ran on, toward the house, having no notion of what he would do when he got there. For all he knew he would run into the very flames themselves.

Something clipped him powerfully on the side of the head and he went to the ground, smacking hard, taking the slam painfully. Suddenly he needed to cry, to sob, but there was no air in his lungs for it and he couldn't manage to pull any in. His ability to breathe had vanished.

He came to his feet again and ran hard toward the house. Ran without breathing, trying with excruciating and futile strain to suck in air. His head began to spin . . .

Suddenly, his breath returned. His lungs, emptied and stunned into paralysis by his fall to the ground, had begun working again, all at once.

He neared the flaming house. The heat seared, feeling as if it might peel the skin off his face.

"Father!" he shouted. "Father! Where are you?"

Someone grabbed him from behind and pulled him into the air. He knew even without looking that it was Michel, come from some hiding place to rescue him and pull him to safety.

He twisted his head to look.

It wasn't Michel. It was a stranger, clad in a fringed rifleman's coat. Red hair. A grinning, freckled, young face.

"Gotcha, injun! Gotcha!"

"No!" Bushrod shouted in Cherokee. "No! Let me go!" Then he realized that this man probably understood none of it. He would speak English, not Cherokee.

Long and dull hours spent at his father's side, crouched over a slate, came back. He sought the right words.

"No . . . let me go . . . please . . . I must find . . . must find my father . . ."

"Hellfire and damnation!" the young frontiersman bellowed, almost dropping him. "You're *white*!"

"I am the son . . . of Jean-Yves Freneau."

The frontiersman reasserted his grip around Bushrod's thin waist, and chortled. "Got me a white one!" he yelled to anyone who could hear. "Got me a white injun boy, son of a Frenchy! *Waaugh*!"

Bushrod struggled but could not break free. The frontiersman, still laughing—Bushrod could only wonder why—ran with him, jolting him along so hard his ribs threatened to break against the frontiersman's bony shoulder. Bushrod's stomach felt like it was trying to crawl out of his mouth.

"Bushrod!"

The boy heard the call as if from a great distance, but when he looked, Jean-Yves was not far away. He was filthy, bleeding, and some of his clothing looked like it had been burned off, and maybe some of his flesh, too.

"Father!"

"Bushrod, I—"

Whatever Jean-Yves would have said, Bushrod never knew. The young frontiersman who carried him threw him hard to the ground. He landed on his face. Rolling over, tasting blood that spewed out his nose and over his mouth, he saw the red-haired man raising his flintlock rifle. Jean-Yves wasn't moving. Just standing, mouth moving with words that Bushrod couldn't make out, one hand extended imploringly.

The shot was louder than anything Bushrod had ever heard. He screamed and spasmed at the sound of it, then screamed again as he saw his father fall, face now a mass of blood, the extended hand falling limply to the side as he collapsed.

"No!" Bushrod screamed. "Father!"

"Shut up, damn you!" the rifleman bellowed. Bushrod saw the butt of the rifle swing down and toward him. He tried to dodge it but couldn't move. It smashed hard against the side of his head, knocking another scream from him, driving him into a darkness, deep as a cavern, where there was only silence and all awareness faded to nothing.

CHAPTER FIVE

Bushrod's head was scabby and painful, he was scared to his core, and wouldn't have been surprised to see someone raise a rifle to shoot him at any moment. But he didn't cry. One thing he'd learned from the men of Coldwater—which now burned and smoldered behind him—was never to cry, especially in the presence of an enemy. The role of a man was to face his enemies with dignity and honor, no matter how hard or how great the cost.

So, with effort, Bushrod kept his face frozen into a blank mask. His lip trembled and his eyes blinked more often than he wished they would, but all in all, he did an astonishing job of maintaining composure. He even managed an occasional glance of contempt toward his firehaired, freckled captor, whose hand gripped one end of a rawhide rope. The other end was leashed around Bushrod's thin neck.

"Caught me one!" the red-haired man would say with a shake of the rope whenever some newcomer came near. "Caught me a sure-'nough white-skinned Frenchy injun pup!"

Bushrod was humiliated to be displayed this way, tied like a dog and laughed at by the red-haired man. What scared him even more than his captor's laughter, though, was the opposite demeanor of the other *unakas*. They didn't laugh. Their looks were dark as old blood.

One of Bushrod's playmates at Coldwater had once told him that *unakas* sometimes captured and ate young Indians. Though he'd been assured by Jean-Yves that this wasn't true,

it was easy to examine the morose faces around him and seriously wonder if he was about to become a meal.

Only one face gave him comfort, that of a tall, wide-chested
man with graying hair, deep blue eyes, and fair skin. Those
large eyes, the first blue eyes Bushrod had ever seen, had a
soft, sympathetic light when turned toward the boy, but a hard
glare when aimed at the man holding the rope. Bushrod locked
his eyes on the sympathetic-looking man, wordlessly pleading
for help.

"Dance, boy!" the red-haired man said, jerking the rope
harder this time. "Do us an injun dance! C'mon, boy!"

Bushrod gagged and choked as the rope tugged against his
neck, but manfully refused to rise. He would not dance. He
would not cry. He was only a small child, but he would act
like a man.

"Up from there, you squat Frenchy coon! Up on them feet!
Dance! Dance for us!" As if to demonstrate, the red-haired
man began dancing, wildly slapping his moccasined feet
about, looking like quite a fool.

The kind-looking man with the blue eyes stepped forward.
"That's enough, Snoddy."

The red-haired fellow ceased dancing. "What?"

"I said, that's enough. You take that rope off that boy's
neck."

Tip Snoddy's freckled face went almost as red as his hair.
He faced the intervenor. "You just tell me why the hell I
should!"

"It ain't fitting that you treat a white boy that way."

"White of skin he may be, but this here's an injun on the
inside. And Frenchy on the outside."

"It ain't fitting."

"Maybe it ain't, Jim Lusk, and maybe it is. Maybe it ain't
none of your damn affair either way."

"What do you aim to do with him?"

"Take him home."

"Why? Ain't nobody else doing that. The women and children got away. This raid warn't about women and children. It
was to clean out a hornet's nest."

"This one's white. He don't belong with a bunch of injuns. Besides, his father's dead."

Jim Lusk stopped arguing with Snoddy and drew closer to Bushrod, at whose side he knelt. "Boy, can you understand what I'm saying to you?"

"Yes."

"So you do speak English?"

"Yes."

"I didn't say you could talk to him, Lusk," Tip Snoddy said to Lusk, pulling back on the rope and choking Bushrod. Without looking at or replying to Tip, Lusk shot out a massive hand, grabbed the rope, and held it slack between his fist and Bushrod's neck. Tip tugged the rope again, but Jim's fist around the rope absorbed the pull before it could reach Bushrod's neck.

"Who was your father?"

"His name was Jean-Yves Freneau."

"He was one of the French traders here?"

"No. His brother was a trader. My father was a hunter and woods runner."

"Snoddy said he killed your father. Is that true?"

"It's true."

"Who's your mother?"

"Her name is Waninahi. She's Cherokee. I have a sister, too. Marie. I saw my mother carrying her away in the fight, but they were lost in the smoke and I don't know what happened to them."

"I know," Snoddy said. "They was killed."

Lusk looked at Snoddy. "I ain't aware of no women nor children being shot here today."

"These was. I seen it myself. The woman took a shot through her middle, and the girl was hit in the head. The woman went off into the trees, dragging the dead girl along with her brains all running out like water."

"Whoa, boy!" Lusk said, reaching out to catch Bush, who had teetered as if about to faint. "Hold up there, young fellow. You got to be a strong young man just now—hear?"

From somewhere Bush found the strength to keep on his

feet. *Dead . . . Marie is dead. Jean-Yves . . . Waninahi . . . dead. I am alone.*

"Son, I'm sorry you've had to hear such news," Lusk said. "The Cherokee woman, was she your birth mother?"

"No. My real parents were white. They died a long time ago. I scarcely recall them. My father—my French father, I mean—told me about them. I grew up among the Indians."

"But there's no true Indian blood in you at all. You don't really belong among the redskins. What's your name?"

"Bushrod Underhill."

"That don't sound like a French name."

"It isn't. I want to find my uncle."

"Sorry. Doubt you can do that. The traders who wasn't killed were took prisoner. We believe the traders were pushing the injuns to raid our settlements and towns farther north. You understand what I mean when I say 'prisoner'?"

"Yes. Am I a prisoner?"

"No, son. You're just rescued from the savages, that's all."

"I don't want to be rescued. If I can't see my uncle, then there's another man, an older Cherokee with eyes going blind. His name is Tuckaseh. Can I go to him?"

"The women and children and old folks have all fled to the woods, and we're letting them be," Lusk said. "There's no such fellow as you describe among the dead or the prisoners."

Tip Snoddy gave another tug on the rope. Jim shot him a fast, hot glance and turned his attention back to Bushrod.

"The French trader uncle of yours, what's his name?"

"Michel Freneau."

"Michel Freneau. I'll see if I can find out what become of him. But you got to know I can't say for sure that he's alive. Some of the French traders ran or resisted, and got shot for it. But there was some who surrendered. Maybe he was one of them."

"If he is alive, can I go to him?"

"Maybe you can go back to him . . . if they let the traders go free. But they haven't decided yet what to do with them. They may shoot them."

Snoddy jerked on the rope again, so hard this time it yanked

Lusk, who floundered onto his rump, and almost pulled Bushrod over, too.

"They are going to shoot them. I heard it said myself, just now."

"You're a liar, Snoddy," Lusk said, coming to his feet. "You ain't heard any such thing. I know for a fact that the General is still debating the matter."

"Well, whatever they decide, this boy ain't going to be with nobody but me, Lusk!" he said, face so crimson his freckles were almost lost to view. "*You* ain't deciding what happens to *my* prisoner! *I* caught him! *Me*! He's *mine*!"

"And what do you need with him?"

"Not a thing. But I caught him, and I'll be the one to keep him!"

Jim Lusk snarled like a panther in Snoddy's face. Teeth gritted, he glared at Snoddy as he untied his sash, dropped it, then pulled off his hunting jacket and the linsey-woolsey shirt beneath it. Snoddy lost much of his abundant color all at once. Lusk advanced and loomed over him. Standing in the shadow of his foe, Snoddy looked small and frail.

"You ain't aiming to fight me, are you? Ain't no call for us to fight, Jim!" he said, forcing a weak smile. "He's my catch, that's all. I just didn't want nobody trying to tell me what to do with him."

"Ain't about the boy no more," Jim Lusk replied. "It's about me and you. I've had enough of your mouthing! And I don't take to being jerked over onto my arse by such as you!"

"I warn't trying to do that—it was an accident."

"Snoddy, get ready to spar! When you messed with me you plucked the blood-red rose of the wilderness!"

Tip Snoddy backed away, still holding the rope. It pulled tight around Bushrod's neck and forced him to his feet. Snoddy kept backing off, Bushrod choking and stumbling after him. "Ain't no call for us to fight!" Snoddy said again.

"Whoa!" somebody said from among the crowd of men, who had begun to form a spontaneous wide circle around the would-be combatants. "Look coming yonder! It's the General!"

One side of the circle parted to admit a keen-eyed, dark-haired man in a rifleman's garb, but with a decidedly military bearing. He walked into the midst of the circle, and without a word evaluated what was going on. He looked at Jim Lusk a moment, a little longer at Tip Snoddy, and longest of all at Bushrod, who was beginning to lose the fight to hold back tears.

"What's the meaning of this?" General James Robertson demanded. "Why is that rope around that boy's neck?"

Snoddy stood silent, mouth hanging open.

Jim Lusk took advantage of the moment to approach Snoddy from the side, pull the rope out of his hand, and knock him flat with a single blow to the side of the face. Snoddy made a high, wavering noise as he collapsed with a shudder and lay stunned.

Lusk turned to Robertson. "I'm sorry 'bout that, General. I just couldn't miss the opportunity."

"You shouldn't have done that, Mr. Lusk."

"I know, sir. But I had to. He was treating the boy bad, and this is a white boy who's been imprisoned among the savages for all his days."

Bush didn't perceive his life up until now as an imprisonment, but prudently kept his mouth shut.

"Even so, you shouldn't have hit him." Robertson paused, then smiled slightly. "You should have stood aside and let me do it."

The surrounding men cheered. Bushrod was both startled and relieved, realizing that those dark looks he had seen on so many faces before hadn't been directed at him after all, but at Snoddy.

Lusk reached down and rumpled Bush's hair in a friendly way, then gently opened the noose and removed the rope. Just then, to Bushrod, it was as if he were looking up into the face of some benevolent deity, and he loved Jim Lusk.

Bushrod said, "*Monsieur* . . . sir, no one is going to cook and eat me?"

Lusk looked shocked, then smiled in a bemused way. "What've these savages been telling you, boy? We don't do that kind of thing! Where in the world did you get such a notion?'' Lusk looked around. ''You all hear that? He thought we was going to eat him!'' Lusk looked squarely into Bush's eyes. ''Nobody going to hurt you, nobody going to eat you. You got the word of Jim Lusk on that.''

Bushrod felt a great, hot tightness rise within his middle and work its way up toward his throat. Tears pressed the back of his eyes, seeking escape. He felt very young just now. He'd lost all the ones he loved. His father, mother, and sister, all dead now, his world changed forever, even his town burned. He felt he could cry and never stop.

But he swallowed it all down. No sobs, no tears. Bushrod Underhill would die before he would weep in the view of his enemies.

CHAPTER SIX

Later that night, alone, Bushrod did cry.

He was almost asleep on a pair of blankets, one given him by Jim Lusk, the other by another kindly soul named Elisha Poler, when the sound of nearing footsteps roused him. He sat up, quickly wiping away his tears, and saw Jim Lusk approaching.

Lusk had hardly reached Bush before the boy was on his feet, asking, "Did you find Michel Freneau?"

"No, son, I didn't," Lusk said. "There was no such a man among the traders held prisoner."

Bush looked down, blinking fast. "So he's dead, too."

"Probably so. As I told you, there were some traders killed."

Bush somehow managed to keep his voice steady. "So what will become of me?"

"Well, I reckon you'll go back to the settlements with us."

"With the fire-hair man," Bush said sadly.

Lusk fidgeted. "Son, I don't know that you have to stay with Tip Snoddy. I mean, he don't own you."

"Don't own me? But he took me prisoner in war. I'm his possession now."

"That's the redskin way of looking at things, son. You're among white men now."

"So I don't have to go with Snoddy?"

"Well . . . not really. Though he wants you to go with him."

"Can I go with you instead?"

Lusk scratched his beard and looked away. "Christmas, son, I wish you wouldn't have asked that."

"I'll be your prisoner. I'll do slave work for you."

"Son, son, I ain't looking for no slave."

"I don't want to have to go with the fire-hair man."

"I don't blame you. But son, listen to me. I can't take on no boy! I don't even have a proper home. You know what I am, son? I'm a hunter and roamer and scout—"

"You're like my father, then. He was a *coureur des bois*."

"What's that?"

"A woods runner. He roamed, trapped, hunted. Mostly just roamed."

"I'll be. Well, yes, that's much like what I do." He paused. "But there's a keen difference between me and your late pap, son. He was amongst the Indians, at peace with them, living like one of them. Me and the Indians, we're enemies . . . or as often as not we are. Right now there's little peace between my people and them you come from among. That's why we had to do this raid."

"I could hunt with you. I'm a fine woodsman. Tuckaseh told me that he'd never known anyone my age with the kind of skill I have in the woods. I've brought in much meat for my family. I'm brave and strong. I could carry your kills for you for great distances, and would never complain."

"Listen to me, boy. Just listen a minute. It ain't like that for me. I do things alone. I got no wife . . . not yet, anyway, and no family. I live here and there in the woods, this shelter and that cave and this holler tree and such, and I serve as a scout for the settlements all along the Cumberland country. I'm out in the forests in the worst times of Indian trouble, and scarce set foot inside a fort or blockhouse unless my rifle's needed for protection. I can't take a boy into such a life!"

Bush might have pleaded, for the prospect of life with Tip Snoddy galled and troubled him so deeply that he might easily forget all pride to avoid it, but he saw it would be of no use. Jim Lusk would not yield.

Bush sank to the ground again, silent, staring at a stone.

"I'm sorry, son," Lusk said. "I wish I'd found your uncle

living, and you could have gone with him." He paused. "No, no, I won't lie to you. The fact is, I think you're going to be glad someday that all this happened. You're best off with your own kind of people."

"My father said that any kind of people could be my people."

"Well, I don't know much about all that. I believe it best for whites to be among whites, and redskins among redskins. But I suppose we can try to get along. But the redskins will seldom let a white man live in peace."

"It wasn't the Indians who burned down Coldwater and killed my family."

"No, but it was the bloody Indians who killed and scalped my own brother, and who've killed more good white men of my acquaintance than I can count, and who won't even let a farming man sow his field without somebody standing guard with rifles." Lusk's tone was changing now. He was breaking away. "I done what I could for you, boy. Just be glad for the better life you'll have one day, thanks to being away from the savages."

Bush lay down, saying nothing more. He stared at the sky.

"See you here and there, son," Lusk said. He turned away and strode off.

Bushrod rolled over slowly, stretching and moving, resettling himself in his blankets. How long now until his mother would make him rise? He wished she would let him sleep until he was tired of sleeping, and get up only when he felt like it. But any moment now, he was sure, he would hear her voice telling him to rise . . .

He opened his eyes as a stab of realization filled him with pain. He would not hear her voice this morning. He would never hear her voice again.

The sunlight was pale and thin, the light of very early morning. Bushrod sat up. The camp was abustle, *unakas* moving about, quick fires being built to warm breakfasts, all the motions of the camp indicating that all was breaking up. Today the frontier army would move on.

Bushrod stood, looking about. There was Jim Lusk, across the camp, looking over some horses. Bushrod recognized the horses as the property of a Coldwater neighbor. He wondered if that neighbor was among the twenty-odd Coldwater men killed in the attack.

A thick cloud of smoke, carried on the breeze, swept past Bushrod from the direction of Coldwater. He turned and sadly inspected what remained of the creekside town. Not much. The houses were gone, smoldering and smoking. The cornfields had been flattened, trampled down into mud. He stared sadly at the place Jean-Yves's house had stood, then in the direction of Michel's trade house, now also a blackened ruin, set ablaze after all the goods were removed.

"Well, look here!" a whine-toned voice said. "Our little Frenchy boy's up and about!"

Tip Snoddy passed by, bearing his packs and rifle. Snoddy glared at Bush hatefully, but did not stop. Bushrod hated him.

There was activity at the river. Partially folding his blankets and throwing them across his shoulders, he headed in that direction.

Several boats had been captured by the raiders; the activity of the moment centered around them. Bushrod walked slowly toward them, trying to be inconspicuous. He found a good spot and crouched there, watching the activity on and around the boats.

The boats were heavily laden with what Bushrod soon realized were the captured goods of the town's French traders. The *unakas* had done well for themselves, and that without the loss of a single man. Bushrod wondered if the goods would be divided among all of the raiders later, or if the leader called Robertson had a right to it all. He knew nothing about the war customs of white men.

His stomach rumbled and he wondered who would feed him. Lusk would surely do so. Bushrod trusted Lusk. He thought that maybe he trusted General Robertson as well, but he'd seen less of him and wasn't sure. And there was the fact that Robertson was the man who had led this expedition.

Michel. There he was, standing in one of the boats. Bushrod came to his feet. Lusk had been wrong! Michel *was* among the prisoners! Bush stared in amazement, but soon the emotion changed to confusion.

Something was happening here, and Bushrod didn't understand it. Why was Michel on that boat?

Don't leave me, Michel! Don't leave me!

"Bushrod!"

Bushrod didn't turn; he knew the voice by now. Jim Lusk came up from behind and slipped his big hand onto his shoulder.

"Bushrod, have you had any food?"

In his distraction, Bushrod spoke in French. "Where are they going?"

"What?"

English this time. "The boats . . . where are they going?"

"I believe they're heading down the river a ways, son."

"Why?"

"Them's the traders who was captured. As I understand it, they're going to a ferry on up a ways, and once there—and again, this is just how I understand it, nothing I know for sure—they're going to give the traders one of the littler boats and let them go free, on up to the Wabash country."

"My uncle is on that boat!"

"No, boy. I looked for your uncle among the traders, and there was no Michel among them."

Or maybe, Bush thought, no one willing to admit to being Michel. Perhaps his uncle had feared that he was in some sort of trouble when Lusk came around calling his name. Maybe he'd just kept his peace and not admitted to Lusk who he was.

And now Michel was going to be free! And if so, Bush knew where he belonged. Excitement filled him, taking his breath.

"Come on back and we'll have us some breakfast, son," Lusk said.

Bushrod was not going back. Not at all. He began striding toward the river's edge, fast losing his reluctance to draw attention. He belonged on that boat, with Michel, heading toward freedom.

"Michel!" he called, waving.

The boats began to move. Michel turned, saw him.

"Michel! Wait!"

The boats moved faster, drifting into the current.

"No, Michel!" Bushrod reached the river's edge. Michel stared at him, not waving, not smiling, not speaking. He was closely packed in with several other men, standing, only his head and shoulders visible to Bush.

Bushrod stepped into the water. "No! Wait for me, Michel! Let me go with you!"

A strong hand grabbed Bushrod from behind. Lusk spoke. "Son, you can't go with them. Can't you see your uncle don't want you? And it's for the best, son. You don't belong among such vermin as them traders."

Bushrod shrugged free and tried to plunge deeper into the river. Lusk caught him again. Bushrod screeched, twisted his head, bit Lusk's restraining hand. Lusk grunted in pain and pulled away. Bushrod splashed out into the water.

"Michel! Wait, Michel! Wait!"

The boats were drifting fast, moving quickly away.

Lusk caught Bushrod again, more carefully, making sure that his hands weren't in biting range. Bushrod yelled and fought. Michel watched silently from the boat, staring at him with the look of a man about to grow ill.

Lusk dragged Bushrod back out of the water. A crowd had gathered, watching it all, most of them obviously amused. Bushrod saw their smiles and hated them. Twisting his neck, he saw his uncle's boat going hopelessly out of range down the river. He hated him, too.

The next few minutes were lost to Bushrod. He sobbed uncontrollably, unable to accept what was happening here. His uncle was floating off down the river, leaving him behind, in the hands of the same men who had killed his father, and burned his town, and changed his life forever.

It was more than he could bear.

"Settle down, son," Lusk said. "Settle down. Nothing gained by crying. Everything's going to be fine for you, son. I promise it will."

He tried to tousle Bushrod's hair, but Bushrod grabbed his arm, pulled it down, and bit his hand as hard as he could.

Lusk yelled. The watching men laughed.

Bushrod hated them all.

They gave him food, but he wouldn't eat it. He sat on his blankets, staring silently, no longer crying, as angry now as he was sad and afraid.

Why had Michel done it? How could he not have taken him with him? His father would never have abandoned him. He would have died before he let them take him away without his boy.

Bush hated everyone around him just now. Even Jim Lusk, in spite of his kind manner and efforts on his behalf, because Lusk had held him back from running into the river.

Bush hated Michel, too. Looking back, he saw all his past relations with his uncle in a startlingly different light. Michel had never cared for him. His affection had been for Marie. Now that she was dead, along with the rest of Bush's family, Michel had no desire to be burdened with Bushrod Underhill, who was no blood kin of his, and never a recipient of any true part of his fondness.

Lusk approached. "I'm sorry about your uncle, son."

"I'm not your son."

"No. You're not." He paused. "But you are in need of somebody to finish raising you. I been thinking some about what you said yesterday evening, and maybe I could consider—"

Bushrod spat at him. Others nearby laughed.

Lusk reddened; veins became visible in his thick neck. "Very well. You was never rightly my worry to begin with, but I took up concern over you out of good Christian kindness. But I won't be spat upon. I wash my hands of you."

Bushrod spat at him again. The veins bulged bigger. Lusk turned and strode away, laughter trailing him.

Bushrod turned and found himself face-to-belly with a grinning Tip Snoddy.

"Reckon you put that big old bastard in his place, eh?"

Snoddy said, leaning over slightly to bring his face to Bush-rod's level. Bushrod stared at him. "Listen, boy. I was mean to you, putting that rope around your neck. And I'm sorry it was me who shot your father. If I'd known who he was I'd not have done it." He grinned. "That's the truth."

Bushrod stared some more.

Tip Snoddy dug long fingers into his fiery hair and scratched at a louse skittering across his scalp. He caught it, pulled it off and glanced at it, then sucked it off his finger and spat it onto the ground encased in saliva. "I won't treat you bad no more, boy, if you want to walk along with me while we're a-heading back."

An odd and unfortunate thing happened to Bushrod at that moment. All the hatred that filled him crumbled away to be replaced by the pure fear that only a young one can know, and an intense, piercing need. Something in him reached out, unquestioningly, to the nearest offer of companionship, even if it came from the same man who had shot Jean-Yves Freneau in the face. It was not a rational decision, but the decision of a very scared boy who knew he couldn't hide his fear much longer without someone, anyone, to lean on. He wished he hadn't driven off Jim Lusk, who would make a much better leaning tree than Tip Snoddy—But Lusk was gone, and Snoddy was here, apparently willing to take him on.

When the northward march began, Bushrod walked at Tip Snoddy's side.

CHAPTER
SEVEN

*Two weeks later, near Eaton's Station on the
Cumberland River*

Tip Snoddy rolled over noisily on his husk mattress, making
a piggish sound somewhere back in his snout. His eyes flut-
tered but didn't quite open. Within moments his respiration
steadied and Bushrod, who had gone breathless when Snoddy
moved, knew he was still asleep.

He stood beside Snoddy's bed, staring at the ugly, freckled
face, and holding Snoddy's own firewood ax in his hand. His
eyes were continually drawn to a particular smooth patch of
freckled flesh just above Snoddy's left temple, near the line
of demarcation between sunburned, speckled skin and the or-
ange forest of Snoddy's hair.

Bushrod imagined the ax coming down at just that spot,
hard enough to break skin and bone and sink into the sleeping
man's head. How quickly would Snoddy die? Would he open
those eyes before he was gone, and know who had killed him?
Would he have a few moments in which to react before life
fled, perhaps just long enough to jerk the ax from his own
skull and bury it in Bushrod's? Tuckaseh had told Bush a story
about a relative of his who had been killed in battle in just
such a way by the very man he'd just tomahawked. Fearful,
Bushrod hesitated to do what he had come to believe, over the
last two weeks, that he must do.

His few days of life in Snoddy's lonely cabin had been quite
sufficient to clear his head and make him think more sensibly
about his situation. Though he remained muddled in grief at
Jean-Yves's death and Michel's abandonment, his mental wa-

ters weren't quite as turbulent as they had been just after the Coldwater raid.

He had reached three major conclusions in the last two weeks, one at a time. The first was that he had been foolish to take up with Snoddy, who had turned out to be just what he had seemed at the beginning—a crude, animalistic lout of a man and a thorough misery to be around. Still not fully answered was the question of why Snoddy had wanted Bushrod with him to begin with; Bushrod suspected by now that there *was* no answer. Snoddy, as best he could tell, had taken him as a living souvenir, even a kind of human pet. He apparently had found the notion of bringing home a white boy raised like an Indian to be quite a novelty.

If so, the novelty had quickly worn off. Snoddy now was mostly hostile to Bushrod, saying nothing to him except in a snarl or curse. This had led to Bushrod's second major conclusion: His future was bleak indeed as long as Tip Snoddy was part of it. Not only bleak, but also potentially curtailed. Bushrod hadn't fully worked it out in his mind, but he had a strong notion that Snoddy might just do away with him when he'd finally had enough.

And thus, inevitably, he had reached his third conclusion only two nights before: Snoddy had to be disposed of, before he in turn disposed of Bushrod. It was simply a matter of self-defense and common sense.

There was another reason, too, to get rid of Snoddy. Snoddy was the man who killed Jean-Yves Freneau. This fact, which Bushrod knew all along, had, for reasons he did not comprehend, failed to fully impress upon him until lately. But some days ago, Bush had reached a moment of clarity when he looked at his captor and thought: *This is the very man who shot my father in the face!*

It was as if he hadn't really known that fact until then. He'd stared at Snoddy until the man noticed, cussed at him, and told him to keep his ugly little face turned some other direction.

From that moment of realization, Bushrod had seen his duty clear. The Indians among whom he had been raised followed a strict, formalized code of vengeance. Snoddy had murdered

Bushrod's father. Blood had been spilt. Therefore, other blood needed to be spilt in turn, to balance things out, and preferably the blood of the very one who was guilty.

Now, with Snoddy sleeping away a rainy afternoon, opportunity presented itself—yet Bushrod was frozen with indecision. To actually ax a man to death was a significant act, to say the least. Bushrod was too frightened to move. He could imagine what he needed to do, but his hands trembled and felt so numb he could barely hold the ax.

He bit his lip and stirred up his will. He *had* to do it! He owed it to his father. He'd kill Snoddy, flee, head back toward Coldwater, find Tuckaseh, if he was still alive.

Maybe he'd even find Michel, if Michel had gone back to the same region after the *unakas* freed him. Not that he was all that certain he really wanted to find Michel, after the way the man abandoned him.

Bushrod gripped the ax in both hands, drew in a breath, raised the weapon . . .

He groaned and turned away, lowering the ax, then putting it back in its place in the rear. He fell to his knees and scooted into the opposite corner of the cabin, shaken by his loss of nerve.

He was glad none of his Coldwater friends could see him now. They would surely mock him as a coward.

Snoddy wakened in a fairly good humor, meaning he only tripped Bushrod and laughed, instead of cussing at him just for being there. Scratching himself, belching loudly, he declared himself hungry and began digging about in the dirty cabin for food.

Bushrod was hungry, too, but didn't dare say so. He could tell that Snoddy resented sharing his food; the ratty man watched with a frown each bite that Bushrod consumed. At such times Bushrod wondered what had possessed Snoddy to take him in to begin with.

Snoddy gave a loud "Aha!" and came up grinning with a moldy loaf of bread in one hand and a scrap of old venison in the other. "Now, there's a meal!" Grinning and scratching some more, Snoddy sat down at the little homemade table, plopped the victuals onto the rough wood, plate or trencher be hanged, and began gnawing away.

Bushrod watched, disgusted. The one good thing about the way Snoddy ate was that it made his own aching appetite disappear for awhile. It was almost as bad a sight as the time he looked out the cabin's one window and saw Snoddy perched atop what he had before taken to be a hitching rail. Snoddy was hanging his bare rump over the rail, loudly emptying his bowels. Bushrod had almost become sick.

Bushrod watched Snoddy finish the food and lick the crumbs off his fingers. Flicking his tongue out to clean the residue from his scraggly beard, Snoddy's eyes caught Bushrod's.

"What are you staring at, boy?"

"Nothing."

"Quit staring at me. I don't like that gaping. What? Them injuns teach you some kind of evil eye, maybe? You trying to hurt me?"

"No."

"Why do you sound so strange when you talk, boy?"

Bushrod, accustomed to hearing the Cherokee and Creek languages, or the smooth, educated inflections of multi-lingual Jean-Yves, thought it was Snoddy who sounded strange. He didn't dare say that, but the silence was as ill-received as the words would have been.

Snoddy slammed the table with his palm. "*Damn* you, boy! Have you got no sense about you at all? Didn't you hear me tell you not to stare at me that way?"

Bushrod quickly turned his head and looked at the door.

Outside that door, Snoddy's three dogs instantly began to bark. The coincidence of timing didn't escape Snoddy's notice. "How'd you make *that* happen?" he asked in an awed tone.

"I didn't."

"The hell! You got some witching in you, boy? Them heathens teach that to you?"

"No."

"What else can you do?"

"Nothing."

"I don't believe that. Look at me again."

Bushrod obeyed, though he found it hard to look at Snoddy when Snoddy was looking back at him.

"You got a strange light in your eyes, Bushrod. I believe you really are some kind of witch."

The dogs barked again, and Snoddy nodded, taking it for verification of what he'd said. The barking, however, continued and heightened for several moments until it was evident the dogs were barking at something or someone drawing near the cabin. Snoddy grunted and went to the corner for his rifle, then to the door, where he pushed back a wooden slide and peered out through the rifle hole.

"Snoddy!" a man's voice called from some distance away. "I want to come have a word or two with you!"

Snoddy hollered, "That you, Magree? Come on in, if it is!"

"Tie them dogs off first! I'll not be eat up by them like last time!"

"Hold on, then!" Snoddy went out to tie up the hounds. They were indeed mean animals, which Snoddy made sure of by treating them badly. Bushrod had almost been attacked by them several times already.

Bushrod watched from the window, trying to stay hidden behind the partially closed shutter. A man he didn't know, but who maybe he'd seen among the Coldwater raiders, came up to Snoddy out of the woods and talked to him. The conversation was out of Bush's earshot, but Snoddy grew quite intense as he heard whatever was told him. His hands waved about, his face reddened. The visitor looked sad, like he was delivering news he didn't really want to tell.

The conversation went on for three or four minutes, then Snoddy, now looking deflated, walked by the newcomer's side back into the woods, talking with his head hanging low, his gestures now limp and small. They were gone for nearly half an hour, and when Snoddy returned, he was alone.

Bush was astonished. Snoddy's face looked like that of a man who'd been crying.

*   *   *

Snoddy kept whiskey, but hadn't drunk much of it during Bushrod's time with him. This night he pulled out the jug and began drinking heavily, growing more moody the drunker he became.

He'd said nothing about his conversation with the stranger, and Bushrod had known better than to ask. At the moment, Bushrod was seated in the corner on the floor, trying to stay out of Snoddy's line of view. He wished he were back in Coldwater, with his father and mother still alive, and with no knowledge of the *unaka* world beyond what he learned from returning Indian raiders.

He eyed Snoddy's red hair, thinking how interesting some of those raiders would find a thatch like that. It would make quite a colorful scalplock, stretched around a red-painted willow hoop.

Despite a gnawing hunger, Bushrod finally fell asleep out of sheer boredom. Just when he had, Snoddy gave a great, loud sob that made Bushrod spasm awake.

"Boy!" Snoddy said, not sharply like usual, but almost tenderly. "Boy, come here and let me take a look at you."

Bushrod wasn't sure he liked this. He rose and cautiously approached.

Snoddy turned to face him; Bushrod was surprised and a little appalled to see tears streaming over the big, blotchy freckles on his cheeks. Snoddy looked Bushrod up and down, and nodded. "Yes, indeed, a fine young fellow you are. So mighty fine and good to have forgiven me for killing your own father!"

It was news to Bushrod that he'd forgiven Snoddy.

Snoddy raised his jug and took a swig. He set the jug down roughly and wiped his mouth with his hand. "Bush, you reckon you'll marry when you grow up?"

"I don't know."

Snoddy sobbed again, then managed to compose himself some. "She's gone and married another man, Bush! The only woman I ever cared about, and she's gone and married some fool out of Virginia, and gone off! Vernon Magree told me all about it today. I can't believe she done it, Bush! I'm all alone! But not really. I still got you to be my friend and comfort. What would I do if you was gone?''

Bushrod would be glad to give Snoddy the chance to find out. It was interesting to see this new version of Snoddy, but he still didn't like him. The drunken persona was certainly different from the sober one, but just as unpleasant in different ways.

Maybe less threatening, though. Bushrod decided to risk a question. ''Am I going to stay here for good?''

''Oh, yes, son, of course you are. Don't you worry! I wouldn't throw you out, not after all the suffering you've done! No, sir! Besides, I need you around to cheer me in my sorrow.''

Bushrod had seen no evidence yet that his presence did anything but annoy Snoddy. He hated to hear that Snoddy wanted to keep him around. He hoped the scoundrel would grow tired enough of him to boot him out, before he chose to shoot him instead. Bush still thought with an Indian's mind, and perceived himself as Snoddy's prize and slave. In the culture in which Bush had grown up, a slave lived entirely at the will of the master. He could be killed at any moment, without recourse or reprisal.

Snoddy pulled his head up and looked into Bushrod's face while rheum ran down his own face from his nostrils and soaked his whiskers. ''You and me, we're partners, Bush! Ain't nobody going to divide us.''

Bushrod wished he had found the will to use that belt ax when he had the chance.

''Bush, I want you to know, son, that I'm sorry about shooting your father like I done. I thought he was coming up to kill me, you see, but I think I was wrong. I can't bring him back, but I'll surely try to take his place. I'll do my best for you. I only wish I could give you a mother, too.'' He sobbed anew. ''Oh, she's gone and left me! Gone and married a jackass from Virginia!''

He let his hands fall away from Bushrod's shoulders. The boy backed off and sat down.

Snoddy drank and cried another hour, then passed out.

Bushrod rose from the corner and walked over to where Snoddy lay with his head on the table, a puddle of drool beside his open mouth. Bush stared at him a few moments, then went to the rear of the cabin, and fetched the ax.

CHAPTER EIGHT

Bush moved through the woods at a speed a healthy hunting dog might have envied, as if he expected Snoddy to show up behind him in pursuit. In fact he knew he wouldn't. Snoddy was in no situation to come after Bush or anyone else.

Bush had brought the ax with him, though he sawed the handle short so he could carry it like a belt ax. The ax head was clean because it hadn't been used. Though the general Indian concepts of vengeance that Bush had grown up with would have justified the killing of Snoddy in retaliation for his killing of Freneau, Bush had again found himself unable to perform that ultimate act. Instead he'd tied the drunken man up very tightly, using every thong and cord and rope and scrap of cloth he could find about the cabin.

When Bush left, Snoddy was on the floor, hog-tied, his forearms bound to one another as well with a strong rope that stretched across his shoulder blades, and further tied to a metal ring pegged deeply into the wall as a place to hook pots and such when not in use. Snoddy would get loose eventually after he woke up, but it would take a day or two.

And by that time Bush would be long gone, miles away in the direction of Coldwater. The more he thought about it, the more sure he was that some of the town's former dwellers would still be about the area. If not, Bush would try to track them. If that failed, he would head east, toward the older river towns, where surely he would find someone he knew, or at least someone who had dealt with his father or uncle. If all went the best, he'd find Tuckaseh.

Two weeks of *unaka* life had been entirely enough to suit him. He was ready to return to the kind of people he'd known since birth, to be Skiuga again instead of Bush Underhill.

He traveled with confidence equalling his speed. Under the tutelage of Tuckaseh, Freneau, and the finest woodsmen of Coldwater, Bush had developed a sense of direction that seldom failed him. Further, he'd kept a close watch on the route from Coldwater, and realized that finding his way back again would be relatively simple even without honed instincts.

The upper half of the route followed a long-established Indian war and trading trail that stretched from the bluffs of the Cumberland River, where Shawnees lived prior to the coming of the white settlements, on down through the Chickasaw and Choctaw country and eventually to the region of the Natchez along the vast river that split the land from north to south, a river Bush had yet to see but about which he had heard much from his father and Michel.

Some miles below the stream that the whites called the Duck River, the path deviated almost due south from the southwest-oriented Indian trail he now followed, and led toward the Tennessee River, whose shoals would identify the vicinity of Coldwater. All in all, it would be a relatively simple journey.

If he could avoid the whites, that is. Now that Coldwater was destroyed, the whites took to the wilderness as they hadn't done in the longest time. The Indian threat was diminished with the destruction of Coldwater, the whites believed, and thus the wilderness was again open for white hunters, explorers, and field-clearers. Bush figured chances were good he might run across some of them, especially in the earlier portions of his journey. But he would not let any of them lure or take him back. He didn't want to live among the whites, and in particular, after what he'd done and all he'd taken, he didn't want to run across Tip Snoddy again.

He had a lot of Snoddy's possessions on him. His trousers were an extra pair of Snoddy's, which he'd hurriedly cut shorter at the bottom to fit. He'd thrown one of Snoddy's old hunting shirts atop his own as well. Hunting shirts hung long by design, but on Bush's frame, Snoddy's reached well below his knees, like a long dress, and Bush had been forced to cinch a lot of it high up beneath the waist sash, also taken from Snoddy. The sleeves were rolled up at the cuffs. His hat, a typical flop, was the one stolen item that fit well, Snoddy being a small-headed fellow.

Then there were the weapons he'd taken. Snoddy's rifle was a good weapon, though poorly maintained. Most frontiersmen cared for their rifles as if they were extensions of themselves, but it fit Snoddy's sorry personality that he'd let his fall into disrepair. It was battered and scratched, the barrel and lock even rusted at spots. Still, it was an adequate .43 caliber, with a maple stock and a nearly 50-inch barrel that was a pretty charcoal blue where the rust hadn't eaten it. The buttplate and flint were in excellent shape. Snoddy had possessed a good supply of powder, patches, and rifle balls, probably materials he accumulated prior to the Coldwater raid.

Bush's moccasins had also been Snoddy's, taken right off his feet while he was passed out. Though Snoddy's feet were a lot longer than Bush's, moccasins had enough give-and-take in them in any case to transfer adequately from one wearer to another. Besides, Snoddy's were new and Bush's were old and nearly worn out. He'd slipped Snoddy's on right atop his own old moccasins, and tied the high flaps above the curve of his calf, just below his knees.

Topping off Bush's outfit was Snoddy's linsey-woolsey hunting coat, which again was too long. Bush had hacked the sleeves short, just like the trousers.

Bush had been raised with a strong sense of morality pounded into him, in their different ways, by both Freneau and Tuckaseh. He had no use for a thief and had once beaten nearly senseless another Coldwater boy who'd stolen a home-made knife from him. But what he took from Snoddy he didn't see as stolen, merely the legitimate booty of war. For all the syrupy, emotional things Snoddy had said to Bush while drunk, he was still Bush's enemy and jailer. And in Bush's world view, an escaping prisoner had the right to take what he needed in order to survive and avoid recapture.

Slung over Bush's back were three blankets rolled together around a rawhide cord. These would provide wraps to sleep in, or if need be, material for a quick lean-to shelter in case of rain.

Just now rain looked likely. Tuckaseh was a master of reading weather signs, and had taught the skill to Bush. From the weight of clouds, their color and heaviness, the way they moved and hung and grew in the sky, Bush could predict with almost total accuracy the approach of worsening weather, how hard the precipitation would be, and how long it would last. He'd traveled almost an entire night and the better part of a day without stopping even to eat, and his prediction was that there would be a substantial rain before sundown. Well and good. A hard rain would blur any track he might have left and make him harder to follow—assuming anybody would bother to follow him at all. Chances were reasonable, it seemed to him, that no one would, unless Tip Snoddy held grudges terribly hard, and was willing to go to a lot of effort to see them vented.

The afternoon waned as clouds rolled in, and he paused to eat, taking very little. A squirrel came by too close, and he dropped it with a single barking shot. He skinned the squirrel quickly and expertly, cutting it around the middle and peeling the rump end of the pelt back over the hind legs, the front portion over the head. Carving off the meat, he laid it aside briefly while he built a fire, sparking it with a few grains of powder laid among the punk and touched off with a spark from the rifle lock. Normally such use of powder would seem a wasteful extravagance, but Bush had plenty of powder and needed to hurry because of the coming rain. He didn't want the fire burning for long and sending out smoke to betray his presence, either. He got the blaze going, considered heating some stones on which to roast the squirrel meat, then opted for the faster, if less satisfactory, approach of spitting the meat on green wood and roasting it directly against the flames. When it was done, he put the fire out and ate hurriedly. He needed to find shelter fast.

He paused near a stream, but moved up from it a good thirty

feet when he noticed he was within the high-water marks left
by past floods. Once above the mark, he selected a level spot,
reasonably clear, and with two small trees ideally situated for
his purposes. Quickly he hacked down three saplings maybe
a couple of inches in diameter, and chopped away the branches
so that he was left with three long, straight poles. One of these
he lashed, horizontally and about four feet off the ground, to
the two trees. The other two poles were placed, one against
each tree, each with one end extending over the lashed-up
pole, the other end thrusting into the ground. He cut small
stakes from some of the branches he'd peeled off the saplings,
and drove them into the ground where the leaning poles
touched the soil. He tore strips of cloth from the excess length
of his hunting shirt and tied the ends of the poles firmly to
the stakes. The upper end of the poles he tied to the pole he'd
lashed horizontally between the trees. The first drops of rain
were beginning to patter, so he worked fast.

He stretched one of the blankets between the leaning poles,
curling the top over the horizontal pole and tying it in place
with more cloth strips. He tied further strips down the sides
of the blanket where it lay over the leaning poles, forming, at
the end, a sloping cloth roof. The second and third blankets
he folded into triangles and affixed to each side of the shelter.
The rain fell in earnest now, but it hardly mattered. He'd made
an adequate lean-to to deflect it, even if it did leave him without a blanket to sleep in. Perhaps if the rain stopped later, he
would remove one blanket from the side of the shelter, fold it
flat, and roll up in it.

He lay down, watching the storm sweep spectacularly
through the woodlands. His feelings were as turbulent as the
electrified sky. Building this shelter had taken him back to a
time when he and Tuckaseh built a similar blanket lean-to
while on a hunt. They'd been caught by a storm, as Bush had
today. Tuckaseh put up the shelter in half the time it took
Bush to put up this one. And together they had rested out the
storm and slept a peaceful night, rising to a beautiful day and
excellent hunting.

It was hard to fathom that such an event might never happen

again. Tuckaseh, like Freneau, Waninahi, and Marie, might be dead. If so, then Bush Underhill was indeed alone in the world. Utterly so.

The storm swept the forest, silencing the birds, sending squirrels, rabbits, and other small game into their hidden burrows and dens. Lightning struck a tree on a hillside somewhere behind Bush. He listened to the magnificent rending of its bulk, the crash of it through the trees, the thrumming, dead jolt of it striking ground.

The wilderness could be frightening. Bush, however, had little fear. He'd been raised in this wild land and was at peace with it. Where he felt fear, where he felt out of place and endangered, was among the *unakas*. The only one he'd met since the Coldwater raid that he could hold much good feeling toward was Jim Lusk.

Bush slept, awakening only once in the night. The storm was long past, the stars winking overhead through the trees. He took down the blanket on one side of the shelter and wrapped up in it, sleeping out the rest of the night in comfort and arising hungry and thirsty, but fully rested.

He went down to the stream and drank, then fished by hand in the shallows. Cleaning and spit-roasting the fish, he breakfasted, eyes ever scanning the land around him. A man on his own in the forest must be ever vigilant, Tuckaseh had often counseled. It is the man who thinks himself safe who dies.

Bush rose, broke down his shelter, rolled the blankets up again and tied them across his shoulders as before. He set out, heading farther down the old war trail toward the Duck River.

Bushrod crouched, as still as a carved figure, his rifle ready, cocked. He peered across the canebrake beside which he hid, his eyes in motion, his ears probing the unnatural silence around him.

Someone was there. More than one person. He'd heard them, sensed them, smelled them.

White men, come in pursuit? Maybe. But why would anyone bother? Unless, perhaps, Tip Snoddy had gotten free of his bonds much more quickly than Bush had anticipated.

He heard movement, a crackling in the cane. Bush tensed and waited—and into view crept two figures. Indians. Crouched, with rifles, looking for him.

Bush's first impulse was to relax. He was, after all, a resident of Coldwater, raised among the combined Creeks and Cherokees of that town.

No. Not anymore. Coldwater was gone. He was clad in white man's garments, and his skin was white. And these Indians weren't familiar; they wouldn't know him. They appeared to be Creeks, one side of their heads shaved, a crest left on the top, the hair on the other side hanging long. To them he was simply an anonymous white. An enemy. And they were stalking him.

This terrified Bush, then angered him. The very notion of being considered one of *them*, the very *unakas* from whose society he was fleeing, was offensive. He might be killed, but he would not be killed in these circumstances!

He held still as ice, watching and waiting. The rifle was heavy in his hands; he felt cold, but his palms sweated. His best hope was that they would move around the brake and not detect him.

But they did. Through a gap in the foliage the first Indian's eyes met Bush's. Everything was perfectly still for a moment, time itself frozen—and then the Indian let out a fearsome cry and began running around the wide canebrake, circling toward Bush. The second one, now seeing Bush as well, yelled and fell in behind. He didn't think they'd seen his rifle, which might prove advantageous. In any case they'd be around the stand of cane and upon him in moments.

Bush fought back panic. He felt very much a scared boy just now, but knew he must act like a man, calmly and courageously. He could not hope to outrun both these Indians. So he dropped to his knee, raised the rifle, and waited for the first Indian to come around the canebrake.

Moments later, he did. The Indian saw Bush kneeling, saw the rifle aimed at him, and apparently saw as well that the man he thought he'd been stalking was in fact merely a boy. After that he saw no more, because Bush's rifle boomed. Smoke and fire burst out into the canebrake, and the Indian fell back, dead, his heart perfectly pierced by the rifle ball.

Bushrod Underhill, not yet out of his boyhood, had just killed his first man.

The second Creek—who, Bush noticed, had a fresh, sandy-haired scalp tied to the waist sash of his breechcloth—fell back after the first went down, and Bush got on his feet to run. At the same time he reloaded the rifle, a trick that Tuckaseh had taught him only a year prior. The old Indian's eyes weren't quite so blind then. "A man never knows when he will have to load while running," Tuckaseh had said. "Knowing how to do so has been the difference between life and death for many a man."

Bush ramrodded patch and ball down the barrel atop a powder charge, and slid the hickory ramrod back into its thimbles without losing a step. The second Indian, having paused only a moment to examine the body of his companion, was coming on hard, but more carefully than the first man. This one would be harder to deal with.

The best bet was to go out of sight, to keep the Indian in view while forcing the Indian to look for him. He dodged into the canebrake, sliding through the tall cane stalks, losing himself quickly. The Indian had seen him enter, but it was always a tricky business to search for a fugitive in a canebrake, and if Bush handled his situation correctly, he had a chance to gain the advantage.

He let instinct guide him to a place that seemed a likely hiding place, and dropped to a squat. The rifle was fully reloaded now, but he took a moment to check the charge in the pan, and refresh it when he found it wanting. Then he settled to wait the Indian's approach.

He heard nothing. It could be that the Indian had given the matter a second thought or two, and decided a mere boy wasn't worth the effort and risk. Perhaps the thought of possibly dying at a boy's hand, like his companion had, was too shameful and he'd turned off the pursuit to save face.

Or perhaps he was still out there, waiting for Bush to move, or cough, or sneeze, or otherwise reveal where he was hidden.

Bush determined that he would do nothing of the sort.

But as he sat there, a pain began to throb in his foot, beginning as a dull ache and quickly turning sharp. Puzzled, he looked down and saw a piece of broken cane penetrating the two moccasins he wore and digging deeply into the flesh. The pain was fast growing intense, and he wondered how it was he hadn't noticed it until he sat still. Probably the sheer panic of flight, the intense concentration on survival, had temporarily robbed his body of the ability to feel pain.

The pain swelled hotter and higher, crawling up his leg, making him bite his lip, hurting so badly he wanted to murmur, to yell, to cry. But he held still, hardly breathing, keeping the rifle trained at the place where the Indian would surely appear.

The cane rustled to his left. He turned his head and saw the Indian entering the brake. The Indian saw him, met his eye, raised his rifle to shoot. Bush tried to whip his own rifle around, but the long barrel struck cane stalks and was obstructed.

The Indian fired. Bush let out a yelp as something stung the left side of his head. He was shot! He groped up, felt blood, then realized the bullet had merely clipped off about a quarter-inch of his earlobe.

The Indian began to back out of the canebrake. Bush came up on his uninjured foot, managed to get his rifle into position, and fired just as the Indian withdrew.

The shot struck the Indian in the belly. He grunted and fell back.

Immediately, Bush began to reload, concentrating so intently that once again his cane-stabbed foot no longer hurt.

He heard the Indian moving on the ground, writhing, but still managing to reload his own rifle. Bush finished his reloading, tried to advance, and received a brutal new reminder of his cane stab. Sharp pain fired up his leg and he fell.

Shots sounded outside the canebrake. Men yelled. White men, speaking English.

Bush felt faint all at once. He struggled against it, but knew he'd pass out in a moment. Before he did so, however, he raised his voice: "Here! I'm in here! Help me, white men!"

"It's a boy!" one of the unseen white men called. "You hear that voice? It's a boy!"

Bush flopped over, losing consciousness for a few moments. When he opened his eyes again, he'd been pulled out of the canebrake and was lying on his back.

Looking down at him were three white men, and one of them was Jim Lusk.

CHAPTER NINE

Bush winced and tried to divert his mind off his painful foot by looking around the stockade. It was a small one as stockades went, and seemed to be getting smaller all the time with the arrival of new people from the countryside around.

The general mood was one of disappointment and anger. The idea that the Coldwater raid had put an end to Indian raids had died a quick and disturbing death. A body of no less than two hundred Creeks had reportedly pervaded the countryside and split up into smaller parties. Raids were hitting farmsteads and isolated blockhouses right and left. Rather than end the Indian hostilities, the destruction of Coldwater had simply roused new anger, particularly among the Creeks, who were angry over what they saw as the unjustified deaths of several of their warriors.

There were rumors that a large Indian attack might come upon the community within the next day or so. And thus the stockade was filling, families fleeing to their safety, bringing with them livestock and what household goods they could. Most of the livestock went into pens outside the fort, the household goods into a general storehouse built against the main fort wall.

Bush's foot, though still painful, felt much better now that the intruding piece of cane had been pulled out. Jim Lusk had taken care of that right at the canebrake, yanking it out without warning, sending a jolt of pain through Bush that was so intense he actually passed out again for a couple of moments. Lusk wrapped the bleeding foot with a temporary bandage, and with his two companions led Bush to their horses, hidden nearby. Bush rode into the stockade with them, his eye all the while on the horse ahead of Lusk's, on which was lashed the scalped corpse of a young frontiersman. He'd run upon the same two Creeks whom Bush had dispatched. A member of Lusk's scouting party, this fellow had been far less fortunate.

The stockade was filling steadily, and Bush, seated on a keg up against a cabin wall with his poulticed and bandaged foot stretched out before him (as soon as he'd reached the fort, a fat, matronly woman had removed the temporary bandage and replaced it with medicated wrappings), noticed that he was receiving plenty of curious glances and seemed to be the object of much conversation. He wasn't entirely comfortable with this. Did these people know his Indian background, and despise him for it?

The truth was quite different, as he learned when Lusk approached and squatted beside him.

"How's the foot, Bushrod?"

"Feeling better."

"Good. You know, you're quite the hero here."

"Hero?" Bush wasn't quite sure of the meaning of that word, though he recalled hearing Jean-Yves use it a time or two in his old schooling sessions.

"That's right. Two Creeks, brung down by a lad! It's the talk of the fort."

Bush thought about it, and had to admit that it did sound impressive. Still below shaving age, and had killed two experienced warriors! The reality of it hadn't quite set in yet.

"Who was the dead fellow we brought in on the horse?" Bush asked.

"Ah, that was poor Jimmy Herndon. A fine scout, though a young man. Those two Creeks caught him while he was drinking at a spring, and killed him. Took his scalp, with the rest of us just over the next rise. We were out tracking them when you had your own run-in with them. That's how we happened to be there so quickly when it was over. Not that we were needed. That was one devil of a job you did at the canebrake, son."

"Thank you." Now Bush knew whose scalp it was he'd seen on that Creek's breechcloth.

"But tell me something, Bushrod. Why were you out there anyhow?"

Bush saw no reason to lie. "I'd run off from Tip Snoddy. Took his rifle, a lot of his clothes, food, blankets. I had it in mind to go back to Coldwater."

"Bush, you didn't kill Snoddy, did you?"

"No."

"That's good. He's hardly worth more than killing, but murder is murder, and I wouldn't want to see you involved in it. But how'd you get away from him?"

"He got drunk and went to sleep like drunkards do. I tied him up and took his things. He's probably still trying to get free."

Lusk flicked his heavy brows. "Well, given this Creek threat, maybe I ought to send somebody out to his place to set him free so he can get here."

"I don't want to see him again."

"I can understand that, after what you did. But don't worry about Snoddy. I'll see to it myself that he gives you no trouble," Lusk grinned. "After he hears about you and them two Creeks, I doubt he'd have much will to cause you problems, anyhow."

"All I did was load and shoot when I had the chance."

"Aye, but it's having the nerve and the skill to do so under such a pressure as you were, that makes the difference between a common man and a woodsman. And I do believe you are a woodsman, son."

"I was well taught."

"Why did you want to go back to Coldwater? There's nothing there. And your people are dead."

"Maybe there's still someone left there."

"I don't think so. They've scattered, or so all the scouts say. The town is nothing but ashes and rubble."

Bush looked away. It was still hard to conceive of Coldwater being gone, even though he'd witnessed its destruction himself. He changed the subject.

"Tip Snoddy will be angry because I took his possessions."

"He may at that," Lusk said. Scratching his beard, he thought a minute. "Well, then we'll give them back. I've got better than he had for you, anyway."

"What do you mean?"

"Jimmy Herndon had no kin at all. He was something of a partner of mine, so I reckon that makes me the closest thing to family there is in his case, and means I can decide what will become of his rifle and gear and so on. I'll give it to you, and Snoddy can have his rusty old stuff back again."

Bush looked into Lusk's face and saw pain barely hidden there. "I'm sorry about your friend being killed."

Lusk grinned sadly. "You've already made up for a lot of it by killing them two Creeks."

A girl, maybe a year or two older than Bush, and quite attractive, walked up slowly and eyed him in a way that made him feel a lot more manly than he'd ever felt before. A slightly younger girl, just as pretty, approached shyly behind her. "Are you the one who killed the Indians today?"

Bush nodded. "Yes."

The girls made little sounds of excitement, looked at one another and giggled. "We think that's truly wonderful," the older one said. They ran off together, grinning, giggling, casting glances back Bush's way.

Lusk looked at him closely. "Maybe living among your own kind has got some possible good about it after all . . . you think?"

Bush blushed, and was embarrassed by it. "Maybe so." He looked away from Lusk.

Lusk chuckled. "I'll go fetch poor Jimmy's rifle and such."

Bush watched him walk away, then caught sight of the two girls still looking at him, grinning and talking to one another.

He stared at his bandaged foot. Oh, well. Couldn't walk just now, anyway. And likely Lusk was right about Coldwater. There'd be nobody there, and if the Creeks were roaming the region, looking for war, it didn't make much sense to undertake such a major journey at present.

Bush glanced up at the girls, then down again.

He figured maybe he could stand to linger among the *unakas* awhile longer, after all.

Two hours later, Tip Snoddy arrived at the stockade, freshly rescued from his humiliating situation by a pair of Lusk's men. Snoddy was wild-eyed, wild-haired, furious and cussing, talking about how he was ready to thrash Bushrod Underhill to his death, how it was his right to do so because Bush was his personal prisoner, and had stolen from him, stolen his very rifle, the very hat off his head, and—

"Shut it up, Snoddy," Lusk said. "You're a scoundrel and a drunkard and not fit to occupy this stockade, and you'll not talk so about a young fellow who's already killed two redskins this very day, and would probably be glad to kill a red-haired fool to top it all off."

Snoddy frowned. "What the hell you talking about, killed two redskins?"

Lusk told the tale with relish, and Snoddy listened with a deepening frown, casting a dark glance or two at Bush every now and then during the narrative.

"Hah!" he grunted when it was over. "Got lucky, I reckon."

"Maybe it was more than luck," Lusk said. "Maybe he had a bit of courage about him. Seems I recall that the last time we was raided around here, you was found hiding in a well, too far down to get out again, and had to be hoisted out." Lusk leaned over and spat. "We should have just left you there."

"If you're calling me a coward, Lusk, I'll—"

"You'll shut up, that's what. And you'll stay well away from Bush Underhill. He's my partner now. Jimmy Herndon, who was ten times the man you'll ever be, got killed today by the same Creeks that Bush took care of. Bush is taking his rifle, his gear, and his place. He's my partner now, and you'll stay clear of him if you know what's good for you."

"What about my rifle? My clothes and such?"

"You can have 'em back. Probably crawling with lice anyhow."

"But look! He's hacked the legs short on my britches!"

"Then do a bit of stitching and add to them. And be glad that because of the young fellow who wore them, there's two fewer redskins roaming this countryside to threaten us."

Snoddy grunted disdainfully and cast a harsh glare Bush's way. But he stayed away from him the entire time the stockade was occupied, and after that, Bush worried about Tip Snoddy no more.

The anticipated attack never came, the large Creek force opting not to work in unison, or to take on the usually futile task of stockade attack. Instead they divided into small raiding bands and struck across the entire area, burning the cabins and barns of several of the people who had taken to the stockades, killing a few stragglers who hadn't forted up, and stealing what horses they could find. Then they faded back into the wilderness, rejoined, and left the vicinity, only a few remaining behind to carry on quick little raids when the opportunity came.

Bush left the stockade limping badly, but able to get by. He had heard what Lusk said about them being partners now, and though they hadn't discussed it between themselves, his acceptance of the slain Jimmy Herndon's goods counted in both their minds as an agreement to Lusk's proposition. Things had progressed a long way since the day Lusk declared he was washing his hands of young Bushrod.

Oddly, Bush found his new situation suited him. The more he was around Lusk, the more he liked him. Lusk reminded him sometimes, in some limited ways, of Freneau, and occasionally even of Tuckaseh. He was a fine woodsman, to be sure; Bush admired his woodcraft and learned something from him daily, simply through observation. And when Lusk praised him for some accomplishment—even something so minor as improvising a button for his handed-down hunting jacket by rolling a leather strip into a ball—Bush felt he received a true compliment indeed.

Almost against his will, Bush found himself falling bit by bit into the kind of life Lusk led, and enjoying it. This accommodation was made easier by the fact that Lusk's life was not much different from that of an Indian, anyway, so there were few mental transitions required on Bush's part.

Lusk had spoken truly when he said he had no one at home. In fact he had many homes, or at least many places to lodge for a night or two. He spent his days hunting, scouting, watching for Indian sign. He was a kind of ghost of the forest, an Americanized version of the *coureur des bois* that Freneau had been. Bush watched the man and the way the settlers responded to him when his path crossed theirs, and realized that Lusk was esteemed almost as a superhuman being, a guardian in the forest who watched, protected. Bush got the idea that many of the people, the children in particular, believed that no Indian could draw near without Lusk detecting his presence. As long as Lusk was out there, all would be well.

In fact, all was not well. The raids continued, the impact of the Coldwater attack falling into ever deeper insignificance. The ruination of Bush's old village and way of life hadn't even accomplished the end the *unakas* had hoped for. So, in a sense, Freneau, Marie, Waninahi, and all the others had died for no reason, even from the viewpoint of the attackers! It made Bush angry when he let himself think about it.

Which wasn't often. As weeks rolled by and he grew ever more comfortable in the woodland life of the hunter and scout, he began to admit to himself that he not only liked being with Lusk, he also liked being an *unaka*. These people, once alien and enemy in his eyes, had suddenly become human beings to him. Personalities. People he could like, and who certainly liked him in return. His shooting of the Creeks had become legend, and he found himself receiving the same kind of veneration that Lusk received.

"The scouting lad," many called him. He liked the ring of it. The scouting lad, the brave fellow who roamed the forest with the great Jim Lusk, surviving unprotected in the woods when everyone else was forted up and afraid, and always coming through. The intelligence that Lusk and Underhill carried to the various stockades along the Cumberland repeatedly saved lives and sent people safely inside in time to avoid attack.

Bit by bit, Bushrod Underhill was turning into a white man, not only physically, as he always was, but mentally. He noticed it at the beginning, but soon ceased thinking about it. After that, the transformation speeded on briskly, until it reached its completion one morning.

Bush, who was growing fast, both in height and muscle, rode at Lusk's side toward a line of rising black smoke in a hollow beyond a high ridge. At the ridgetop they paused and looked down upon the scene they had expected to find: a farmstead, smoldering and black, the barn burned to the ground, the cabin almost gone. Dead cattle, a dying horse, and in the yard, three corpses.

They rode down slowly. There was no reason to rush; the raiders had already vanished. Dismounting, they walked up to the first corpse. A woman, hacked nearly to pieces, her scalp torn away, her mouth wide open, her eyes half so. Flies buzzed about her, settling and feasting in the clotted blood that covered her.

Nearby, a boy, equally mutilated. His scalp had come off raggedly, leaving his skull exposed in a particularly ugly fashion. The raiders had taken time to carve off his genitals and lay them across his neck. The father of the family, who died closest to the house, was so thoroughly roasted by the heat that it was harder to tell what they'd done to him.

Lusk and Bush walked from corpse to corpse, saying nothing at first. Then Lusk sighed, shook his head, and said, "You know, Bush, I know you were raised among the Indians, and I know you see them through different eyes than I do. And I admit I've known many a fine Indian in my day, men just like this Tuckaseh you talk so much of. But on the whole, son, looking at them as a breed, I got to say I got little use for a redskin. Any that does such as this, and takes such relish in it, I can't say I find much affection for in my heart."

The words were spoken slowly, in a controlled voice. Bush knew that Lusk was struggling to avoid saying what Bush knew he was feeling at that moment: That he hated the race of Indians. Most white men did, Bush had learned. They felt toward the Indians the same disgust and bitter fury that the Indians felt toward them.

Bush looked over the carnage, and realized something that surprised him, and disturbed him, too: He was beginning to see how a man could come to hate Indians; to see that it might even be possible, if he saw much more like this, for him to hate them himself.

CHAPTER
TEN

June 1792, near the Cumberland River

As hard as he tried, Bushrod couldn't move. He stood affixed to the bank of the river, reaching his hand toward the boat that sailed swiftly away. He struggled to lift his feet and plunge into the river, but he seemed rooted. The boat, well-laden, moved farther from him, and inside it, at the edge of a small crowd of passengers, Marie Underhill reached back toward her brother, crying, trying to get to him. But she was held back by the arms of a man behind her. Michel Freneau.

Bush shouted for her, and she called his name . . . and then he opened his eyes and sat up, breathing fast and feeling his heart throb at full pace inside him.

The dream again. More distinct and memorable than ever. Bush glanced about, trying to recall just where he was. Oh, yes. One of Jim Lusk's many wilderness hovels, this one nestled beneath a riverside bluff. He and Lusk had been hunting and scouting through the area all the day before. He glanced at the rough wall, and through chinks and holes saw the dim light of a new morning.

He glanced across the little shelter and saw that Lusk was gone. Sniffing the air, he smelled smoke and the scent of cooking fish. After his disturbing dream, the prospect of a good breakfast cheered him.

What was less cheerful was the realization that there would be fewer such meals with Jim Lusk before long. Within days, Lusk's life was going to make a dramatic change, and Bush's, therefore, would change as well. For about five years now he'd been Lusk's partner, almost always at his side, growing out

of the last of his boyhood and gaining the stature and girth of
a man. Without conscious design, Lusk had become Bush's
new mentor, taking the role formerly filled by Freneau and
Tuckaseh. Under Lusk's straightforward guidance and teaching, Bush had almost forgotten the life he lived before.

Almost . . . but he hadn't forgotten Tuckaseh, who maybe
was still alive out there, somewhere. And he hadn't forgotten
Marie, who was dead, except in his increasingly frequent and
vivid dreams.

Bush exited the hovel, rising, stretching, yawning. Lusk was
at a fire nearby, roasting fish on a small metal cooking grate
he carried about in his pack.

"Morning, Bush."

"Morning. Fish smells mighty fine."

"It's nearly done. Hey, I heard you give a yell in there just
now. Everything well with you?"

A yell? Bush hadn't realized he'd yelled, and was embarrassed. "Everything's well. Just another dream."

"Marie again?"

"Yes."

"Which one? The one in your uncle's trade house, or the
fire, or the one where she's being taken down the river?"

Bush was again embarrassed. Did he really have so many
dreams of Marie that even his companion could categorize
them? "The river dream. My uncle holding her, taking her off
in the boat."

"I recollect that day quite well. Him floating off, you shouting for him. But no little girl in the boat."

"I know. But it's the oddest thing. When I see her there in
the dream, it's awfully real. Like a memory, not just something
I've thunk up. And I get to thinking: Might she have really
been on that boat? It was crowded. If she was standing with
my uncle, she'd have been hidden to me by the others standing
in front. And Michel always loved Marie. It would have been
like him to take her along with him."

"But he didn't take you along, and you were as much family to him as she was."

"Yes, but he never cared as much for me. She was always his favorite."

Lusk turned the fish. It dripped and sizzled and sent off a wonderfully scented smoke. "But she's dead, Bush. You know that. Her death was witnessed and reported."

"By Tip Snoddy. Not the most reliable fellow I could think of. I wish I could ask him more about it. He might have made it up." But nothing could be asked of Snoddy. A year before he'd been killed and scalped while hunting along the Harpeth River.

"Bush, you're letting a dream overtake your good sense."

"I believe she might be alive, Jim. I can't help but think it."

Lusk gave Bush an evaluative look. "How old are you now, boy?"

"You know I don't know that, not knowing for sure the year I was born."

"About what, though?"

"I figure maybe sixteen, seventeen. Somewhere in there."

"Then you're as good as a man. And a man knows when to quit hoping when the hoping becomes nonsense."

"I'll never quit hoping my sister is alive, Jim. You may as well not get to expecting that."

"I don't. I don't."

Bush made a visit to a nearby thicket, relieved himself, then came back to the fireside. "So, how many days now?"

"Oh, I don't know. A week or so."

"Just a few more days to be a free man, then old Jim's going to go into the pen and close the gate behind him."

"It's not a pen, Bush. It's marriage, and that's one gate I'm eager to close. You know, you make for fine enough company, partner, but I been married before, and believe me, a good wife's better company than you'll ever be." He chuckled, but took a glance at Bush's expression, and added, "Don't get fretful over it. You and me will still be scouting together, hunting, all that."

"It'll be different, Jim, and you know it. You'll have a wife to look after, and before long, a family. You'll have to get careful, not be roaming around taking all the chances we do."

"Bush, I don't believe you want me to get married."

In fact Bush didn't. He liked the free-roaming life he and Jim Lusk had lived for half a decade, and didn't want to see it end. But he knew that his partner was deeply in love with the attractive young widow named Nancy Carter, and that, like it or not, the marriage was going to take place. And on a deeper level, he was happy for Jim Lusk. The man had been lonely for a lot of years, having lost his first wife and family to ague and other illnesses years before. "I'm glad for you to get married, Jim. I hope only the best for you, and her, too."

"Thank you. Fish is ready."

They ate slowly, washing it down with cold spring water and accompanying it with dried biscuits. There was no conversation until the eating was done. Lusk's mood, however, visibly declined by the time he was finished.

"I'm worried about the rest of this year," he said, wiping his fingers on his trousers.

"Me, too," Bush said. "It was right peaceful last year, but this year . . . I don't know."

Indeed it had been a violent year so far. In January two hunters were fired upon and badly hurt by Indian raiders. The pair managed to get away and crawl to Bledsoe's Station, one of the several stockades in the Cumberland country. Later, however, one of those same hunters was tomahawked to death while he slept in his cabin with his family. The family died, too, except for one girl taken captive. The blame was laid on a Chickamauga band, and Bush wondered ever since if any of the guilty ones included men he'd known in Coldwater. Odd, how different his attitude was toward such Indians now.

The massacre of the hunter's family, unfortunately, was only a prelude for another death, when a young man named Purviance was slain and scalped by Indians less than a month after he moved to the region from North Carolina. His corpse was found by his pregnant wife. Bush had seen his gravestone: "John Purviance, Age 24 Years, Fell by Indian Barbarity May 7, 1792." The bereaved family had already moved away.

"Jim, I ain't just talking when I say you'll have to be more careful once you're married. What we do is dangerous, poking

around here in the woods while Indians are raiding and killing—if you don't watch, you'll end up like that Purviance,
with your wife a widow for the second time.''

"Always the optimist, ain't you, Bush?"

"I'm just speaking the truth."

"So you're saying we should cease our rangering and scouting?"

"I'm saying maybe you should."

"And leave you out here alone to do it, you just being a
boy?"

"You were talking like I was a man just a minute ago."

"Sixteen ain't a man."

"Maybe I'm seventeen."

"The point don't change. Bush, don't make too much of
this marriage of mine. We'll still be partners."

Bush kicked at a stone. "I been thinking that maybe I
should head out, maybe see if I can find out more about what
happened to Marie."

"What?"

Bush kicked the stone again.

"Bush, you know what happened to Marie. She was killed
in the Coldwater raid, and God only knows I've felt a weight
of guilt over her dying, even though I didn't do it, thank the
Lord. I've seen how you've thunk about her, dreamed and
yelled out in your sleep. It's bothered me, Bush. I can't deny
it. But it'll bother me a lot worse if you go out looking for
something you can't find. She's dead, Bush. You got to face
the truth."

"I know. I know. But what if—"

"Forget about that, Bush. Please. And let's get on away
from here. I got a feeling."

"Indians?"

"Yes. Just a feeling."

"You trust that feeling, Jim?"

"I've learned to."

"I have a feeling about Marie."

Lusk shook his head, smiling. "Bush Underhill, you could

drive a man to drink. Now, come on. Let's move along toward Zeigler's.''

The preacher's name was Atchley. He performed the ceremony out of doors on a warm afternoon, while Bush fidgeted nearby and kept watch on some clouds rising in the western sky. There would be rain before long, and if Atchley didn't speed up his marrying, it might strike before Jim Lusk became a married man.

The marriage made it in advance of the rain, though, Lusk planting a kiss on his new wife's lips just as the first drops fell. Afterward the entire party of participants and onlookers headed for the nearby house of Joseph Wilson, a few ducking into Jacob Zeigler's place. Food and drink came out. Bush, at Zeigler's house with the Lusks, stood off to the side, nibbling at roasted turkey and trying to look cheerful.

Lusk approached him. ''Bush, you going to congratulate me?''

''Of course I am. I'm pleased for you. Sorry you can't do any traveling to celebrate.''

''Too deuced dangerous, with all the Indian sign we've seen. But this station is home to Nancy. Staying here will do us just fine. You'll be staying close by, too?''

''Thought I might scout a bit for a couple of days.''

''I don't like you getting out and doing that alone.''

''It wasn't me who got married, Jim. I don't have a wife to stay home for.''

''You be careful if you do go out there, son.''

''I will be. It'll be easier, in one way. I won't have to worry about anybody but myself, you being safe and sound here with your wife.''

''Ain't no place safe and sound these days, Bush. Not even here.''

Two days later

Bush leaped over a boulder and came down in the stream, splashing across the shallow water and onto the bank beyond.

He moved his long rifle adeptly, avoiding the brush and branches, and dodged on moccasined feet up a leafy forest slope toward the top of the next ridge.

A man behind him clambered atop the same boulder and stopped, panting, face red. "Devil . . . with it," he said to himself, aloud. "I can't . . . keep up . . . with that . . . and I ain't trying . . . no more."

He sat down, let his breath return, then stood and walked slowly across the creek. His job had been merely to find Bushrod Underhill and deliver an urgent message to him, not to keep pace with him on the mad race back to the station. He'd delivered the message, and if Underhill felt compelled to run all the way back to Zeigler's he'd just have to run alone.

But as he stepped slowly across the creek, the messenger heard sounds behind him in the forest that sent a chill up his spine. He speeded up, and once over the far bank, was on the run again himself. The countryside seemed a dangerous place just now. What lay ahead at Zeigler's Station proved just how dangerous.

Bushrod, meanwhile, pounded over the final ridge and stopped. Looking down, he felt stark horror, followed by a vague sense of sickness, rise inside.

"No," he said. "Oh, no."

He bounded down the slope, the long queue of dark, braided hair bouncing on the back of his head, the fringes of his linsey-woolsey rifleman's frock flapping and flying, his rifle pouch and powderhorn swaying, swinging as he ran.

The scene he entered was black and smoldering—an all too familiar vista for a young man who witnessed firsthand the horror of Indian raids along the Cumberland for five long years.

A man with a vacant look stepped out from behind the smoldering remnant of a log shed and gazed at the newcomer. Bush grasped his shoulder. "Where's Lusk? Jim Lusk?"

Without a word the man gestured, listless as a sleepwalker, toward one of the remaining standing buildings. Bush raced toward it and burst through the door.

Jim Lusk looked up slowly at him with hollow, red eyes,

then down again at the terrible thing that lay stretched on the ground before him. Bush felt his gorge rise when he took in the blackened, twisted, stinking object that only hours before had been the living, beautiful person of Nancy Carter Lusk.

"Jim . . . no."

"She died so bad, Bush." Lusk's voice was like that of a different man. "She died so bad, so hard. She burned. My wife burned."

"I'm sorry." The words were so inadequate that they seemed little better than mockery to Bush even as he spoke them.

"It was a white man who led them, Bush. A white man turned Indian."

"Tom Turnbridge."

"Yes."

Bush knew of the man, an Irishman who had left the British military service during the Revolutionary War and taken up with the Cherokees. He was a chief now, married to a Cherokee woman and fighting the whites right along with the most radical Chickamaugas.

"I was married to her two days, Bush. Two days! And now she's gone."

"How did it happen?" Bush looked away; he couldn't bear the sight of Nancy Lusk's burned corpse anymore, with its arms pulled up tight against her chest, like a pugilist, the head burned away to the skull, the legs gone entirely.

"Michael Shafer was in the field, working. The Indians fired on him from hiding. Killed him." Lusk sounded extremely weary, his voice so soft Bush had to strain to hear it. "Others went to get his body . . . the Indians waited for them, drove them back into the fort. They shot at the fort all day. I was gone, Bush. Out hunting, too far away to hear. Hunting, while my wife was trapped in a fort, under fire . . ."

"You didn't know, Jim."

"That was when Turnbridge came up, maybe two score warriors with him. They demanded surrender . . . it was turned down. They fired some of the buildings. The fire spread drove them out . . . the Indians killed some, captured some. Zeigler

was killed. A couple of slaves burned to death. . . . and my
Nancy. My Nancy. She's dead, Bush. My wife is dead.''

"I don't know what to say.''

"Where were you, Bush?''

"Scouting. Hunting.''

"Scouting . . . but you saw no sign?''

"None.''

A pause, and then Lusk's voice, and his eyes, transformed.
"None? *None?* Then what the hell kind of scout are you?''

Bush jerked slightly, reacting. "Why do you ask that?''

The fury came as if from nowhere and mounted fast. "I ask
that because if you'd been worth a damn as a scout, you'd
have seen sign of Turnbridge and his savages. You'd have
given warning, and my Nancy would still be alive!''

"Jim, you know there's not always clear sign. You've said
that very thing to me time and again!''

"Hell, maybe you know old Turnbridge. Maybe you think
he's a fine fellow, living amongst the savages even though
he's a white man. You know a bit about that kind of thing,
after all! Hell, you roll around with swine, you come up stinking. And you rolled with the cursed savages enough years to
reek—you and that Indian-loving Frenchy 'father' you put so
much stock by! And that blind old Cherokee turd you speak
of like he was some kind of damned prophet or something!''

Bush stared, voiceless, at this stranger who was once his
partner, unable to believe what he was hearing.

"Get the hell out of here, Bush! Get out of here and give
a man some peace!''

Stunned into silence, he blinked, then turned and walked
slowly out the door, closing it behind him.

CHAPTER
ELEVEN

Bush dismounted and knelt, examining the tracks he'd spotted on the ground. John Harpool came to Bush's side. They were part of a little scouting band in pursuit of the Zeigler's Station raiders, in advance of a military party.

"That's their trail, sure as shooting," Harpool said.

They were south of the Cumberland River, having followed the Indian sign closely all the way from the burned station. "How many children did they take?" Bush asked.

"Ten, maybe a dozen."

Bush evaluated the ground again, as two more scouts, Peter Loony and John Carr, joined him and Harpool. "It appears to me that all the children are likely still with them. Let's just hope that none of them begins to balk."

They remounted and continued. Some distance later, they made a new discovery.

Stashed up in the branches of trees they found many packs, wrapped up in bark to protect them from the rain. They took some of these down to investigate them and discovered they contained booty taken from the station.

"Why'd they leave them like this?" Harpool asked.

Carr answered, "Because they're short of horses. Too hard to carry all that on their backs. They're planning to come back for it later, pick it up."

"Well, it won't be here when they do," Bush said. "Now let's move on."

"You seem right driven about all this, Bushrod," Loony said.

"I am. I saw what happened to the wife of my partner."

A bit farther on they found more tracks, plus sign indicating the Indians had stopped to smoke and rest. There were more tracks of the children, but with a difference: They wore moccasins this time. The same Indians who had besieged the station with such ruthlessness had paused in the middle of their flight to make footwear for a group of weary children.

"They have a bit of humanity about them after all," one of the scouts observed.

"Of course they do," Bush said. "An Indian can be as kind as anyone you meet. That they show humanity shouldn't be a surprise, them being as human as me and you."

"You would think that way, I reckon, considering they got their fingers into your mind so early on."

"It's not just Indians who can be cruel. It wasn't an Indian who shot my mother and left me and my sister to starve, nor an Indian who killed my unarmed father during the Coldwater raid, nor an Indian who shot my small sister in the head while she was being carried away from danger by my mother."

"I'm surprised to hear you talking so kindly about redskins, considering what we've seen back at Zeigler's."

Bush was a bit surprised himself. His mind had been turned in a different direction for some years now, and he wasn't quite sure why he felt a compulsion just now to extend any good will toward the very people he was chasing. Apparently Jean-Yves's early teaching about the common humanity of the human race had stuck deeper in Bush's mind than he had realized.

Harpool intervened in what promised to grow into an argument. "I swear, Bushrod, you got such deep ways of thinking that I often forget how young you are. You seem older than your years, like I've heard Jim Lusk say many a time. But I say the time for preaching and philosophizing is Sunday-go-to-meeting, not here and now. Let's move along."

They followed the trail farther, but as they did so, began to have doubts about the wisdom of attacking this force. Returning to the small army of frontiersmen following them, they conferred with the leaders.

"To fight this group would probably endanger the prisoners. Let them go on into captivity, and be traded off or ransomed later," Carr said. "The Indians no doubt want these prisoners for that very purpose, and if they see them about to be taken by force, they might retaliate against them rather than let them be took."

This argument, backed by Bush and all the scouts, carried the day. The combined band of scouts and armed frontiersmen turned, rather reluctantly, back toward Zeigler's.

The dead were buried by the time they returned. Bush found Jim Lusk waiting for him.

"Glad you made it safely back," he said.

Bush, feeling defensive, wondering if Lusk was about to work up to another harangue, merely said, "Thank you."

"Bush, I'm sorry for the things I said to you earlier on. I didn't mean them. I had no right to be angry with you. And I wasn't, not really. If I'm angry, I'm angry at myself for being out hunting while my wife was in danger. I'm maybe angry at the Lord for letting such a thing happen to her, and letting her suffer so. But I ain't angry at you. I know you for the scout you are. If there'd been sign of this to be found, you'd have found it."

"I'm only sorry I didn't, Jim. Maybe if I had scouted a little better, the whole thing wouldn't have—"

"Pshaw! You're the finest scout I know, Bush, and I include myself in the comparison."

"I'll never be the woodsman you are, Jim."

"Son, you had me passed up by the time you was sprouting your first crotch hairs, and you and me both know it. Now, if you can see it in your heart to forgive a sad old fool for saying what he shouldn't have, I'd be obliged."

"You're forgiven, then."

"And I'd like to be your partner again. Scout with you like before. I don't want nothing like what happened here to happen again to nobody, without warning."

Bush felt greatly relieved. Sad as he was for his friend's

loss, he was glad to have him back as partner. He stuck out his hand. "Like it used to be."

Lusk nodded and shook the offered hand. "Like it used to be."

But it wasn't like it used to be, because Jim Lusk wasn't the same man.

Some weeks after the Zeigler's Station tragedy, Bush had occasion to share a private conversation with John Harpool about the matter.

"He's careless now, John," Bush said as he carefully chipped out a new rifle flint. He and Harpool were seated in one of the stockades around the area, Bush working on his rifle, Harpool cutting out tanned hide for a new coat. "He misses sign, makes noise, seems like his mind's a hundred miles away most all the time."

"It's the grief," Harpool said. "He's missing his Nancy."

"More than missing her," Bush said. He glanced around, then spoke lower. "I swear, John, I believe that way down inside himself, Jim's trying to get himself killed."

"What? Why?"

"To go be with her, that's why. He misses her that bad. He wants to die and join her."

"No! Are you telling me true?"

"As best I can see it. But I don't want Jim Lusk dead. He's my partner and my friend, and as much credit as he gives me as a woodsman, there's a lot I still want to learn from him. Besides, I'm afraid that if he gets himself killed, I might get killed right along with him."

"That's a true problem you got there, Bushrod. You talked to him about this any?"

"Some. Not quite as direct as I am to you right now. But right direct. And he declares it foolish, like you might expect."

Harpool did some awl-work and thought it over a while. "You know you can't stick by him if he becomes dangerous to you."

"No. But I can't leave him alone, either. He'll sure 'nough get killed then. I wouldn't say this if it wasn't true, and I ask you not to repeat it, but I've had to save his skin three times since his wife burned up. He almost walked right into an Indian camp twice, and nigh got shot by a hidden one another time.''

Harpool poked the awl through again, then held up his handiwork to evaluate the hole he'd made. ''Bush, let me give you some advice. You'd best talk straight to old Jim, and fast. He's too good a man to lose, and you're too good a boy. Hell, you're too good a *man*. You quit being a boy by the time you was twelve.''

''I ain't going to be anything, boy or man, if Jim gets me killed.''

''Don't let that happen, Bush. Don't let that happen.''

One week later

At the first sound of gunfire, Bush came to his feet and kicked dirt onto the small campfire, swept up his rifle, and took to the nearest clump of trees. As soon as he'd removed his moccasins he tied them to the stock of his rifle, following old woodsman advice from Jean-Yves Freneau. Now as he looked around, trying to ascertain from where the rather distant shots had come and whether they had the sound of hunter activity or human violence, he quickly put them back on. He was clad only in the moccasins and his trousers, having washed his shirt and rifleman's frock out in a nearby stream. They hung on branches near what had been the campfire.

More shots, and the sound of a yell.

Indians. Bush knew it at once. And someone was under attack.

''Oh, no, Jim . . . don't let it be you.'' He'd gone off scouting alone, something he'd insisted upon though Bush had advised against it. Bush trembled all of a sudden, but forced himself to take back control. Slipping the straps of his pouches and horns off the end of the ramrod, he hung them across his bare shoulders and advanced back through the camp clearing, heading in the direction in which the shots had come.

He heard more shots, another Indian yell. A triumphant sound to this one.

Bush moved as swiftly as he could through the brush, reaching the river bottom and its mixed stands of river birch, willow, sweetgum, and slightly above, on higher ground, beautiful oaks of several varieties, walnut trees, and hickories. Bush, a child of the forests, loved the marvelous variety of the trees among which he lived and roamed, but today his mind was fixed entirely on reaching the site of the battle going on ahead of him.

Thus he was surprised when something moved abruptly on the incline next to him. A shot blasted so close to him that his left ear went momentarily deaf.

The shot ripped past him, through a green alder thicket. Bush reacted at once, wheeling leftward, raising his rifle, and firing at the retreating Indian who had just failed to hit him.

Bush's shot was better. It caught the Indian in the middle of his back, driving right through his spine and penetrating his lungs and heart. The Indian fell limply and rolled halfway down the slope, landing on his back with his face turned toward Bush. Bush gazed into that face and watched the light of life leave the dark eyes, but not before a different light passed through. The light of recognition.

He knew this Indian, and was sure that just as he died, this Indian knew him.

There was no time to linger and ponder, however. Bush, already beginning to reload, bolted around the green alder. He had the rifle ready for use again as a tumult just ahead, nearing, told him that he need not rush into the battle as before, because the battle was coming to him.

He dropped to one knee behind a stump just as a white man, his face twisted in terror and ivory as parchment, came bursting through a thicket and into the little rivulet that ran near Bush's hiding place. His mouth was wide open, eyes big and glaring in fear, hands stretched out before him like he was trying to feel his way in a dark room, while running at full speed. In his right hand was a flintlock pistol.

A man running that hard was surely being pursued, and

closely, so Bush edged up a little, leveling his rifle atop the stump, preparing to shoot whatever Indian appeared on the fleeing man's track.

He would later rebuke himself many times for his timing and two faulty assumptions he made at a crucial moment: One was that the fleeing white man was so terrified he would continue to race right by, never seeing him behind the stump; the second was that the man's flintlock pistol had probably already been shot empty.

In fact, the fleeing man first caught sight of the Indian shot moments before by Bush. Though the Indian was obviously dead, the man in his panic failed to notice this, because he screamed and diverted his path, which brought him into visual contact with Bushrod. Another scream and, before Bush could show more of himself to reveal that he, too, was a white man, the little flintlock came up and fired.

Bush did not know where he was, but he was in motion. Turbulent, up-and-down, rough motion. He also seemed to be moving forward. Yet not under his own power. His body felt heavy and lifeless, almost indiscernable except for a dull, hot pain in his right side.

He opened his eyes and saw a man above him. Familiar and yet strange. He squinted, trying to focus. Carried . . . he was being carried by this man. The face looked down at him. It was Jim Lusk. His face was wet with sweat and blood, and his scalp was gone. Bush closed his eyes again.

He awakened in greater pain, inside a cabin. His eyes felt grainy and weak. He shifted them from side to side, and groaned. Instantly he heard a feminine voice, with the inflections of a slave, shouting that he was awake, he was awake, he was awake . . .

Gradually he began to remember, and to understand. The man with the flintlock pistol had shot him. And Jim Lusk must have found him, and carried him here . . .

Jim Lusk . . . minus his scalp. The battle, the shots he'd heard . . . Bush had to learn more.

He had awakened in daylight but now it seemed to be dark.

Time had passed, apparently, with him hovering in and out of consciousness. He called out. John Harpool appeared from somewhere, looking down at him.

"What happened, John?"

"We don't entirely know, Bush. We were hoping you'd be able to tell us."

"There was a fight . . . a man with a pistol . . ."

"Yes, yes. We found that same fellow. He'd been toma-hawked, the pistol still in his hand. It was him who shot you? Not one of the Indians?"

"I think so . . . I remember the pistol coming up at me, fir-ing. After that . . ." He coughed, fitfully. It hurt. Harpool went away a moment, then reappeared with a dipper full of water. He held Bush's head up slightly, helping him drink.

"This fellow who shot you was killed, as I said. And two other white men with him. Strangers. Nobody knows where they came from, nothing at all. My guess is they were come unannounced to put up a cabin and settle, and got caught by the Indians before they met anybody, so they died strangers."

"Jim Lusk . . ."

"Jim saved your life, Bush. He carried you all the way here, and if he hadn't, that ball in your side would have worked its way in deeper and killed you. I'm sure of it. But Jim saved you."

"His scalp . . ."

"They'd done took it, sorry to say. He'd been hurt bad, scalped alive, and yet he carried you. He was a great man, Bush." Harpool's voice changed. "You'd said he wanted to be with his Nancy. I guess now he is."

Bush's throat went tight. For a moment he couldn't really think, only slowly comprehend the significance of what Harpool had just said. Tears rose and streamed down his face.

"I also said he was likely to get me killed . . . and now he's saved my life. He's dead, and I'm alive, because of him."

Harpool nodded. "He was trying as well to save them three strangers. He wasn't so successful at that. But he did kill a couple of Indians. One was shot through the head back where the attack had come. The other we found lying on his back on a slope near a little stream.''

''I shot that one,'' Bush said. ''He came over the ridge and I shot him. He was—''

''What?''

''He was going to shoot me. So I shot him first.''

''Ah! I see. Well, that much is clearer, anyhow. The rest is going to stay unsure forevermore, I suppose, with the strangers all three dead, and Jim dead, too. And you didn't see much of it all, I take it.''

''I'd heard the shots, was on my way to see what was happening. Oh, God . . . Jim's dead.'' The tears came harder. Bush always thought nothing could shame a man more than crying before another, but now he couldn't hold back. Harpool didn't show any sign of looking down on him for it.

At length he asked, ''How you feeling, Bush? The wound and all.''

''Hurts. How bad is it?''

''Bad enough. But it ain't festered and is already starting to heal. You'll make it through.''

Bush nodded.

''Sorry about Jim.''

''Me too.''

Bush dreamed about Marie again that night. Not the usual fantasy of her on the boat with Michel Freneau, but a memory. Marie as a very young child, playing under his supervision near Coldwater Creek. Bush had spotted a possum waddling off into the woods, had gone after it. Suddenly, he sensed something wrong, left the possum, and went running back.

She'd fallen into the creek, but had already been rescued. A handsome young warrior called Te'wa had gone in after her and dragged her out. He'd seen her floating facedown in the water, unconscious.

The incident had terrified Bush and haunted him for many nights thereafter. He'd dreamed of Marie floating in that water, imagined her dead. Even to the present he could recall no worse nightmare than that recurring one. Yet he'd almost forgotten it with the passing years. And almost forgotten Te'wa.

The memory had come back after he killed the Indian who came over the ridge. That Indian was Te'wa, several years older, but looking hardly any different than he did the day he went into Coldwater Creek after Marie Underhill, and gave Bush back his beloved sister, alive rather than dead.

Now Bush had killed him. It somehow didn't make sense.

But he was a different person now, Bush reminded himself. He lived in a different world and had new loyalties. Like Jim Lusk said years ago, after Coldwater, Bush didn't really belong among the redskins. He was white by blood, and blood counted above all other considerations.

Bush told himself that now, as he lay grieving and healing. But he wasn't sure he fully believed it.

Thinking now about both Jim Lusk and Te'wa being dead and gone—with no real good reason for it that Bush, for the life of him could see—he wasn't sure what he believed about much anything.

CHAPTER TWELVE

Storm clouds had rolled in a couple of hours before, as the sun began its westward tilt, and had thickened and blackened until it was evident that the biggest thunderstorm of the year was about to descend upon the Cumberland country.

Bush Underhill walked slowly out of the cabin and looked around the enclosed yard. He was at Campbell's Fort, a relatively new, small stockade fort to which he'd moved a couple of weeks after being carried in wounded. Bush had received an offer of a little cabin inside the stockade from Tyler Campbell, patriarch of the family for whom the fort was named, and a man who had become a sort of unofficial judge in the region in the year-and-a-half he'd lived on the Cumberland. He accepted the offer to rest there until his wound healed, and since moving in had regained much strength.

Enough so, in fact, that he was beginning to grow quite restless. He was pining for the forests again, the wilderness and free-roaming he and Jim Lusk had enjoyed. Then he'd recall that Jim Lusk was with him no more, and the oddest kind of unsettled, directionless feeling would come over him.

Feelings not too dissimilar would also strike him whenever he caught sight of the two beautiful daughters of Tyler Campbell. Rachel and Mary, ages fifteen and sixteen, respectively, were dark-haired, dark-eyed, tall and slender, and pretty. Both of them knew they had Bush's eye and seemed to enjoy it. He suspected they in turn thought him a fine figure of a young man, but they were generally haughty around him, in a way that let him know there was a bit of pretense in it.

Folks told Bush he seemed older than his years—though not even he could say exactly how many his years were. As best he could guess, he was probably seventeen or so, certainly more man than boy. And though his life in the forests and preoccupation with staying alive and scouting out signs of Indian presence had left him little time to even think about females, much less develop any kind of relationship with that lovely breed, the death of Jim Lusk set him to thinking about changes, and time, and the passing of years.

Maybe it was time he gave up the woods, and settled down to some kind of life with a good, young, pretty wife. One of the Campbell girls, maybe.

He liked the idea of the company of a pretty wife, but the settling down part made him shudder. He'd not lived for more than the occasional winter season or two in a true house or cabin from the day he left Tip Snoddy drunk and tied up. His homes had been Jim Lusk's widely scattered shelters. He spent almost an entire summer living inside a cave, and one autumn took up housekeeping in the huge, hollow trunk of a great sycamore.

He wasn't sure he had the experience in normal living that a man should have to take a wife. He wasn't sure he even *wanted* one.

But change was coming. Of that he was sure. The passing of Jim Lusk had been a milestone, the full significance of which he couldn't yet quite see. Something was building in his life, just like those thunderheads gathering and stirring in the west.

He couldn't recall when he felt quite so restless.

The rain began to fall, pattering down hard. Wind rose, sweeping the treetops, chilling the air, making leaves turn up their undersides and whip like gray-green flags in currents of air. Lightning flashed on the hillsides and thunder cracked like cannonfire.

Bush stood in the doorway of the open stockade, letting the rain drench him. He'd loved the feel of rain on his skin since he was a small child, and standing here like this took him back to Coldwater. Smelling the smoke whipping into the stockade from the cookfire of some nearby cabin, he could close his eyes and imagine himself as a child again, smelling the scent of Waninahi's cooking, feeling the wash of rain heavy with the evaporated waters of the Tennessee River. Jean-Yves was in his cabin with his books and his deep thoughts, Michel was displaying his wares for some visiting band of Cherokees and trying at the same time to charm some lovely Creek maiden, and Marie was playing with pretty stones at the edge of a puddle, enjoying the rain just like Bush did.

It was a good fantasy. Bush stayed out in the storm despite the lightning, leaning on the walking stick he was just about ready to throw away, once he'd healed a little more.

He turned his face skyward, eyes closed, and let the rain wash over it.

The Campbell house stood outside the stockade, but within easy running distance, and many was the time the Campbells had made that run on occasions of Indian alarm. From the loft of the Campbell home, a good view of the stockade gate could be had from a shuttered window that stayed open most of the time during the summer.

Rachel Campbell looked out that window and watched Bushrod Underhill standing in the center of the stockade gate, face turned up as the rain hammered down and lightning sizzled in the sky above.

"Why you reckon he's doing that, Mary?" she asked her sister. "Is that some kind of peculiar Indian religious something that he picked up when he was raised a savage boy?"

"I don't know what it is. All I know is, he surely does look pretty. Prettiest young man I believe I've ever seen."

Rachel watched in silence a few moments. "He is at that. Oh, Mary. Sometimes when he looks sweet at me I just know he loves me!"

"You're too young, Rachel. I'm closer to his age than you are."

"Well, maybe you are. But it don't matter, 'cause he ain't been looking at you. But he looks at me."

"Indeed he has looked at me! I've caught him watching me many a time! More than he looks at you!"

"I'm going to marry him."

"You'll never!"

"You wait and see. Pap has said himself that Bushrod Underhill would be a fine fellow for me to marry. He says Bushrod Underhill is the best tracker and hunter and Indian fighter to be found anywhere along the Cumberland, and him as young as he is. He says that two Indians tried to kill Bushrod Underhill at a canebrake when he was just a boy, and he killed them both—and they'd just killed and scalped a white man! Pap says there ain't no young men around to match Bushrod Underhill."

"You sure do like to say the name 'Bushrod Underhill' a lot, don't you!"

"I do. I think it's a pretty name. And my name will be Underhill, too, one day before long. Don't you like the sound of that?"

Her sister didn't answer, busy mouthing her own name attached to Bushrod's.

They watched him until the rain declined and he turned to walk back toward his cabin in the stockade. "I do wonder why he stood out in the rain like that," Rachel said.

"I don't know," Mary replied. "But ain't he pretty to look at!"

Bushrod finished the last bite of his third slab of roasted pork, remembered to dab the grease off his lips and light beard with one of the Campbell family's linen napkins, imported all the way from Charleston, and nodded politely at Tyler Campbell's wife, Susanne.

"Mighty good food, Mrs. Campbell. I appreciate you letting me dine with you." He flicked his eyes toward the two Campbell girls, self-conscious as they stared brazenly at him. His eyes connected with Mary's, and from her look he judged she found something significant in the moment. He quickly looked away, more uncomfortable than before.

Tyler Campbell filled his pipe slowly and lit it, puffing

smoke into a great cloud around his bulbous head. He smiled at Bush, who was examining a flintlock pistol hung on pegs on the wall, and asked him to join him outside to enjoy the evening breeze and watch the sunset.

A planned presentation was about to come, Bush sensed. He flicked another glance at Mary and wondered.

"There's a clay pipe on the mantle," Campbell said as they walked toward the door. "Take it and break off that old chewed stem, and we'll have a smoke together."

Bush seldom smoked, but accepted the offer simply so he'd have something to do with his hands during the coming conversation.

"Beautiful day today, eh?" Campbell asked, settling his somewhat bulky form onto one of two log-section stools set conveniently in place beneath a spreading oak.

"Yes, sir."

"You're healing well, I take it."

"Yes, sir. And I appreciate the use of the stockade cabin, and all the food and such you've given me."

"My friend, I consider you a hero. Your scouting, and that of poor Mr. Lusk, has saved more lives than any of us will ever know. And your skill at killing Indians is worthy of the admiration of all."

Bush stared at the bowl of his pipe. "I take no particular pleasure in killing Indians. None at all, in fact."

"Well, of course not. Pleasure is the wrong word, I'm sure. But . . . satisfaction, perhaps. The knowledge that you've rid the world of one more dangerous savage."

Bush puffed the pipe. The tobacco tasted bad and he removed the stem from his lips. "I grew up among the Indians, you know. Among what most consider the worst kind."

"The Chickamaugas?"

"Yes, sir. In the town of Coldwater."

"It was Mr. Lusk who brought you out, I believe."

"Not precisely so. My father—not my blood father, who died long ago, but the French woods runner who took me in—was shot dead by a man named Tip Snoddy. I was taken prisoner."

"You lost family, then . . . so to speak."

"Not just 'so to speak,' sir. Jean-Yves Freneau was the only father I'd ever known, and a fine one he was. My mother, my Cherokee mother, died as well."

"But they weren't blood kin."

"They were kin nonetheless. And my sister, who died as well, was blood kin, if you consider that so important."

"I've offended you, I think."

"To be truthful, you have."

"I ask your pardon, then. I admit to having a very low view of the Indian race."

"Most do hereabouts, I've noticed."

"You've killed quite a few of the breed yourself."

"When it was necessary. As I said, I took no pleasure in it."

"Now that Mr. Lusk has been taken from us, what are your plans?"

"I don't know."

"I'm sure you've thought about it?"

"Yes. But no decisions."

"I hope you'll consider staying around our region. You've endeared yourself to the people here."

"I don't know what I'll do."

"Have you thought about your future in marital terms?"

Here it came. "I suppose someday I'll marry."

"A healthy, beautiful young woman is a treasure any man should be glad to find."

"No question about that, sir."

"Bushrod, this is perhaps a bit forward of me, but I'm a forthright man. I always have been, and take a certain pride in it. And therefore I want to ask you to give some thought to my own lovely daughter, Mary. She's a fine young woman, and perhaps someone who could—"

"Mr. Campbell!" A shout from the road, where it curved around a copse of maples beyond the stockade.

"What the devil?" Campbell stood, gazing at the young rider speeding his way. Bush stood, too.

"I think that's Mark Randall," Campbell said. "I wonder what has him in such a state?"

The rider reached them and came down lithely from the saddle. "Mr. Campbell, sir, I'm sorry to be bothering you, but there's some Indians been captured, and nobody is quite sure what to do with them."

"Indians! Raiders?"

"We think that was their intention, yes sir."

"How many caught?"

"Two."

"Wounded?"

"One of them. The other one was knocked senseless with a blow to the head, but seems to be well enough now. The hurt one took a slight wound to the leg. Them and three others was caught trying to steal horses. William Cavett has both of them locked up in his blockhouse just now, and he's talking of shooting them. His brother says no, they ought to be held for trading off for white folks the Indians hold and so on."

"I agree. Did they send for me?"

"They've agreed to stand by your judgment on the matter, sir. And they request you come at once."

Campbell put down his pipe and nodded. "Indeed I will. Bushrod, would you join me?"

"Yes, sir." Bush would have welcomed any reason to break off the conversation that Campbell had just engaged him in, but this reason was interesting in itself. Except after full-fledged battles of the Coldwater variety, Indian prisoners were only infrequently taken.

"Go on back, young man," Campbell told the messenger. "Tell them to do nothing further with the prisoners until I arrive."

"Yes, sir." The young man climbed back into his saddle and rode away in the direction he had come.

The Indians were locked away and out of view. Campbell, along with two armed men and an interpreter, entered the blockhouse to talk with the captives. Bush lingered outside, talking quietly with some of the men about, getting a fuller version of the capture story than what he'd heard.

Campbell emerged at length and announced that he retained his initial judgment: These men would be secured as prisoners, then turned over into military custody to be held for exchange of white prisoners. Bush was glad to hear this. There were always a few hotheads about ready to kill any Indian captured, which would do no good at all for relations on either side.

"Mr. Campbell, sir, I'd like to take a glance at them, if I could," Bush said.

"Why is that?"

"There's always the chance I'll remember someone from my early years."

"I see no harm in it. Step on over, young man, and have a look."

Campbell accompanied Bush over to the blockhouse door. An armed guard opened it, and the pair entered.

It was dark inside the blockhouse. The Indians, typical of most Indians Bush had ever seen in captivity, were quite still and impassive, their faces fixed stoically. Bush paused a moment to let his eyes adjust to the shadowy light, and studied the face of the first Indian. A stranger. He turned to the second and looked closely.

"Hello, Ancoowah," he said, speaking in Cherokee.

The Indian nodded at him, looking puzzled at first, then as he looked at Bush more closely, recognizing him. "Freneau's son!" he said. "So, you are still alive, Skiuga. And much older and bigger."

"I am. I'm sorry to see you a captive, Ancoowah. And I'm sorry your companion was wounded."

"You live among the *unakas* now, Skiuga?"

"I'll be!" murmured Campbell. "I believe you *do* know him!"

"Yes, I do. Among my own kind of people. I was taken captive by the whites after Coldwater was burned. I never knew what became of you, Ancoowah."

Ancoowah, about ten years Bush's senior, said, "I was hurt, but escaped. My brother died there, and my mother's brother."

Bush turned to Campbell, who was listening with interest,

but with no understanding, to the conversation under way in Cherokee. "Mr. Campbell, sir, might I speak to these men in private?"

"You want me to leave you alone in here?"

"I know Ancoowah. He knew me when I was a child in Coldwater. He'll do me no harm, and I'm sure the other will not try to, either."

Campbell nodded. "Very well. Raise a shout if you need help and we'll be in in half a moment." He left the blockhouse. Bush heard the lock bar fall in place again outside.

"Ancoowah, I'm glad I've seen you today, even if I am sorry you have been caught. There are questions you may be able to answer me, about Coldwater."

"If I can answer, I will."

"You remember my sister, just a child. I was told she was killed there. Do you know?"

"No, I'm sorry. I don't. I can tell you I didn't see her after."

"What about my mother, Waninahi?"

"I didn't see, but I was told she was killed."

Bush took in a slow breath. So that much of what Snoddy said was confirmed, at least, and if that part was true, then probably his report of Marie's death was true as well. "What about Tuckaseh?"

"Tuckaseh still lives."

"He lives! Where?"

"In Nickajack Town, in the house of his daughter. He is much older and slower, and now he sees nothing at all with those bad old eyes of his, except shadow and light."

"Tuckaseh . . . I wish I could see him."

"And he would be glad to see you, Skiuga. He still talks of you after all these years. But he believes you are dead. He grieves for you, even now. He says he will die soon, but he's been saying that for years now." Ancoowah paused. "But he is older. Perhaps this time he truly will die."

Bush paused. A future that had been uncertain and directionless suddenly pulled itself into a path—one that was distinctively different from marriage to a Campbell daughter. "I must see him."

"To see him, you would have to go to Nickajack. It would be a fool's journey for an *unaka* to go there alone."

"Then make me your prisoner, Ancoowah. Take me there as your captive, and give me your protection. I must see Tuckaseh before he dies."

"How can I take you as my prisoner if I am a prisoner here myself?"

Bush spoke low. "You won't be a prisoner long. I'll see to it myself. If you will pledge to me to molest no *unakas* here, I'll get you free of here. But you must take me to Nickajack, and you must give me your protection."

"I can offer it to you, but I can't assure it. There are many at Nickajack who hate all *unakas*, and who would seek blood vengeance for those they have lost in war."

"I know the ways of our people." *Our* people. Bush would notice only in recollection, much later, that he had spoken so. "I'll take the risk, if I can see Tuckaseh."

Ancoowah said, "I agree to what you say."

Bush said, "Keep yourself ready, then. We'll go away from here as soon as we can. I'll offer my service as guard outside, and when it's dark and the way is clear, we'll go. Be ready, both of you. You'll not be prisoners here long. You have the word of Skiuga."

The news spread across the region the next day. Bushrod Underhill was gone, as were the two captured Indians who had been held in the blockhouse.

Rumors and conjectures flew. The prevailing sentiment was that the prisoners had somehow gotten the drop on Underhill while he was guarding them in the night, and had gotten away. Underhill was possibly still in pursuit of them, but more likely dead. Had he pursued them he probably would have sounded an alarm for help, and none had been heard. Probably he had been wounded as the Indians got away, had stumbled off somewhere and fallen, unseen. Dogs were in use already in a search for his body.

Others said darker things. More likely Underhill, who had grown up among the savages, had known these Indians and engineered the escape himself. Small circumstantial clues supported this. He'd asked Tyler Campbell to leave him to speak to them alone in the blockhouse, even though they were conversing in Cherokee, of which Campbell understood only a smattering. Then there was the ready, almost hurried way in which he had volunteered to stand night guard over the captives, as if he wanted to be sure that he and no one else was in charge of them during the night. No one had perceived these things in a questionable manner at the time, of course—this was, after all, Bushrod Underhill, the finest young scout on the Cumberland and a famed fighter of Indians—but in the wake of the escape, everything about his actions seemed to have a slightly different smell about them.

Campbell had nothing to say on the matter. It was known by all that he had cast his eye on young Underhill as a potential husband for his beloved eldest daughter. His views of the escape and attitude toward Underhill he was now keeping to himself, quite glumly. His daughters weren't so circumspect. They wailed shamelessly, Mary in particular, and declared that Bushrod couldn't have possibly done such a vile thing as free Indian prisoners, much less run off with them.

Many were inclined to agree. Bushrod Underhill had become famous as a boy killer of Indians, and had grown into a free-roaming protector of the Cumberland settlers whose constancy and faithfulness had been unwavering. He'd known the Indian life as a boy, this was true, but he'd lived the life of civilization, too, and thus knew its superiority first-hand. Such a fellow as Underhill would never, never consider going back to the savages!

It was just too inconceivable.

CHAPTER
THIRTEEN

*Nickajack, in the Five Lower Towns of
the Chickamaugas*

The interior of the cabin was shrouded in shadow and smoke. It seemed to Bush an appropriate setting in which to meet his old Cherokee mentor again, for the first time since the Cold-water raid.

Tuckaseh looked older now, but mostly because his hair had grayed considerably and his eyes had grown more clouded and marbled. The crevices of his craggy face had been deep as long as Bush had known him, so there was little change to be seen there.

The house was that of Tuckaseh's daughter—in the Cher-okee world, house ownership was the domain of women, not men—but no one was present except the old man himself. Tuckaseh, who had been told by Ancoowah that his beloved Skiuga had come to find him, raised his head slowly when Bush entered, and looked at him. For half a minute neither spoke.

"Do you see me, Tuckaseh?" Bush asked.

"Yes, Skiuga. I see your form, your shadow. And I hear you. Your voice is very different . . . but I know it all the same."

"I'm glad to see you," Bush said. "I've thought about you many times for many years, and never knew what became of you. I was afraid you were killed at Coldwater, or died since."

"My time to die will come soon, but I remained alive be-cause there are things I hoped to see before I die. And one of these was you, Skiuga. I wanted to know you were alive."

"I was taken captive at Coldwater by an *unaka* named

Snoddy. He's dead now. After him, I became the friend and partner of another *unaka*, a good one, like my father was. But he's dead too, now, killed in a fight with our people." *Our people*. Bush noticed he put it that way without really thinking about it.

"And you've come back now to me, in my old age."

"I learned from Ancoowah that you were still living. He was a prisoner in a blockhouse near one of the Cumberland stations, but I helped him escape and made myself his prisoner so I could be brought here."

"It's not safe for you, even under his protection."

"Seeing you is worth danger. Besides, there's nothing for me back among the *unakas*, now that my friend has died. There was a young woman I might have married, if I wanted."

"But you didn't want her?"

"In one way. She was very pretty to look at. But I don't want to be married. At least, not nearly as much as I wanted to see you again."

Tuckaseh's wrinkled old mouth bent into a smile. He nodded. "I am a happy man. Skiuga is back."

"And I'm happy, too." Bush drew closer and sat down cross-legged in front of Tuckaseh, who was in a similar posture. "Have you liked living as an *unaka*?"

Bush thought about his answer. "I've liked some of it. I was a scout and ranger, living mostly in the woods, which pleased me very much."

"Yes. You were made for such a life, my friend."

"Other parts of the life I've lived . . . I don't know. Sometimes I don't know what world I should live in."

"Your skin is a white man's, but I think your soul will always be an Indian's."

Bush hesitated, then admitted, "There were times in the past years when I was able to hate Indians, Tuckaseh. I've fought them and killed them. The first two I killed barely after Coldwater. They were Creeks, stalking me while I tried to return to Coldwater."

"You tried to return?"

"Yes. But I didn't reach it."

"Why did you try to return to a town that was destroyed?"

"Because I hoped I would find you still there, or nearby. You were all that remained for me then. My father was dead, my mother, Marie—"

The old man cocked his head. "Marie?"

"Yes . . . she was killed. Shot in the head while my mother tried to carry her away."

"You saw this?"

"No. I was told about it by someone who said he saw it."

"Who saw it?"

"Snoddy. The same man who killed my father and took me captive."

"Do you believe him?"

Bush paused. "Yes, I suppose I have believed him." He paused again, thinking of his vivid dreams of Marie alive on the boat carrying the captured French traders, reaching for him while he was fixed in place on the bank, unable to reach her. "But sometimes, no. Sometimes I've felt sure that she was alive, and almost close enough for me to reach . . . but I can't reach her. Just a feeling, that comes with dreams. Not a feeling to be trusted."

"Perhaps you've trusted the wrong things, Skiuga. Because I didn't hear that your sister died," Tuckaseh said. "I heard that she lived."

Bush came to his feet. "She lived?"

"I heard she lived. As I told you, I didn't see for myself."

"But if she lived, where did she go?"

"Again, Skiuga, I didn't see, only heard talk. But the talk said that she was taken away from Coldwater by your father's brother, Michel Freneau."

Before dawn, the next morning

Bush jerked awake, eyes flashing open. He stared up into the darkness above him, not realizing for a few moments that he was holding his breath.

He exhaled in a gust, then drew in a deep breath. His brow

was damp with perspiration. Sleep had been a long time coming, thanks to what he'd learned from Tuckaseh, and when it finally came, was turbulent with dreams of Marie.

Bush stared across the cabin with thoughts of her. Ancoowah, ostensibly his captor but in that role actually his protector, was kindly allowing him to sleep on the floor of his wife's house. It was still hard to conceive of Marie as alive, after thinking for so long she was dead.

Even now, though, he really didn't know. Tuckaseh had merely heard, not seen. He wasn't sure. All this could be a vain hope based on nothing but an old man's misconception.

He sat up, leaning his chin on his knees, and thought hard. How could he learn the truth? The best answer he could come up with was to seek out others here who had been in Coldwater, and see if any of them could confirm what Tuckaseh had said.

And what if they did? What was the difference in having a sister who was alive rather than dead, if she was equally lost to him either way?

Thinking that way made Bush feel selfish. Of course there was a difference, for Marie if not for him. Yet he couldn't deny that there would be something infinitely frustrating in discovering that his sister was alive, but out of his reach. It had been a long time since Coldwater. Any trails left then would surely be cold and gone by now.

Sleep wasn't about to return tonight, and Bush's well-developed sense of time told him morning was little more than an hour away. He got up and left the cabin silently, disturbing no one, and walked through the town of Nickajack toward the huge, dark mouth of the cavern than overlooked the town and gave it its name.

Bush reached the mouth of Nickajack Cave and paused, letting his eyes adjust to the even deeper blackness inside. Walking in a short distance, he sat down on a rock that allowed him a view of the town, and thought about Marie. He stared at the sky, and thought: Same sky that's arching over her, wherever she might be, if she's really still among the living.

He pondered in silence as the night grew darker then began to lighten. Morning broke slowly to the rising music of birds and a new briskness in the breeze. Bush relaxed, enjoying the best view of Nickajack he'd had since his arrival. Apart from the gaping cavern that overlooked it, the town looked much like any other Indian town, with cabins, earthen winter houses, open and airy summer houses, a council house, storage buildings, a chunkey yard, garden areas, stock pens. There was something unreal to Bush about sitting in this cavern mouth and observing a town occupied by those who had been his enemies for the last several years.

But not his enemies now. Or they didn't seem so. They were simply who they were, as the *unakas* were who they were. And Bush himself was both . . . and neither. He wasn't sure.

Among his dimmest memories was that of Jean-Yves Freneau, talking of how one day his adopted son would be a citizen of all worlds, all people his people, no race or way of life extending an exclusive claim on his allegiance. At the time Bush made no sense of it, but when he grew older came to realize that it stemmed from Freneau's most idealistic side. Now Bush wondered if he was fulfilling that very ambition of Freneau's. Indeed he seemed capable of moving back and forth between races and cultures. But did this flexibility mean he was a citizen of all worlds, as Freneau dreamed, or merely that he really belonged nowhere?

Bush contemplated the question and reached the surprising conclusion that it really didn't much matter. The important issue for him was not whether he was Indian or *unaka*. The important issue, he decided, was not race or society, but family. He needed family, someone to whom he was bound by blood or by nature. In short, what mattered was his lost sister, Marie.

The possibility that Marie still lived intrigued but also troubled him. If she were alive after Coldwater, and Michel had taken her, she would have been on that boat with him. But Bush had not seen her. On the other hand, the boat had been well-packed, men standing before Michel. If Marie was there, maybe she was hidden from sight. Maybe Michel kept her deliberately hidden to keep her from growing upset at seeing her own brother left behind on the bank.

If Marie were still alive, Bush wondered if she remembered him, if she ever thought about him and wondered what had become of him. He hoped so. He would not like to think that she had forgotten him.

As the sun broke fully free of the ragged horizon, Bush made a decision. He would seek his sister. He might be able to discover here whether she really survived Coldwater, though even if so, he could not know if she lived all the years thereafter. In any case, he would look for her, no matter how hard or how far, or how cold the trail.

Bush was leaving the cave to find Tuckaseh, when a man in breechcloth and headdress stepped out from behind some rocks and positioned himself in his path. Bush immediately thought some bitter Chickamauga had decided to avail himself of this moment of seclusion to take out upon him some anger felt toward the *unakas*. A glance at the man's face, however, revealed to Bush's surprise that this was a white man.

"Howdy," the man said in a strong backwoods accent that sounded very out of place coming from someone dressed from head to toe like a typical Cherokee.

"Howdy," Bush said. "You're a white man like me, I see."

"That's right. Name's Kendall Saws, but here I'm called Kennesaw, for no other reason, I reckon, than that it's a Cherokee name that happens to make a pretty close match to my real one."

"Good to meet you, Kennesaw." Bush put out his hand. "Name's Bush Underhill, but here I go by Skiuga."

" 'Ground squirrel,' eh?"

"That's right." Obviously Kendall Saws had been among the Indians long enough to pick up at least some of the language.

"I seen you coming up here earlier, and followed. Been wanting to meet you since I heard you was brought in prisoner.

Looks like you're going to be a fortunate one, lots of free rein.''

"I'll tell you the truth. I'm not truly a prisoner. I was raised among the Cherokees and Creeks at Coldwater Town, and was taken back to be among the whites when that town was destroyed. I'm here now because I want to be.''

"The hell! Why would anyone want to be among the savages?''

Bush thought that an odd question for this man to ask. As a white man, Kennesaw was either a captive himself, or an adoptee into the tribe. Given that he obviously had the freedom to move about as he wished, Bush would assume the latter.

"I'm here because there was an old man, Tuckaseh, who was almost a father or grandfather to me when I was young. I'd feared he was dead, then found he was alive, and here. I came to find him again.''

"Have you?''

"Yes.''

"Well, good. And now here you are, amongst the Indians. You aim to stay?''

"No. Not for long. There's someone else I have to search for.''

"Going to leave your old man friend here, then.''

Bush, who was beginning to find this man's nosiness annoying, hadn't really thought out that angle of his decision. To search for Marie would mean leaving Tuckaseh behind again, this time maybe for good. Tuckaseh was old and talked a lot about dying. "I don't know what I'll do. I'm not going anywhere right off.''

Kennesaw looked around as if about to reveal a great secret, and pulled close to Bush. "Wouldn't be staying too long, if you're truly free to go when you please.''

"Why?''

"Just take my word for it. You won't want to be here for long.''

What Bush didn't want at the moment was to be around Kennesaw for long. But the man had his curiosity up.

"Just who are you, Mr. Saws, or Kennesaw, or whatever you want yourself called?"

"In the eyes of them savages down yonder in that town, I'm one of them. Took into the tribe and made an injun."

"Were you a captive to begin with?"

"Let me just tell you about myself. It's quite a story, if I do say so. When I get back into the real world again, reckon I might write it down, it's so good."

Bush looked around, found a rock to sit on. Kennesaw seemed the talkative kind, and this might take a few moments. But Bush was curious, for when one found white men among the Indians, there usually was an interesting story attached to the circumstance indeed.

"It begun, Bush—can I call you Bush?—when Cap'n Sam Handley was sent by the territorial governor to defend the Cumberland country against the savages. Old Middlestriker set up an ambush for us and we walk right into it. Only three got killed, but the ambush put a fright into our men, and they fled. Me not among them, I'm proud to say, though if I'd run I might have been better off today. The Cap'n got captured while he was trying to rescue one of our men who was hurt, and I got took at the same time after my rifle misfired on me.

"I wasn't too keen a prize, but them savages was tickled to have caught the Cap'n, him having fought at Point Pleasant and been on so many Indian campaigns and such. They hauled us both back to Willstown, where their big chief Watts was laid up with a wound, and they commenced with meetings and such to figure what to do with us. Me and Cap'n Handley both figured our time was up, and when they told us we had to run the gauntlet, we got ready to die.

"I come through the gauntlet right well, though Lord knows I don't know how, but Cap'n Handley was nigh beat to death, and they took him in and patched him up so he'd be healthy for the fate they'd decided for us. They aimed to burn us to death, Bush. Ain't that a devil of a thing—patching up Cap'n Handley to get him well enough to kill!" Kennesaw spat on the ground. "Damned savages!"

It crossed Bush's mind that if Kennesaw had in fact been

adopted into the tribe, the conversion hadn't gone much more than skin deep. His heart and soul certainly weren't in it.

"Bush, there's no way to tell what that's like, hearing you're to die by torture! But so it was for us, and we tried to ready ourselves for it as best we could.

"When the day came, they tied us to a stake and got ready to burn us. The squaws come and cussed at us, flung dung and piss and spit and God knows what all upon us, and me and the Cap'n just taunted them back, cussing all the Indians, cussing their mothers and fathers and doing our best to make them so mad they'd shoot us in anger instead of burning us. Then all at once there come up a storm and drenched that wood so that there couldn't be no fire built. That rain saved our lives. They hauled us off and held us prisoner for a few days more until they'd have a good chance to give it another go.

"Finally the day for the second try came around, and they put us back on the stakes again. I didn't figure we'd get no providential rainstorms this time around, so I was sure it would be over soon. We was up there cussing them again, trying to make them shoot, when out comes old Watts, just about healed up from his wound, to watch the show.

"Him and the Cap'n took to talking, and the Cap'n tells Watts, 'You know, you're a brave chief, Mr. Watts. All us white folk love brave men, and we all love you. Why, I've heard the very men you've fought most talk about how brave you are, how fine a leader you are and how it's a shame we have to fight each other. But these warriors of yours, that's a different tale. They're a bunch of cowardly women, or else they'd never put brave men like me and Kendall Saws here to death by the fire. They'd shoot us as brave warriors.

"All at once old Watts got teary-eyed on us. Surprised me to no end. He says, 'You speak the truth, Cap'n Handley. It's a damned shame that brave men have to die when it ought to be cowards who die.' And he up and cut us away from the stakes right there. I couldn't believe it. And you know what, Bush? Them other Indians all at once become just as friendly as they could be. Shook our hands, fed us, told us they'd adopt us. And sure enough, they did. Put me and the Cap'n both into the Wolf Clan. Made us regulation Indians! That's how I come to be in the position I am, with a free run.

"The Cap'n only stayed among the Indians for three months—and you know, his hair had went from dark to white in that short span of time!—before he was turned back over in exchange for some Indian prisoners being released. Me, I'm still here. Not at Willstown no more, of course, but still among the savages."

Bush said, "I don't understand why you are. You can go anywhere you want to. You'd have plenty of chance to run off if you wanted to take it, and I can tell you got no love for the Indians. But you're still with them. Why?"

Kennesaw looked slyly around and spoke more softly. "Because I aim to see some fire and brimstone fall on this place before it's through."

"What do you mean?"

Kennesaw smiled. "I've said enough. You remain around, and you'll see what I mean. But if I was you, I wouldn't remain around." He yawned and stretched. "I'd best be going. See you later, Bush."

Bush watched him go, giving him plenty of lead time. Kennesaw's tale was certainly interesting, but the man himself was unpleasant, and there was something ominous and bitter in him that Bush didn't relish.

He wondered what Kennesaw's obscure warnings meant. Maybe nothing. Perhaps he was the kind of man who was filled with delusions, touched in his mind. The Indians generally respected folks like that, and didn't molest them. Perhaps that was why Kennesaw was still here and enjoyed such freedom. Maybe some of his story was nothing but fantasy.

Bush soon forgot the man, his mind turning back to Marie. He had work to do here. He would roam among the people of Nickajack and see if he could learn more about what happened to her after Coldwater. Perhaps somebody would know as well what had become of Michel Freneau. If he could find Michel, maybe he'd find Marie, too.

CHAPTER
FOURTEEN

When Bush went back to the cabin of Tuckaseh's daughter, the old man was gone.

The daughter, a fat, slovenly, unpleasant woman with warts on her hands, looked at Bush with open distaste and said, "He's not here. He'll not be back. He's gone off to the woods to die."

"To die?"

"Yes. He says that it is a good time to die now that Skiuga has come back to him and his life is complete." She said the name "Skiuga" with a slight disdainful rise in her voice, and Bush remembered why even as a child he'd despised this miserable female.

"And you'll not go after him?"

She wrinkled one side of her nose and made a little gesture with her pudgy hands. "If it's his time to die, who am I to stop it? And he goes out to die very often. He'll be back again when he gets cold, eating more of our food and filling our space."

"Where would he be?"

She gave minimal, grumpy directions. Bush set out at once, irritated at her and thinking how he, too, might look forward to dying if he were blind and had to live, unwelcome and unloved, in the house of such a daughter.

Sure enough, Tuckaseh was sitting just where his daughter said he would be, with a blanket over his shoulders, his blank eyes staring across a beautiful, rugged woodland landscape he could barely see.

Bush approached him and sat down nearby. "Hello, Tuck-aseh."

"Hello, Skiuga. I'm glad you've come to see me here at the end of my life."

"You are planning to die?"

"Yes. It's a good time to die when your happiness is complete. And mine is complete now that I know you are well and with me again."

"But if you die, my own happiness would be ruined."

"I'm an old man. It's right that old men should lay down their bones with their fathers."

"Don't die now, Tuckaseh. There are things I want to talk to you about."

"I'm still living and able to talk now, if you are ready."

"I am. I've decided that I must find my sister . . . if she really is alive."

"Yes, I agree. This would be a good thing to do. But how do you plan to find her?"

"I'm going to talk to the old men and women here, and in the other towns, if I must, who were at Coldwater. I want to know if any of them saw Marie die, or if any know where she might have been taken."

"That's a wise plan."

"And I'll see if anyone has heard of Michel Freneau in recent times, and where he might be."

"Yes. If he took her, then she might be with him still, or he might know where she went."

"And when I find out the truth, then I'll go look for her."

"Even if she didn't die at Coldwater, she may have died since."

"I know. And if that is the case, I'll try to find out. But I must search for her. I must."

"Yes, you must."

"And now, you must come back to Nickajack with me."

"No. It's my day to die."

"No. The wind is too cold, and it will be raining later. Come back with me, and die some day when it will be more comfortable."

Tuckaseh considered it, and nodded. "Very well. For you, Skiuga, I'll delay my dying."

"That's good news. Now come. I'll walk with you."

Bush didn't anticipate a long residency at Nickajack. His plan to find his sister filled him with excitement and a direction he'd never known before. As planned, he spoke to the older inhabitants of Nickajack who had been at Coldwater, and found all to be in agreement: Marie Underhill had not been killed, but had been taken away by Michel Freneau, who in turn had been taken prisoner. What became of her after that, none of them knew, of course, but one thing seemed certain: She was with Michel when he was captured.

Bush thought back to that hectic, terrible day after Coldwater and tried to envision what might have happened. It seemed most likely that Marie, as a young white child, would have been taken away from Michel, a hated French trader, and placed in custody of some settler's family in the "Hair and Horses" country. Had that happened, however, Bush would certainly have learned about it long ago, since he ranged the entire region for years in the company of Jim Lusk, and came into contact with virtually every family in the settlement areas. So Michel must have kept her, and she must indeed have been with him that day on the boat. Perhaps he told his captors that she was his daughter, and as such, she was allowed to stay with him.

If Bush were to find Marie's trail, he'd first have to find that of Michel Freneau, and this he couldn't do at Nickajack. He needed to leave, but found himself caught in a bind. He couldn't leave Nickajack without leaving Tuckaseh, and he wasn't willing to do it. Tuckaseh's daughter and her husband treated the old man hatefully, so much so that Bush actually feared for Tuckaseh's safety in their household. If Tuckaseh were younger and not blind, he might consider bringing him along while he sought for Marie. But this was out of the question. Tuckaseh was too old and too blind to become a traveler. Besides that, he was an Indian; he'd be no safer roaming the *unaka*-infested countryside with Bushrod Underhill than he would be with his spiteful, foul daughter.

So Bush was trapped at Nickajack, unable to leave in good conscience. Eventually he built a small cabin outside the town and took Tuckaseh in. The old man actually gave up his talk about dying then, though he finally worked around to it again, and continued making periodic visits to the place he'd selected for his death site. Bush would head out after him and bring him back. It wasn't particularly morbid—for Tuckaseh approached the whole idea of dying rather matter-of-factly—but it was often troublesome, particularly in bad weather.

Bush was out retrieving Tuckaseh in this way on the day that Kennesaw disappeared from Nickajack. When Bush heard the news, his thought was only: Good riddance. He disliked the man intensely, and mistrusted him, too. He had developed the idea, completely speculative, that Kennesaw remained in Nickajack as a sort of spy, gathering information about the Chickamaugas and their haunts, their relative strength, their leadership, their plans. If Bush hadn't been distracted by his dealings with Tuckaseh and his frustration over being unable to launch in earnest his search for Marie, he might have addressed these suspicions once Kennesaw had vanished.

The raiders had ranged far and enjoyed much success. Bush sat beside Tuckaseh as evening fell on Nickajack, and listened to an oratorically-inclined warrior named Nontuanka describe the achievements of the foray. With great gestures and big words, Nontuanka told of cabins burned, *unakas* killed and scalped, and pitifully ineffective defenses breaking down under Indian attack. Nontuanka was an intriguing speaker, but his talk roused the occasional sly look and knowing nod among his audience members when he wasn't looking. Everybody knew that Nontuanka loved exaggeration almost as much as he loved whiskey, but none questioned or teased him. He had proven himself time and again in raids, and before his house many hoop-stretched *unaka* scalps were displayed.

Bush had lost interest in Nontuanka's overblown story quite some time back, but lingered to listen mostly because some of the territory that had been raided was familiar to him, the same country in which he lived while in the white settlements on the Cumberland. Occasionally, in Nontuanka's descriptions, he would recognize places and even cabins, but the warrior's characterizations of the victims were too imprecise for him to surmise whether he knew any of them.

Bush was almost dozing when Nontuanka reached a particularly dramatic narrative moment, punctuating it by lifting a scalp in one hand and a pistol in the other. Bush glanced up through glazed eyes, saw the pistol, and instantly became fully awake.

It was as if someone had just kicked him in the pit of his stomach.

Later that night, Tuckaseh asked Bush what was troubling him. Bush made denials at first, but Tuckaseh was not fooled. He could detect more, it seemed, than could many who had far better eyes than he.

At last Bush told the truth. "When Nontuanka was talking, he showed a pistol he had taken, and the scalp of the man he had taken it from. I recognized the pistol."

"Ah. And so you knew who the scalped man was."

"Yes. His name was Campbell. He always kept the pistol displayed on his wall. I didn't know him that long, nor that well, but he seemed a good man. He wanted me to marry one of his daughters, I believe."

Tuckaseh's dark brows arched. "Yes. And so again, you wonder in which world you belong, this one or the one you left to find me."

"Yes. I do. I find myself confused. The only thing that is clear to me is that I must find my sister."

Tuckaseh paused. "And I keep you from doing that."

"What? No, no. Of course not."

"Yes, Skiuga, I do, and we both know it. You would have been gone from Nickajack long ago if not for me."

Bush couldn't lie to this man. "I can't abandon you to a family who treats you as badly as yours does."

"I think I'll be dead soon, and then none of it will matter anymore."

"Tuckaseh, I mean no disrespect . . . but every morning you wake up and declare it a good day to die. You'll live to see many moons and suns rise and set."

"No. I don't believe so. I believe we will soon see trouble here."

"Why?"

The old man paused, his blind eyes moving back and forth. "A sense. Just a knowledge."

"I don't understand."

"You should leave Nickajack, Skiuga. Go back among the *unakas* and search for your sister. And have no sorrow for me. I am at peace with the end of my days."

"I'll not go. I can't."

"You must."

"No. I spent too many years without the pleasure of your company, Tuckaseh. I'll not abandon you to die alone."

"We all die alone, Skiuga. No matter how many may be with us, the boat that carries us on that journey is made to hold only one."

The army moved like a great, white serpent along an ancient war trail worn by the feet of generations of warriors. Passing an ancient stone fort whose origins no one knew, the frontiersmen crossed the Cumberland Mountain and camped by a spring.

Their next twilight saw them at the wide Tennessee River, which they crossed by swimming or clinging to floating debris, pushing and pulling their weapons over in oxhide boats. A fire blazing on the opposite shore guided them, set by four men who had swum across ahead of the others. One of them, Joseph Brown, was the chief guide for the expedition, having spent time in Nickajack itself as a prisoner of the Chickamaugas while he was still a boy. Another guide had come from Nickajack much more recently. His name was Kendall Saws.

Crossing the river was slow; by morning only half the soldiers were over. The first army didn't wait for the rest to cross.

Nickajack was not far away; the element of surprise must be retained.

At approximately the same time in Nickajack, Bush Underhill set out on a familiar path to find Tuckaseh, who had again left to die. But to his surprise, Tuckaseh was not at his usual place. Retracing his steps to the town, Bush inquired of a woman who was grinding corn outside her cabin in the crisp early autumn air, and learned that Tuckaseh had passed by, apparently headed for the river.

The river . . . Bush worried instantly. Thanking the woman, he hurried toward the river himself, moving, without knowing it, directly toward the mouth of a serpentine army.

Fog began just outside of town and thickened the nearer he drew to the river. Mists were common in this mountainous river country, but this morning's fogbank was unusually thick, oddly threatening. Bush found his bright mood dimming the deeper he plunged into the rolling whiteness.

Bush paused suddenly, listening. Something different and strange was out there in the shrouding fog.

He slid to the ground behind a tangle of ivy growing around a deadfall.

Less than a minute later, phantom forms slid through the fog, moving in a great, silent mass toward Nickajack. All armed, all intent, all clearly heading for battle.

For a moment Bush was a child again, back in Coldwater. He must warn his father, his mother—and then he remembered. They were gone. But there were others there. People he knew . . . *his* people.

Right now, Bush Underhill felt thoroughly Indian, and this *unaka* army, which for all he knew contained many a man he'd fought alongside during his time with Jim Lusk, was an army of enemies.

He wondered if they'd run across Tuckaseh already at the river, and what might have become of him if they had.

He must get back to Nickajack at once, and give warning. His head hammering, he rose and circled toward a place where he could enter the town without being seen by the white army.

He was sure they would soon surround Nickajack; it was vital that he reach the town before they cut him off from it.

He wished he'd brought his rifle. He was armed only with his knife and belt ax. Aware of his vulnerability, Bush moved as fast as he could, with caution. To be captured would end any hope of warning the hapless people of Nickajack.

He heard shots, and knew he was too late. The *unakas* had reached the town, the attack had begun.

Throwing aside caution, Bush broke into a dead run, heading toward the battle.

Though he expected to encounter a wall of *unakas* at any point, Bush came out onto a low hill overlooking the cornfields surrounding much of the town, without meeting resistance. Pausing at the crest of the hill, his belt ax in hand, he watched the attack upon Nickajack unfold.

He saw mostly confusion and carnage. As at Coldwater, the attack came in almost complete surprise, and no defense was ready.

Women and children screamed and ran in all directions, seeking refuge. Warriors who in a more prepared moment would be fearsome foes were impotent, scrambling for weapons, heading for the river in hope of escape by canoe, only to be shot down by frontiersmen positioned specifically to stop them.

The design of the attackers was evident. They had split into three divisions and were approaching the town from different directions, squeezing in like a giant, constricting snake. As the frontiersmen finally entered the town and the fighting became hand-to-hand, the bloodletting was great, with far more Chickamauga blood than white being shed.

Bush had seen enough. He would join the battle, and he would surely die—but there was no question about where his loyalties were on this day. He would fight to the death with the Chickamaugas.

As he raced into the fray with his belt ax swinging, he saw Nontuanka, the drinker, orator, and braggart, positioning himself to fire at one of the invaders, his weapon being the very pistol he had taken from Tyler Campbell. Poor Nontuanka! Bush knew what would probably happen, because he knew that pistol. It misfired more often than not, which was why Campbell had relegated it to the status of wall ornament. And sure enough, the flint snapped without setting off the charge, and Nontuanka, a stunned look on his face, was brought down by a flurry of belt ax blows while still holding the useless weapon.

No apparent effort was being directed against the women and children, Bush was glad to see. Many were fleeing into the forests.

A yelling frontiersman came toward Bush with a knife lashed, bayonet-style, to the muzzle of his rifle. He probed and Bush dodged, making a graceful turn and swinging his belt ax into the man's head. He heard the crack of bone and the man fell twitching. He was still alive, Bush thought, but would not fight any more today.

Bush ran on, beating a frontiersman off the very woman he'd seen pounding corn earlier. She vanished into the cornfield as the man went down. The fellow swung with a pistol aimed at Bush, but Bush broke the man's arm with his weapon, and took the pistol away from him before he could fire it. He struck the man a blow with the flat of his belt ax, not really wanting to kill him if he could avoid it. Then he looked around to see an *unaka* blowing the head off of the husband of Tuckaseh's daughter. Bush raised the pistol, aimed, and the *unaka* lost the back of his own head almost at the same moment his own victim fell.

Something caught Bush's eye. He wheeled around and saw—

He set out running into the cornfield, beating down stalks with his body, closing in on the man he'd spotted.

"Kennesaw!"

Kennesaw, who had just beaten to death a sickly man almost as old as Tuckaseh, turned from his bloodied victim and pulled back his thin lips to reveal his yellow teeth. The look was fright and viciousness combined. When he saw it was Bush, he looked relieved.

"Bushrod Underhill!" Kennesaw said. "Today the white man takes his vengeance, eh? A great day!"

Bush roared and came at him with the ax. Kennesaw side-stepped, went for his rifle. Bush grabbed it by the muzzle and pulled it right out of Kennesaw's hands, flipped it end over end into the corn. Kennesaw, seeing now that he'd misapprehended Bushrod's sentiments, pulled a long knife from his belt and took on a fighting posture.

"Well, well!" he said. "Seems the white's turned red! You want to fight on the side of savages, you can die with them!"

"Did you guide this army here, Kennesaw?"

"I did, and I'm damned proud of it!"

"Then the army can carry you away to bury you." Bush closed in.

Five minutes later, Bush emerged from the cornfield, cut and bloodied, the head of the ax red with gore. He'd left Kennesaw lying beside the body of the old man he'd beaten to death. And he'd taken Kennesaw's scalp; not because Bush Underhill kept such trophies, but because Kennesaw didn't deserve the honor of retaining his scalp in death, while all around him better men than he were losing theirs.

Bush was about to plunge into the thick of the battle when fingers yanked his hair from behind. Moccasined feet kicked his ankles, making him trip and fall. He tried to turn and swing the ax, but something hit him hard on the side of the head. Stars exploded with brilliant light in the field of his vision and he went numb.

He slumped earthward, feeling the hands in his hair tighten their grip, and the cold, sharp edge of a blade touch the base of his hairline, and begin to press in.

CHAPTER
FIFTEEN

Three days passed before Bush was aware of the world around him. He opened his eyes and saw overarching tree branches that moved against the sky, as if the forest was marching past him. He pondered this mystery for a time until his mind began to clear and he realized it was not the trees that were moving, but himself. He was strapped onto a tandem litter, riding along on his back between two horses, unable to move, stiff and sore. His head hurt.

He fell asleep and awakened near nightfall, lying on the ground now. When he regained consciousness, he drew a burst of attention from a group of grizzled, dirty strangers, all of them obvious backwoodsmen. They crowded around him and introduced themselves with amber-colored, gappy grins. The eldest, a long-bearded fellow with a hook nose, was one Packer Bledsoe; the others were his sons, the names of whom passed by without lodging in Bush's addled memory.

He caught the gist of what they told him. He was saved, just shy of a scalping, by Packer Bledsoe, or maybe by one of his sons—or maybe *from* one of his sons—and spared because he was white-skinned and obviously a captive of the "heetherns," as Bledsoe put it. After the battle was over, the Bledsoes made a litter, tied him on it, and were now hauling him back to their home, wherever that might be, to recover from his battle wounds.

One sentence of Bledsoe's came through clearly. "You surely were fighting hard to get free of them savages, young man. We couldn't let such a feller of spirit such as yourself just be left to lie, no sir, not with you being a white man."

Clearly there was a misunderstanding here about which side Bush had been fighting for, but Bush realized this was to his advantage. He whispered out a "thank you," which seemed to please old Bledsoe very much.

The weeks that followed, Bush would gladly put behind him. The Bledsoe home proved to be a small cabin on the road between Knoxville, Tennessee, and Abingdon, Virginia, far away from Nickajack. The lengthy journey was almost as hard on Bush as the battle injuries themselves, especially after the Bledsoes switched from tandem litter to travois, a much bumpier way to haul a man, but which required only one, not two, horses.

Once at the Bledsoe cabin, Bush was placed under the care of the ugliest female he'd ever seen, Bledsoe's daughter, Nancy. She was maybe twenty years old and bore an unfortunate resemblance to her father. There was no Mrs. Bledsoe about; either Packer Bledsoe was a widower, or perhaps his wife had abandoned him.

Nancy, now the woman of the house, talked to Bush until he could hardly stand to hear her voice. He suspected that she had designs on him beyond seeing him mended, which motivated him to heal and make a quick departure.

All in all, however, he was grateful to the Bledsoes. They saved his life, and their kindness and generosity in the midst of a grinding poverty they hardly seemed to notice was touching.

Nancy Bledsoe wept the day that Bush was well enough to leave. Packer Bledsoe made Bush a gift of a rattle-boned old horse—not much of a beast, but better than walking for a man still regaining his strength after long weeks of recuperation.

Bush actually felt some authentic regret about leaving the Bledsoes, even though he was sure he couldn't have endured another day with them. If he were laid up for life in that drafty house, smelling those smells and abiding Nancy's unending chatter, he would surely begin harboring thoughts of suicide.

Among the emotions Bush felt as he left the Bledsoes was a great heaviness of heart over the siege of Nickajack. It astonished him that twice in his life, he'd experienced a devastating raid on an Indian town in which he resided, and twice his white skin had helped protect him. As at Coldwater, he was left with many unanswered questions, the biggest of which was: What had become of Tuckaseh?

He was afraid that this time, Tuckaseh was dead.

He never even had the chance to tell him goodbye.

Just a few miles from the Bledsoe place, where a new tavern had been built, Bush's old horse started showing signs of fatigue. Since he'd set out in the afternoon and didn't have much day left in which to travel, anyway, he turned his beast into the tavern yard and headed in to do some negotiating. He had hardly a cent to his name, nothing sufficient to pay for tavern lodging or for a meal. All he had to offer was a willingness to work.

The tavern owner was a rather bleary-eyed man named John Crockett, and unfortunately for Bush, he had a houseful of strong sons and daughters, so there were few jobs left undone. Still, Crockett had a soft side to him and said he would give Bush's horse a stable and feed, and Bush supper and lodging for a night, in exchange for some firewood chopping. Bush accepted gladly and began hacking away. This was harder work for him than it would have been normally, weak as he was from his long recuperation at the Bledsoe house.

Bush chopped a huge stack of firewood and was wondering where he would find the strength to keep going, when at last Crockett came around, nodded his appreciation, and called Bush in for supper.

It was plain fare but good, pork and corn and potatoes. Bush sat between a couple of teamsters who were too weary to do much talking, which suited him. Across from him sat some of the assorted Crockett children. The boys ignored him; the girls cast him some lingering, interested glances. Bush did not respond, mostly heeding the food, which was seasoned to his taste and reminded him pleasantly that not all the world was as grim and dirty as the Bledsoe place.

He was eating a last bite of cornbread when a tumult outside made John Crockett glance knowingly at his wife. "Lordy . . . sounds like the Buckner boys," he said, and rose, heading for the door. He looked out. "Yep. Buckners. And they've got 'em another one in their stocks."

"Who are the Buckners?" asked one of the weary teamsters.

"They're trouble, that's what they are," a young Crockett answered. "They live way back in the hills, stay to theirselves mostly, but every now and again they'll get mad at somebody and throw them in their stocks and haul them down here to find a crowd to watch them give their man a whupping. They'll not whup a man unless there's folks to watch them do it."

Bush thought this all sounded odd enough to merit a look. He swallowed his cornbread, nodded his thanks to Mrs. Crockett, and headed for a window.

He'd never seen a sight quite like this one. Three bearded men with long, dirty black hair and whiskers, faces the color of dirt, and narrow, squinting eyes, were walking toward the tavern door, their wagon parked on the road. Bush would have thought it impossible, but these fellows made the Bledsoe family look downright urbane.

"I wonder what the poor fellow in the stocks done to them?" John Crockett said.

Bush looked at their wagon. On the back of it was a full set of stocks, homemade and rough, and in them a man with dark, slightly graying hair and a pained, hopeless expression.

"John Crockett, are you in there?" bellowed the nearest Buckner.

"John, go out there before they come in—you know I can't bear to have them in the place." This from Mrs. Crockett.

John Crockett sighed and went outside, nodding greetings to the ragged newcomers.

"Got us one!" said the nearest Buckner, apparently the family spokesman, gesturing toward the man on the wagon.

"What'd he do, Abraham?" Crockett asked.

"Caught him trying to steal whiskey from our stillhouse," Abraham Buckner said. "When we chased him down, he cussed us, and tried to bust Willard with a stick. We knowed we had one for the stocks then. We says, let's go down to Crockett's with him and put us on a prime whupping show for all the folks!''

"Abraham, you can't just go putting folks in the stocks and whupping them when they make you mad," Crockett said. "Ain't civilized. There's courts of law for such as that."

Buckner didn't even seem to hear. "Got you anybody in there wants to see the whupping show, Crockett?"

"I wouldn't care seeing it," one of the teamsters said, with more vigor than he'd shown so far. He came out of the tavern behind Bush. The second teamster said nothing, but looked interested.

"Well, fine!" Buckner said. "Willard, limber up that whup and let's get to busting!"

Bush, meanwhile, moved around to one side, looking intently at the man in the stocks. The fellow refused to look back at him, tugging and twisting, trying to get free.

Bush fixed his gaze on the prisoner as one of the Buckners made a show over at the tavern door of uncoiling the bullwhip that had been hanging over one shoulder.

Bush glanced at the Buckners, then leaped into the wagon beside the prisoner. Grabbing him by the hair, Bush jerked his head up and stared silently at the face.

"Hey! What you doing up there?" one of the Buckners demanded.

"You be ready to jump," Bush quickly instructed the prisoner. He hurriedly examined the stocks, finding them locked shut with a peg pin positioned so that the person in the stocks couldn't possibly reach it. He quickly yanked it out and threw the stocks open.

Cursing and yelling, the Buckners reached the wagon just as Bush and the freed prisoner jumped off the opposite side. They ran hard together across the road, over a stone fence, and into a field beyond. The Buckners chased them all the way across the field, but Bush and the freed man, leaner and faster, and motivated by self-preservation, lost their pursuers in the woods.

They ran on long after the cursing Buckners had fallen back, just to be sure, then stopped and collapsed onto a mossy patch, out of breath and immediately unable to speak.

Finally the freed man managed to get a few words out. "Thank you . . . thank you, sir. They would have whipped me near to death, I'm sure. I don't know why you saw fit to do what you did, but I'm grateful."

"You don't know why I did it?"

"No. But as I said, I'm grateful."

Bush stared closely at the man. "What's your name?"

"Michael Fray, your grateful friend indeed."

"No. No, I don't think so. You're no Michael Fray. Look at me. Don't you know me?"

The man frowned at Bush. "No. I don't know that I've ever seen you . . . yet . . ."

"It's me, Bushrod! Bushrod Underhill."

Michael Fray went pale and sank back onto the moss, his look that of a man sighting ghosts.

Bush grinned at him. "It's good to see you again, Michel. It's been many a long year."

Though Bush burned with curiosity and questions, he allowed Michel time to absorb the fact that the young man before him was indeed his brother's adopted son from so many years ago.

"I can see now, Michel, that there really is such a thing as fate," Bush said. "I've been wanting to see you for a long time."

Michel shook his head. His eyes began to redden. "Oh, no, it's not fate," Michel said. "Unless fate is the tool of the devil, doled out to a man who deserves punishment and is now receiving it. I'm glad to see you alive and well, Bushrod, and grateful to you for saving me just now . . . but this meeting should never have come."

"I don't understand, Michel. Are you angry with me?"

"No, no. It's you who should be angry with me."

"Why?"

"Go away from me—I'm a wicked man." He began to rise, making as if he were about to leave.

"No!" Bush said, grabbing at him, holding him. "No, you must not go. You and I have to talk. It's a wonderful thing that I've found you, Michel. You're the only man who can answer questions I've carried with me for years."

"Please, please let me go. Let the past be gone, like my name was until you called it tonight—a name I haven't heard in years. I've been living before the world for years as Michael Fray. Michel Freneau is long forgotten."

"Your accent, Michel, it's gone. You sounded so French when I knew you in Coldwater. Now you sound American."

"Much has changed with me, Bushrod. Much has changed. I'm not the man I was. But the changes are for the worse. I'm a wicked man, and you should go away from me." To Bush's surprise, Michel began to cry.

Bush remembered what the Buckners had said about Michel seeking to steal whiskey from them. "Michel, have you taken to drink?"

"Indeed. I'm a drunkard, Bushrod, and worse. Please go away from me. Don't make me speak anymore. It's best we're apart. You don't know me now."

"No. I'll not let you go this quickly. I have questions, and I think you owe me answers."

"Sometimes it's best not to know every answer." He paused, then sighed. "But I can see I'll not get away from you. So if we're to talk, why don't you begin? Tell me what has gone on with you since Coldwater."

"At Coldwater I was captured by the *unakas*. I watched you float away on the boat with the other captured traders that were set free. I called for you, but I reckon you didn't hear."

Michel looked down.

Bush briefly recounted his captivity, his escape, his years with Jim Lusk, his recent return to Nickajack and its fall. But he hardly cared that Michel know his experience—the question that burned in him now rested on the tip of his tongue, ready to be asked. Yet he was afraid. The answer he received might shatter his hopes of ever seeing his sister again.

"Michel, there is something I must know. I was told after Coldwater that Marie was killed, but in Nickajack, Tuckaseh and others from Coldwater told me it wasn't true. He said that she had lived, and that you took her away with you. Is this true?''

Michel seemed reluctant to answer. He hung his head a moment, then said, ''It's true.''

Bush's heart thumped harder. ''So Marie is alive!''

''She was alive when last I saw her. Two years ago, it was.''

''Where is she now?''

''I don't know . . . I only know where I left her.''

''You left her?''

''Yes. In Kentucky.''

''But why?''

Michel looked at him. ''You've told me your story. I'll tell you mine, and Marie's, though I wish I didn't have to. It's true that I took her with me from Coldwater. She was always dear to me, you remember that.''

Bush did remember. As a child he noticed quite clearly the greater affection his uncle held for his sister than for him.

''I took her, claimed her as my own child, and they allowed me to keep her with me when they put us on the boat. She lay at my feet in that boat, scared, crying for her mother. For years after that she was with me, under my care, and I did well for her, I believe. At first. I gave her all the affection and love I could, trying to serve her and give her safety—such a young girl, and she'd lost so much! I felt a great obligation for her good.''

Oddly, Bush felt a burst of jealousy. Though being raised by Michel Freneau would never have been his first choice, it stung a bit to realize that Michel could have felt such pity and responsibility for his niece without feeling similarly for his nephew.

''She grew strong and lovely—such a pretty child she was! You remember how beautiful she was when hardly more than a baby, Bush? She only became all the more so as she grew older. And her manner, her gentleness and kindness . . . they were as beautiful as her face.''

''Why did you leave her?''

''Because of what I had become. Liquor took a hold on me,

Bush. I make no excuses for it. It's merely a fact. I wasn't fit for her. She was too pure, too good, and I was just going to bring her harm."

"So you abandoned her?"

"I let her go for her sake . . . I did what I thought best. But I won't deny to you, Bushrod, that every night since, she's haunted me. And I've worried for her, wondering if I did what was right and what was best, and if she is well. Or even if she is still alive."

"You've never gone back to see?"

"It's best if I stay away."

Bush seldom cried, but hot, angry tears began to rise in his eyes as he looked at a man who had once abandoned him, and now had abandoned his sister as well. In a slightly quaking voice, Bush said, "I want you to tell me where you left her, as exactly as you can. The name of the town, the community, the people there."

"You're going to go looking for her?"

"I am. And I'll find her, and when I do, I'll not abandon her to anyone else."

Michel nodded. "That would be good. That would be right. You have grown up to be a better man than me, Bushrod. Maybe it was the hand of God that brought us together tonight, for the sake of Marie."

"Then tell me, right now, where you took her."

Bush left Michel an hour later, with mixed feelings. After Michel told Bush all he could about where he left Marie, he related a little more about himself. Bush, angry as he felt at this man, couldn't deny that Michel's story was fascinating and unusual.

After Coldwater, Michel, despite all his earlier declarations never to leave the world of the Indians, had done just that, drifting into the society of the white American settlers. With effort and cleverness he'd shed his French accent, learned to speak flawless English, and become Michael Fray rather than Michel Freneau. He invented a past for himself and Marie, presented her to the world as his daughter, and supported her by a variety of means ranging from straight-out theft to honest, hard labor.

"I often thought that Jean-Yves would have been proud of me, at least for my cleverness and adaptability, if not for some of the other shameful courses I followed," he said with one of the few fleeting smiles that Bush saw cross his face. "But all I did, I did for the highest reasons, and for Marie's good as best I could see it. That includes taking my leave of her. You must believe that, Bushrod. You must."

Bush thought it over, and nodded. "I do." He studied Michel as the last light in the woods began to fade. "You are far from the carefree rover I knew when I was a boy."

"Farther than you can ever know. Don't follow the path I've taken through life, Bushrod. It leads nowhere."

"Michel, would you come with me to find Marie?"

Michel thought about it, then shook his head. "No. It wouldn't be the best for her. She's best off free of me."

"Tell me something, then. Does she still have the mark upon her neck?"

"Yes. And always will. She often hides it, but the mark is still there."

"Then I'll know her by that, if in no other way."

"Yes."

"Goodbye, Michel."

"Goodbye, Bush. God go with you."

And then they parted. Strange, Bushrod thought, withdrawing from this man so soon. This, he was sure, would be the last meeting between himself and Michel for the rest of their lives.

Bush headed back to the road. The Buckners were gone, so he returned to the Crockett tavern, and made up an excuse about why he'd freed the prisoner. The Crockett children, unsatisfied, buzzed with questions, but he evaded them and retired early to his narrow bed, a trundle. It was uncomfortable, but at least he didn't have to share it with one of those teamsters.

Tomorrow morning would be like no other morning, because now he had a trail, a clue. There was no certainty he could find his sister, but there was reasonable hope. He was so excited that sleep was unlikely to come quickly.

But a long road lay ahead, up into Kentucky. He needed his rest. Willing himself to lie still and relax, at last he fell asleep, and dreamed about Marie.

CHAPTER
SIXTEEN

The weeks that followed were ones of great poverty, hard trials, long journeying, and deep uncertainties, yet also of the strongest sense of purpose Bushrod Underhill had ever known.

Possessing no weapon, almost no money, little more than the clothing he wore, and a tired old horse that did well just to plod, Bushrod could not undertake a journey almost all the way to the Ohio River in one sweep. It was necessary to work his way up slowly, pausing in one settlement and the next to pick up whatever work or trade he could, gradually bettering his situation while putting a few more miles behind him.

By the time he made Cumberland Gap, Bush had earned a pocketful of change, and received many a warning to beware the thieves that haunted the Wilderness Road on the other side of the mountain gap. He also managed to obtain a battered old flintlock and its related gear, paying for this by hewing out a dozen logs for a cabin under construction. Once armed, he fared better, being able to hunt small game, and also felt safer.

Beyond Cumberland Gap he found a fine horse roaming free, saddled it, and spent two days trying to locate its owner. Having no luck, he felt justified in claiming the horse for himself. He was nagged by a grim, worrisome fear that the horse's owner might have come to some poor end at the hand of a trail bandit, but this he couldn't know, and so he put it out of his mind.

He continued this way for weeks, traveling, working, and learning. Bush discovered in himself abilities he hadn't known he possessed. Not only could he handle more varied kinds of work, but he also made out well with people, charmed them, made obvious good impressions on them. This was something of a revelation, a brightening of his horizon that he had not expected.

Bush always knew he was among the best of woodsmen. Perhaps he had it in him to be among the best of civilized men as well.

As Bush penetrated deeper into Kentucky, he began asking questions of those he met. Did anyone recall meeting a dark-haired young lady, not yet twenty years old, with beautiful features and a dark birthmark upon her neck? Her name was Marie, and she might be going by the surname of Underhill, or perhaps Fray.

No one he met could recall ever seeing such a young lady.

Bush traveled on, covering miles and weeks, working, searching, asking, and despite a seeming utter lack of progress, never losing his resolve to find Marie.

In a tavern a few miles south of the Ohio River, western Kentucky

The man had a weasely, keen-eyed look to him that Bush didn't trust. He looked like a liar, the kind to toy with a man and give him the answers he wanted to hear, in hope of reward.

Even so, Bush couldn't quell his excitement. This spare-framed tavern weasel named Jaeger was the first man he'd met who declared that he'd indeed laid eyes on a young woman matching the description of Marie Underhill.

"Aye, yes," he said. "It was in this very place I seen her. She was with a man at the time, older than she, maybe her father. He drank a mite, this man, like I do, and we shared our cups a bit in yonder corner, the girl quiet as churchtime and prettier than a kitten, just setting there, looking about and fetching the eye of every man who entered the place."

"Did you hear her name called?"

"No, that I didn't. But this fellow, I recall, went by the name of . . . oh, Lordy. My mind fails me."

"Sir, I must tell you, I'm a poor man and have traveled a long way, mostly on my wits. I've got nothing to pay for information. It's my sister I'm seeking, and it's been many a year since I've seen her. All I can do is appeal to your kindness."

"I'm not dancing for a coin, young man," Jaeger said, not seeming offended. "My mind truly fails me as to his name."

"Might it have been Fray?"

"It might have been, or Smith, or Jones, or Gee-wilickers. I have no recollection."

"And do you know what became of them after you met them?"

"The man, no. But the girl I did see again. This time in the company of a family name of Simpkins who'd settled up near the river maybe five mile from where we sit."

Simpkins. The very family name that Michel had given Bush as the people with whom he'd left Marie! Unfortunately, Michel had not been able to give exact directions on where to find their dwelling—Bush figured that Michel never learned those facts, either because he wanted an excuse not to return, or because he had been too drunk when he parted with Marie—so the information he was gathering here was valuable indeed.

"So you know where the Simpkins family lives?"

Jaeger turned up his cup, took a swallow, then wiped his whiskered mouth on his cuff. "Not lives, sorry to say. Lived."

"They've moved on?"

"Aye, yes. Moved on to eternal glory or eternal damnation, whichever it was that awaited them, and I'd not presume to know which."

"They're dead?"

"Aye, yes."

"All of them?"

"I'm afraid so, young man."

Bush looked at the tavern corner, blinking fast. "How did it happen?"

"Some say Indians, some say a band of ruffians come down from Cave-in-Rock or off some river-pirate flatboat. Such sometimes will give an Indian look to their murders, trying to hide their tracks. I'd place my bet on it being robbers rather than redmen who did in the Simpkins clan." He took another swallow.

"Do you know for a fact that the young woman with them died, too?"

"No, I don't. I have no idea of that one. But if she was with them, then probably die she did. If not, then she was carried off by the ruffians who did the killings, and God above knows it would be better for any woman to die than to go through what such as that breed will make her endure."

Bush swallowed hard, feeling vaguely nauseated all of a sudden. "How can I find out for sure about the deaths of the Simpkins family, how many there were killed and such?"

"There were five of the clan that I'm aware of, but maybe more. That was a family with a lot of coming and going, and kinfolk of theirs were sometimes living with them, sometimes not. I don't know how many died."

"Are there no graves?"

"There's but one grave for them all. Buried all together, bones side by side, in the ground beneath their cabin. There was no floor, you see, and nobody wished to live in such a place after so many died there, for it seemed sure to be haunted. So them what found them dug up the floor, laid the corpses away, covered them over, and burned the cabin down atop it. It seemed as fitting a grave as could be made under them circumstances." He paused for another swallow and wipe of the cuff. "And sure as day, that spot has been haunted by ghosties and ghoulies ever since that day. A year and a half ago, I believe it was, that they died, the Simpkins."

Bush stared at his own mostly untouched tankard. "I want you to take me to the house."

"What house?"

"The burned-out house." He looked up at Jaeger. "I'm going to dig up that floor and look at those corpses. If my sister is there, and if there remains any flesh to her, maybe I can tell it by the mark on her neck."

Jaeger turned pallid. "No, no, I'll not see you do something so foolish as that! My Lord, young man, them spirits is already restless! What do you think they'll do if you go disturbing their earthly remains?"

"I'm not worried about ghosts. I have to know."

"I'll not be the one to take you. No."

"I'll pay you."

"You already told me you have no money."

"I have some money. And I have a fine rifle, and a good horse. I've worked hard for them all during my journey here, and I don't want to give them up. But they're yours if you'll take me to this cabin."

Jaeger looked very afraid, but Bush noticed that he didn't give an immediate "no" this time. He squinted at Bush. "All I need do is take you there?"

"That's all. And stand guard for me, in case anyone should come along who might not like what I'll be doing."

"Or any*thing*."

"I've never put much store in ghosts. Will you do it?"

"The rifle, and the horse?"

"That's right."

Jaeger drained the last of his drink. "I'll do it."

They reached the place in the waning hours of an afternoon that was darker than normal because of an incoming storm. With a very nervous Jaeger on foot before him, Bush walked along, leading his horse, on which a couple of picks were strapped, along with a wooden grain shovel, the best he could do in the time he had.

Bush had grown up in the wilds and knew no fear of forest or wilderness, but this place indeed did have a ghostly quality about it. A half-burnt log barn stood as a backdrop against a line of ugly, leafless trees, and before it was a heap of black-ened logs. Black ash had been pounded by the rain into a hard crust that covered everything within reach of the fire. The only intact structures in the clearing were a corn crib and lonely woodshed.

"There she is," Jaeger said, staring at the burned-out cabin. "That's all that remains of the house, and beneath it you'll find all that remains of their flesh, which I'll warrant won't be much after all this time."

"Probably not," Bush said. "But still I have to see for myself."

"You want me guarding you, you said?"

"Just keep your eyes open, make sure nobody comes along who'll give me trouble over digging up a burying place."

"I'll keep watch, but I'll go no closer than this."

Now that he was here, Bush found Jaeger's superstitious fearfulness annoying. "Look, just go on with you, if you're that concerned. I can take care of everything myself from here on."

Jaeger eyed Bush. "Go on . . . and take the horse and rifle anyway?"

"Take them! Just leave me the tools."

Jaeger was glad to accept this bargain. He removed the tools and laid them on the ground, and accepted from Bush the long rifle, horns, and pouches. Smiling now, he nodded thanks, wished Bush good luck, and climbed into the saddle.

Bush watched him ride away. The sky darkened further and thunder rumbled loudly. The storm would strike within the hour.

Picking up his tools, Bush went to the burned-out cabin, pushed aside blackened, fallen timbers, and began to dig.

An hour later, Bushrod stood drenched and exhausted in the hole he had made. The broken little shovel had been tossed aside and his hands were clotted and bruised from scooping mud and stone. Around his feet lay the dead. Just bones now, and a few scraps of cloth, rich and heavy black earth where once flesh and muscle had been. The driving rain washed over the remains as he knelt and dug among them by hand, looking for any evidence that might tell him whether one of these was Marie.

He found few clues, time and decay having obliterated most individuality these remains might have possessed. But here and there were indicators: a large bone that struck Bush as likely belonging to a male; a scrap of fading, decayed hair that still bore some of the original color as it clung to some stubborn, not-quite-decayed bit of scalp; a crumbling, tiny moccasin that had obviously been a child's.

He dug further, gradually uncovering the face of another skull. Delicate, well-formed, perfectly balanced. A woman's skull, probably. Bush smoothed away more mud, washed the face of the skull clean in the water gathering at the bottom of the hole. He studied the face in the gray-orange light.

There was still hair on this one, a single patch of thick, black hair. Hair as black as Marie's had been.

He gently laid the skull aside and dug further, looking for more of the skeleton. He prayed he would find enough flesh remaining to examine the skin of the neck. The birthmark, whether there or not, would tell the story.

But there was no flesh left, other than the one patch of skin clinging to the skull. It might be Marie . . . it might not.

So, after all his effort, his long journey, his obsessive quest, he still had no answer. The trail seemed at its end, as cold and dead as the unfortunates whose bodies he had uncovered.

It was more than Bush could take, and tears came.

He was still standing in the rain, sorrowful and frustrated, when Jaeger returned, riding in fast on Bush's horse, his face pale, screaming that he was pursued, that something was coming. The horse bucked; Jaeger fell, got up, and disappeared into the woods again.

Bush clambered out of the hole. Just now he didn't care who or what might be chasing Jaeger. He didn't care if there really were ghosts here, or terrible demons with fangs and a thirst for death. Nothing much seemed to matter, now that the search was at its end.

All this labor, all this journeying, all this hope . . . and now, nothing.

He watched as the brush at the clearing's edge yielded to a rider who emerged silently. He was astride a big chestnut horse, a tall, muscular figure with ebony skin shining from the rain that streaked it. He rode slowly to Bush and looked down at him.

"Howdy."

"Howdy," Bush said back.

"Why you been digging up the dead?"

"I've been searching for my sister. I'd hoped I'd find proof either that she was dead, or that she was alive, but I've found neither."

"Huh." The man seemed neither sympathetic nor hostile. "You going to leave that hole open?"

Bush hadn't really thought about that. Now that he did, he realized it was certainly improper to disturb a grave and leave the bones exposed. "No. I'll cover the bones again."

"What makes you think your sister is among the dead there?"

It was far too long a story to tell. "I had cause."

"So maybe she is there, and maybe she ain't."

"Yes. So I'm left not to know."

"You know what I'd do, if I was you?"

Bush, listless and preoccupied, felt the first stirrings of interest in this strange black man. Who was he? What was his concern with this place of death, and Bush's business in it? "What?" Bush asked.

"If I didn't know for a clear fact she was dead, I'd assume she was living. And I'd keep looking."

Bush thought about it and nodded. Lightning flashed, splintering a tree a hundred yards away from them, but neither man did more than throw a glance in its direction. "I'll do that. I will."

"I wish I could do the same for my own sister. But I know for a fact she's dead. Matter of fact, she's one of them laid away in that hole you just dug up."

"I'm . . . sorry. I didn't know." He paused. "This was a colored family?"

"No. But my sister was with them, a servant, when the raiders struck. Some talk of Indians, but that's foolishness. It was white men. Ruffians off the river. That's who did this."

"Why are you here?"

"Same reason as you, I reckon. I was drawed here because of my sister. I had to come see where she lay. Didn't expect to find a white man digging her up."

"I'm sorry. But you understand why I had to do it."

"I do indeed." The black man swung down from his saddle. "My name's Frank. Cephas Frank. And in case you're wondering, I'm no slave. I was set free ten year ago, and got the papers to prove it."

"I'm no slave hunter. I don't need to see any papers." Bush stuck out his hand. "My name's Bushrod Underhill."

"Pleased, Mr. Underhill."

"Call me Bush."

"Call me Cephas."

"Sorry I disturbed your sister's bones. I only wish I knew if I'd disturbed my own sister's bones as well."

"Maybe you'll find her yet, alive and well."

"Maybe so."

"I'm going to go fill up that hole again, Bush, if you don't mind. I don't like her bones being flooded over like that."

"I dug it, I'll fill it."

Bush did the work, and when it was finished, for good measure, fashioned a cross from some of the burned cabin timbers and placed it on the grave. Cephas Frank watched him and seemed to appreciate the gesture.

"Who was that who run from me on that horse yonder?" Cephas asked.

"The man who guided me here. I reckon he took you for a ghost. I'd given him the horse and my rifle to guide me here, but it appears he's left the horse behind."

"Your rifle, too. It's laying at the edge of the clearing yonder."

"I don't know about you, Cephas, but I could use a bit of shelter, and some victuals."

"Then let's go find us some."

Bush fetched his horse and found his rifle by the flare of lightning. He mounted. Jaeger's horse and gun now, he thought, but if the man was going to abandon them, Bush wouldn't leave them to go to waste.

He and Cephas Frank rode out of the clearing together as the skies grew dark and the storm began to die away in earnest. There were dry, open caves nearby, Cephas said. Good places for men on the move to pass a night and dry out from a storm.

PART II

THE DEVIL'S BACKBONE

CHAPTER SEVENTEEN

Near the Chickasaw Bluffs of the Mississippi River, just after the turn of the 19th century

Bush flicked his knife one more time on the piece of cane, held the cane to his eye, and looked down it. Good and straight, and cut just below the joint so the bottom of the cane section was enclosed. Perfect. He laid the cane section, about a foot in length, aside, and picked up a straight piece of hardwood already partially whittled into the shape of a pestle, or plunger.

Bush glanced up and around, wondering where Cephas was. He'd been gone too long, already over an hour beyond their rendezvous time. Bush wondered if he'd made a mistake and come to the wrong rendezvous point. He thought hard. No. This was the right place. He and Cephas Frank had rendezvoused at this same point along the river many a time over the past six years.

Six years. Hard to believe that much time had gone by since the dismal, rainy evening they first met at the burned-out cabin where Bush had dug for the bones of his sister, to no avail. Six years of searching, of question-asking, praying, and hoping, and he was no closer to learning whether Marie Underhill was living or dead.

He whittled on the hardwood plunger a little more, then test-fitted it to the piece of cane. It fit in, sliding all the way to the enclosed bottom, not too loose, not too tight. Perfect so far.

Noise near the river made him look, wondering if Cephas was arriving at last. No, just a possum prowling around lazily. Bush looked around and wondered again what had become of his partner.

Old Cephas. A rather peculiar stranger to him that first day, and now one of the closest friends Bush had ever known, every bit as close as Jim Lusk had been. Bush and Cephas had much in common, despite their different races and backgrounds, and Bush had always thought that was what made them get along with one another so well. Neither fit well into the dominating society around them. Both were far more comfortable in the wilderness than in towns and society, both were capable, natural woodsmen, and both appreciated the privilege of freedom more than most.

And both had lost sisters. That more than anything seemed their strongest common bond. Cephas's sister had died during the raid on the Simpkins cabin and lay buried beneath it. Bush's sister, who could say? Perhaps some of those bones under the cabin had belonged to her. Maybe the raiders who struck the cabin had hauled Marie away. Or perhaps she had already gone from the Simpkins house, on her own or with someone else, before their arrival.

Bush was tired of not knowing, and though he hadn't said anything of it to Cephas, he was beginning to think of giving up. He'd hoped against hope that they'd somehow pick up some bit of Marie's trail, but so far years of effort and countless miles of travel had failed to turn up a thing. And for Bush, hope was beginning to wear thin.

He picked up some hemp fibers he'd gathered and prepared, and began wrapping them tightly around the large end of the plunger he made. What he was up to was something of an experiment, dreamed up years ago by Jean-Yves Freneau, who never had a chance to try it, because his life was cut short by the raid on Coldwater. Bush always wanted to carry out the experiment himself, but only now got around to it.

He looked about for Cephas again. The day was waning. If Cephas didn't come in soon, he probably wouldn't see him this day at all, and Bush would spend the night worrying. They often separated to go on individual hunts and explorations many, but never before had Cephas failed to show up at the designated time and place.

I'm getting to be like an old woman, Bush thought. *Cephas can take care of himself.*

Bush wrapped the pestle until it fit so snugly into the cane section he couldn't muscle it in farther. Good. He popped it out again, then from one of his pouches produced a little wooden container filled with grease. He smeared the grease liberally over the tightly wrapped fibers on the end of the plunger. Then to that end, he attached a little ball of charred tinder. He placed the plunger against the open end of the cane section and pushed it in. Lubricated by the grease, it went in more easily this time, but the fit was airtight.

"Well, let's give your idea a try, Father," Bush said to the spirit of the man who raised him.

He rapidly pushed the plunger into the cane section, giving it a lot of force. Pulling it back up again, but not quite out of the cane section, he rammed it down one more time. Again and again he pushed and withdrew the piston-like plunger, compressing and decompressing the air inside the cane section.

The cane began to grow hot in Bush's hand. It was working!

When his instinct told him to, Bush pulled the piston out of the cane section with a loud popping sound, and to his delight found the tinder glowing and sparking. Jean-Yves Freneau, with that philosophic and scientific mind of his, had been right! Through the compression of air alone, a man could generate enough heat to build a fire.

Bush blew the tinder into a flame and applied it to yet more tinder piled and waiting beside him. As the fire caught, he added kindling sticks, then gradually, larger pieces of wood. The fire burned nicely, a fire created by nothing more than muscle-power and air.

Bush grinned as the flames rose. Jean-Yves Freneau would have been proud to see this.

Above and around, shadows descended. The sun was edging westward over the river. Pleased as Bush was with his successful experiment—and the fact that he now possessed a very practical new fire-making tool—he was still preoccupied with concern for Cephas Frank.

He surely hoped everything was all right.

*   *   *

Three miles downriver, Cephas Frank crouched in the brush on a high bank and looked down on a scene playing out on a roughly made flatboat moored below him. Though this craft, hardly more than a raft with a low-ceilinged, flat-topped shed built in its center, seemed hardly worthy of any kind of name, someone had given it one: *The George Washington* was painted onto the side of the shed.

Three men on the flatboat were talking with a fourth; occasionally some of their conversation would be loud enough for Cephas to hear. What he heard troubled him. As best he could tell, the three men were striking some sort of bargain with the fourth, and the object of the deal was a dark-haired, pretty woman who stood at the door of the shelter. Cephas looked closely at her. Her face was sad. One of the saddest he ever seen.

She turned slightly. Cephas peered more closely at her, and whispered, "Sweet mother of—"

"Well!" a man's voice behind him said. "What've we got here?"

As Cephas began to rise and turn to face two men, who'd come up unheard behind him, the second said, "Looks to me like we got us a nigger poking about where he got no business."

Cephas had laid his rifle on the ground beside him while he watched the flatboat, but picked it up as he rose. He shifted it just a little, ready to bring it up for use if need be.

"Is he right, nigger? You been watching our boat? Or maybe you been eyeing that white woman down there! Ain't right, you know, a darky looking at a white woman. What's your name, darky?"

"I go by Cephas."

"Got you a last name, or are you just one of them one-name slave darkies?"

"He's a runaway. Sure as hell."

"I'm no runaway."

"We supposed to take your word? There might be a reward for you, nigger. You're coming back to the boat with us, and then you can explain why you been up here watching us. And maybe we'll make you pay for staring at our woman. She don't come for free, you know.''

Silence. Followed by a sudden charge in the air. One of the intruders cursed and moved at Cephas, who raised his rifle. His position and close quarters in the brush worked against him, though, and he was unable to get the rifle raised before the second man moved in, much faster than the first, and got his hand around the barrel, pushing it away, making it impossible for Cephas to aim.

The first man brought up his arm; there was something in his hand. The arm flashed down, and Cephas felt a jolting, painful thud against the side of his head. He staggered, losing his strength and his grip on the rifle, which was pulled away from him.

He stumbled backward, fighting not to pass out. He saw the glitter of a shiv's blade. His opponents moved toward him.

Cephas put up his arms to fight as the world danced and moved before his unfocused eyes, and a dark numbness began to descend upon him. He went down, and even before he fully passed out, they were upon him, cursing, the shiv rising and then falling, once, twice, three times.

Something's wrong, Bush thought. *Cephas should be here by now. Something's surely wrong.*

He rose and put out the fire he so cleverly built, hefted up his weapons, and set out for Cephas. When they'd split up, Cephas had headed south and he north, so now Bush turned southward.

The farther he traveled the more unsettled he felt. It was just an intuitive feeling, but Bush couldn't shake it off. He searched, called Cephas's name, though not too loudly. Along the river, one never knew who was within earshot, or what kind of response one would receive.

The sun was almost to the horizon. Bush pressed his search all the harder. Another hour, and he would have to give up and go back to the rendezvous point in hopes that Cephas was merely late.

Ten minutes later, he found the first evidence that something was amiss. A wooden powder horn plug, lying on the ground in a clearing, proof of recent human presence. Bush picked it up and examined it. Cephas's powder horn plug, no question of it. The plug had a distinctive shape and a chip off one side.

Bush examined the clearing and detected that there had been some significant activity here. Branches were bent and broken, grass and young tree sprouts mashed to the ground. A scuffle, maybe.

Soon Bush located evidence that something heavy had been dragged through the brush. There was blood.

Hurrying along in the waning light, following the sign, Bush soon found him. Cephas was on his belly, having dragged himself nearly a quarter of a mile from the clearing where Bush had found the powder horn plug.

"Cephas . . . Lord, Cephas, what's happened to you?"

Bush dropped to his knees beside his partner and carefully rolled him onto his back. The moment he saw Cephas's puffed, bruised face, he knew it was bad. There was blood coming out his nostrils and crusting around his mouth.

"Bush . . . Bush . . . listen to me . . ."

"You shouldn't try to talk, Cephas."

"Listen . . . George Washington . . . flatboat . . . saw them . . . saw them there, and I saw—" He cut off, blood coming up his throat in a great gush, filling his mouth, choking him.

Bush turned Cephas's head to one side, letting the blood clear from his throat. "Lie still, Cephas. I got to find us help."

Cephas would not lie still. He pulled his head back to its previous position. "Got to . . . listen . . . brothers . . . it was them . . . saw her, Bush. On the boat . . . George Washington . . . woman . . . saw her . . . the mark . . . I could see it, clear . . . knew she was . . . she had to be . . ."

Cephas was almost unconscious, his words coming harder, making less and less sense. George Washington? What could that mean? Bush was sure his partner was babbling because his mind was failing him as his life drained away.

Bush pulled open Cephas's shirt and winced. Puncture wounds, small and deep, like those a riverman's shiv would inflict. They'd bled much, but were now closed and crusted. Most likely the story was quite different deep inside Cephas, though.

"Cephas, don't die. Don't die." Bush didn't want to weep, but tears came.

"Bush . . . two of them . . . hit me, cut me . . . and they, they . . . she was . . . they was . . ." A new gush of blood came up from inside, cutting his voice off, filling his mouth, spilling over. Cephas's head rolled slowly to the side and his eyes went glassy.

Bush knelt over him and wept like a child. Cephas Frank was dead. Another friend and partner lost, as he had lost Jim Lusk.

Bush buried his partner where he had died, and for all the next day, lingered in the vicinity, numb with grief at the loss of a friend, angry at the world for its unfairness and cruelty, and sorrowful for Cephas Frank himself, his life cut short.

He thought over Cephas's final babblings, trying to make sense of them. Much of what Cephas had said Bush already forgot—he'd been in such shock at Cephas's condition that most of it had sailed right past him—but some of it, maybe, made sense.

Cephas had probably been trying to tell Bush who hurt him. The "George Washington" reference Bush could make no sense of, but there'd been something about a flatboat, and brothers. "It was them," he'd said. Them. The ones who'd hurt him, he must have meant. Men from a flatboat. A couple of brothers, Cephas's words indicated.

Standing by Cephas's grave, Bush collected his thoughts, then spoke to his departed friend. "I'll not let this pass, Cephas. Somehow I'll find whoever did this to you. I'll see they receive their due punishment, if only from me." Bush's throat grew tighter, emotion filling him. "For three years you and me have roamed, hunting, trapping, fishing, working the river. For three years you've kept my hopes up about Marie when I was ready to give up. You've told me time and again that I should never think her dead until I know she's dead, and that if me and you had switched places, and it was your sister who maybe was still alive out there, somewhere, you'd hunt for her long as you lived.'' Bush rubbed his eyes. ''Well, Cephas, I appreciate all of that, you keeping me going, keeping me thinking that maybe I can find her someday. But three years is a long time, time enough to drain a lot of the hope and spirit out of a man. And now that you're gone, I don't know I've got any spirit left at all, nor any will to keep trying. So I'm going to give up looking for Marie for now. Maybe for good. I'm too weary of it to keep up, and tired of having my hopes rise only to get pulled down again. I'm letting Marie go, Cephas. From now on, the looking I'll do is for the ones who did this to you. And that's one quest I won't fail in. I promise you. I promise.''

He took up his rifle and packs, looked for a last time at the grave of another friend and partner, and turned his steps southward.

CHAPTER EIGHTEEN

It was easy now for Bush to understand what had overtaken Jim Lusk in the last days of his life.

Lusk had lost a wife, a greater loss, Bush knew, than that of a friend and partner, but the grief was similar. And with the passing of Cephas went his sole source of encouragement to keep up the seemingly vain search for Marie Underhill, Bush felt a double bereavement.

As he watched himself over passing weeks, he began to wonder if the soul of Jim Lusk had mystically replaced his own.

Bush found he simply wasn't the man he was. He began making mistakes, losing the edge of perfection that always marked his woodcraft. His mind wandered; at times he became lost in areas he'd traveled a score of times with Cephas Frank.

It was just like Lusk had done.

One new thing entered Bush's life that hadn't entered Lusk's in his last days. Bush began to drink, much more than he ever had. He'd never really had much fondness for liquor, drinking it minimally, never getting drunk, and many times taking a simple glass of cold water in honest preference over stronger drinks others clamored for. It was different now. He left the woods behind, began haunting the dives of riverside communities, drinking, brawling, acting and even looking so different from his prior self that he sometimes went initially unrecognized by men he'd met on the river years before.

Bush forgot much of himself as days passed, even stopped thinking about Marie, who'd occupied at least some back cor-

ner of his attention almost constantly since that day at Nickajack when he'd pledged to find her, no matter what. But he
never forgot what happened to Cephas Frank, and his vow to
find and punish his killers.

Bush got it in mind to go to Natchez. There, in the hellholes
and dens of infamous Natchez-under-the-hill, he would have
a better chance of finding the sort of river trash who would
murder a man such as Cephas.

He continued working his way southward, living on what
he could kill, and twice, to his astonishment, on what he could
steal. These thefts were not large, just a loaf of bread in one
case and half a pie in another, but they were atypical of Bushrod Underhill, who'd had honesty drilled into his soul by Jean-
Yves Freneau in his earliest days, and reinforced by Jim Lusk
and others since.

Bush was half-drunk one late afternoon on a saloon barge
that had pulled to shore about halfway between the Chickasaw
Bluffs and Natchez, when he found what he was looking for.
He'd been seated on a keg at the edge of the barge, looking
out across the water and drinking from a dirty pewter cup,
when a flatboat came into view up the river. He watched it
idly as it drifted along at the speed of the current.

A friendly young boy, son of the owner of the saloon barge,
came over to Bush and sat down crosslegged beside him.
"Look yonder at them clouds sweeping up," the boy said.
"There's going to be a devil of a storm this evening."

"Believe so," Bush said, taking another swallow.

The boy said no more for a while, watching the rising storm,
then turning his attention to the same flatboat that Bush had
been casually observing.

"George Washington," the boy said.

Bush, frowning, looked down at him. "What'd you say?"

"George Washington. See? It's writ there on the side of
that flatboat. I read it off myself." The boy smiled, proud of
his literacy in a day when many an older soul than he couldn't
read a word.

Bush came to his feet, dropping his cup, staring at the flatboat. "Lord . . ."

With both heart and mind racing, Bush stared at the flatboat as it neared, wondering if it might swing toward the bank so those aboard it could take advantage of the saloon barge. The boy's father, hoping to stir more business, went to the side of his barge and called across the water, encouraging the flat-boatmen to stop in for "fine libation."

A call came back, carrying loud over the water: "Not today, friend! 'Nother time!"

Bush turned to the boy and grabbed his shoulders a little too roughly. The youngster's eyes went wide. "Son, I need a canoe, something I can use to get over to that flatboat."

"Only canoe we got is right yonder, but that belongs to— hey!"

Bush, releasing the boy, had already gone for the canoe, which sat on one end of the barge, tied upside down. He loosened the ropes and prepared to put it into the water.

The barge owner approached. "You, there! What the deuce are you doing? That's my canoe!"

Bush wheeled, knife in hand, and held it toward the man. "I got to borrow it. I'll bring it back."

"That canoe ain't available for loan."

"Then I'll rent it, damn it! Now you stand aside. Boy, go fetch my rifle and such over yonder. Bring it to me, easy and careful, and don't think of trying any tricks with it."

The boy turned. "Ain't no rifle."

Bush looked. The boy was right—his rifle and packs, left near the place he'd been seated, had disappeared. Some other patron of this floating establishment had made off with them while he was drunkenly unaware.

Taken aback, momentarily unsure of what to do, Bush watched *The George Washington* moving on past in the river. Men stood on the deck. He saw a woman there, too, dimly. One of the men turned to her and pointed at the shelter on the middle of the flatboat. She entered it and Bush saw her no more. One man who had ordered her inside took up a spyglass and looked through it at the people on the shore.

"If my rifle's gone, then it's gone," Bush said. "Mr. Saloon Man, just consider this canoe my compensation for what was stole from me while I was at your fine establishment here.'' Bush put the canoe into the water and took up the paddle.

A burly fellow with a flintlock pistol beneath his belt came up and said to the barge owner, ''You want me to stop him?''

''No,'' the man said. ''This fellow's a madman. Just let him go. Ain't much of a canoe anyway.''

Bush pushed away from the barge, turned the canoe in the water, and began paddling toward the flatboat, adding the speed of his own muscle to that of the current, gradually closing in on *The George Washington* as the men on its deck watched him coming.

Bushrod Underhill usually would never have been so reckless as to single-handedly attack a flatboat with no more than a canoe and knife. But it wasn't Bushrod Underhill as he had been. This was Bushrod Underhill transformed and maybe ruined. Bushrod Underhill transformed into something utterly different from the man he'd been before.

The canoe came within talking distance of the flatboat. A tall man, dark-haired, with a clean-shaven face, called out to him: ''Who are you, pilgrim?''

''What? Don't you know me?'' he grinned harmlessly, knowing he had to get on the boat, and that it would be almost impossible to do so without permission.

''I can't say I do.''

Bush cast his eyes skyward, saying, ''It astonishes a man how quick his old friends forget him!''

''We don't know you.''

Bush looked heavenward again, the image of an exasperated man, and said, ''Surely you recall old Jim!''

Another man, much younger than the prior two, said, ''I can't say I do.''

Bush shook his head. ''Gents, my feelings are nigh to getting hurt. I can't believe you can't remember old Jim Lusk!'' He looked back at the nearing storm, clouds whipping in low and close, lightning beginning to flash in the distance. ''Can I come aboard?'' He glanced left to right, and grinned wickedly. "Got me some money . . . and I hear you got something to sell."

The attitude of the men instantly changed. "Jim! Now I recall you! Come on up and join us."

Aided by the youngest of the flatboatmen, Bush got the canoe up against the boat and climbed aboard. There were five men aboard besides him, and the unseen woman inside the shelter. All the men appeared to be brothers, their features and coloring quite similar.

It came to Bush's mind that he might not leave this flatboat alive. If he determined that these men, or some of them, had killed Cephas, he intended to do all the damage he could with his knife. He was a good fighter, but five against one was five against one.

A moment of doubt—then he was past it. Tuckaseh had told him once that it's too late to think of dry land once one has already jumped in to swim. And there was some biblical quotation Jean-Yves had been fond of, about not looking back once you've put your hand to the plow.

He grinned and nodded at those around him, trying to look a little drunker than he really was. Best to seem a bit of a buffoon just now, rather than a threat.

"You fellers are all looking healthy."

The one Bush had pegged as the eldest spoke. "Let's end the bilge. We don't know you, though maybe you do know us. We meet a lot of men on this river. We're in business, you see. And if I heard you right, I believe it's business you got in mind?"

Bush stepped back one pace and covertly put his hand on the handle of his knife. "The truth is, I came because I believe I owe a debt to you gentlemen."

"What debt?"

Bush looked from face to face. "The debt I owe at least two of you for killing my partner on back up the river. He was a black man, beat and stabbed to death . . . but before he died, he told me the pair who killed him seemed to be brothers, and he called the name 'George Washington.' "

The older men stared stonily, but the face of the youngest

told the story, and a moment later it wouldn't have matter if it hadn't, because he chuckled nervously and said, ''That nigger. He's talking about that nigger.''

The eldest one swore at the youngest, telling him to keep his mouth shut.

So now it was confirmed. Bush pulled out the knife. ''Cephas Frank was my friend and my partner, and I swore above his grave that I'd make the men who killed him pay, no matter what the cost.''

The eldest brother produced a pistol and leveled it at Bush. ''That cost is going to be quite high for you, sir.''

''No,'' the youngest said, pulling a long knife from beneath his waistcoat. ''Don't shoot him. This one's acting like a knife-fighter. Let *me* have him.''

The eldest glanced at the others, shrugged, and put away the pistol. ''As you please.''

With a grin, the young man edged to the low, flat-roofed shelter, which wasn't high enough for anyone above a child's height to stand in. Bush thought of the woman within it. Lying down or sitting, no doubt. Probably watching out a knothole.

If so, she was going to have the privilege of witnessing a death, he thought morbidly. Maybe his own.

''Up on top,'' the young one said, nodding at the shelter. ''Good fighting platform.''

''You first.''

The challenger put one hand on the shelter top, heaved himself up lithely, and was on the shelter so quickly Bush didn't quite see how he did it. ''You next.''

Bush, wishing he hadn't drunk so much earlier, gave it a try, and to his pleasure succeeded. On the shelter, with the storm now almost over them and the river moving faster because of heavy rains that had already fallen to the north, Bush confronted his foe, and readied himself to die.

The young flatboatman made the first lunge. Bush jumped back, then forward, slashing. His blade caught his enemy on the side of the face and laid open a shallow cut.

At first the young man, who obviously considered himself a fine knife fighter, looked shocked. He wiped the blood from his face and backed away. He regained his composure quickly, though, a grin spreading across his face. His teeth were perfect and white, which for some reason made him look all the more dangerous.

He lunged and slashed. Bush dodged back, almost too far, nearly dumping himself over the edge of the flatboat platform to the lower deck. He caught himself just in time. The boatmen whooped and hooted and urged on the knife-flourishing combatants on the platform, which was actually the roof of a shed built in the middle of the big raft-like cargo vessel.

"What's the matter with you, my dear and blooming peavine?" the younger fighter mocked from behind those pearly teeth. "Are you looking for a coward's haven to run to? You'll find naught on this boat! You've bit into the flesh of Beelzebub when you met me! I'm the mud hen of hell's darkest thicket! I'm the very child who put the fork in the serpent's tongue! Waaaauuugh! I'm a screamer! I'm damnation and redemption! I'm brimstone! I'm a gouger! Whoooop! Run from me, coward, while you can!"

"I run from no one," Bush said. "You're nothing but the murderer of a fine man, not fit to boast of anything. As for me, I don't brag. Any boasting to be done my blade does for me."

The pair circled and lunged and feinted and snarled, though neither made contact with the other. Lightning flashed and thunder pealed. On the farthermost shore, trees whipped wildly in the wind and birds cawed and called; dogs barked faintly in the distance. The air was wet and crisp, almost crackling with the energy of the approaching storm. Darkness was falling fast, the river flowing faster.

"I'm seeing some prime dancing, sweethearts, but can you fight?" someone bellowed.

"Cut his gullet!" another yelled. "Show him who's the true Orleans fire-belcher!"

The young man barked like a mastiff and slashed, and Bush danced back suddenly with a red line across his bare chest. The cut was not deep or even painful, but sufficient to make the momentum of the fight shift away from Bush.

For five minutes they danced and dodged and slashed, neither gaining much advantage over the other. If the flatboatman had thought he would have an easy opponent, he learned otherwise. Bush Underhill wasn't easy to kill.

But Bush was worried. Even if he prevailed over this one, there were four others. Short of a miracle, he was a doomed man.

The storm caught up with the flatboat, hard rain gushing down all at once, lightning striking somewhere beyond the far bank. Two more lightning flashes came in fast succession. The first splintered a tree on the closer shore, beside a cabin on the very brink of a badly eroded bank. The second struck farther away, but illuminated a sight that made both combatants break their gaze from one another and look landward: the bank beneath the cabin gave way, sliding with a dull roar into the river, carrying the cabin and dumping it into the water.

Lightning ripped through the sky just as Bush looked back at his opponent. His heart jumped throatward as a monstrous and impossible vision appeared before the flatboat and behind the younger man: a gigantic hand. The great claw reached up from the river, bending down toward the deck and crew, ready to snatch as many men as possible into the river.

The boat jolted hard against something. Timbers moaned and cracked, the boat turned completely about, tilting slightly. The great hand knocked several men to the deck, and suddenly the flatboat tilted the opposite direction.

It wasn't really a hand, Bush realized after the initial shock, but a gigantic tree, broken loose and floating free in the water. It had chanced to reach an unseen sandbar at the same moment as the flatboat. The tree was wedged against the underwater obstruction. Its trunk wrenched in the current so that long branches grappled out across the boat while it slammed hard against the spit of sand.

Bush's opponent unexpectedly screamed. A new flash of lightning revealed to all that the young knife-fighter had just been impaled on a sharp branch of the tree. It poked into his back and out of his belly, crimson and wet, some of his stomach pushed out on its end. The force of the racing flatboat had driven the branch completely through him from behind.

The boat twisted on the sandbar and moved forward again. The knife-fighter's bloody form, lodged on the branch, came at Bush and went past him. Something closed around Bush's middle, picking him up. He yelled and scrambled madly but could find no footing.

The boat moved out from beneath him and the tree that held him twisted down, turning him sideways and plunging him beneath the dark and cold water.

Bush, caught in the limb of the same tree that had killed his opponent, struggled underwater for a moment, then broke free. He had no idea whether he was upside down or right side up, so he merely flailed and kicked. Moments later, he broke through the surface of the water. He'd somehow washed right over the sandbar and now was free in the river, being pushed helplessly along in the current.

As he turned and twisted, struggling to gain control, he caught intermittent glimpses of the flatboat being wrenched about on the sandbar. Voices cried out frantically; receding, barely-visible figures grappled about on the deck. Then, miraculously, the boat came free of the bar and bumped around it. Twisting back into the main current and down the river, it kept pace with Bush as he washed along—though far off to one side of him—then steadily outpaced him and drifted toward the opposite bank.

The miracle he'd needed had come; he was out of reach of those on the flatboat. But the river was just as likely to kill him.

A branch brushed against him and he grabbed it, but it was far too small to float him. He let it go and swam some more. The flatboat had gone out of sight, though he heard the occasional snatch of a voice carried to him like a wind-borne zephyr.

Bush struggled in the water as his feet and hands went numb and his body began to feel heavy. Muscles cramped all over his body, wracking him with pain.

He knew he was going to die in this river. Dead and gone

in his mid-twenties, a life cut short before he even had time to figure out what it was all about.

A log bumped his shoulder and pushed him beneath the surface. He twisted, kicked, and came up again. The log had already passed by, but, working with the current, he managed to catch up with it and get a hand around a stub where a branch had been. His fingers slipped away and again the log went out of reach, but with another great effort Bush managed to reach it and, this time, hold on.

Pulling himself forward, he hooked his other arm around the log and dragged himself slowly up over it. He relaxed as much as possible, letting the log keep him above water.

Now, he thought, he would just float, loosen his muscles and after a few minutes, see if he could kick the nearer bank.

The log began to turn beneath him, almost throwing him back into the water. He held on tighter, then looked up just in time to see a big sawyer poking out of the water right at him.

He tried to maneuver the floating log around the sawyer, but he had seen it too late. One log bumped another, and Bush was thrown free, back in the water again.

Despair swept him in. He knew his strength would never last, unless he could reach the bank.

Something made Bush turn his head and look behind him.

Floating at him through the storm was something huge, black, and heavy, rolling like a big wheel in the water, moving too swiftly and taking up far too much river on each side for him to hope to escape it.

He surrendered. No hope now. Whatever this was, it would be on him in a moment, slamming him senseless and pushing him under the water.

He closed his eyes and waited to die.

Moments later, Bush was thinking: This thing must have a mouth, whatever it is, for I swear I believe it's just swallowed me!

He opened his eyes as his body was thrown up against something rough and hard. He rolled over, splashing into water, then bumped against another hard surface. Debris rushed around him. Then it felt, as sure as the world, as if someone had slapped his face. Not particularly hard, just a flat, wet slap, palm and fingers.

Bush found a handhold and pulled himself farther up onto the hard surface, out of the water. The thing he was in steadied and stopped rolling, floating now at a cock-eyed but steady angle. Looking around in nearly pitch blackness, broken sporadically by lightning flashes, Bush suddenly made sense of it all.

He was inside that cabin he'd seen fall off the bluff. The deuced thing had floated down the river, and somehow he'd gotten inside of it!

As best he could guess, the cabin must have rolled over him in just the right way to draw him in through a door or window. He laughed at the absurd luck of it—moments from death, and he was rescued by a floating cabin!

The cabin twisted sideways and something hit him hard on the side of the head. He caught it—a three-legged stool. He saw it drop, in the brief white moment of a lightning flash, into the water below him, and float about, trapped like Bush himself inside the cabin walls. A stout cabin, this one. Obviously spiked together instead of merely notched.

Bush scooted up farther; he was somewhere at the top of an inside wall, just under the edge of the roof. He bettered his handhold, tried to wedge himself as securely as he could, and hoped the house wouldn't roll over again.

It did. The wall to which he clung suddenly pitched downward, dipping into the water and pulling him with it. Then he was out, looking down at the water again, losing his handhold, and falling into the murky wet.

Something fleshy and soft was next to him. He pushed the thing away as the cabin rolled over yet again, then resettled.

Bush was half in, half out of the water. Lightning flared, and he found himself looking into the face of a man who stared back at him but did not see him, for he was dead, the back of his head crushed like a dropped egg. For a moment Bush thought maybe this was the knife-fighter, washed free of the stabbing branch, but it wasn't. The face was different.

Bush pushed the corpse away, disgusted, and scrambled back up the wall again.

The house moved along, rolling no more, though it did twist continually. Bush kept an eye out for the corpse, as if by its own power it could climb up the wall and slap him again like before.

The cabin leveled somewhat as it moved down the river and Bush was able to position himself more steadily. He noticed, however, that the cabin was also riding lower in the water. Before long it would sink, and take him down with it.

At length the cabin angled up enough to bring its puncheon floor, which was spiked to the base logs of the wall, mostly out of the water. Several puncheons were missing; through the gaps he saw the sky go white with each lightning flash. He would work his way out through that opening, climb atop the cabin, and keep his eye open for some alternative support, before the cabin went fully under.

Bush began to climb. He made slow but steady progress, then slipped on the wet wall logs and slid into the water again.

Solidity gave way beneath him and he went down, falling out a submerged window into the cold river below. For a few moments he was wedged in the window, competing for space with something else—the corpse! Then he was through, but found himself under the cabin, and stuck.

He struggled to find a way out from under, but part of his clothing was stuck on some protrusion from the cabin, keeping him below water level. He ached for air, struggled for freedom, and at the last possible moment before the surrounding blackness became unending, the cabin rolled again, pulling him up and out of the water and freeing him from whatever had trapped him.

He gasped, and sucked in huge, welcome breaths. Suddenly, he was tossed into the water again. But as he fell it seemed to him that the eastern bank was not nearly as far away as before. Blindly, he began to swim, realized he was going the wrong way, then turned in the current and pulled himself in the other direction. He swept downriver much more swiftly than he managed to move across it.

Farther ahead in the river, the cabin gave one more roll, wrenched into pieces at last, and vanished. He kept swimming. The bank seemed no closer. He was growing very, very tired.

CHAPTER
NINETEEN

Bush walked in darkness through a light rain that had begun in the wake of the storm, with no clear memory of having made it to the bank. He was weak, sore, lost, and very disoriented.

He was also weaponless and shoeless; his footwear had come off sometime during his river ordeal. Staring across the river, he looked for the flatboat he had fallen from, but saw nothing. Too dark. Eventually, the rain stopped, the clouds opened to let through the moon, and the broad river shimmered with reflected light. Still no flatboat visible, just assorted floating trash and refuse discarded by the storm.

As bad luck would have it, Bush had washed onto an unpopulated area. Not a cabin was in sight, not a distant glimmer of a settlement or camp—nothing but black Mississippi forest.

Finally Bush quit walking, realizing he'd best wait until daylight and hope for aid from some passing boat. He'd build a fire on the shore, see if he could snare a fish or roust up some other game come morning, and make his way downriver however he could. He'd not gone more than twenty feet when he caught a glimmer of light coming from deeper in the woods. He peered closely. A campfire? It appeared so.

Stepping gingerly because he was barefooted, Bush began moving toward the light, pushing aside branches and brambles, wincing when his foot trod on a stone or burr. The light grew brighter and bigger and soon he began to smell the delicious scent of cooking meat. He listened for voices but heard none. Either the campers were not talking, or there was only one.

Bush stopped, panting. His strength was nearly gone. Whoever started the fire, he hoped they were friendly, and wouldn't be overly startled to see a battered, half-clothed figure such as himself appear.

When the campfire was close enough that its smoke stung his eyes and the smell of the cooking meat made his stomach rumble, Bush cleared his throat and called, "Hello, the camp! Hello! I want to come in, if I may."

No reply came. Bush cleared his throat again and repeated himself, only louder.

Still nothing. Could the fire have been started by lightning, with no one about at all? It didn't seem likely. Not a confined, controlled blaze like that one. Then he sniffed the cooking meat again and knew that the fire had to be man-made. Lightning didn't spit-cook squirrels.

A burst of light-headedness caused Bush to stagger. He leaned against a tree and decided he would have to take his chances and go on in even without permission.

"I'm coming in . . ." His voice was weaker. "I'm a friend . . . I'm coming in."

He advanced, reaching the edge of the woods and the small clearing where the fire burned. Pausing, he looked about for whoever was camped here, and saw no one.

A mystery indeed, but Bush wouldn't try to solve it. Feeling he might pass out at any time, he walked into the clearing and slumped down near the fire. He was intensely weary, almost too tired even to eat. The scent of the meat was too rich to be ignored, however, and he took the squirrels from the fire, waited until the meat was cool enough to eat, and took a bite.

When he was sated, he tossed the remnants aside and lay out flat on the ground, drifting quickly into a deep slumber.

What awoke him he could not say. His eyes opened; he was facing the fire, but it had mostly burned down. Red embers, spewing smoke and sparks.

Bush was not alone. He felt it.

Sitting up, he sucked in his breath, a reaction to an army of pains that marched up and down his battered body in a short span. Slowly he twisted his head and looked into the darkness just outside the glow of the fire.

Somebody out there. Watching.

Bush rolled over slowly and sat straight up, then came to his feet unsteadily.

"Your camp, I reckon," he said into the darkness.

No response.

"I ate the meat you'd roasted. I'm sorry."

Still nothing.

"I'm hurt . . . got knocked off a flatboat in the storm, and nearly drowned."

Nothing. Silence.

"Is there anybody there?"

The darkness itself seemed alive and ominous.

"If there's somebody there, I'd sure be obliged if you'd show yourself. I'm unarmed. I'm no threat."

The darkness moved; a piece of it advanced. Not quite fully into the light, but just into the fringes of it. A ghostly, black figure, hard to discern.

"Howdy," Bush said, honestly wondering if it was, in fact, a ghost he was seeing.

The figure held its silence. Bush squinted and tried to see him better. Or was it a man at all? So vague was the image that Bush could not even discern the sex.

"My name's Underhill," Bush said. "Bushrod Underhill. Most just call me Bush for short."

No answer.

"Please, friend, I'd like to ask you to come more into the light if you would. I can't see you well enough to tell a thing about you."

The figure did not move for a moment, but then stepped forward.

Bush stared at the strangest human being he'd seen, either in the world of white men or red. Tall, gaunt, the man had black hair that hung thickly around his narrow face and past his shoulders, as unkempt and uncut as Samson's. The beard was just as long, reaching to the middle of his chest, and black as the river depths by night.

His nose was narrow and protruding, his eyes intensely dark and indefinably strange. Almost unblinking—yes, that was the strangeness of them. They hardly blinked, just gazed ceaselessly.

The clothing was as black as the hair and beard. Loose, dirty trousers, a bulky black coat over an equally colorless waistcoat, and if the shirt had ever been white, it was now dirtied to an indistinct buff.

"Sir, I tell you again that I'm sorry I ate your meat."

The man did not speak.

"I'll be glad to pay you for it, sir, as soon as I can get my hands on money. I've lost all my possessions, you see. They're still on the flatboat I had the misfortune to be knocked off of, and the boat is no doubt long down the river by now."

The figure moved to one side and slowly bent over until he was seated on his haunches. An uncomfortable looking position, but it didn't seem to bother the stranger.

"Sir, do you speak English?"

The man, who, with his long coat draping past his knees, seemed to be floating on air, still said nothing.

Bush asked him his name in French, to no avail, then dug fragmented German out of the dustiest memories of his days with Jean-Yves Freneau, and repeated his question. Bush even asked in Cherokee. Still no reply.

Bush sat down again, watching the man mistrustfully, thinking him surely the oddest living being on the river. Why did he not answer? Was he deaf?

Bush shifted his position so that he could keep the man in the corner of his eye without staring openly at him, but within minutes the man rose and moved around to face Bush again, with no look of apology about doing so. Bush grinned at him, hoping to earn one in return. He didn't.

The remainder of the night seemed longer than two. Bush didn't dare sleep with this stranger watching him endlessly, saying nothing, looking malevolent with those dark and probing eyes. The pair of them remained as they were, each watching the other in silence. Bush, thinking he must have roused up a forest demon of some sort, scanned through all the Cherokee legends he could recall to see if he could find a match. Nothing quite did. He maintained the fire and made sure he always kept the stranger in sight.

By the pitch-black minutes of pre-dawn, Bush was mentally exhausted by the extended staring game, and thought it might be better if he abandoned the safety of firelight and heat to take his chances in the forest alone. But with daylight so close, he had developed a superstitious curiosity about what would happen to this vampirish creature come sunrise. Would he vanish like smoke? Retreat into some cavern or hollow tree?

Bush had actually dozed off when the first rays of morning came streaming over the horizon. The stranger, who had been seated on the ground on the opposite side of the fire, suddenly came to his feet, walked to the edge of the clearing, and faced the rising sun. Bush, startled awake, watched him closely.

The man raised his hand skyward, lifted his face toward the clouds, and bellowed, "I thank you, oh Father, for the morning, and I thank you, oh Father, for life and sun and survival through the night. And I thank you, oh Father, for my new companion Mr. Underhill, who you have sent to me for his good and mine. All praise to Father, Son, and Holy Ghost. Amen."

The man turned so quickly that Bush jumped to his feet, expecting to see a pistol come out from under his coat. But the man was empty-handed, and extended those empty hands his way. "Mr. Underhill, I welcome you to my camp. And there is no need to apologize for having eaten my meat. What I have is given me not to hoard but to share. And I'm very sorry about my rude silence. I'd vowed to the Lord that I'd be silent until day, you see, and was simply fulfilling what I'd promised."

Bush was so taken aback to hear a voice coming out of the raven-like man that he hardly knew how to reply. "Sir, who are you?"

"My name is Moses Zane."

"Zane . . . I've heard that name before, sir. You're a preacher, I think, one my late partner, a free black man name of Cephas Frank, told me of. You're the man folks say can—"

"Can summon up the devil himself and by the power of God make him dance at my command? Or so people say. Yes, I'm that same Moses Zane." He smiled, and seemed a little less odd for it. "And now, Mr. Underhill, how about you and I enjoy a bit of breakfast?"

From behind a tree Zane produced a large leather pouch, and from it pulled half a loaf of hardened but unmolded bread, a hunk of cheese, some nuts, jerked beef, and even a small jug of cider. To Bush it looked like a king's feast.

Zane fished out two crockery cups, scratched and lacking handles. He uncorked the cider and poured some into each cup.

"You do enjoy cider, Mr. Underhill?"

"Yes sir."

"Good, for I have no other beverage to offer you, unless you want to try to find some pure water after such a terrible storm as the mighty Lord sent us last night. I don't think you'll have much success if you do, as much mud as was stirred up." He took a small sip of his own cider while handing Bush the other cup.

"What kind of preacher are you, Mr. Zane?"

"My confession, do you mean? I'm Methodist by doctrine, though at the moment I'm not a part of any official circuit or under the authority of any church structure other than the one true and universal church of Almighty God." He sipped his cider again. "In short, Mr. Underhill, I've been put out of the ministerial fold and must make my way as an independent. Are you hungry, Mr. Underhill?"

"I could eat the very grease off a wagon axle."

"Well, I hope you'll find my fare, such as it is, better than that." Zane distributed the food. A very different man he seemed now from the silent, looming vampire he had been in the darkness. "I normally eat rabbits and squirrels and other small game, saving this food for those times I enjoy the pleasure of human companionship."

"You're alone a lot?"

"Never. My God is always with me. But in the sense in

which you meant the question, yes. I'm alone quite often.''

"May I ask why you'd told the Lord you would hold silent until morning?"

"Certainly. In my prayers yesterday, I implored the Lord to see to my aid in my time of distress and give me guidance. There came to me at sundown the strongest impression that I should remain silent until sunrise, and during that silence I would find the help I needed. So I made my promise to my Father, and was bound to keep it until the sun came up.'' Zane ate a handful of nuts.

"What 'time of distress' are you talking about?"

"I was put off here, Mr. Underhill. A crew of keelboatmen found my company to be intolerable. They were not agreeable to hearing the truth that changes souls.''

"So you prayed for help. No offense, preacher, but I don't see the Lord has answered your prayer.''

"Of course He has! You've come.''

"I just fell off a flatboat, sir.'' Zane needed to know no more than that. "I rode some distance down the water in a cabin that'd come off the bank and was floating down the river with a corpse in it. That cabin rolled right over me in the water and swallowed me like that Jonah fellow with his big fish. I don't know quite how I got out without drowning.''

"You were protected in order to be sent to me. And now we must decide what to do now that you've come.''

"I know what I have to do,'' Bush said. "I have to move down the river and look for somebody.'' He didn't intend for the men who'd killed Cephas Frank to escape him.

"And so we can see providence at work! It happens I need to head downriver myself.''

"You may not have noticed, Reverend, but I got no boat. I'm afoot just like you. I ain't even got shoes! I lost my boots in the river.''

"I have an extra pair of boots in my pouch. They pinch my feet, but may do better for you.''

Indeed they did. Moments later Bush was admiring a pair of boots finer than those he had lost, fitted nicely over his feet. If Zane was peculiar, he was also generous.

Zane said, "I have a proposition for you, Mr. Underhill. You and I will remain together for now and see if we can't find some good passage down the river. Your company and protection will be welcome to me."

It was absurd. Bush couldn't be hampered by company as he tried to track down Cephas's killers, but the preacher had him hooked as a partner for now simply because Bush felt indebted to him for the boots, and he certainly had no money to pay for them. So he heard himself saying, "Well, I reckon we can travel together—for a time."

"Good! Then let's be off, shall we?"

"Where to?"

"Down to the river. Providence has already sent you to me by way of the river. Let's see what else might come floating along."

As they broke camp, Bush made the pleasing discovery that Moses Zane owned a good flintlock rifle, an almost equally good pistol, two fine knives, and a hatchet. They had been out of sight before, tucked away behind the same tree that had concealed the leather supply bag.

"Please, take the weapons with my blessing," Zane told him. "I make them a gift to you. I hate the cursed things. I rarely use them except to occasionally kill small game, such as those squirrels you found on my fire. Most of what I eat is either fish I catch, food good people along the way give me, or rabbits and such I snare."

Bush was astonished that a man would give away such fine weaponry to a near stranger. "Sir, I don't think I can take such a gift as this."

"Nonsense! It's my pleasure to give you the guns, and it should be yours to take them. You lost what you had in the river, I'd be willing to wager—though don't take that literally. I don't favor wagering."

After they had hiked about two miles, the preacher pointed to something Bush had just spotted himself—something caught in tangled brush on the bank. Bush trotted over and found a dugout canoe trapped there. Just the right size for two men.

"God provides!" Zane declared.

Bush reached into the canoe and pulled out an odd item: a dented old hunting horn. Putting it to his lips, he tested it, sending a piercing blast across the water. "Has an unusual sound to it. Clearer and louder than most. Wonder how it came to be in there?" he mused aloud, examining the instrument.

"For a reason, I'm sure. Maybe it will prove to be something I can make use of in some way." Zane looked at the horn and rubbed his chin. "You know, I think perhaps there is a good use for this instrument. I can use it to sound the call for my meetings. Here, let me try a blow on that."

Bush handed the horn to Zane, who drew in his breath and blew, with pathetic results. With greater effort, he tried again, doing a little better this time.

Suddenly Zane changed. His eyes bulged, his face reddened, and his mouth fell open. The horn dropped from his fingers. Bush went to Zane's side as the man began to collapse slowly to the ground, hand on his chest as he gasped for air.

"Preacher, what's wrong with you?"

"Back . . . away from . . . the river . . ." He collapsed.

Bush swept the man up in his arms and ran.

Zane sat slumped on a rock beneath a spreading, moss-draped tree, looking at the ground and breathing deeply. "Thank God," he whispered. "That time I didn't know if I would make it through."

"What happened?" Bush asked.

"My lungs," Zane replied softly. "Since my boyhood I've struggled with it. My wind sometimes is cut off, my lungs seem to close, and I struggle to draw my breath. An attack of Satan, who always tries to silence me."

Bush looked up and down the preacher's gaunt frame, studying the sallow, narrow face. He looked like someone who had known weakness and sickness all his life. It was no surprise that he was asthmatic.

Zane lifted his gaze and looked gratefully at Bushrod. "Had

you not been there, my friend, I might have never breathed again.''

"I didn't do a thing," Bush said. "You commenced breathing again on your own."

"Because you carried me away from the river," Zane said. "There seem to be times and places that cause it to happen. Excitement, sorrow, fear can all bring it on. And being near rivers can do it as well, though not all the time. Generally, I'm quite able to function normally, or at the very least to have only minor difficulties. This one was . . . different." He shuddered and looked down again. Despite the preacher's apparent tendency toward religious bravado, it was evident to Bush that this man was thoroughly shaken by what happened.

"Reverend, has it crossed your mind that maybe you ought to find some place other than the river country to do your preaching? There's some folks who can't do well for their health in certain places, certain kinds of air. I knew a man once who'd break out in red patches every time he'd walk through a copse of maples, and get wheezy in the chest if ever he breathed air from a cave."

"It's here I belong, Mr. Underhill. Nowhere else. And I've never suffered such an attack while preaching. I believe I'm protected then."

"I wish you'd call me Bushrod instead of 'Mr. Underhill.' "

"Very well, Bushrod. And you may call me Moses." And he went straight into another asthmatic attack. Bush hustled him farther away from the river until his breathing again settled.

Bush grinned at the preacher when he was well again, but he wasn't happy at the moment. He ached to continue his pursuit of *The George Washington* and its murderous crew, but suddenly this puny preacher was, as it were, tossed into his lap, giving gifts and making Bush feel obliged to him. He had no impression that Zane was trying to manipulate him—but he'd hooked him all the same. He couldn't abandon a man who might smother to death at any given moment.

It appeared that, for the short term, he had himself a traveling companion.

The fire was strong, and in its warm glow Zane didn't look nearly as weak and pale as he had in the white, color-stealing light of morning.

"So, Bushrod, where are you from?"

Bush didn't really want to enter that rather complicated history. "A lot of places. I was born near what's now Nashville, in Tennessee."

"I see. I've never been there. What profession do you follow?"

"I've been a lot of things. Mostly now I hunt, work the river some, flatboating and all. And live off the land."

"I see. Sounds, in some ways, like my life. Much wandering."

"Yes, there's that."

"Do you have family?"

"No wife. My parents are dead. I have a sister—had a sister."

"She's dead?"

Bush paused, looked down. "Yes."

"I'm sorry. Was she a Christian?"

"I never had the chance to know her much, preacher. We were separated early on in life."

"You've had some sorrows, my friend."

"I have."

"How did you become separated?"

Bush was just opening his mouth to respond when the brush on the far side of the camp clearing opened, and a man stepped out of the woods with a rifle raised, aiming it squarely at Moses Zane's head.

CHAPTER
TWENTY

Bush scrambled for the rifle, which lay propped against the preacher's bag on the ground beside him.

"No, you don't!" the intruder ordered. "You freeze yourself right there, freeze yourself stiller than ice, or I'll blow you to hell where you sit!"

Bush glanced longingly at the rifle, considering his chances—then yielded, knowing the risk was too great. He cursed himself for his carelessness. He was too good a woodsman to have let some forest bandit sneak up on his camp.

He expected to hear Zane gasp asthmatically again, or see him topple over in fright like the tremulous weakling he appeared to be. Instead Zane leaped to his feet and faced the intruder with a defiant demeanor worthy of a mountain cat.

"Forbear!" Zane bellowed, lifting his right palm toward the gunman. "Forbear, or pay the price!"

The gunman, surprisingly, backed off a few steps. "I know you . . ."

"In the name of Almighty God who gives me my authority over you, I command you, dark one, to arise and devour this villain who dares threaten the servant of the Most High . . ."

"You're that Zane preacher, the one who can summon up the devil . . ."

"Summon him, indeed, and make him obey, make him devour my enemies and dance like a whirlwind of hell on their graves! Dark one, I bid you *come!*" Zane flung his other hand in the direction of the fire, which flared and spat dark smoke in a big puff, startling Bush as much as the bandit.

The latter leveled his wavering rifle at Zane. "You back away, now, you don't come near me . . ."

"Inhabitant of the nether regions, I summon you to arise, come to me under the power of the Almighty, come to me to do my bidding and that of none other—"

"I'll kill you! Don't you call no devil on me!"

"—and if he should harm me or my companion, dark one, pursue him, pursue him, pursue him through a tortured life and then dine on his soul for all eternity in the foulest pits of hell . . ."

The man's eyes flicked back and forth from Bush to Zane. "All I want is money. That's all I come for. You stay away from me, Zane! You keep your demons to yourself!"

Zane threw back his head like a howling wolf, and let out a loud, echoing, mournful cry, a wail that might have emerged from some ancient chamber of torture. Then he laughed the most maniacal laugh Bush had ever heard. "He is near . . . he is near . . ."

The gunman turned and fled into the woods.

"Pursue him!" Zane screamed. "Pursue him, my dark and thirsty demons! *Pursue!* And if he should stop—*devour!*"

Off in the woods they heard the gunman running wildly, thrashing through the brush as if nothing could stand in his way. His sounds faded away, and all was silent.

Bush stood slowly, picking up the rifle. Looking at Zane, he shook his head and said, "In all my born days, Reverend, I ain't never seen the like of that."

Zane smiled slightly and nodded, a talented showman humbly accepting the praise he had earned.

"I swear, preacher, I thought he'd kill you when you came up before him that way."

"It was a risky tactic, and I wouldn't have done it had I not recognized him as soon as he stuck his head out of the trees. I'd seen him before in Natchez while I was preaching on the street. He stood mocking, but with a look of fear he couldn't hide. I knew he had heard the stories about me."

"About those stories . . ."

Zane lifted one coy brow. "Can I really do those things? Is

that the question?'' He grinned. ''I've always found it to my advantage to leave that question unanswered.''

''What made the fire spark?''

''Maybe it was a manifestation of my power. Or maybe it was a bit of the gunpowder that I always carry loose in my pocket. It generates quite a strong reaction from crowds to talk about the fire and brimstone of eternal hell, then to suddenly toss a bit of it into the nearest torch or bonfire.''

''You're quite the trickster, preacher.''

''It's my view that, while my duty is never to lie, it doesn't necessarily extend to correcting every false conception that may already exist.'' He smiled. ''Especially when they prove themselves as useful as they did tonight. That scoundrel who just fled will tell every vile friend he meets that I conjured up a devil before his eyes, had it chase him for miles, and opened the mouth of hell at his feet. And some of them, I daresay, will believe him.''

''All I ask, Reverend, is that if you ever really do roust up the devil, do it when I'm nowhere around.''

''I promise you, quite sincerely.''

They returned to the canoe the next morning, warily, the preacher taking cautious breaths. No asthmatic reaction to the river air this time. Zane was obviously relieved.

With Bush at the oars, they launched into the river. The sky was clear, the sun bright, the wind cool and brisk. Bush, with nothing to warm him but his dirty waistcoat, envied the heavier garb of the preacher.

Zane began to sing, his voice surprisingly rich and strong. Bush marveled at the man, stricken down by the atmosphere of the river one day, seeming to thrive on it the next.

Bush knew no hymns, so it was a novelty and entertainment to listen to Zane go through one after another. The river current caught the canoe and they moved rapidly, Bush keeping his eyes on the river, dodging the abundant garbage still floating on it.

The preacher was in the middle of another Isaac Watts standard when he cut off abruptly and pointed. "Bush . . . what is that?"

Bush looked closely. Caught in the tangle of a huge "raft" of floating trees was the body of a man. Very dead, and, Bush thought, familiar.

"Preacher, should we stop?"

Zane frowned in silence. "He was once a living soul. I think we should."

The corpse, puffy, decayed and sodden, would have been unrecognizable even if they had known the man in life. Distorted and stiffened, he lay on the bank, Zane and Bush looking at him.

"I'm sure it's the same corpse who was in the cabin that floated down the river," Bush said.

"I wonder who he was?"

"Maybe I should look for something on him, you know, to tell his name."

"Yes." Then Zane, momentarily overcome by the stink and gruesomeness of the sodden remains, walked away and stood with his back turned, breathing slowly and praying beneath his breath.

Bush moved away a few steps, sucked in a lungful of clean air, then began a hurried search of the body. He found some coins, which he guiltily pocketed. He had almost no money, having spent and drunk most of it away. He needed whatever he could find, but it made him feel terribly guilty to take it, especially with a preacher right at hand.

He found a few soaked, folded papers, too. He tried to open them, but they were too damp, and clung together. Bush showed the papers to the preacher. "We'll have to let these dry out some. Maybe they'll tell us who he was."

The preacher, steeling himself, returned, knelt beside the corpse, and prayed aloud. A gentle, mournful prayer, speaking of the shortness of life and the length of eternity and the importance of every man's soul.

They had no means to bury him, and so took the body to the woods, where they worked it inside a hollow log. Afterward, they returned to the river. The current caught them again and they swept on toward the sea.

They camped overnight and set out again the next morning. The day was beautiful and crisp; the canoe moved along easily under just enough clouds to keep the sun from scorching. Zane seemed strong, no wheezing or shortness of breath.

Later Zane lay down in the bottom of the canoe, curled up as much as the space would allow, and fell asleep. Bush paddled, watching the river, occasionally glancing down at the sleeping man.

He couldn't figure why, with only the vaguest notion of what moved and drove this strange man, he couldn't help but like him. The gentleness of his prayer over the corpse of that stranger had told him much of the heart of Moses Zane.

A couple of miles down the river, Bush recognized something lodged against the far bank. It was a half-wrecked flatboat. Bush guided the canoe toward it. In a few moments he saw the name ''George Washington'' on the side.

Bush looked around. Where were the brothers? The woman who'd been in the shelter during the fight? He saw no sign of anyone close by. Probably they'd abandoned the boat after it was damaged by the storm. They might be traveling on foot, or maybe had caught themselves a ride on some other craft.

Bush pulled the canoe up to the ruined flatboat and tied it off, then climbed out and clambered across the tilted craft. He squatted on the shelter roof and realized how fortunate he was to have survived his foolhardy attack on this crew of killers. If not for that sawyer sweeping him off the boat—and conveniently killing his opponent, too—he would certainly not have survived. A close call indeed.

Maybe the preacher was right about there being an unseen hand at work.

Sighing, he turned back to the canoe, in which Zane still slept.

It was gone.

Bush stared at the place the canoe was supposed to be, dis-

believing. He looked down the river, and saw it, floating free
and now very far away.

Zane wasn't visible. He was probably still asleep, oblivious
to his situation. And blast it all, the rifle and supplies he'd
given to Bush were in the canoe with him.

Bush stared helplessly, watching the canoe become a tiny,
distant speck on a vast and merciless river.

Maybe the preacher had just received another favor from
the hand of providence, being swept away like this. People
who aligned themselves with Bushrod Underhill seemed to
come to bad ends.

Bush sat down on the ruined flatboat again because there
was nothing else he could do, watching until the canoe was
out of sight.

He sure hoped that preacher would be all right.

Bush watched the traffic of the river as the morning went
on. At first the river was empty of human life and craft, looking as it must have when none but the aborigines of the country knew it. Before long, boats came into view, flatboats and
keelboats, occasionally pirogues or rafts. Bush sat and watched
them pass. They were far across the river from him, all too
distant to be hailed down by a poor stranded woodsman.

Eventually, however, a canoe headed his way, rowed by a
lone man. Bush stood as the canoe pulled in at the flatboat.
Its rower tied it off, tilted back a hat, and studied him openly.

Bush felt wary of this fellow. He was quiet, broad-faced,
sunburned, very ugly. An odd bump or tumor disfigured the
upper left portion of his face, and he stared at Bush with an
animalistic lack of self-consciousness.

"Howdy," he said at last.

"Howdy."

"You stuck here." A statement, not a question, so Bush
didn't answer.

"Why you there?" the man asked.

"Got to be somewhere."

"This your boat all smashed?"

"No, not mine. Who are you, friend? Why are you so interested in me?"

"I'm Auty Tuck." Brown eyes danced up and down, sizing Bush up. Tuck scratched at the bump on the side of his face.

"My name's Underhill. Bush Underhill."

"I'll give you a ride in my canoe."

Bush had already decided two things about Auty Tuck: he was dim-witted, and probably a robber. The first he deduced from a dozen obvious signs in appearance, language, and manner; the latter he based on gut feeling and the furtive looks with which he evaluated Bush.

"I'll stay here for now. Thank you all the same."

"I stay too, then." Tuck clambered out of the canoe and onto the boat.

"Mr. Tuck, there's no call for you to stay here."

"Want to do it." He climbed up close to Bush and settled down in a cross-legged squat. He stared at Bush some more and scratched at the tumor.

Bush grew annoyed. "Look here, Mr. Tuck. No offense intended, but I don't want you on this boat. I figure you have it in mind to rob me first chance." On impulse he dug out part of the money he'd earlier taken off the dead man. Thrusting it at Tuck, he said, "Here. I'll spare you the trouble of robbing me. You take that free and clear, with only one condition, and that's that you get back in that canoe and get on down the river and away from here."

Auty Tuck looked at the money, at Bush, then grinned and scratched some more. Nodding, he took the gift, stood, and went back into his canoe. Bush watched him paddle off down the river. Tuck looked back several times, nodding and grinning. Bush was glad when he was out of sight.

By sunset he wished he hadn't been so quick to send Tuck away. The canoe ride Tuck had offered would have been very helpful.

Bush looked at the darkening sky, felt the painful grumbling of an empty belly, and sighed. He wished he hadn't come across this flatboat. Then he wouldn't have been separated from the canoe. He and Zane would be far downriver now.

Night fell. Bush left the boat and made himself as content

as possible on a mossy patch of ground. He closed his eyes and tried to sleep.

It was going to be a long time until morning.

An hour later, his eyes snapped open again.

Someone was approaching, moving through thickets and trees toward him.

"Moses? Moses Zane?"

"No," came a whisper in reply. "Hush!"

Bush came to his feet. "Who are you? What do you want?"

"It's Auty Tuck. Come with me, before they get here." Tuck's voice was a tight whisper.

"Before who gets here?"

"No time to be talking. Come now. You, me."

"I don't trust you."

Tuck appeared from the brush, just an outline in the night. "There's men, robbers, who'll be on you soon unless you come."

"I don't trust you," Bush repeated.

"Got to trust me." Tuck tilted his head. "Listen!"

Bush heard more crackling brush, the sound of forms moving near in the darkness. A wicked, sinister sound.

"You gave me money, so now I help you. Come on with me!"

Bush weighed his options. Tuck looked like some misshapen troll of the night. Probably all this was a setup, and it was Tuck's co-conspirators who now approached.

But perhaps not. Bush made sure his hold on his knife was strong, and nodded. "I'll come with you. And if this is a trick, you'll die. I vow it."

Tuck didn't sound at all distressed by the threat. "Come with me, and stay quiet."

Ten minutes later, Bush was crouched in a stony crevice with Tuck at his side, listening to the hoarse whispers of angry and disappointed men. They were swearing and fuming over the strange disappearance of a man they had obviously planned to rob and kill—a man Bush knew was himself.

Bush listened to Tuck's wheezy breathing, heard the faint *scritch* of his nails scratching at the lump on his face, and thought how strange it was to feel grateful to so repellent a creature.

The half-dozen or so deprived ruffians finally departed. Only when they were evidently well away did Bush speak.

"Mr. Tuck, I'm mighty obliged to you for your warning. If not for you, I'd likely be a dead body dumped in the river by now."

"You gave me money, so I help you," Tuck said again.

"Mr. Tuck, you offered to give me a ride in your canoe today, and I turned you down. Yet you came back to warn me of danger. I appreciate it, sir." Bush wondered if anyone else had ever called Tuck "sir" in his life.

"Watched you," Tuck said. "Rode on down the river, tied up the canoe, come back and watched you."

Bush felt his skin prickle. "Watched me? Why?"

"You gave me money. Wanted to see if you had more."

"Why? Were you thinking about robbing me of it?"

"No. You gave me money. Makes you my friend. But there was others who would rob you. Black Aleck and his men. This is their part of the river."

"Black Aleck . . . is that who those men were?"

"That be Black Aleck, yes. He's a hard one, Black Aleck is."

"Will Black Aleck come back?"

"Don't think so, no. They figure you run off."

"I'm obliged for your warning, Auty."

"I'm always glad to help my friends. Bewley says a man should help his friends."

"Who's Bewley?"

"My brother. You wait, you see Bewley. I'll tell him you're my friend."

CHAPTER
TWENTY-ONE

Neither Bush nor Tuck slept any more that night, but as soon as dawn spread pale gold across the river's broad surface and the landscape on either side, Tuck curled up like some gigantic dying bug and began to snore, rumbling away in his ragged, dirt-colored clothing, looking for all the world like a little bit of the earth itself come to life and laid down for slumber.

Bush watched him and wondered who he was, where he had come from, and what had made him whatever he was. The river crawled with such odd characters; he and Cephas Frank had seen plenty of Auty Tucks sweeping past on arks, flatboats, keels, or peering out the windows of seedy riverfront dives. Each one much like all the others, each destined to a short life remembered by few, yet each one also distinctive, with his own sorry story to tell, or more often, to keep hidden.

As Tuck slept, Bush set some snares, improvised a fishing line from some twine and hooks he found aboard the flatboat, and after two long hours had the makings of a meager fish and rabbit breakfast. He skinned the rabbit, cleaned the fish, built a fire, and began cooking. Auty Tuck snored on.

Bush let him sleep, wondering if this were his usual pattern—roaming by night, sleeping by day. If so, it tended to confirm Bush's initial suspicion that Tuck was a robber. But Tuck had done him a good turn in the business with Black Aleck. Just now Tuck's companionship was about the only asset Bush possessed.

Bush ate his half of the food and left the rest for Tuck. Settling back, he drowsed off a few minutes, then shook himself awake. Tired as a sleepless night had left him, he didn't like the idea of both he and Tuck sleeping in such an obviously dangerous locale. To keep himself awake, he dug those dead man's papers out from beneath his waistcoat and opened them.

They were pages of a letter, it appeared. Poorly written, apparently with some kind of improvised quill and ink, the latter having suffered in the Mississippi River water. That, however, didn't entirely account for the poor legibility. The letters were badly formed, either by a man who was a terrible penman, or perhaps who was very sick or hurt when he wrote them. As Bush puzzled through what words and lines were legible, he began to lean toward his second theory.

The letter was unfinished and therefore unsigned, and the name of the writer appeared nowhere else on it. It was, however, written to a woman named Lydia, in Natchez, obviously the writer's wife. The names Lethy and Walker, apparently a daughter and son, appeared in the body of the letter. Bush studied the scribblings closely, and felt his spirits steadily decline.

The letter was the last record and confession of a hurt and dying man. Bush pieced it together slowly as he read. The writer had been away from Natchez on some business matter, and upon returning with significant money in his possession, had been robbed by some ruffian band. He resisted and was wounded, and made his way to an abandoned cabin to write to his wife and family because he knew he probably would not live to see them again face-to-face. The letter became more illegible as it went along, the writer's strength clearly fading, but what came through clearly was a deep sorrow and an even deeper love, a man throwing his soul into his final words.

The unfinished letter simply faded out shortly after the statement: "God grant that someone find this letter and convey it to you, my dear wife."

Bush put down the pages and wished he hadn't read them. He folded the letter and placed it back in his waistcoat, picturing the writer doing the same as he realized his end had come. Bush wondered if the man had been alive when that cabin washed off the bluff, or if he had already died from the injuries received in the robbery.

Bush sighed, and lay flat on his back, staring at the sky. In a few moments, despite himself, he dozed off again.

When Bush awakened, maybe an hour later, another man had joined Tuck.

"There he is, Bewley," Tuck said, pointing at Bush when he sat up. "He's him. The one I been telling you about. Bush, this here is Bewley. He's my brother, Bewley is."

Bush rose, came over, stuck out his hand. "Howdy, Mr. Tuck."

"Call me Bewley," the other said back. "What's your last name, Bush?"

"Underhill. Where did you show up from, Mr. Tuck—Bewley?"

"Auty and I have been planning to meet up along this stretch of river for some time now," Bewley Tuck continued. "We always meet up hereabouts when we've been apart, and lately, I've had to be away, on business. Auty just now told me about you, Bush, how you'd given him money and befriended him. I do appreciate it, sir. Not many are kind to my poor brother."

"I try to be a good man to all who'll let me," Bush said.

"Are you hungry? I've got a big hunk of bacon just waiting for cooking."

The insufficient breakfast had long since ceased to satisfy. "Sounds very good. Thank you."

A while later, Bush was gnawing on bacon, listening to the brothers talk. Bewley Tuck seemed to have a gentle and kindly manner in dealing with his inferior brother, a fatherly sort of sweetness in how he talked to him, and even more than that, in how he listened.

Bush, eager to keep moving downriver in hope of picking up the track of Cephas's killers, was ready to board the canoe and head out. But the Tuck brothers evidently had no plans to travel this day. Long and frustrating hours passed, during which Bush considered saying his farewells and striking out on foot, or maybe trying to hitch another ride. But as the day ended, he was still with the Tucks.

As night fell and Bush sat by the campfire, the Tuck brothers droned on, talking about relatives and events and the river—never about robbery. Never about any subject one would expect to arise between criminals.

Bush decided that he must have been wrong about these men. Apparently they weren't robbers after all. Never be too swift to judge, Jean-Yves has always said, and he had surely been right.

He traveled with the brothers the next day in the canoe, more relaxed and comfortable around them, now that he'd concluded they were good men after all. His mind turned toward Natchez, where he hoped to find out more about the brothers, surname still unknown to him, who had killed Cephas.

Bush spoke little with the Tucks, who seemed content to converse between themselves, and not intrude on his business. He made a point not to intrude on theirs, either. However, the close quarters of the canoe made it unavoidable for Bush to pick up some details of their past.

The pair had grown up in Pennsylvania, apparently among Quaker relatives. Their parents had been dead for many years; the brothers had lived a few years in South Carolina, a briefer time with an uncle in Virginia, and then divided most of their adult lives between New Orleans and Natchez. Obviously, Bewley, older and sharper-witted, took care of mentally-deprived Auty.

Bewley spoke several times of his "business" and "work," but never said what it was. Bush did not ask. He was ready to believe the best of the Tucks and assume the business was legitimate.

They cut travel short, at Bewley's command. "We'll make our camp early, and a little further inland than before," he said, pleasant as a well-fed parson, beaming at Bush.

"Why are we stopping at all?" Bush said. "We might make Natchez by nightfall if we press on."

"Well, there's some things we must do, and a stop to make

at some quarters we have in these parts. I think you'll like it, by the way. Much better and more comfortable than the hard ground we've slept on until now."

Bush, helping pull the canoe onto the bank, looked down the river. "How long until you go on to Natchez?"

"Soon, soon. As early as tomorrow, perhaps the next day."

"Gentlemen, perhaps I should simply go on by foot. We're on the right side of the river for it."

"Please, Bushrod. Don't leave us just yet. Believe me, if you decide to stay, you'll be glad of it."

"Why?"

"Trust me. And please, don't rush off just yet."

Bush sighed and looked down the river again. "Very well."

The "quarters" Bewley had described were merely a simple cabin that stood much farther from the river than Bush had anticipated. Built in a thicket, it was rugged and dirty, containing no more furniture than a table, a big wooden box, and a couple of beds with mattresses stuffed with leaves. Bush looked around the place, puzzled and displeased.

"Your home?" he asked Bewley.

"One of three places where Auty and I reside. We move around a bit."

"Bewley, pleased as I am to be here, I think the best would be to move on toward Natchez. It's important that I get there. There's men I need to find, and the longer it takes for me to begin searching, the longer it will take to find them."

"We're talking about one evening, Bush. That's all. What's the hurry? You'd not make it far before the day was gone. Stay with us. I insist."

Why was Bush feeling unsettled? He didn't want to be here. "Thank you, Bewley, but no. I'll be moving on."

"Let me put it straight to you, Bushrod. It's my intention to reward you for the help you gave to Auty. But I can't do it immediately. There's something on its way here that will allow me to do so."

"I don't understand."

"And you never will, if you leave us. It's a business matter,

Bushrod. While I was away from Auty, I was quite busy. And I can tell you that, with a little patience, you can see yourself placed in a much better position to go looking for whoever it is you're looking for. At the moment you have almost no money, no food, and as best I can tell, not even a change of clothing.''

"And you'll provide those things for me? As some kind of reward for giving Auty a little bit of cash from my pocket?"

"I always try to reward those who deserve it."

"Auty already rewarded me by leading me away from trouble. The balance is even."

"At the very least, stay long enough to have some food with us."

"Well, I see no reason I can't at least do that."

Bewley beamed again, and Bush thought this whole affair was taking a very bizarre and uncomfortable turn.

Supper wound up not being worth the wait. Jerked beef boiled in tallow. No bread, no drink but springwater. Bush ate in near silence, thinking he'd made a mistake even to stay this long. There was something in the atmosphere he didn't like.

When he was finished, he nodded and thanked the Tucks, wished them success, said he hoped they would run across one another again, and turned to go.

"No," Bewley said lifting a pistol matter-of-factly and aiming it at Bush's chest. Auty, meanwhile, rose and positioned himself at the cabin door. "You'll not be leaving us tonight, Bushrod. We have a job for you to do."

"What is this?"

"Very simple. We're holding you at gunpoint, and tomorrow you'll do us a service by robbing a certain well-heeled traveler whom I know to be traveling right now down from Nashville. He should be coming through within the next day or two on the Boatman's Trail. We'll be waiting for him."

Bush wondered if this was some sort of absurd jest. "You really believe I'll rob someone for you, just because you tell me to?"

"I believe you'll find yourself persuaded when the time comes."

Bush laughed. The unreality of it all was so great as to make it hardly more than funny. "I'm walking out of here, Bewley. And you're not going to shoot me. And I'm hanged if I intend to commit a crime on your behalf." Bush headed for the door. "Out of my way, Auty."

Auty pulled out a knife, stabbed it shallowly into Bush's forearm, and pulled it out again. Bewley clicked the lock of the pistol.

As Bush pulled back his bleeding arm, Bewley said, "Don't think we won't kill you here and now, Bush. We've killed before. All it would take from me is one word to Auty, and he'd cut your head off with that knife."

"He might find the task a little harder to achieve than he might anticipate," Bush said.

"Sit down in that corner, back toward me, and your hands behind you."

"No."

Bewley pushed the pistol forward, threateningly. "Mr. Underhill, you're unwise to try my patience."

Bush stalked toward Bewley, insolent in anger. Bewley, who'd been squatting on the floor, came to his feet and backed away. "Auty!"

Auty lunged at Bush, who stiff-armed him away. With his other hand he reached for Bewley's pistol, defying the man to shoot him. He was betting that Bewley wouldn't discharge the pistol and risk missing or inflicting only some minor wound, leaving himself unarmed.

He was right. Bush closed his hand around the pistol and shoved it to the side as Bewley went pale very fast. A moment later, though, something clouted the back of Bush's head very hard, stunning him. He fell, groaning, and saw Auty with a stout piece of firewood in his hand. Bush had not anticipated that Auty could move as fast as he had.

"Tie him up!" Bewley commanded. "Tie him tight, Auty!"

Bush struggled, but the stunning blow left him too disoriented. Auty hit him again and almost knocked him cold. After that, Bush's contentions were in vain. Auty had him tied before he could even clear his head.

"You shouldn't have struggled, Bush," Bewley said, leaning over him. "You are a fool. You could have made this all much easier with a little cooperation."

"I'll not . . . cooperate with you. I'll not do it."

"I think you will."

"Cords are too tight . . ."

"Your voice is slurred, Bushrod. Auty dealt you quite a blow. I'm afraid I can't understand anything you say." He walked away, laughing, and sat down as before. Bush was far too tightly bound to hope to escape, but Bewley kept the pistol close at hand.

The night was long and painful. Bush was bound in a misery-inflicting posture, with cords that left his arms numb from the elbows down. Though he tried to work the ropes loose, it proved impossible.

The hours dragged by in suffering. But Bush only grew more determined not to cooperate with these specimens of vermin.

When morning came, two strangers appeared at the cabin. Grizzled, foresty characters these were, long-bearded and flint-eyed. Bush had persuaded himself in the night that once he was unbound, and feeling returned to his extremities, he'd find some way to overcome Auty and Bewley. These new arrivals ended any hope of that. Two he might best, four he couldn't.

He felt disgusted, having counted on Auty and Bewley working alone. He should have realized when Bewley indicated advance knowledge of a particular traveler coming down from Nashville that the pair were merely part of some bigger criminal web.

"Caught you one, I see," one of the newcomers said, walking over to Bush and looking down at him. He nudged him with the toe of his boot. "Looks stout enough." Leaning over, he spoke to Bush. "You do what you're told, you'll be fine. You don't, we'll cut the bowels from you."

"Let me up from here, give me a knife, and we'll see who does the cutting," Bush replied.

The man grinned and turned to the others. "Got him some spirit! He'll do fine."

The two new men had brought food with them, the best feast Bush had seen in many a day, and all of them fell to eating, Bush not included. He was ignored, left lying where he was. When all the food had been eaten, Bewley went to Bush, carrying a chicken leg with most of the meat gnawed off. He held the leg down to Bush's mouth, but Bush shook his head and refused it.

Bewley shrugged and nibbled at it himself, then tossed the bone aside. "Listen here, Bush, and let me tell you a story. What we're doing here we've done before, and it's worked just prime. Except for once. We caught us a fellow like you, sent him out onto the Boatman's Trail, had him rob some Kaintucks coming down that way, the rest of us hid along the trail, watching. This fool decided to turn noble, tried to warn the folks he was robbing. So you know what happened? We all squeezed our little triggers and opened up, that's what, and killed every one of them dead, our Judas friend and all the folks he was robbing, too. Had he done his job like he should have, they'd all have lived. You keep that in mind when you're out there on the trail, doing the job."

Bush saw their game now. Innocent folks such as himself were captured, forced to commit crimes for these men while the men themselves remained safely hidden, unidentifiable. And if the unwilling participant rebelled, it brought instant death not only to himself, but to the innocents being robbed. A bold, madman's scheme these men had worked out, but it made its own kind of sense.

"You going to cooperate with us, Bushrod?"

Bush hated Bewley Tuck, hated Auty, hated the two strangers. Hated himself for allowing the Tucks to fool him so thoroughly and get him into this situation. Mostly he hated the situation itself, because he saw no way out of it.

"I reckon I got no choice," he said.

"You don't, that's the truth. So you're going to be a good robber for us?"

"I'll do what you tell me. Just as long as you hurt nobody."

"That's the whole idea, Bush. We get what we want, and nobody gets hurt."

"Except me, if I'm identified to the law as a robber."

"Well, all worthy things carry a certain risk. But we can help you even there. Got us an Indian-looking suit of clothes for you, and we'll even paint up your face so nobody'll be able to tell what you look like. You rob the folks we tell you to rob, turn what you get over to us, and everybody's happy, everybody's safe."

"And then I go free?"

"Then you go free."

CHAPTER
TWENTY-TWO

For Bushrod, the robbery was a nightmare that seemed to carry out on its own, as if someone else animated his body. It was humiliating, infuriating, having to do such an unnatural thing. He'd not felt so helpless since the day he was swept away by the invaders of Coldwater, and Bush didn't like to feel helpless, not one bit.

He was grateful for his disguise, an absurd, so-called Indian outfit that at least helped mask his true appearance. His face was blackened with charcoal and clay, and he tried to disguise his voice as he held a rifle—an empty rifle—on his victim and demanded money and valuables.

The victim was a distinguished-looking, silver-haired man whose most extreme reaction to the theft was a calm, haughty lifting of one brow while he held his hands aloft. Bush, already ashamed of what he was doing, felt even more so under this disdainful and fearless gaze. He had to remind himself throughout that what he was doing was not his choice, and that to do anything other than obey his captors would only get this man killed, along with the three slaves who traveled with him, and Bush himself.

The robbery fetched a strongbox, which Bush directed the victim's slaves to place on the ground near him. He ordered the whole pack of them to move on, eager to get them out of the way, even though he was unsure of his own fate once they were gone. Bewley had promised he would be freed after the robbery was complete, but what was the promise of a thief worth?

Bewley and company emerged. They broke open the strong-box and found it full of several small sacks, each of which contained gold coins.

Ecstasy reigned. The robbers howled in delight, dancing about, slapping shoulders and yanking beards, stomping the ground in imitation of an Indian dance. The celebration was brief. They gathered their wealth and bounded for their hide-out. Bush remained on the trail, wondering if they really meant to abandon him. But Bewley turned and ordered him to follow.

"I was promised my freedom!" Bush said.

"You want freedom while you're still wearing a robber's clothes? Come put on your own clothes, and give us those back."

The cabin was miles distant, but they traveled nonstop and made good time. Once inside, Bush got out of the Indian garb and into his own clothing as fast as possible, and headed for the door.

"Leaving us, Bush?" Bewley asked. "Have a happy journey, then!" He laughed sardonically.

Bush, ignoring him, exited the cabin without a word and strode into the woods, expecting to be accosted.

This didn't happen. They were really allowing him to leave unmolested! Maybe even scoundrels sometimes kept promises.

He'd gone only fifty yards farther when one of the two late-comers to the criminal band stepped from behind a tree to face him, rifle in hand. In his eagerness to get away, Bush hadn't noticed the man's absence from the cabin.

He exhaled slowly. *I should have known they'd not just let me walk away.*

"Time to die, young man," the outlaw said, raising the rifle.

No time to devise a plan, so Bush acted by instinct. He jumped to the right, behind a tree that was too small to cover him, but the abrupt movement was enough to make his opponent hesitate before firing. The man lowered the rifle slightly, and Bush came out again, hurtling toward him with shoulder out and head low. The rifle came back up, blasted, the flare of the gunpowder stinging Bush's face but the ball going past, missing. A moment later Bush's shoulder caught the man in the chest and drove him down. Bush grabbed the rifle, wrenched it free. There was a cracking of buttplate against forehead. The man went out cold. Bush freed him of his weapon, powder horn, and bullet pouch, slipped the straps over his shoulders, and took off in a run, reloading as he went in case he was pursued.

He doubted that he would be pursued. These men, who robbed in hiding and tried to kill their unwilling accomplices in ambush, would probably lack the courage to pursue an armed woodsman. Anyway, they probably assumed the shot they'd heard had killed him. If so, it would take them some minutes to ascertain otherwise.

Bush put a mile behind him before he stopped, by then certain he was not pursued. He found the nearest creek and washed his face clean, and felt exhausted.

He also felt ashamed. Having been manipulated by such low vermin was humiliating, infuriating, shameful. But they'd had him in a most unusual bind.

So Bush knew it wasn't really his fault. Even so, he felt responsible. It had been his hands that held the rifle, his voice that barked the demand for valuables. He'd caught a glimpse of the amount of gold in that strongbox. A small fortune, lost to its owner in one moment, at Bush's hands.

After resting a few minutes, Bush began his trek toward Natchez, trying to think how he might at least partially recompense the man he'd robbed. His Cherokee upbringing had ingrained him with a strong sense of the balance of things. He'd disturbed that balance by robbing the silver-haired man, and felt compelled to restore it as much as possible. It seemed a hopeless prospect. He would never be able to replace the kind of wealth contained in that strongbox.

Natchez was a town of two levels and two personalities. Atop the bluff were the fine houses, places of commerce, and government. Below were the dives, the dance halls, and gambling establishments, the prostitute cribs and tippling houses. A dismal and dangerous pit was Natchez-under-the-hill, but immensely popular with the boatmen who were its most frequent visitors.

Bush went to Natchez-under-the-hill first, but not to drink. The ordeal he'd just endured and barely survived made him see how much he had changed after Cephas Frank's death. By turning to liquor and a grim, sorrowful attitude about life, Bush had been on the edge of something dangerous and self-destructive. A few more months of liquor and bitterness, and he might have become as amoral and worthless as the Tuck brothers.

He was determined not to let that happen. He vowed to himself: No more liquor, no more carelessness and bitterness. From here on out he would undertake even his pursuit of Cephas's killers differently. He'd proceed carefully, not impulsively. No canoeing out to flatboats with nothing more than a knife to challenge a gang of murderers. No letting the likes of the Tucks get the upper hand over him, ever.

Bush was drawn to Natchez-under-the-hill by a slender promise of assistance. He'd been to Natchez's riverfront district twice before; once when he and Cephas traveled to Natchez on foot for no better reason than that they felt like it, and another time when the pair of them took on work as keel-boatmen and traveled down the river. He'd made a friend in Natchez that second time, a saloon operator who went by the name of Choctaw Charlie, even though he was blond and fair, with no trace of Indian in him. Choctaw, as he was usually called, ran a dive called the Indian Camp.

Bush found the tavern, same place, same run-down condition, but with a new, classier name: The Emporium. Bush feared the change of name indicated a change of ownership, so was relieved to see Choctaw Charlie still behind the bar. He'd built the bar of timber taken from the flatboat that had borne him to Natchez years ago. The wood still smelled like the river after all this time. Choctaw looked no different from the last time Bush had seen him, beyond the missing upper half of one ear—probably a souvenir from some disorderly patron, Bush guessed. Choctaw recognized Bush the moment he walked in.

Bush received an eager and encouraging greeting, and re-
treated with Choctaw into a rear room to talk over his situation. He recounted the death of Cephas Frank, which shocked
Choctaw, and said the murderers were two of several brothers,
names unknown, one of whom was killed when their flatboat
met up with a sandbar and sawyer. The flatboat had been
named *The George Washington.* Did Choctaw by chance know
of such a craft, and who its owner might have been?

Choctaw said he didn't know, though Bush wasn't sure he
could believe that. Choctaw had an unwavering policy of
keeping his mouth closed, revealing nothing to no one. A pru-
dent policy in Natchez-under-the-hill, and Bush never held it
against him, as much as he might like to know how much
Choctaw *really* knew.

"I'm out of money, Choctaw," he said. "I've had a turn
of bad luck, beginning with Cephas getting killed. I need some
kind of work."

"All I can give you is tending the bar and throwing out the
trouble-makers, which is what gave me this," Choctaw said,
pointing at the mutilated ear. "There's not much money in it,
but a bed and lodging for you, if you want it. Little cabin out
back of the place. Used to keep a sporting woman out there,
but that's something I ain't selling no more."

"I'll take whatever you can offer," Bush said. "I've got a
debt to pay."

"What? You gambled yourself into a hole, Bush?"

"No. No gambling. It's different from that." Bush thought
of that strongbox, all that gold. More of a fortune than he'd
ever hope to make in a lifetime of trapping and hunting, much
less through a meager job in a Natchez dive. But it was a start,
a way to keep himself alive and maybe lay aside a few coins
while trying to figure out a better solution. Though he knew
he could never repay the silver-haired man for all he'd taken,
he believed he was obliged to do what he could.

He had another obligation in Natchez, too. Though somewhere amid his misadventure with the Tucks, he'd lost the
letter found in the pocket of the dead man, he still remembered
the mournful message, and the name of Lydia, the wife to

whom it was directed. And the children, Lethy and Walker. Residents of this town. He would begin asking around until he tracked them down, then deliver the sad news to the family.

In the meantime, he would work for Choctaw, live in the hovel out back, and see what he might learn about the men who'd killed Cephas. What a change it would be from the life he'd known! Bushrod Underhill, son of the wilderness, was for the first time in his life about to become a townsman.

He'd worked for Choctaw less than a week before he finally learned the identity of the man he'd robbed on what some called the Boatman's Trail, others the Nashville Road, and still others, who had experienced the trace's dangers first hand, the Devil's Backbone. The victim, true to his distinguished appearance, was a man of some prominence, and once he had reached Natchez, was not at all timid about sharing what had happened to him and his gold on the trace.

He was a former Tennessee judge named Randall Borham. Having returned to the private practice of law, the wealthy jurist had come to Natchez on extended business, anticipating a stay of nearly a year while he prepared the legal groundwork on a massive yet little known business venture being constructed by investors from far up the river. He rented the lower floor of a large house above the bluff, and already was working his way into the center of Natchez commercial, legal, and social life. His wife was scheduled to join him in Natchez within weeks, traveling by river.

Bush wondered if there were any chance the judge would recognize him if they met on the street. He hoped not. Everywhere the judge went, he talked bitterly about the unknown man, the "Indian Bandit" who'd robbed him on the trace, and his determination to see him punished.

When Bush wasn't busy dispensing liquor to his clientele or tossing them onto the street, he asked questions. Anyone know any brothers, apparent low-lifes and prostitute suppliers, who ran for a time on a flatboat called *The George Washington*? He received plenty of blank stares, and quite a few looks that weren't so blank, but no information. He ran up against the same code of the riverfront that had kept Choctaw silent. It dictated that a man's business was his own, and that most questions were best left unanswered, especially when they had the smell of trouble about them.

Bush fared no better when asking about Lydia, wife of the dead man in that floating cabin. In the rough environs of Natchez-under-the-hill, people seemed to assume that every query was backed by some bad intent, so if Bush was asking about this woman, he probably meant to bring her problems she didn't need.

It grew annoying. Bush began to wonder if he was wasting his time in Natchez.

The barrier of silence finally broke concerning the widow.

Bush's work at Choctaw Charlie's Emporium reversed the pattern of his life, turning him into a night bird who caught up on sleep in the morning. For a woodsman who'd risen before dawn since boyhood, it was a difficult transformation.

About ten o'clock one morning—probably the latest hour, barring times of ill health, that Bushrod had slept until in his life—he awakened to the sound of a squabble on the other side of the wall. Peering out his window into the alley between his hovel and the Emporium, he saw a big, rough boatman, already drunk this early in the day, vying with a boy for a loaf of bread. Cursing and threatening, the boatman demanded the bread, emphasizing his demand by touching the handle of a shiv tucked under his belt.

Bush had never been able to bear the bullying of the young and innocent. He went outside and ordered the boatman to leave the boy be. The answer he got was a curse, to which Bushrod replied in turn with his fist. The punch caught the much bigger man in the jaw at just the right angle to break it and send him to the ground, stunned and nearly unconscious. Bush relieved the fellow of his shiv, slapped him awake, and sent him on his way.

"You hurt, boy?" Bush asked.

"No, sir," the boy replied, clutching his loaf of bread.

"Son," he said, "I admire your grit in refusing to give up

the loaf to that fellow, but you shouldn't have done it over no more than bread. That loaf ain't worth getting stabbed over."

"I'd not have done it, sir, except that the bread ain't for me. It's for Lethy and Walker, and they need it bad."

"Who'd you say?"

"Lethy and Walker Maloney. They're friends of mine."

"Is their mother named Lydia, by any chance?"

"Yes, sir. Lydia Maloney."

"Is there a Mr. Maloney?"

"There is . . . or there was. He's been gone quite a long time. He was supposed to have been back home with money for them all, but he ain't never come. Mrs. Maloney still watches every day for him, but he ain't never come and probably never will."

Indeed that was true, as Bush well knew. "Son, my name is Bushrod Underhill. What's yours?"

"Jack Calhoun."

"Jack, could you take me to meet the Maloney family?"

The boy frowned. "Why?"

"Because I know why Mr. Maloney ain't never come home."

The boy frowned at Bush a few moments as if wondering whether to believe him.

He nodded curtly. "I'll take you to them."

She was a pretty woman, dark of hair and eye, her lips full and naturally ruddy, her skin slightly olive. A few shades darker, and Bush might have taken her for Cherokee. In fact, she reminded him of the beautiful Cherokee woman he saw pounding corn at Nickajack the day of the raid, and the association gave this moment a certain poignance.

Lydia Maloney's beauty was marred just now, because she was crying. Bush sat silently at a table across from her, feeling out of place and maybe a little despised, particularly by the children, as a bearer of the worst of news. Lethy, an adolescent daughter who seemed destined to grow into the image of Lydia, cried at her mother's side. The son, Walker, maybe a couple of years older, successfully held back the tears, but it clearly required a great effort.

Bush remained silent, letting Lydia weep as she adjusted to the knowledge that she was—as she had surely suspected now for weeks—a widow. Bush caught himself wishing he could reach out and tenderly hold her hands, which were clasped together before her on the table. He dared not, of course.

A minute or so later, she pulled herself together and managed to quell her tears. In a faltering voice she asked, "Did he suffer, Mr. Underhill?"

Bush wished he could say no, but it would hardly be credible. The man was robbed and fatally wounded, and yet lived long enough to write a fairly lengthy message to his family. Of course he had suffered. "I think he must have borne whatever pain he had very well," Bush replied. "He was in good enough condition to write."

"Where is the letter now?"

"It was lost," he said. "I'm sorry about that, though it was beyond my control. But what he wrote, and your names, have stayed with me. It's been my plan to find you here and tell you what happened."

She smiled at him. "You are a good man to go to such trouble for strangers."

"It's no more than most would do."

"How did you find him?"

"Me and a companion were traveling down the river and saw his body washed ashore. I was looking through his clothing for something to identify him when I found the letter. By the way, ma'am, the man who found Mr. Maloney with me that day was a preacher of the gospel, so he was prayed over proper."

"You buried him?"

"Yes, ma'am." Bush figured it wasn't really a lie; they had interred him in a hollow log, which could count as a burial of sorts. It was best these folks think of their dead loved one as properly laid to rest.

"Mr. Underhill, he was to have brought us money. Had the thieves gotten it all?"

"Not all. There were a few dollars still on him, money they must have missed. I had to use some of it myself, but I've earned money since, and I can make it up to you." He reached into his pocket and pulled out all he had earned from Choctaw Charlie. He handed it over.

"Thank the Lord," she said, slowly taking up the meager pile of coins. "This is more than we've had at any one time since Jacob went away."

Bush looked around the little cabin, which was outside the worst part of Natchez-under-the-hill, but still far from the upper and more decent part of town. "How have you been getting on this last while?"

"I've taken in laundry, done seamstress work. Walker here, my strong young man, has found work at the levee, unloading flatboats and keels and so on. We've struggled, but survived. Sweet little Jack Calhoun, a friend of Walker's and Lethy's, has sensed our situation and done little kindnesses—bringing food, odd items of clothing, this and that. A wonderful boy. He's made it much easier. And always there's been the hope, of course, that Jacob would show up eventually with the money, and the struggling would end." She paused. "Now, I suppose, it won't." She closed her eyes and new tears came.

Bush looked at her clasped hands. Red and rough, a working woman's hands, but still beautiful, gracefully shaped.

"Ma'am, it's a pain to me that I've been the source of such sorrowful information for you."

"It's better to know. The uncertainty has been dreadful. I think that in the back of my mind I've known for a long time now that Jacob was gone. What you've told me isn't a total surprise."

"Still, I'm sorry." He paused. "And I want to help you all I can."

She seemed surprised. "Mr. Underhill, that is the kindest sentiment I've heard in the longest time, but truly it isn't your responsibility to take care of us."

"A man can take on responsibilities, can't he? I'd be honored if you'd let me help you out in these difficult times. I don't have much, and don't know how long I'll be in Natchez, but what I can do for you, I'd like to do.''

"Sir,'' she said, ''you are a saint. Surely you are a saint!''

"No, ma'am. Just a man who knows all too well what it is to lose those you love.''

CHAPTER
TWENTY-THREE

Bush spent his night's labors at the Emporium in a state of distraction. Thinking about her. Her sorrow. Her bereavement. Her children.

Mostly, just about her.

When his next packet of pay came to him, he took half of it to her at once, and made her take it over protest. He knew she needed it, and Bush had never cared a lot about how much money he had, as long as he had shelter and food. The Emporium gave him both.

The next evening, he'd just tossed a rowdy drunk onto the street and was turning back to reenter the saloon when a stout river-country wind blew a newspaper in his direction. The dirty page hooked around his middle. Bush was about to throw it off when the name of Randall Borham jumped out at him from a headline. He folded the paper instead of throwing it away, and took it inside to read the story by lamplight.

He was impressed and pleased by what he learned. Judge Borham, whose wife had arrived in Natchez two days before, had celebrated the occasion by donating a large amount of money to a local church that was establishing a fund for the local poor.

Bush was impressed by Borham's generosity, especially after losing so much in the robbery, and pleased to see that Borham obviously wasn't on the verge of destitution despite all the gold taken from him. It eased some of Bush's guilt over his role in the judge's loss. He was also glad to see that

Borham was a philanthropic man, who obviously cared about those in poverty.

This set Bush to thinking. It was indeed unrealistic to think he could ever repay Borham for all that lost gold, surely worth thousands. But perhaps, by joining him in helping out some of the downtrodden folks, he could at least make a symbolic restitution. And who was more downtrodden than a widow with two children and the meagerest of incomes?

It wasn't a perfect recompense, and didn't help the judge get back what he'd lost, but it was the best Bush could hope to achieve. He figured the judge himself would support the notion if he knew the whole story. Almost at once the idea took on the firmness of resolve.

Bush noticed a second item about Borham elsewhere in the same newspaper. The judge was offering a reward of one hundred dollars in gold for the capture of the "Indian Bandit" who had robbed him on the trace north of town. This gave Bush a chill, but he reminded himself that he'd been well-disguised. No evidence could possibly link him to that crime. Bush folded the newspaper and laid it beneath the bar.

About eleven that same evening, the saloon door opened and a man in a black suit and tall hat entered with practiced theatrics, not saying a word, drawing every eye in the place to him. He looked about in a cavalier pose, and said loudly, "The veil of the future opens tomorrow! For those who seek the revelation of what lies ahead in their lives, come two lots down tomorrow evening, beginning at the hour of six, and have your questions answered—if you dare!" He cocked up his chin, spun on his heel with a dancer's dexterity, and left the saloon.

Laughter erupted after he was gone, along with abundant exclamations that were, basically, all variations on the question: "Who was *that*?"

Bush grinned as he wiped the surface of the bar with a rag. Natchez was an odd town and drew the oddest of people. He figured the man who'd just come in was some sort of traveling fortune teller, here to bilk the gullible, particularly those with an interest in the gambling tables.

Bush wished there were people who really could reveal life's mysteries as simply as fortune-tellers claimed to do. If he could find one, he'd have a good question for him: What's likely to become of a man who comes to a town in search of murderers, and instead maybe, just maybe, finds himself falling in love?

And how can that man know if it's really love he's found, and if the one he loves loves him in turn?

He visited Lydia the next day at noon, gave her a little more money, and shared a meal with the family. The children, who'd at first seemed so cold to him, treated him now like a beloved uncle.

By the time he left, Bush believed maybe he really did love her, and she him. His own feelings clarified in his mind each time he looked at her face, and he detected a matching response in her look and touch, in the subtleties of her voice.

Yet Bush was left troubled by all this. He wondered on what her affection toward him was based. She'd only been recently widowed. She was afraid and alone, with children to care for. He'd been supporting her with money, hardly more than a pittance, but certainly more than she would have without him. Did she really love him, or merely what he was doing for her? And how could he be sure he himself loved a woman he didn't really know?

Further, where might this lead? He gladly fled even the hint of matrimony to old Campbell's daughter back in the Cumberland. Was he ready to reverse course now? If he and Lydia began to eye marriage, could he really bear to live without the freedom he had known for years? Would he have to become a townsman for life—a prospect that repelled him, just as becoming a woman of the wilderness would probably repel her? And how would he search for Cephas's killers if he had a family tying him down? What about Marie? If someday her track should reappear, how could he follow it with a family to attend to?

Many questions. Much to think about.

Bush shook his head. He was making too much of too little,

too soon. A few meaningful glances over a midday meal didn't equal impending marriage.

As he made his way down the street toward Choctaw's Emporium, he saw the strange fortune-teller fellow who'd appeared in the saloon the night before. He was getting ready to trade nonsense for money over in the empty lot down from the saloon. Bush glanced at the lot. A sign stretched overhead:

THE EYES OF THE BLIND SAVAGE PROPHET SEE WHAT IS TO COME.

Bush looked from the ridiculous sign to a lone figure standing beneath it, slumped and ancient, head bowed.

Bush stared for a long time, and tears came.

It was Tuckaseh.

Bush walked slowly toward the lot, overwhelmed. The bent, withered form was far different from the man who'd taught him to make fish traps years ago. Tuckaseh bore the weight of his years heavily.

Bush walked past a man, jostling him by accident. The man swore at him. Bush didn't even hear.

At the edge of the lot he paused, and said, "Tuckaseh."

The old head came up, and glassy eyes turned, unseeing, in Bush's direction.

"Tuckaseh, it's me. It's—"

"Skiuga?" He had a withered, raspy voice now. "Skiuga!"

Bush approached the old man and put his hands on his shoulders, then embraced him. "Tuckaseh, I was sure you were dead."

All at once, the old man couldn't speak. The strangely pale, blind eyes were moist now, and the humped body trembled.

"What the hell are you doing?"

Bush turned to see the showman who'd entered the saloon the prior night now coming toward them, frowning. "The show's not on yet, friend. You come back tonight if you want to consult my redskin there."

Bush ignored him. The man laid a hand on his shoulder. Bush shrugged him off. "Get away from me."

"This is *my* redskin, friend, and you'll stay away from him until I say different!"

Bush wheeled and faced the man. Silence. The showman looked into his face, moved his lips, and backed away, glowering but unprotesting. What he'd read in Bush's eyes didn't need to be spoken aloud.

Bush turned back to the old Indian, and spoke in Cherokee. "Do you want to stay with him, Tuckaseh?"

"No, no."

"Are you well, or sick?"

"Sick, Skiuga. Weak and old and sick."

"Then come with me."

The old face wrinkled into a smile, and Bush had the distinct feeling that it had been a long time since this ancient face had worn that expression.

Bush slipped his arm over Tuckaseh's shoulder. The old man's form was terribly shrunken. They walked together onto the street, with Bush guiding the way. Tuckaseh was completely blind now, he could tell. Not even glimmerings passed through those glassy eyes.

The showman came up behind. "You can't do this! This is theft!"

Bush looked over his shoulder. "Go away."

"I'll have the law on you!"

"You don't own this man. Now go away."

"I'm damned if I'll—"

"*Go away!*"

The showman said no more, stopped where he was, and slinked off.

There would be no prophecies made in the empty lot this night.

Bush never made it to the Emporium that day. He took Tuckaseh to his home and gave him food. The old fellow didn't eat much, but what he ate, he ate ravenously, and Bush wondered how much deprivation he'd endured while that blustering huckster used him.

When Tuckaseh was finished eating, he sat back, stared

blindly ahead, and nodded. "It was good, Skiuga."

"Tuckaseh, where have you been all these years?"

"Many places. Many miles. Too many to tell. I was captured at Nickajack, near the river. I have no wish to talk of all that happened to me after that."

"Then tell me how long you've been with the showman out there."

"A long time. I don't know. He has me tell lies to people, who give him money. He calls my lies prophecies. He's quite rude to me, and doesn't give me good food."

"No more of that for you, Tuckaseh. From now on you are with me."

Tuckaseh smiled again. "That is good, Skiuga. But I won't burden you long. Very soon, I will die."

He'd heard it before, of course. At Nickajack, Tuckaseh had been declaring almost weekly that his death day had come. This time, however, was quite different. Bush could look at his old friend and see that death truly was near. Surely the unseen forces that guide men's lives and paths must have brought Tuckaseh to him at this unlikely place.

He would not desert him, and this time, there would be no invading army to drive them apart.

"I don't want to die in a white man's town, Skiuga. The smell of a white man's town makes my nostrils choke. I want to be in the woods when I die."

"Then you will be."

"It's good that we've found each other again, one last time, Skiuga."

"It is indeed, my old friend."

Bush spoke briefly to Choctaw Charlie. He'd found an old friend and was going away with him for a time. He didn't know when he would return.

Choctaw was an easy-going man. He let Bush know he was welcome any time. If there was work available, fine with Choctaw if Bush wanted to take it. Who was this old friend, anyway?

Nobody Choctaw would know. Bush thanked him, and departed.

He had one more visit to make.

Lydia listened intently as Bush told her about Tuckaseh. But to tell her this much led to telling her more, and slowly, Bush's entire story laid itself out. Lydia listened intently, fascinated, silent, to the history of the man who she'd come to love without really realizing it.

When he was finished, she asked, "You truly were raised among Indians, savages?"

"Among Indians, yes. If they were savage, well then, I've seen white men equally so."

"And your father—a Frenchman, a white man, who left his own people and chose the Indians?"

Why was she asking this? He'd just explained it all quite thoroughly. "He was an unusual man. He did what he did for reasons of his own."

"But he rejected his own kind."

"He saw the idea of 'kind' based more on, on . . . common humanity, I suppose, not just common race."

She looked away, troubled. "Tell me again, did you say this Cephas, Cephas—"

"Frank."

"—Cephas Frank, was a nigra?"

"What point are you getting to, Lydia?"

"It seems wrong to treat a man of that race like a partner."

Bush rose slowly, suddenly wanting this conversation to end. "Lydia, I must go."

"Will you be back?"

"Yes. Of course. Then we'll talk more. About all these things."

"Yes . . . that would be good."

"Goodbye, Lydia. You'll be able to get on well enough for a while, you think?"

"We got on before. We can do it again, while you're away with your Indian."

He looked at her, taking in more than the words themselves, and she knew it. She'd intended it.

"Goodbye, Lydia."

"Goodbye, Bushrod. You be careful of that Indian."

Bush and Tuckaseh traveled slowly, the best the old man could do. There was a sense of finality around all they did, but no sense of urgency. They traveled many miles, seeking the solitude of wilderness. When they reached the right spot, they both simply knew it.

Bush built a shelter for them, and as different as this humid, often-swampy terrain was from the mountains of the old Cherokee country where they'd spent their earlier years, the feeling was the same.

Bush and Tuckaseh talked much in the days of solitude that followed. Bush described his life since he and Tuckaseh had last parted.

"Do you believe that Marie could still live, Tuckaseh?"

"Who can say? You must keep looking for her. And don't let this quest to find the killers of your friend stop you. Don't waste your years looking for vengeance that can gain you nothing, and miss finding your sister, who can give you happiness. Your friend, Frank, was a wise man. Until you know beyond any question that your sister is dead, you must believe she is alive."

"Are you telling me not to seek vengeance?"

"Vengeance is of little value when a man is old, like me," Tuckaseh said. "Or perhaps it has always been of little value, and I'm only now old enough to learn it. Skiuga, in a man's life he finds many quests he might pursue, but he can't pursue them all. Sometimes he must choose between them. You may search for these murderers, or you may search for your sister. It's up to you to decide which is of the greater value. But I know which is better. And so do you. Choose wisely, Skiuga. Because sometimes, the time to choose comes only once."

CHAPTER
TWENTY-FOUR

Two weeks later, Bush returned to Natchez in the misty glow of a dawning day. The town was quiet at this hour, peaceful. A man could move about in it unseen and unmolested.

The load of grief was heavy on Bush. When at last the long-predicted day of dying had come, he'd laid Tuckaseh away with his own hands, turning his face northeastward, toward the Overhill Cherokee country, far away, where the old man was born. For a day thereafter Bush lingered by the grave, then headed back toward Natchez.

The river drew him, so he headed for the levee, where he seated himself on the end of a pier and watched the wide water flow by. It was good that he'd had time with Tuckaseh. His vision was clearer now.

He would not stay in Natchez. He couldn't. He wasn't a townsman, and never would be. The matter of Lydia Maloney was uncertain. He still experienced strange, unique feelings inside when he thought of her, and pictured her face. Yet he was troubled. There were suggestions in their last conversation, things revealing themselves in Lydia that could not be seen with the physical eye.

He just wasn't sure. But he knew this: If he and Lydia did end up together, she would have to leave this place. He was not made for streets and alleys and buildings, the stench of humans pressed together like arrows in a quiver, when there was a wide, untouched land stretching west beyond them. If Lydia loved him, she would have to accept him as he was. And who he was.

When the sun was higher and the town began to stir, Bush rose from the levee and walked back onto the street. The Emporium, which opened its doors by afternoon and closed them by dawn, was locked and barred, Choctaw sleeping by now in his ratty bunk in the unfurnished upstairs room that passed for his home. Bush headed around to his hovel and found no one had taken his place as its resident. He opened it, went inside, flopped down on his own bed and stared at the ceiling.

"I miss you already, Tuckaseh," he whispered. "There's so much more I could have learned from you if we hadn't been driven apart."

Bush wasn't one to lie about, so he took a lengthy walk around Natchez, up onto the higher parts, and meandered amid the fancier dwellings there. A man came by, carrying a stack of newspapers. Bush had a bit of money and bought one, wondering what he might have missed during his time of isolation with Tuckaseh.

Most of the news was uninteresting, but as before, the name of Judge Randall Borham caught his eye. He read the story, and lowered the paper slowly.

It was the worst news he could have received.

He approached her house, dreading the meeting.

Ever since his forced participation in the Borham robbery, Bush had moments when dreadful consequences crept into his mind. But always he reminded himself that his face and body had been well-disguised during the robbery, even his voice distorted. He had nothing to fear. No one could link him to the crime.

There was one scenario, however, that he'd not considered. The very one he now faced.

But first there was Lydia to tell—and he dreaded that almost as much as what would follow.

In no hurry to enter the unpleasantness ahead, Bush leaned against a tree, in the shadows, and watched her house.

She came out, carrying a big wicker basket laden with laundry, and headed for the long clothesline strung from one exterior corner of the house to a tree thirty feet away. Bush smiled, watching her work, her experienced hands nimbly clipping the clothes onto the line with pegs split halfway down the middle so they would slide across the line.

He figured she might be angry if she caught him watching her, and was about to speak up, when a young Indian boy, perhaps a Natchez or maybe a Choctaw, came walking up a path leading from a nearby woods. With him was a puppy, leaping about his feet, yapping and energetic. An appealing child, a cute pup. Lydia looked up, saw them. Bush noticed no smile.

The puppy, catching sight of the flapping clothes, ran away from the boy, angled across the yard, jumped, and clamped its teeth onto the corner of a hanging sheet.

"Damn you!" Lydia screeched, kicking the pup so hard it yelped and flew a good ten feet before rolling and tumbling to a stop. "Damned cur!" She wheeled and faced the Indian boy, who had frozen to a halt when she kicked the animal. He was halfway across her yard, having tried to catch and stop his puppy as soon as it raced away from him.

Lydia raised her finger and pointed it at him. "You damned little savage, I ought to kill that dog, and you, too! Curse your soul, child! Does your kind not even know how to control a dog? Miserable little heathen! And who said you could set your red foot into my yard?"

She reached down and picked up a stone, which she threw at the boy. He dodged it and ran. The puppy came near her, trying to get back to its master, wagging its tail and ducking its head as it neared her. She saw it and kicked it again, even harder. It howled, tumbled again, and raced to join the Choctaw boy, who was already beating a path away from the house.

"Damn you, savage!" she screamed after him. "You let that pup come around here again, and I'll shoot it! You hear me?"

Still muttering and cursing beneath her breath, she returned to her work.

Bush, still unseen, quietly turned and walked away, never to return, and deeply saddened.

*   *   *

The yellow-haired jailer was dozing in his chair, no longer hearing the whimpering and complaining of the prisoner locked in the flat-barred cell behind him. His feet were propped on the desktop, his hands folded on his belly, his head bobbing as he slipped between semi-wakefulness and sleep, and back again.

He jerked to alertness when he sensed the presence of a newcomer in the room. A slender, muscled, dark-haired man in his mid-twenties stood before him, looking for all the world as sad as a prisoner himself.

"Can I help you, friend?" the jailer said in a sleep-hoarsened voice.

The newcomer looked at the prisoner in the cell, who was looking at him in turn. "Is that man the one who's been arrested as the thief who robbed Judge Borham out on the Devil's Backbone?"

"That's right, sir. The very bird. Gault Marchell's his name. Who are you?"

"My name's Bushrod Underhill."

"What's your interest in this case, sir?"

Bush stared at the man in the cell. "Just the interest of a citizen who once brushed up against a robbery himself. May I talk to the prisoner?"

"Why?"

"Just personal reasons. To see if maybe I know him."

"Well . . . fine. But let me run a hand over your pockets first, just to be sure, you know."

Bush lifted his arms and underwent a quick search, then advanced to the cell.

The prisoner came to the bars. "I know you. I seen you somewhere before," he said to Bush in a whisper.

"Yes, you have," Bush replied. "I remembered you the moment I saw you. You recall one night when you walked into a camp with a gun, ready to rob two men, and one of the two turned out to be the preacher Moses Zane?"

"I remember. He rousted up a devil that chased me through the dark woods for nigh a mile. And you were the man with him."

"That's right."

"They're claiming I'm the man who's robbed so many folks along the Trail all dressed in Indian clothes. But it ain't true. I found that redskin suit hid in an empty cabin. Sure, I give it a try, putting it on, and damned if I didn't still have it on when they caught me. Just some men trying to get some reward. Brought some tall silver-haired man in here and he looked at the suit and says, 'That's the one.' So I says, 'Put the damn suit in jail, then.' None of them laughed."

"You're in quite a fix, friend."

"I know it. I ain't no saint, but it wasn't me who was that Indian bandit, I swear! Can you help me, mister? You a lawyer, maybe?"

"I'm no lawyer."

"The hell! Then why'd you come here?"

"Because I'm the one man in the world who can help you. I'm the one man in the world who knows you're telling the truth."

"What? How you know that?"

But Bush had no more to say to this man. He walked back to the jailer.

"I need to talk to you. But I'd like to have a lawyer do it with me, if I could. You know any good lawyers?"

"Yes, sir. You want me to send for one?"

"I do."

"What is it you need to talk about?"

Bush paused. "I need to make a confession. Of a crime."

Gault Marchell leaned against the bars of his cell and stared at its only other occupant, who was trying to ignore him.

"I don't know why you did it," Marchell said. "You didn't have to come forward at all. Who am I to you?"

"An innocent man."

Marchell glanced toward the jailer, then lowered his voice. "But I ain't innocent. Maybe I didn't rob that judge, but I've robbed aplenty of others. Would've robbed you and the preacher if it hadn't turned out to be Moses Zane!"

"I did it because it was the only thing I could do."

"You're a saint. You're a good and fine man. If you and me should be so fortunate as to get out of this jail, Mr. Underhill, I'll tell you one thing: I'd never leave your side. Not for no reason. Not after what you done, coming in here and taking my part when you could have walked away. But answer me this: If you don't mind stealing from folks, which ain't right, why you so worried about doing the right thing for me?"

"I don't steal from folks. I was forced to do it. There were men in the woods around, who would have killed me and the man I was robbing, too, if I'd not done as they told me. They took the gold when it was done, and tried to kill me besides. But I got away from them."

"Who were they?"

"Two brothers, name of Tuck, and a couple of others I never heard names attached to."

"I've heard of the Tucks. Seen them, too, I think. One got no wits about him, and a bumpy kind of thing on his face?"

"That's right."

"I've seen them, then." Marchell thought it over. "Huh. Clever scheme, that one. I'd have never thought of it."

"If you get out of here, don't go trying it."

"I don't know that I'm going to get out. You've come in and claimed to have done the crime, and I'm still here."

"There'll have to be some kind of something done in a court of law, I reckon. But you'll get out in the end."

"They'll never believe your story about being forced, you know. How you going to prove there was men hid in the woods, going to shoot if you didn't go along?"

"I can't prove it."

Marchell said, "Glad as I am for you coming here, I swear, I don't understand why it would matter to you about somebody else taking the blame."

"That's the difference between me and you."

"I guess you're a holy kind of man, considering you was running around that time in company with that devil-raising preacher."

"He didn't raise a devil. He just talked spookish and threw gunpowder in the fire to scare you."

"Oh, there was a devil, sure enough! He chased me the longest way, big old long teeth, claws, breath like a fire—oh, I never want to see the like again!"

Bush rolled over on his side, back toward Marchell. He'd talked all he could stand.

He slept, but awakened, sensing a presence. Looking up, he saw Judge Randall Borham standing on the other side of the bars, looking at him.

Bush sat up, brushing back his long hair with his hands, and looked back in silence at the man he'd robbed.

Borham, unsmiling, lifted his brow, just as he had out on the trace, and said, "You've become the talk of all Natchez, you know."

"I didn't know."

"Oh, yes. It's a noble thing, taking one's due punishment just so some piece of backwoods rubbish like that man yonder won't have to."

"Even backwoods rubbish deserves not to be falsely accused."

"Why'd you do it?"

"Because I've got a conscience, I guess. Best answer I can come up with."

"No, the robbery, I mean. Was it really you?"

"Yes, sir. It was."

"Then why? You're obviously a moral man, doing what you've done. Why would you commit such a crime?"

"To save your life, sir."

"I beg your pardon?"

"To save your life, and mine. There were men around us in the woods that day. Armed. Ready to kill us all if I didn't do what they said. They took the gold when it was done. I barely got away from them alive."

"You have evidence to back this?"

"None."

"Then how do you intend to support your story in a court of law?"

"I suppose, sir, it won't be supported. And I'll end up taking the punishment."

"It doesn't quite seem like justice, does it?"

"No, sir. But justice is like money. Hard to get, and never quite enough to go around."

Borham made a faint grunting sound, and was for a moment silent and thoughtful. "Indeed. Good evening, Mr. Underhill. We'll meet again."

" 'Evening, judge. And I'm sorry about the gold you lost."

The judge walked out. Bush lay down again and closed his eyes.

When morning came, Bush sat up, yawned, and looked over at Marchell in the next cell. To his surprise, Marchell, who looked as likely an illiterate as any man could, was lying on his bunk, reading a small pamphlet.

"Morning," Bush said. "What you reading there, Marchell?"

The other man sat up and held up the pamphlet. "It's new. Published by your own friend, the Reverend Zane. Jailer give it to me, said some lady with Bibles and such came by yesterday and left some copies to be give to prisoners."

"Do tell!" Bush was glad to hear that Zane was alive to be writing pamphlets. He'd been unsure until now what had become of Zane after the canoe drifted away with him, and feared he might have capsized and drowned. "What's it about?"

"It's the story of him coming down the river awhile back, and meeting an angel."

"An angel?"

"That's right. An angel in the form of a man, who joined him and give him aid and encouragement after he'd been tossed off a boat by some folks who didn't like his preaching. Huh! I'd say it wasn't the preaching, I'd say they probably didn't like the devils he raised on them, that's what I'd say!"

Bush was thinking hard. "How'd he come to believe this man was an angel?"

"Because they was traveling along in a canoe, and Zane

lays down to sleep, and when he woke up, the canoe's sailing right on, and the man had vanished. Old Zane's got him a hunting horn now that he and this angel found together, and he uses it to call folks to his camp meetings. Really draws them in, he says. He believes it's an angel trumpet.''

"I see." Bush lay down and looked at the ceiling. "An angel, you say. And an angel trumpet." He slowly began to grin, then a chuckle welled up, growing into full, extended laughter, which thoroughly confused Marchell.

"What are you laughing at?"

Bush didn't reply, but just kept on laughing.

CHAPTER
TWENTY-FIVE

The following midnight

A hand jostled Bush awake. Sitting up, he saw a figure in the darkness, beside his cot, another in the door of the cell. A door opened. Beyond, in the blackness of the jailer's area, other men moved.

"What's happening here?" Bush asked, and as he did, fear hit him. Men breaking into a jail at night, opening cells—was he to be hauled out and hanged? It happened sometimes to captured robbers. Justice didn't always await the verdict of a court or the guidance of formal sentencing to be carried out.

There was no light. Bush could see no faces and could barely discern forms. Someone grabbed his arm and pulled him up. Resisting by instinct, he reached out and touched a face shrouded in a mask—and suspicion became certainty. He was being taken from this jail by force. He wondered how death would come—rifle, blade, noose?

"Up from there! There's no time to waste," an unfamiliar voice said. "The jailer will be back soon."

Bush found nothing objectionable in that. He wanted the jailer here. Right now Bush loved the stringencies and rules of official law and punishment. He believed in jailers and closed cells with fervor. If they provided punishment, they also provided protection.

Bush aimed a fist at the place from which the voice had emanated, but in the darkness, missed. His knuckles merely brushed the cloth of a mask. He drew back to strike again, but someone hit him hard on the temple, driving him back down onto the bed, stunning him, paralyzing him.

He sensed rather than felt that they were dragging him out of the cell, and then out of the jail. He struggled to open his eyes, saw a black open sky above him, and felt the breeze against his skin.

At least he would be privileged to die in the open air. Maybe it was better this way. Maybe it was better to die in the freedom of open space than to live in misery in the close confines of a cell.

Something cold and wet struck his face, making him grunt, pulling him out of his stupor. Arms pulled him up and made him stand on his feet. He staggered and leaned against something that moved away from him just a little. Warm, with coarse, short-haired hide. A horse. Saddled.

"Come around, damn you!" the same voice as before said. "Into that saddle."

So this was to be it. He'd be placed on a saddled horse, the rope tightened around his neck, the horse driven from beneath him.

"I'd rather you just shoot me and be done with it," he said.

"Shoot you? Don't you know what's happening here, you fool? You're being set free!"

He took it in emotionlessly, unable to comprehend. Someone came to his side. This voice he recognized. Gault Marchell.

"It's true, Mr. Underhill. They've busted us loose, both of us. They have these horses for us. We can ride away."

"They'll shoot us, send us riding off, shoot us out of the saddles. Say we were escaping."

"You don't have much trust in your fellow man, do you, Mr. Underhill!" the masked man said. "Are we going to have to hire a lawyer to persuade you that you can go free?"

Bush was trying desperately to clear his head. He looked around at the dimly visible forms around him. The horses moved and snorted, ready for their riders, and Marchell was already clambering into his saddle.

"Why?" Bush asked. "Who?"

"Never mind that. All you need to know is that you have a friend with a bit of influence, who found it in his heart to drop a bit of money to a certain jailer so as for him to step out for a while this evening, and just happen to leave his cell keys lying on the floor.''

Bush wondered if he were dreaming all of this.

''Into the saddle, Mr. Underhill. Sorry I struck you so hard. Are you able to ride?''

Bush blinked hard, trying to clear his head. ''I'm able.''

He pulled himself into the saddle. He was dizzy, but things were beginning to become clear.

It was really happening. He was really being freed.

He looked down at the masked man, surrounded now by his associates, also masked. ''Who are you?'' Bush asked.

''You think that's a likely question for men in masks to answer? Who we are don't matter—we're hired men.''

''Who hired you?''

''You ride north, then west, and come to the river at the Westerman Point, and maybe you'll find that out, if he wants you to. It ain't up to me. Now, sir, you'd best ride.''

Bush rode, Marchell at his side.

There was food in the saddlebags, and even money and fresh clothing. Once they were well away from Natchez, Bush and Marchell paused long enough to examine what they had, and to marvel together over the unexpectedness of it all.

''But I can't figure who would do this,'' Bush said. ''Who would care enough to go to this trouble, and to scoff at the law besides, just to break loose two highwaymen?''

''You heard what the man said. Somebody who didn't want you locked up.''

Bush chewed on some of the dried beef from his saddlebag. ''Where was it he said to go? To the Westerman Point?''

''That's right. And I know where that is.''

''So do I.''

They mounted and rode north, then turned westward and followed the trail that led to the Mississippi River bluff called Westerman Point.

With their horses tethered nearby but out of sight, Bush and

Marchell lay on their bellies on a little grassy hill and looked down at a tiny cabin on the riverbank.

"Look—the door's open," Marchell said. "And there's something in there, like maybe a box or a bag or something."

"Let's go on down. I don't see any sign of life anywhere."

They advanced to the cabin, looking around as they went. Bush felt edgy, not fully confident that this wasn't all an elaborate trap. But if it was, whoever had set it up had done so at some risk, in that there had been nothing to force them to come to Westerman Point at all. Once out of jail, they could have ridden off anywhere and vanished forever.

The cabin contained a crate containing more supplies—food, extra clothing, even a couple of good knives. The goods were obviously left for Bush and Marchell, but there was no clue about who had left them, or why.

"I don't understand this," Bush said. "It makes no sense at all."

"Bush . . . look."

Marchell was looking out the door, where a subtle change in the light indicated movement outside the cabin. The shadow shifted again, Bush and Marchell instinctively drawing away into the corners, brandishing their new knives.

A man stepped into the doorway, silhouetted against the light outside. But Bush thought he recognized him at once, and when he heard the voice, was sure of it.

"Judge Borham!"

"Good day, Mr. Underhill. Mr. Marchell."

Borham stepped farther inside. Now that they all shared the same kind of light, they could see him more clearly. He was unarmed.

"Sir," Bushrod said. "I don't understand."

"It's quite clear to me, Mr. Underhill. I'd be a greater villain than any trail bandit if I let you be tried and punished after what you did. You see, I believe you, sir, when you tell me you were forced to commit the crime. And I believe your act of nobility in turning yourself in on behalf of Mr. Marchell here reveals your character to be far from that of a criminal. Yet you would never have successfully defended yourself in a court of law. Your story had no evidence to back it.''

"So you broke me out of jail based on a hunch I was telling the truth?''

Borham smiled softly. ''Mr. Underhill, I've been a jurist for many years of my life. I've learned to recognize the truth when I hear it. Furthermore, I've seen men accused of every kind of crime, and I've seen innocent men locked away and even executed. But what I've seldom seen, on either side of the law, is true nobility. But in you, Mr. Underhill, I've seen it. And I could not, cannot, simply stand by and see such a man as you wrongly punished.''

"What you've done, sir, could create problems for you, should the story get out.''

"Then I'll count upon you and Mr. Marchell not to let it get out, hmmm? Blast it all, Mr. Underhill! Give an old man the opportunity to do something he never had the freedom to do while he was bound by the strictures of law! Many times, sir, I've seen injustice administered in the name of justice, and wished I had the power to throw aside tradition and rules of procedure and simply to *act* on what I knew, by pure intuition, was right! I've never done such a thing before, but by all the eternal, I have now. I have now.'' He looked from man to man, and nodded. "Your act of courage and self-sacrifice, Mr. Underhill, has gained freedom for you and your companion both.''

Bush hardly knew what to say. He was being set free by the very victim of the crime that had caused him to be jailed! "Thank you, sir,'' he said. Marchell mumbled something about being obliged.

"Come out here, gentlemen,'' Borham said, waving them toward the door. "There's something I want to show you.''

They walked out into the light. The judge led them to the edge of the river. "Look yonder,'' he said, pointing westward. "You see that land beyond the water? That land stretches for more miles than a man can count. That land is the future, my friends. There's a place for you there, a place for anyone. A man can start over beyond the river. I have advice for both of you: Go out yonder and begin again. Go into that new land

and make a new life for yourselves. Make it the gloryland! Cross this glory river and never turn back.''

Bush looked at the distant landscape. ''Yes,'' he said. ''I'll do it.''

''A man can lose himself in a land that big,'' Borham said. ''I suggest to both of you, considering your circumstances as accused criminals who have now escaped jail, that you do just that.''

''How will we get over?'' Marchell asked.

''There's a raft down yonder, big enough for you and your horses. See it?''

Bush smiled. ''You planned this right thoroughly, sir.''

''I'm good at planning. It's what gave me success in life. Take that raft on across, then let it go. Let it float away while you keep heading west. Put everything behind you that's come before. Start a new life.''

''It's a good prospect, sir. But there's one further thing I must talk to you about. After the robbery, I had it in mind to try to recompense you in some way for the loss, but the amount of money was far too great for me to hope to repay it. But when I found you were a man who cared about the poor folks around him, I decided maybe the best penance for me was to help out a poor family I'd run across. A widow, two children, hardly any money. Her name is Lydia Maloney. If you could maybe see that they're among those who benefit from some of your charity, sir, I'd truly appreciate it.''

''Consider it done, Mr. Underhill.''

Bush reached out and shook Borham's hand. ''Then I thank you again, sir.''

''Indeed. My pleasure.'' He pulled a little closer to Bush and spoke so that Marchell couldn't hear. ''Your companion here has little chance to make much of himself, I'm afraid, whatever side of the river he's on. I suggest you part company with him as soon as you can. But you, Mr. Underhill, are a different story. The nobility you displayed, as well as your concern for this poor widow, shows it. Don't waste your opportunities, sir.''

Bush looked across the water. "The glory river, eh? Is that what you called it?"

"That's what it *is*. Now go. They'll be looking for you soon. I've got to get back to Natchez and make sure all my own tracks are properly hidden—wouldn't want it out that an old legal dog like me helped two jailed men escape! Goodbye, Mr. Underhill. I'll not be seeing you again."

"Bless you, sir. I'll not forget you."

"Off with you now. Get across that river, and keep going."

Bush made two vows to himself once he was on the western side of the Mississippi. The first was never to return to Natchez or its vicinity without an utterly compelling reason. The second was to rid himself of Marchell as fast as he could. It wouldn't be easy. Marchell still declared himself attached to Bush forever because of the grand act he'd done for him. Bush couldn't imagine a worse fate than having Marchell become his lifetime shadow.

He'd decided that the only likely escape would be to get Marchell passed-out drunk, then slip away. An unexpected and ironically appropriate alternative, however, presented itself three days after they had crossed the Mississippi.

Riding into a little riverside community by twilight, they heard the clear blare of a horn riding the wind across the level land.

Bush pulled his horse to a halt. *He knew the sound of that horn.*

"I'll be," he said. "I believe the Reverend Zane is calling folks to meeting."

"Zane!" Marchell declared. "Why you say that?"

"That was the angel horn I just heard, that's why."

"How'd you know that?"

"Why shouldn't I? I'm the angel who gave it to him."

"The hell! You ain't no angel."

"How do you know? What do you know about angels? All you know about is devils who chase you through the woods."

Marchell was looking at Bush very strangely. It was difficult for Bush not to laugh. Any man as gullible, superstitious, and suggestible as Marchell could probably consider almost any wild tale to be true. If this man could honestly believe he was chased through the woods by a demon, why shouldn't he believe Bushrod Underhill was a heavenly being come to earth?

"Come on, Marchell. We're going to meeting."

"Meeting! With *Zane*? No, sir, not me!"

"Of course you are. Me and you ride together, don't we? If I'm going to meeting, you have to come along."

"No, sir. I'm scared of that man. I know his power!"

"He's not a man, Marchell. Any more than I am."

Marchell's eyes did strange things. He gripped the reins very tightly.

"Moses Zane and I have seen things you'll never see, Marchell. Things no man has laid eyes on, things done in the halls of high glory long before the world was ever made."

Marchell swallowed hard and looked rather pale.

Bush's face took on a somber expression. "And it's not only Moses who brought down with him the gift of summoning and controlling the devils." Bush launched into a chant, random words in Cherokee strung together. "*Kunu'nu . . . nu'na . . . a'wi . . . a'gana . . .* " Bullfrog . . . potato . . . deer . . . groundhog . . .

"What are you doing?"

"I'm calling up a devil to chase you, Marchell. You're a wicked man, and I can bear your presence no more. *Kunu'nu . . . nu'na . . . a'wi . . . a'gana . . .* "

"Don't do that! Hellfire!"

"Then run—*run*!"

Marchell turned his horse, dug into its sides, and was gone into the night within moments. Bush listened to the hoofbeats fading away.

"Goodbye, Mr. Marchell," he said. "Our partnership is hereby dissolved. May the angels guide your steps from here on out."

He rode off in the direction in which he'd heard the blare of the horn.

* * *

Preaching was already under way when Bush rode onto the hillside overlooking the meeting ground, set up in a great concave circle of land like a vast, shallow bowl set into the earth. Without dismounting, Bush sat on the western rim of that bowl and looked down at Zane, who was walking back and forth on the back of a wagon set up as a platform. His Bible was open in one hand, and his fist pounded its pages, as he bellowed out his sermon in a voice loud enough to reach beyond the remotest of his listeners.

Bush grinned. He liked Zane, and was glad he'd come through his solo canoe journey safe and sound. It would be interesting to talk to him, to find out what happened to him after they parted, and what had led him to cross the river. But to talk to Zane would involve shattering the preacher's now-published conviction that he'd actually met an angel. It would embarrass him, maybe even disillusion him. Bush didn't want that.

So he just watched the preacher at his work, and listened a few minutes to the ringing voice, just as loud and distinctive as the sound of that "angel horn."

Bush was about to turn and ride away when Zane saw him. The sermon stopped abruptly; Zane stared. The members of his audience glanced at one another, puzzled, and finally followed his gaze up to Bush, there on the edge of the rim.

Bush knew his features were indiscernible, but apparently Zane recognized his form. Bush lifted his hand slowly, and held it above his head, waving slightly at the preacher.

On the platform below, Zane made the same gesture back again.

Bush rode away, out of sight, wondering if this incident, too, might make its way into another Zane pamphlet. "The Night the Angel Visited the Camp Meeting." Bush could imagine it easily.

He grinned, heading across the flatlands toward a distant line of dim, flickering lights. With any luck, it would be a community, and there would be a gunsmith with stock to sell. Judge Borham had provided Bush plenty of money, but no rifle. He aimed to buy one the first chance he got.

CHAPTER
TWENTY-SIX

There was no gunsmith, but there was a tavern, the only place in town—if this barren stretch deserved the name—that was open in this evening hour.

Bush entered it out of thirst, but his only goal was a cup of coffee. When he'd sworn off drinking back in Natchez, he'd meant it. He would take no chances at getting himself caught in a downward cycle again.

There was no coffee to be had in this place, unfortunately, and Bush was about to leave and seek out a good cold spring when an uproar exploded from the back corner of the tavern.

Bush turned and took it all in. He soon wished he hadn't. His head was aching from the blow he received during the jail escape, and he was in no mood to get into a fight.

He couldn't stand by, though, while two stout, healthy men laid into a smaller fellow with his right arm in a splint. The fellow with the splint was not small by average standards— in fact he was burly—but the men attacking him were one step removed from bears, and with that injured arm, he didn't stand a chance.

Bush shook his head and walked back toward the commotion.

"Let him go," he said quietly to one of the two big men.

"What?" the man said through a disbelieving grin, while administering a blow to the side of the victim's head.

"I said, let him go."

The man turned and shoved Bush on the chest with both hands. Bush staggered back but did not fall.

"Get off with you," the man said, turning back to the battle, which had gone from being a true fight to a one-sided beating.

Bush was on him before he'd made a complete pivot. One fist smacked an ear, the other hand grabbed a bulging Adam's apple, both feet entwined around the brute's ankles.

He went down like a mountainslide.

Bush dropped, knee-first, and delivered his full weight against the fallen man's kidney. Rolling off, he landed a kick into the fat belly, before dancing back.

With a roar the man arose. He'd forgotten his original battle; Bush had his full attention. Like a great bear he came Bush's way.

Bush ducked and came in low, landing two more blows on the pillow of a gut. The man gave out two great "oofs!" and took a step back, but got in a blow of his own. Bush felt a moment of weakness, but kept to his feet.

Taking the offensive, he went for the face this time, landing one fast right on the bulbous nose, another on the jaw. The brute waddled backwards into a stool and fell over it, smashing a table.

The tavern keeper protested, but no one heard.

Bush glanced at the other fellow and was surprised to see him doing fairly well, considering he had only one working hand. Using his feet and one good fist, he put the other fellow on the defensive—the two brutes apparently didn't function well when separated.

The fight continued for another five minutes or so, the advantage shifting back and forth, but mostly swaying in Bush's direction. With a final burst of aggression, Bush came in with a jolting blow to the right jaw of his foe. He saw a tremor run through the fellow all the way down to his toes. By then Bush had gotten in two more blows, and it was over. The man sank to the floor, groaned, drooled, licked blood from his lips, then passed out.

Bush turned in time to see the man with the splint lay a punch into the center of the other brute's face and bring him down just like the first. Bush and the stranger looked down at their work, panted, sweated, then looked at one another.

"Obliged," the man with the splint said.

"Think nothing of it."

The man began to stick out his hand, but it was the splinted one, so he withdrew it, and put out the other. Bush shook it.

"Bushrod Underhill."

"Becker Israel. Mightly grateful for the help."

"What were those two on you for?"

"Thought I'd cheated them on a dice roll. I think they were just looking for trouble."

"What do you say we get out of here before they come around again? Somehow I figured they're going to be right annoyed when they rejoin the living."

"So what happened to the hand?" Bush asked as he and Becker Israel rode along slowly, horses abreast.

"Wagon rolled over it. Heard it crunch like a bug on an anvil. But it's mostly healed now. I expected to be using it soon. Hope it won't be too stiff."

"It will be for a time. Where you from, Mr. Israel?"

"Call me Beck. I hail from Kentucky, myself. You?"

"Born near the Cumberland River." He would say no more just yet, nothing about Coldwater or Nickajack, until he knew Israel's attitude toward Indians, and whites who lived among them.

"How you make your way in this world, Bush?"

"Mostly I let the world make a way for me. Live off the land, usually. Hunting, fishing, trapping. I spent the last three years or so living all up and down the river country with a partner name of Cephas Frank. But for the last little while I've—"

"You've run with old Cephas?"

"You know him?"

"Spent a good winter's hunt with him way up in Kentucky some years back! Fine woodsman, that Cephas! How's he doing now?"

"Sorry to tell you, but Cephas is dead."

"No!"

"Afraid it's true. He was killed, best I can tell, by a couple of brothers who came off a flatboat.'' Briefly Bush told him of the ill-fated rendezvous that had led him to search for Cephas, the terrible condition he found him in and the almost indecipherable things he said, before the final gush of blood spewed from his mouth, and death descended.

''He called no names other than 'George Washington,' which made no sense until I ran across a flatboat with that name on it. I went aboard and had a little prayer meeting with the men on board, and one of them all but said he'd killed Cephas. Called him 'that nigger.' ''

''This fellow who said that, young or old?''

''Youngest of five brothers, if I counted right.''

''That probably would have been Coley, then.''

Bush pulled his horse to a halt. ''What? You know who these men are?''

''I've got a likely notion. I saw that same flatboat myself, you see, and recognized the men on it as some scoundrels from my own parts. Five brothers, name of Morgan. Coley's the youngest.''

''*Was* the youngest.''

''What do you mean?''

''He's dead now.'' Bush described the knife fight and the impalement.

''I'll be!'' Israel whistled softly. ''That's some sorry way to die! But you couldn't have found a more deserving soul than Coley Morgan. Or any of his brothers, for that matter.''

''Tell me what you know about them.''

''Well, they come from the west part of Kentucky, same area I do, and they're a fearful bunch. Their folks died early, so the two eldest, Zachary and Rafe, pretty much raised the younger ones, and taught them all how to be the same kind of hell-demons they are. Them Morgans have stole, robbed, burned down houses and barns, murdered—mostly raped, though. Raped women and stole away more than a few, forcing them to turn whore along the river. It's a sorry gang, I'll tell you.''

Bush halted his horse. ''Mr. Israel . . . Beck, I'd like to learn more about these men. I been hoping to find them, further settle that score over Cephas—though a wise old man told me I ought to let it go. Don't know that I can do that. But right now, you and I need to make a camp and have us a long talk."

When the horses were dealt with and a fire built, a conversation ensued that would leave Bush sleepless for a night, and lock its every word into his memory.

Becker Israel filled a pipe and continued what he'd started. "After Zachary and Rafe Morgan, there's Trey, whose name really is William, but nobody ever calls him that. Juniper's the next to the youngest, and odd as that name sounds, it's the one he was given at birth. Coley, the youngest, has a streak of meanness that goes all the way up him. Or had, I should say, him being dead now."

"When you first gave indication you knew the name of that flatboat gang, I was afraid they were friends of yours."

"In no way, Bushrod. I come from the same part of the country they do. I know how bad them boys are. That's what drew my attention to them when I spotted Trey on that 'George Washington' flatboat."

"Why would they have named their flatboat that way?"

"They probably didn't. None of them would care a stone about George Washington or the nation or nothing like that. They'd probably stole the boat from somebody who'd named it."

"If it hadn't been for that name, I'd never have suspected they were Cephas's killers."

"You know, Bush, you're fortunate to be living. Coley had a reputation as one of the best and meanest knife-fighters on the river."

"He didn't fare too well when he come up against that sawyer stob."

"Best killing the river ever done, and that river's killed thousands, if you count Indians. You reckon they're still on that boat?"

"No. The boat pretty much got ruined on a sandbar. I found it laid up to the bank a day or so later. Abandoned. They'd gone off."

"Took their woman with them, I suppose."

"Must have. There was no one at all aboard when I found it. I saw that woman, by the way, while I was canoeing out to the flatboat. They made her go inside the shelter."

"Dark-haired woman?"

"I believe she was."

"I saw her, too. She was standing near Trey when I first recognized him. I spied them all out with a glass I carry. Pretty gal, she was. Too pretty for the kind of life they're no doubt putting her through. Mighty beautiful." He puffed his pipe. "Only thing wrong with her I could see was a mark, right here, on her neck. Birthmark, I suppose. Funny thing, them birthmarks. The redskins believe they come about because the mother, when she's got the child in her, maybe sees a—hey, there, Bushrod! What's wrong?"

Bush had risen suddenly and lurched away. Bending at the waist, he became sick on the spot. He staggered away a little farther, then sank to his knees, panting, his back toward Israel.

Israel approached Bush slowly, unnerved and mystified by the strange display he just witnessed. He came around Bush and looked at his face. Tears were running down Bush's cheeks, but he was grinning.

"Old Tuckaseh was wrong for once," he said. "He told me I'd have to choose my quest—find Cephas's killers, or find Marie. And now I find out that when I'm looking for one, I'm looking for the other. The same quest!"

"What the deuce are you talking about?"

"The woman you saw—probably the same woman I saw too, though not so clearly as you—I believe she's my sister, Marie."

"Your *sister*?"

"That's right."

"Why do you think that? Oh . . . the birthmark. That it?"

"Right. The only way I'd possibly know her for certain today would be through that birthmark. I ain't laid eyes on Marie since the Coldwater raid."

"Coldwater? The old Indian town that got burned down?"

"That's right. I grew up there, as long as it lasted, anyway."

"Amongst the *savages*?"

"That's right. I'll tell you about it if you want to hear."

"I believe I do."

Bush rose, having collected himself a bit, his color coming back. But he was trembly. Israel might as well have hit him with a club as with the unexpected news of Marie.

"Sorry I spewed up like that," Bush said.

"Think nothing of it. Now get over here and tell me this tale of yours."

Bush returned to the fire and sat down, staring into it. He began to tell his story, from the day Jean-Yves Freneau found him, on through to his recent time in Natchez. He spoke most clearly of his longstanding desire to find his sister, a desire that at times had been an obsession, and other times, when he was discouraged and the trail was cold, a wistful and hopeless longing.

"Cephas and I searched for six years for Marie while we hunted and trapped and such. Did some river work. Asked questions everywhere up and down the river, just in case she really was took captive by whatever river pirates raided that burned-down cabin with the bones beneath it. But we never found a trace, not a sign. I was ready to give up, but Cephas would always tell me I should think her alive until I knew for a fact she was dead. And we just kept going. And then the day he was killed—oh, Lord."

"What?"

"I remember now, among the things he said at the end, just babbling with his mouth full of blood and his mind fading out on him . . . he said something about a woman . . . and a mark. Lord, I see it now! He'd seen her, Beck, on that boat! And seen the mark on her neck and knew it was Marie! He must have been getting ready to come back and tell me when the Morgans caught him."

"So what do you aim to do now?"

"I reckon I aim to find my sister. If they've forced her to sell herself—Lord, what kind of hell has she been living in!"

Israel tossed a twig he'd been toying with into the fire, and cleared his throat. "Bushrod Underhill, I don't know you and you don't know me, but I know your character from how you stepped in and helped me out in that fight, not to mention that you used to run with Cephas Frank. That speaks well of you right there. And I know the Morgans, what they are. They were a terror in Kentucky for years. Folks there were glad when they left and took to the river."

"What are you getting at, Becker?"

"That if you're willing, I'd be glad to help you look for the Morgans and your sister."

"You mean that?"

"I got nothing better to do."

Bush scratched his chin. "Why do you even care?"

"I told you, I know the Morgans. And I've known families who suffered because of them. I despise them, body and soul."

Bush said, "I'd be proud for you to help me, Becker."

"Partners, then."

"Reckon so."

And so they searched, as Bush and Cephas had searched before, months rolling upon months, mile upon mile. There was a difference this time, though. This time Bush *knew*.

Marie was out there. Alive, though in the company of wicked men. But men he'd seen, spoken with, and could identify. These new certainties added fuel to Bush's furnace, and he pushed the search like never before.

Finally, they found the Morgans' trail, but with a disappointing end. The Morgans, they learned, were gone from the river country, back to their native Kentucky. They made such retreats periodically, Bush and Israel discovered, and how long they were gone was always unpredictable.

Bush was ready to go into Kentucky after them, but Israel dissuaded him. In the vastness of the Kentucky mountains there was no hope of finding the Morgans. "They'll come back to the river, Bush," Israel said. "And when they do, we'll find their trail again. And we'll find *her*."

"And in the meantime, what? I'm supposed to sit on my rump-end while my sister may still be their captive?"

"We can't help Marie until we find her, and we can't find her until the Morgans come back to the river country. In the meantime, I hear there's fine country up on the Missouri River. I'd like to take a look, maybe set a trap or two. Old Dan Boone himself is living up there these days, with all kinds of his kin. It's good country. What do you think, Bushrod?"

"I can't just stop looking for her, Beck."

"We ain't stopping. We're waiting, like hunters at a blind. You have to face the facts: we'll never find the Morgans in their own mountains, where there's people who'll protect out of kinship. Or fear. Come with me, Bush. Let's go up the Missouri River a bit. Do some trapping and make ourselves some money. We'll journey to St. Louis real frequent, and when we're there, we'll ask questions and such, and if the Morgans are back working the river, we'll learn it. And who knows? Maybe we'll run across some part of Marie's trail in the Missouri country. Somebody who can tell us something. There's a lot of people heading into that country these days, coming in from all over."

Bush thought it over. It was frustrating, thinking of idling along, waiting, still with his questions unanswered. But Beck made sense. Effort would do no good if it was misdirected.

Bush nodded. "Let's go see that Missouri country, Beck."

PART III

EARTH OF EDEN

CHAPTER TWENTY-SEVEN

*The Territory of Upper Louisiana, future state of Missouri,
early 19th century*

Bush had just set the trap in the shallows of the stream when
a rifle ball struck him. It felt like the wallop of a club against
his shoulder, a numb and burning sensation. The shot came
from the edge of a wooded grove behind him. The worst of it
was, the bullet knocked Bush down and made him step into
his own trap, which bit into his left ankle and would not let
go.

As many years as he'd been out of the society of Indians,
Bush still carried their legacy, and thus did not yell despite
the intensity of the pain. He slammed his hands down in front
to catch himself, then turned his head to see who had shot at
him.

He caught a glimpse of a young man, looking at him from
the woods. Sandy hair, light whiskers, coat made of buckskin.
Bush took in all he could see of the fellow and branded it into
his mind, because unless this fellow had shot him fatally, or
planned on finishing the job, Bush had a few words to
exchange with him.

The young man drew back into the woods and vanished.
He made quite a lot of noise running away. Well, Bush
thought, he didn't come out and shoot me again, anyway.

He forgot the young man at once and turned his attention
to his predicament. The rifle ball had entered his right shoulder, nipping through the fleshy bulge just above his bicep. It
was bleeding like the devil, but he didn't think the ball had
lodged, just ripped right on through.

The ankle was a greater worry. A trap could damage a

man's muscle and bone, and, if left clamped on long enough, cut off the blood flow, leading to putrefaction and loss of limb or life. Bush had no ambition to lose either just yet.

Slowly he turned, seeking a position that would allow him to reach his trapped foot. The pain was worsening fast. His biggest concern was fainting, falling back in the stream, and maybe drowning, suffering precisely the fate of the creatures the trap was intended for. He finally came to a seated posture, the knee of the trapped leg bent up before him, the other outstretched, helping balance and steady him in the water.

He touched the trap, looking for a place to grip it and pry it open. But just touching the trap moved its jaws enough to make him weak with pain. Bush closed his eyes, biting his lip, as the water around him began to grow pink.

He was aware of someone coming. Becker Israel, he hoped. Israel had been out setting traps on a different, nearby stream. It wasn't Israel who was coming, though, but a young black man, dressed in the common garb of a settler.

"Mister, you hold still," the young man said, as he ran up, right into the water, kneeling to examine Bush's trapped ankle. "You hold still, and I'll get that off your leg."

"Obliged."

The black man reached down and gently laid his hands on the squeezing jaws of the trap. Bush winced even at this small jostling. "You're shot, too. I seen it happen. How bad?"

"Not bad, I don't think. I think it may have glanced off my shoulder bone."

"Balls will do that, I know for a fact. Had a brother once had one glance off his skull. Didn't even hurt him beyond busting the skin. He died of the consumption a year later. You brace yourself, sir, and I'll take this off now. You be ready to pull that foot out real fast."

Bush gritted his teeth, steeled himself, and the black fellow pulled open the trap in a single fast motion. Bush lifted out his foot and rolled to the side, overwhelmed by a strange mixture of relief and renewed pain as blood, now fully unencumbered by the clamping trap jaws, rushed into the wounded area.

Bush must have passed out, because he never remembered moving from the stream to the bank. He figured the black man must have carried him. Bush looked around and found himself under a tree, the black fellow having stripped off his own shirt and used it to wrap the injured ankle.

"We'll keep that blood from running out too much, and I'll carry you to Granny," he said. "From the look of it, I believe you were lucky, sir. I don't believe the bone is broke."

"I can try to walk a bit, if you'll support me on my left side."

"Sir, it'd be better if you didn't try. Let me carry you." Before Bush could even respond, the black man moved up, placed one arm under the crook of Bush's knees, the other below his shoulder blades, and lifted him as if he weighed nothing.

"You're a remarkable man," Bush said, fighting light-headedness and a new wave of weakness and pain. "My name's Underhill. What's yours?"

"Macky, sir. Macky Tork. Pleased to know you."

He shifted Bush's weight a little and set out toward the woods, moving almost as fast with his burden as he had when first coming to Bush's aid.

Bush felt rather like a child in the arms of its father, and quite a strange feeling that was. Macky Tork carried him to a small cabin standing at the edge of a copse of trees, surrounded by small, recently cleared fields and a few rugged log outbuildings.

"Granny's inside," Macky Tork said. Amazingly, he was hardly panting despite having run for almost a mile with a grown man in his arms. "If there's anybody can heal you up, it's Granny."

But Bush didn't hear. The pain in his ankle, combined with the loss of blood, rendered him senseless for the moment.

The next sight he beheld was a withered, deeply creviced face, obviously the face of a person long dead, eyes closed and sunken, jaw gone rigid, lips clamped together, skin gone dark. A corpse—a woman's corpse, shriveling away in a homemade, high-backed wooden chair pulled up right next to a bed. Bush himself was on that bed.

He moved, causing a new spasm of pain that made him grunt.

The corpse's eyes opened. Stared at him. For a moment or two, Bush was astonished and more frightened than he'd be proud to confess.

He promptly realized that this was no corpse at all, but a living black woman, very old. Older, maybe, than any person he'd ever met, if he was to judge by looks alone. But she stood without excess effort, and came nearer to him, bending down and looking into his face with those sunken eyes. Bush realized that he'd just met Granny.

"You alive and peeping again, sir! I knowed you'd be coming back with us afore long."

"Where am I, ma'am? Is this Macky's cabin?"

"Yes, sir. Macky brung you in here, and says, 'Granny, here's one needs to be patched.' So I patched you, sir."

Bush looked down at his ankle, now nicely bandaged with rags, but clean and well-wrapped ones. The pain wasn't bad now. In fact, it was absent. He moved his shoulder, also bandaged, and found it didn't hurt, either. "You did a fine job. Thank you."

The door opened and Macky walked in. Seeing Bush was awake, he came over and grinned at him. "Hello, Mr. Underhill," he said. "You're looking a lot better already."

"I'm obliged to you, and your grandmother here, too." He eyed the cabin. "Fine house you have."

"Thank you, sir. Built it myself."

"Just you and Mrs. Tork here?"

"Oh, I ain't married. It's just Granny and me."

"That's who I was talking about."

Macky laughed. "Oh, yes, sir! Granny's been just plain Granny so long, I never think of her as 'Mrs. Tork.' Yes, sir, it's just me and Granny, trying to make our way and stay to ourselves."

"You're both free, then."

"That's right, sir. We been free for years, and got the papers to show it. They was writ up by the man who had us, saying that when he was dead, we'd be free, and he's dead now.''

"You said at the creek you saw me shot. Did you see the man who did it?''

"Seen him poking his head out of the woods after, Mr. Underhill.''

"So did I, but he was a stranger to me.''

"Not to me, sir. That was Willie Squire, and it surprised the very fire out of me that he done it, for he don't seem the kind to shoot somebody.''

The old woman sat down slowly in her chair and closed her eyes again. Bush watched her fall asleep within the span of two seconds, as the very elderly often do.

"Squire, eh? I don't know that name.''

"He must have known you, Mr. Underhill. Or maybe thought he did.''

Bush thought it over, mystified. Glancing at his ankle again, he was equally mystified by the lack of pain. "I don't know what your grandmother did to my ankle and my shoulder, but they don't hurt. Not even a little. I don't understand that.''

"I ain't surprised. Granny's good with wounds and sickness. She got the gift of the healing touch, and she knows the secrets of plants and such. But she ain't really my grandmother, sir. My grandmother dead. Granny, she's my dead grandmother's mother.''

"She outlived her own daughter?''

"Yes, sir. And her granddaughter, too. And likely she'll outlive me.''

Bush studied the sleeping old woman's prune of a face. "I doubt that. You seem a young and hardy fellow, and she's getting more than well on in years.''

"Granny knows the secret, though.''

Bush didn't follow that, and let it drop. "You have any idea why this Squire fellow would do such a thing to me, then run off and leave me?''

"No, sir. I'm wondering if he thought you was some enemy of his, shot you, seen he was wrong, got scared and run.''

The old woman awakened as quickly as she'd gone to sleep,

stood, and looked deeply into Bush's face with an utter absence of self-consciousness. She also lacked that wary manner, which members of her race usually displayed in the presence of whites. In this cabin and situation, it was clear that she considered herself in charge.

"Since you're awake, sir," she said, "I believe I'll go on and dose you now. I been thinking about that ankle, fearing it might fester. We need to tonic your life-spark, sir. Make it strong. You'll heal up fine then, with no festering."

She hobbled across the cabin. "What's she going to do?" Bush asked.

"I believe she's fetching the Eden box, sir."

"What's an Eden box?"

Macky didn't answer, because Granny was shuffling back to her chair, holding an item of some sort inside an old cloth sack whose opening was puckered shut with pull ties. It was small, square, and as broad as a hand in width, depth, and height. A box, apparently. And this was confirmed when the old woman opened the sack and pulled it out.

"Fetch me a spoon, Macky," she said as she settled into her seat, the closed box on her lap.

He brought her a wooden spoon, which she laid across her knees. Her gnarled hands curved around the box, touching it almost reverently. She untied a twisted thong that held it shut, and opened it slowly.

Macky, standing behind her, craned his neck to look inside the box, staring as if it contained pure gold. "Not as much of it left now, Granny."

"No, boy," she said. "But enough. Enough."

She picked up the spoon and dipped it into whatever the box held. Macky slipped over to Bush and helped prop him up.

With one hand, the old woman set the box aside onto a stool, and closed the lid. Her other hand held the spoon, on which there was a small heap of what looked like common dirt. Though her hands had vaguely trembled when she was simply sitting in her chair, the hand that now held the spoon was steady as stone.

She stood and walked over to Bush, bringing the spoon toward his lips.

"What is it?"

"Something that will make you heal fast, sir, and maybe do even more for you," Macky replied. "There's life in it."

"Looks like dirt."

"It is dirt."

"I ain't eating a spoon of dirt!"

"Then that ankle may fester and you may lose that leg, sir," Granny said. "This ain't no common dirt. Now open that mouth."

Grudgingly, Bush opened his mouth. The soil had an oddly sweet taste, and went down more easily than he would have supposed.

He slept well that night. The ankle didn't hurt at all.

The old woman put a poultice on Bush's chest after breakfast, and told him to lie still and let it do its work.

Bush could not understand how a chest poultice could have any possible effect on healing an ankle and shoulder, but so far Granny Tork's remedies had been so astonishing that Bush wasn't going to argue with her.

An hour or so after the poultice went on, the old woman came to Bush with a cup that smelled almost as bad as the herbs on his chest. "Drink this," she instructed.

"Why?"

"It'll help you heal." She put the cup to his lips and poured it down him faster than he wanted, almost choking him. Furthermore, the stuff tasted utterly hideous. She smiled when he got it all down.

"Woman, you nigh choked the life out of me!"

"You'd have never took it all if I hadn't poured it down fast. The taste would have sure made you spit it all back out."

"Well, I might have. What's in it, anyway?"

She put up a hand for silence and lifted her head sharply. "Somebody's a-coming this way."

She rose, went to the door, and pushed aside the slide covering the rifle port. Peering out, she nodded. "There he is. I don't know him."

Macky had been outside, but reentered. "Rider coming."

"We done heard him," she said.

Bush listened. "I recognize that horse's rhythm. Is it a white man, tall and thick, dark brown beard and flop hat?"

"It is indeed, sir."

"Becker Israel," Bush said. "That's my friend and partner."

Granny Tork met Israel at the door and let him in. He swept inside quickly, looking at Bush with concern, and then at the poultice with puzzlement. "Bush, did you step in a trap or come down with the ague?"

"Hello, Becker," Bush said. He noticed all at once his tongue was thick. Probably that drink she'd poured down him. "She's got odd ways of patching up a man. She's already fed me a mouthful of dirt and poured some kind of poison down my gullet. But I've felt no pain, Beck."

"Glad to see you alive and healing," Israel said. "I found the sprung trap and blood on the ground, but no tracks of any kind of critter. Then a young fellow comes up and told me that somebody had shot you and drove you into your own trap, and that a nigra fellow name of Tork had come along and helped you out."

"A young fellow—he would have to have seen me carried off by Macky to tell you that."

"Must have been Willie Squire," Macky said. He described Squire to Israel, who nodded.

"Sounds like the one."

"He's the same man who shot me," Bush said.

"What!" Israel exclaimed. "You telling me true?"

"I am. Which makes me wonder why the same man who shot me and left me stuck in my own trap would turn around and tell my partner where to find me."

"If I had to guess, I'd say his conscience got to hurting him," Macky said. "Mr. Squire probably got worried about what he'd done, come back, and seen me carrying you off."

"Why would he have shot Bush to begin with?" Israel asked.

"I can't figure, sir, unless he mistook him for somebody. Mr. Squire's a hard-working man, good farmer, good hunter, brave when there's Indian threats. Got a wife name of Lorry, and a child. Always keep to theirselves, always leave folks alone, but get on good with people when they do have doings with them."

"We'll see how he deals with me when we meet next time," Bush said.

"You aim to avenge yourself, Bush?" Israel asked.

"It ain't a matter of vengeance. It's just that, when somebody shoots me and leaves me lying, I want to know why."

Granny removed the bandages and examined Bush's ankle and shoulder the next day. Bush wasn't worried about the shoulder to begin with, it being no more than a minor wound, but dreaded seeing the ankle. He was stunned to find it healing remarkably well.

Becker Israel had a different response when he saw the wound. "You mean to say you've been laid up here for *that*? If you're so puny as to let nothing but that get you down, Bush, I've got half a mind to find myself a new partner with more gravel in his craw."

"It's the cures what done it, sir," Macky said. If it warn't for Granny, that leg would have festered up and he'd have lost it."

Israel grunted skeptically.

In a way, Bush was glad for Israel's attitude because it gave him grounds to hurry up his exit from the Tork household. Though he was grateful to old Granny for her nursing and obvious care, she was still coming at him regularly with odd concoctions, and after some days he suspected she was beginning to experiment on him.

When the ankle was healed up enough for him to depart with Israel, Bush tried hard to pay the Torks for their care, feeding, and lodging. All offers were firmly refused. At last Bush was able to talk Macky into accepting a skinning knife.

"You come back through here, you stop and see us," Macky said. "Any time at all."

"I'll be seeing you," Bush said. "Beck and me aim to establish a fixed camp hereabouts. Probably build us a stout cabin for wintering over."

CHAPTER TWENTY-EIGHT

Two days later

"That's him, sure enough," Becker Israel whispered to Bush. They were standing in a patch of forest, watching quietly as a young man and woman, apparently man and wife, worked hard with a big double-handled saw, cutting through run after run of logs in the wall of their cabin. Judging from where and how they were cutting the opening, they were preparing to put in a fireplace and chimney. Already a great heap of sticks were laid aside for the chimney, which initially would be made of sticks and mud and probably replaced later by more lasting stone, a typical progression for settlers. "That's the very fellow who told me about how you'd been hurt and where I'd find you."

"That's also the very fellow who shot me," Bush said. "It happened fast, but I did get a good look at his face."

"I reckon that must be his wife."

"Yep. Pretty, ain't she?"

"She is. Too pretty for a scoundrel like him. Well, you going to talk to him or not?"

"He's got his rifle standing close by. I'll wait until he's not close to it. You never know what he might do when he sees a man he's shot once already coming at him out of the woods. Especially with a big ugly savage like you with him."

"Huh. Funny man, you are."

The opportunity came when the young man entered the woods to answer a call of nature, leaving his young wife back at the house. Bush glanced her way and noticed a toddler come around from behind the cabin and race away toward the woods, laughing. The young woman went after the child. For the moment, both Squires were out of reach of the rifle.

"Let's go pay a call," Bush said.

When Willie Squire came out of the woods, hitching up his trousers, he froze in place to see two woodsmen waiting for him, and his wife out of sight. He went pale when he saw Bush.

"Mr. Squire!" Israel boomed abruptly, very loudly. "A word with you!"

Squire looked stunned and said nothing, his eyes flitting about, looking for his wife.

"You remember me, Mr. Squire?" Israel said.

"Yes, I—"

"You told me where I could find my friend, who'd been shot. I did find him. I also found out you didn't tell me how he come to be shot, and who'd done it!"

Squire looked like a trapped rat, glancing toward his rifle, which was well out of reach.

Bush stepped forward. "Mr. Squire, since we've last met, I've heard some good things about you, believe it or not. Which raises the question of why you shot me, and why you left me with my foot in a trap."

Squire swallowed. "It was a mistake. I'm sorry."

"Right big mistake," Israel said. "Do you usually go shooting at strangers from hiding?"

"I didn't think he was a stranger. I thought he was someone else. And after I shot him, and realized my mistake, it scared me . . . I ran off. But I came back almost right away. And I saw Macky Tork carrying him away."

"How'd you know to tell me about him when I showed up?"

"Because of where you were, looking along the stream. I guessed you were looking for him, and apparently I was right, you two being together now."

"Who did you think I was, anyway?" Bush asked.

Squire seemed reluctant to answer. "I thought you were a man name of Juniper Morgan."

Bush and Israel stood wordlessly for a moment. Then an

inhuman-sounding voice screeched behind them, and something hit them from behind, knocking them to the ground.

Willie Squire reached his rifle before Bush and Israel had time
to realize that what had struck them from behind was Squire's
wife. The men scrambled away from the wild woman, while
Willie Squire cocked his rifle and the child squalled in terror.

"Lorry, get away from them!" Squire yelled. "And you
two, hold still where you are."

Israel, now on his knees, had managed to swing up his own
rifle, however, and barked back at Squire: "Drop that rifle, or
I'll kill you."

Bush leaped to his feet, waving his hands. "No! No! Nobody shoots anybody—please!"

Israel said, "I'll put my rifle down if he will."

Squire said, "I want to know your intentions before I do a
thing. I've got a wife and child to protect here."

Bush said, "Our intentions aren't vengeance. Just information—especially after what I just heard you say."

"What do you mean?"

"The name you said. Juniper Morgan."

Squire looked from Bush to Israel and back again. "That
name means something to you?"

"It does indeed."

"You *are* a Morgan, ain't you! I thought I saw the Morgan
look in your face!"

"God only knows I hope I bear no resemblance at all to
those foul devils, if it's the same Morgan family we're talking
about, and surely it is. I'm no Morgan. My name is Bushrod
Underhill. Now, please, both of you, let's lower those rifles
and set them aside. We've got some talking to do."

The three men conversed through lingering tension and mis-
trust.

"You said you mistook me for Juniper Morgan," Bush said
to Squire. "I know such a man, or know of him. Does the
Juniper Morgan you speak of have brothers?"

Squire glanced at his wife. Just a flick of the eyes. "No. No brothers."

"It's hard to believe there would be two men with such a name as Juniper. The Juniper Morgan I'm aware of is from Kentucky and has four brothers. Well, three now. One's dead."

Bush saw Squire twitch a little at the news, saw his lips begin to form the question *Which one?*, then saw him catch himself just in time. And Bush knew then that Willie Squire was building a false front.

Another glance between the two Squires. "Not the same, then. The Juniper Morgan I know is from Virginia."

"You're sure of this?"

"I should be. Juniper Morgan from Virginia murdered my brother."

"Ah! I see. I'm sorry." Bush shook his head. "Amazing that there would be two men, both of them scoundrels, with such an odd name."

"I hope you can see why I'd take a shot at someone I thought was Juniper Morgan."

Bush thought about it. "I can."

"I'm very sorry I did it. And sorry I didn't act more proper after it. I shouldn't have run. I should have gone straight to you and helped you. I did come back, I did. But Macky Tork had already come by then."

"Yes." A pause. "There's no question that the Morgan you know has no brothers?"

"No question." Squire looked at his visitors. "That all you need to know?"

"I reckon," Bush said.

"You seem disappointed," Squire said.

"I've been looking for Juniper Morgan—the one I know—and his brothers for a long time. My situation is a bit like yours, Mr. Squire. I lost someone, not a brother, but a partner who was close as a brother, to the Morgan brothers. A murder. As best I can tell, it wasn't Juniper who committed it, but some of his brothers. One, I'm sure, was Coley Morgan, the youngest. The other Morgan brothers are named—"

"Please," Squire said, too abruptly. "There's no need for you to tell things that trouble you on our account."

Bush stared at the man, trying to understand him. "Very well. But I'll add this: It's my belief that the Morgan brothers had, maybe still have, my own sister in their company. Maybe against her will. Maybe involving her in things the thought of which *does* trouble me indeed. And that, sir, is my reason for such interest in the name Juniper Morgan. And if it should ever come to mind that maybe the Juniper Morgan you know is, after all, one of the brothers I'm looking for, and if you should learn where I might find them, I hope you'll do the kindness of telling me."

Squire looked down. "I think we've probably said all we need to say to one another, sir."

"Good day to you, sir. Ma'am."

"Good day."

When Bush and Israel were away from the cabin, Bush said, "He's lying, Beck. You and I both know there's not two Juniper Morgans walking this globe. You saw the way he and the woman both twitched and glanced when I named the other Morgan brothers. And how quick he cut me off before I could even voice the names of Zachary and Rafe. He didn't even want to hear those names spoken."

"Or maybe didn't want his wife to."

"What are you thinking, Beck?"

"That the Morgans, being the kind they are, have hurt a lot of women in their time. Maybe Squire's wife is one of them. Maybe he didn't want her being reminded of it by hearing the name of the one who done it."

Bush and Israel began to put up their own cabin the next day, only a couple of miles from both the Tork place and the Squire homestead. It would be basic, not hewn or even barked, its purpose being to serve a function, not provide a home in any domestic sense. The two woodsmen had long since ceased to think of any particular plot of land or collection of walls as "home." Home was the open country, wherever they might be.

As they worked on the cabin over the next several days, Bush could see that Israel was growing agitated with him. He didn't blame him much. Bush's mind was far away, not on his work, and often his ax would fall silent as he cut a tree or notched a log; he would drift off into reverie, his work coming to a halt for the duration.

He couldn't stop thinking about the Squires, and the obvious fact that they knew something about the Morgan brothers. Willie Squire's lies were obvious, and it was eating at Bush's mind, wondering what the truth was.

What if Willie Squire knew something about the Morgans that could lead Bush to them, and to Marie? Might he know their location by now? Did the fact that he mistook Bush for Juniper Morgan mean he had some reason to believe the Morgans to be in this very vicinity? The country was opening fast; there was no reason the Morgans might not be among the new influx of citizens. Scoundrels often followed the growing edge of the frontier.

These thoughts dominated Bush's mind, keeping him quiet, preoccupied, and of little help to his partner in cabin-building. When the cabin was at last finished, Israel had had enough. He was weary of the labor, irritated at Bush and about ready to find a new partner, or maybe do without one. Hang it, maybe he'd just go find a woman and get married, build a proper cabin, and leave worthless Bush Underhill alone with his daydreams!

Bush held his silence while his partner launched his justifiable complaints. But when Israel was finished, it was evident that Bush hadn't heard much of what he'd said.

His mind was drifting off again, sailing into the sky like an eagle, looking down over a vast wilderness, looking for his lost sister.

A day later, Bush had a fever. He hardly knew what to make of it—he'd been laid up with injuries more times than he liked to recall, but sickness had always been almost totally alien to him.

He didn't like the feeling. "I'm going to see Granny Tork,"

he told Israel. ''Likely she'll have something that can put me right again.''

''You really believe in that crazy old woman's cures?''

''I know that I recovered from a wounded ankle and shoulder with hardly a twinge of pain. I don't question what works.''

Bush, recalling that Jean-Yves Freneau used to ''walk out'' his occasional fevers, chose to walk rather than ride to the Tork cabin. By the time he got there he was exhausted, drenched in sweat. The old woman, who loved to tackle a sickness the way most people craved fresh honey on new-baked bread, was delighted.

''Set down right here, Mr. Bush,'' she said, pointing to a stool. ''I got something that'll have you right before morning.''

It tasted as foul as it smelled. Nevertheless, Bush submitted to it, then begged for water. Three dippers later, he said, with a shudder, ''I think I like the fever better.''

''You just wait. You'll feel it working in you this very evening.''

''Where's Macky, Granny?''

''You don't know? He's took off on a long winter hunt up the river. He and Willie Squire together.''

''I didn't know. So you're left here alone? And Squire's wife, too?''

''That's true.''

Bush frowned. He didn't think Macky had done right, leaving such an old woman to fare through a winter by herself. Then again, Granny Tork seemed stronger than most folks half her age, and certainly didn't appear worried about the prospect of getting by on her own.

''Tell you what, Granny. I'll look in on you from time to time, if you don't mind. Maybe bring you some meat and such now and again.''

''I'd surely be obliged, Mr. Bush. Not that I can't hunt my own meat.''

Bush grinned, hoping he'd do so well in his own old age, assuming he made it that far. ''I'm sure you can, but with just me and Beck to feed, we'll often have more than we need. In fact, why don't you just let us throw up an extra room on our little cabin—it's not much, but it's stout—and you come stay right there with us while Macky's gone?"

"Thank you, Mr. Bush, but I like my own home."

"I worry about the Indian troubles some are seeing lately. You may be safer with somebody else about."

"I can fight and shoot, and if any Indian kills me, I'm ready to go. Me and Jesus got to be good friends many years back."

"Well, I will look in, though."

"I'll always be glad to see you, Mr. Bush."

As promised, Bush was fine by morning. He was up before Israel even quit snoring on his cot in the corner, cooking up pork and biscuits for breakfast. He went over and kicked Israel awake.

"Get your lazy hide up, Beck. You and me got a short trip to make."

Beck sat up, rubbing his face. "Where to?"

"Going to visit Mrs. Squire."

"With her husband away?"

"I told Granny Tork I'd be looking in on her. No reason not to do the same for Squire's missus. And there is that child of theirs, too. I'd hate for them to be in want of anything with nobody around to help them."

"I suspect you got more reason than that."

"Now, look, Beck, I know she's a pretty woman, but she's a married woman, too."

"I ain't talking about that. I'm talking about the Morgan business. You're hoping she'll talk out a little more, with her husband gone."

"If she does, all the well. If not, I'm just being a good neighbor. Now get up and eat. I'm feeling prime today, and eager to move."

CHAPTER
TWENTY-NINE

It was not the reception Bushrod had expected.

Based on that one prior call to the Squire home, Bush had anticipated that Lorry Squire might be downright hostile, at best cold and unwelcoming, when he and Israel showed up. Instead she seemed happy, even relieved, to see them.

"Ma'am," Bush said, tipping his flop hat and dismounting well away from the cabin. She'd come to the door as they rode up, with a rifle in hand, but she set it aside as soon as she saw who they were. "I was visiting with Granny Tork, and she told me that her Macky and your Willie have gone off hunting together. Mr. Israel and me thought it might be neighborly to stop by here and just ask if there was anything by way of victuals and such you might be lacking."

"We're well-fixed for now, but I'm glad you came by," she said. "I've had it in mind that we need to talk a bit more than what passed between us the other day."

Bush glanced at Israel, who looked as surprised as he did. "Ma'am, it struck me that such things were delicate matters to you and your husband."

"Yes . . . but maybe more so to him, in some ways, than to me. And what you said about your sister has weighed on my mind. I must talk to you. If you hadn't come here, I would have come to find you, while Willie was away."

"He'd object, you think, to you talking to us?"

"It doesn't matter, Mr. Underhill. It's something I must do."

Bush glanced again at Israel, whose look said, clearly as

words: *We should leave. If the husband would object to further talk on that matter, then we should honor that.*

Bush knew he was right. He also knew that he couldn't turn away from information that might pertain to Marie's captors. He nodded at Lorry Squire. "Would you wish to talk out here, ma'am?"

"It's cool. Come inside. Sariah is asleep, so we'll speak quietly."

Israel frowned at Bush. Here they were, entering the house of a married woman in the absence of her husband. If neighbors were within eyeshot . . .

But Bush led the way and Israel trailed in after. They sat down on a bench against the wall as Lorry Squire pulled up a three-legged stool and quite elegantly settled herself onto it.

"Mr. Underhill, what Willie said to you the last time you were here wasn't fully true. In fact, much of it was false. The Juniper Morgan he mistook you for and the Juniper Morgan who is one of the brothers you've been seeking are one and the same, despite what Willie claimed."

"Not trying to question your husband's honesty, ma'am, but I suspected the same. The name's too odd for more than one to have it."

"He had reasons for not wanting to discuss the Morgan brothers. Even to talk about them brings a great suffering to him. He hates them that deeply. Most of the reason we left Kentucky and came here was because of the Morgans. They stay on the river most of the time, as I understand it, but sometimes they come back into Kentucky, around the area they grew up in. The same area we lived in. And Willie and I both knew that if we were in Kentucky and the Morgans showed up, he'd do just what he tried to do when he thought you were Juniper. He'd kill one of them. Or maybe get himself killed."

"I understand his feelings," Bush said. "If my brother was murdered, I'd be the same way."

"He had no brother murdered. That was another lie. He said that because it's easier to talk of murder than of . . . rape."

"Oh."

"Willie's sister, you see, was raped by one of the Morgans. The eldest one, Zachary. Did you notice how Willie cut you off before you could call Zachary Morgan's name?"

"I did."

"He didn't want the name spoken in his presence. That's how deep his hatred for the Morgans is."

Bush glanced at Israel, who'd reached that exact conclusion after the first visit to the Squire place. Bush remembered Israel's other speculation as well—that the Morgans might have molested Lorry Squire—and hoped he wasn't equally on the mark with that one.

"Ma'am, what do you know of the Morgans' whereabouts these days? Did your husband have reason to think they were in the area, and thus was quick to mistake me for one of them?"

"No. As last we heard, the Morgans have returned to Kentucky. And all I can say is, God help the people of Kentucky. But I'm grateful they aren't here. Believe me, if there were any reason to think they were, Willie would have never gone hunting with Macky Tork."

"How long will they be gone? A full winter?"

"I don't think so. Willie becomes worried after a time, and he'll come back to make sure all is well with us. But I'm glad he went. He needs to get away from people, and let his mind clear. He stays full of hate and anger because of what the Morgans did to—," she paused oddly, as if catching something before it could escape her lips, and said, "his sister."

"And how is Willie's sister now?" Bush asked. "After such an awful thing, is she well?"

Lorry Squire's eyes suddenly filled with tears. "Sometimes she is," she said. "Sometimes."

As they rode away, Israel said, "It's her, you know. Not any sister."

"I know," Bush said. "I suspected it before, and knew it for a surety when those tears came up."

Israel leaned over and spat on the earth, then ground his teeth as he did when angry. "It makes me hot inside, thinking of such devils treating such a lovely woman in that way. I understand how her husband hates them so.''

"Beck, you think that baby could be—''

"No, no. She'd hate the child, surely. She'd see it as Zachary Morgan's child.''

"Maybe not,'' Bush said. "Maybe she'd just see it as her own.''

"She's mighty lovely, ain't she?''

"She is.''

"That Willie Squire's got himself a woman any man would be glad to have for a wife.''

"So he does. Indeed.''

Over the next weeks, Bush spent much of his time hunting; most of the meat went to Granny Tork and Lorry Squire, until finally Granny bade him stop bringing her so much. An old woman by herself could hardly eat half of what Bush was providing.

So Bush just took more to the Squire cabin. Soon, Lorry Squire was even more overstocked than Granny Tork, but unlike her, didn't ask Bush to stop coming. She seemed glad for every visit, and the way she smiled at Bush brought sunlight into every dark place inside him.

And guilt. He knew it was wrong. He was falling in love with a woman already married.

He should stay away, he knew. Send Beck Israel to bring the victuals and so on in his place. But he didn't stay away.

What puzzled him was the manner of Lorry herself. She seemed quite an upright, decent woman. More than once he found her reading a well-worn Bible when he came by. Furthermore, the embroidered samplers on her wall all quoted scriptures and moral dictums.

This was not the kind of woman to let herself become romantically entwined with someone who wasn't her husband. And yet there was never anything in her manner to suggest the slightest hint of guilt on her part for the obvious encouragement she was giving Bushrod to pursue her.

He got on well with little Sariah, too. He'd not been around children much in his years, and the blonde little beauty was a delight to him, which was novel and satisfying. He began carving her little toys, and making dolls out of rags and bits of hide to give her whenever he stopped by.

"You've got to put an end to this, Bush," Israel told him time and again.

"I know," Bush said. "But I can't. I can't do it, Beck."

"You're in love with a married woman."

"I know. I know."

"It's wrong."

"I know."

Yet he kept coming back. He was glad Jean-Yves, who'd been as moralistic as a preacher when it came to fidelity, wasn't around to see this. Or Tuckaseh. Though the Indians had quite an easygoing attitude about relationships between men and women prior to marriage, they were sternly rigid after marriage occurred. Adultery was a serious offense.

So far it hadn't come to that with Bush and Lorry. And he had no plan to try to take the matter in that direction. To cross that line would cause such a hopeless quagmire of emotion and moral issues that he'd never find his way out again. And he wouldn't for any reason destroy the marriage of a young woman he cared as deeply about as Lorry.

Still, he just couldn't stay away. Weeks rolled by and he was still visiting.

Before long, he knew, Willie Squire would be home, and it would be over. He wondered just how Squire would react when he found out who'd been caring for his family in his absence, and with what intensity and depth of interest.

Bush was cutting wood in Lorry's yard on a late December day when Beck Israel rode in, his horse dripping lather despite the cold. He came down from the saddle even before the horse could reach a full stop.

"Bush, you got to come. And bring the woman."

"What's wrong?"

"It's Willie Squire. He was found an hour ago by the river, on up a good distance. He's been shot, and the fever has done set in. When I left him he was talking out of his head.''

"Dear Lord . . . who's with him?''

"A hunter, same one who found him. I stumbled upon the both of them maybe ten minutes after he'd found Squire.''

As they rode swiftly along, Lorry Squire's face was as colorless as the winter-gray clouds that stretched from horizon to horizon. Bush held young Sariah in his arms, balancing her while still expertly guiding his horse. Beck Israel was ahead, leading them. Bush heard Lorry whispering prayers as they hurried along.

When they reached the place, they found the hunter had constructed a quick blanket shelter around Squire. As soon as Bush saw Squire's face, he knew death was inevitable. There was a blue-gray look around his eyes that was too deeply set to ever be removed. Lorry Squire looked at him and put her hand over her mouth, and Bush knew that she realized the same thing he had.

"Oh, Willie!'' she said, dropping to her knees at his side. "Oh, Willie . . . who did this to you?''

To Bush's amazement, the eyes slowly opened. Willie Squire looked up at Lorry, then over at Bush, then back again at Lorry. His voice was a whisper. "It was the Morgans . . . Juniper, and Trey.''

Bush felt something cut into his hands. He looked down and realized it was his own fingernails, digging into his palm because he'd just squeezed his fists together so tightly. He, too, came down to his knees at Squire's side. "You're certain?''

"Yes . . . saw them clear . . . it was Trey who shot me.''

"Where's Macky Tork?''

"Shot him . . . too . . . but he got away . . . going to his house . . . medicine from Granny . . . says it will make us live . . .''

"How long since he left?''

"Don't know . . . been passed out some . . . Mr. Underhill, go after him . . . I think the Morgans followed him.''

*　　*　　*

Bush rode with his head low, eyes scanning the ground. Macky's sign was obvious, and even a neophyte tracker couldn't have missed the stains of blood that marked the way with ever-increasing frequency.

The Morgans were *here!* Was it chance, or had they come for a reason? What could have drawn them?

The possibility that came to mind made his stomach feel like it was full of broken glass. *Maybe they came looking for Lorry. Maybe Zachary Morgan had enjoyed what he did so much that he came looking for more.*

He found Macky not five minutes later, and as he dismounted, knew the finding came too late. Macky lay crumpled on the ground, face down, eyes and mouth half open. His hands were extended forward, as if he'd died crawling, and the sign he'd left behind him indicated he had. Bush looked up. Macky had died within view of his own cabin.

With the heaviest of hearts, Bush bent and picked up the limp, dead-weight form, and carried Macky toward the home he'd not quite reached.

Poor Granny Tork. He dreaded telling her. This time, she was about to face something that even she couldn't overcome, and no herb or magic box of soil could cure.

He reached the cabin door and gently laid Macky down. He'd not let Granny learn the grim truth by seeing the corpse of her only remaining loved one. He'd tell her first.

Bush knocked. "Granny Tork! It's Bushrod Underhill!"

No reply came.

"Granny? Are you in there?"

He thought he heard something, the faintest of groans.

Bush shoved open the door. She was on the floor, bloodied and beaten, her clothing ripped and her withered back exposed. They'd tormented her terribly, kicking her, hitting her. There were the marks of burns, as if they'd knocked out hot pipe ashes on her. The cabin was ransacked. Granny's precious dried herbs pulled down and scattered. Crocks and baskets and bottles broken and crushed and emptied.

She was alive, though, and groping for that same box from which she'd given Bush that bite of soil.

Bush rushed to her. "Granny, don't move. There might be bones broken."

"Box . . . the box . . ."

He reached over and got it. In the midst of pain she smiled, and it was ghastly to see. "Open it . . . put some between my lips . . ."

"Granny, it's too late for such things. You need to see a real physician."

"Please . . . between my lips . . ."

He pinched up some of the soil and did as she said. Her tongue pulled it in and her gums worked around the soil. He saw her throat move as she swallowed it.

"Granny, I'll get you help."

"No . . . no . . . if I'm to live . . . I'll live now . . . because of the box."

"Granny, it's nothing but a box of dirt."

"If I die . . . Mr. Bush . . . give the box to Macky . . ."

She doesn't know, he thought. *They didn't tell her. Thank God at least for that.* And he wouldn't tell her either, not if her death was coming as quickly as Bush believed. There was no reason for her to leave the world burdened with the knowledge that her beloved great-grandson had died at the hands of the same fleshly demons who had killed her.

"Rest, Granny. Close your eyes and rest."

She did. He held her hand in his and cradled her head on his lap. He forced himself not to weep, though he felt like it. The tears would not please her, he thought.

They remained that way, silent, for five minutes or more. Her eyes were tightly closed and Bush was sure they would never reopen when—they did.

"Granny?"

"I'm not going . . . to live, Mr. Bush. I can . . . tell."

"Hush, Granny. No need to talk."

"No . . . no . . . need to tell you. The box . . . if you can't give to Macky for some reason . . . if he don't come back from his hunt . . . then you keep it."

"I will. I will."

"Once a year, Mr. Bush . . . once a year, first of the year

. . . take you one bite of that soil . . . long as it lasts. And you'll live . . . live like I have . . . for a long, long stretch of years.''

Surely she was going out of her head, talking nonsense. But he held her tight and nodded. "I will. I promise."

"It's the Eden soil, Mr. Bush . . . the very last of the true earth of Eden . . . no more to be had in this world . . ."

Earth of Eden? Impossible! But again, Bush wasn't going to argue with an old and dying woman.

"There's life and healing in that soil, Mr. Bush . . . same soil that fed . . . the Tree of Life . . . same soil as Adam trod . . . same soil as God gathered and made into the form of man . . . treasure that soil, Mr. Bush. For when it's gone . . . there's no more."

"Yes, Granny. Yes. Now you rest, you rest . . ."

She closed her eyes. "I'm old, Mr. Bush . . . too old now even for . . . the Eden box to save me."

He held her a little tighter.

"I'm going on now," she whispered. And she did.

CHAPTER THIRTY

The posse was small, consisting of Bush, Israel, and the hunter who'd found Squire, an overly cocky man named Joe Milliard. They made a quick attempt to round up others, but because there'd been a mild Indian scare the day before, the two men they were able to reach were unwilling to leave their homes. There was no time to search for others.

Otherwise, Luck had been good. The two Morgans, probably not expecting that anyone would find their victims before they were far away, hadn't moved fast; Bush's posse had soon picked up their trail. Now the trail was showing signs they were moving faster, indicating they'd realized pursuers were closing in on them.

Willie Squire had managed to share a bit more information before slipping into a coma from which he obviously would not emerge. Trey and Juniper Morgan had been alone, and once they'd recognized Willie Squire, had toyed with him cruelly after wounding him. The other Morgans were camped on an island farther down the river, Trey had said, but they'd surely be back, all of them—and Zachary would be mighty pleased to meet up with Lorry again. They'd tried to glean from Willie and Macky where Lorry was to be found, but both had resisted hard, and neither had told.

Bush knelt and examined the ground, then rose and climbed back onto his horse. "They've come through here, no question about it, and not long ago." Bush looked around, then pointed at a rocky knoll nearby. "I don't know we'd be wise to circle that there knoll. They've seen us by now, and may be thinking ambush. Or maybe just to hide until we go by. Either way, I don't believe they're on the move anymore. I believe they're yonder, up there.''

"I suggest we consider taking a different approach than they expect us to, then,'' Israel said. "Like maybe up and around the back of the knoll.''

"We'd be wasting our time,'' Milliard contributed. "There's three of us, two of them. They won't be thinking ambush. They'll be trying to make it back to that island, where they've got the others to reinforce them.''

"Well, I'll say this: I'm not willing to risk a rifle ball to the head by riding through there without knowing they're not on that knoll,'' Bush said. "I don't consider it wasted time to explore a likely possibility.''

"Gents, you want to go poking in hiding places, you go ahead. But in the meantime, watch me,'' Milliard said. "When I pass through there safe, you'll know I was right.''

"Don't try it, Mr. Milliard,'' Israel said.

"You'll be thanking me in a moment,'' the surprisingly cocky woodsman said.

"Mr. Milliard, I have to insist that you—''

Milliard had already turned his horse and rode out at a good clip onto the clearing in the trail that had brought them up short. Bush and Israel watched him, unhappy that he'd done such a risky thing, but curious about what would happen.

"I believe he's going to make it, Beck,'' Bush said.

"So he was right and we were wrong.''

"Believe so.''

Milliard, once clear of the knoll and positioned so that he couldn't be hit even if anyone hidden up there did take a shot, wheeled his horse and waved at his companions.

"Well, let's go,'' Israel said.

"I don't like it,'' Bush replied.

"Bush, they didn't take a shot.''

"They're up there. I can feel it.''

"Bush, are we following tracks, or feelings? Come on. Let's go on across.''

Bush hesitated, then said, "What the devil. Let's go.''

They rode out—and Bush knew it was a mistake a half-second before the first shot fired.

Beck Israel grunted and grabbed at his right calf. Bush set his own horse into a run, and slapped the rump of Israel's as he passed. The men raced forward, heads low.

Milliard, seeing what had happened, leaped from his own horse, came back into the clear space, dropped to a knee and raised his rifle.

"No!" Bush yelled at him. "You'll never hit them from that angle!"

Another shot cracked from the top of the knoll. Milliard took the ball through the upper chest, fell back, and died with a long, loud sighing noise.

Bush and Israel made it across and dismounted.

"How bad?" Bush asked, peering through the bare treetops toward the knoll top.

"Bad enough," Israel replied. "I should have trusted those feelings you were talking about."

"You should have, that's true. But you didn't. And now it's two of us against two of them, and one of us wounded."

"What do you think, Bush?"

"I think you ought to position yourself behind that there oak tree, and keep your eye on that notch in the rocks up there. If they try to come down, they'll probably have to pass through it. Meantime, I'm going up the back."

"Against both of them?"

"That's right. But I'll need Milliard's rifle. And it's out there in the clear. I want to be able to get off two quick shots."

"Don't go after that rifle. They'll plug a hole through you. Look on Milliard's saddle there. There's a pistol."

Bush had it in hand almost as quickly as he'd seen it. "Wish me luck," he said, and set off around toward the rear base of the knoll.

Ten minutes later, Bush was wondering if he'd wasted his time. He'd heard no shots from below to indicate that the Morgans had moved through the notch in the rocks. Israel would have shot at them if they had. So they were still there—

but Bush hadn't caught even a glimpse, and was growing nervous about getting much closer.

There! A flash of movement in the rocks—and then again. Bush ducked his head for a better angle of view. Yes, a face, looking down the slope in his general direction, perhaps suspecting—

Another shot, and a rifle ball spanged off the stones in front of Bush. He dropped, but only a moment. Coming up with his rifle, he took aim swiftly, waited for his moment, and fired.

The face he'd seen disappeared, but not before he saw the clean, black dot that marked the place where his rifle ball had entered the man's forehead.

Bush went back down under cover again, and wondered which Morgan he'd killed.

"Trey!" a voice called above. "Trey, you hit?"

So that was the one. Trey Morgan was a dead man now, thanks to Bush Underhill. He had no relish for killing in itself, but on this occasion, remorse was hard to find.

He anticipated quick action by the remaining Morgan. A shot from the other side of the hill told him that Israel had found his opportunity. Bush came up and advanced up the hill, holding the pistol in his right hand, the empty rifle in his left, keeping low but moving fast. He knew Israel's skill as a marksman and was reasonably certain that he'd hit Juniper Morgan. But suddenly another shot sounded, this one from Morgan.

Bush wasn't sure, but he thought he heard a yell from the other side of the hill.

Throwing aside caution now, he ran up the slope, but Juniper Morgan wasn't there. He'd made it through the notch in the rocks. Bush leaped up into it, looked over, saw Juniper Morgan running, partially sliding, down.

"Morgan!" Bush yelled.

Morgan lost his footing and rolled the rest of the way down, somehow keeping hold of his rifle, but it was empty, having just been fired at Israel below. Morgan leaped to his feet at the bottom. Bush aimed the pistol at him and fired, but the pistol was poorly aligned and the ball sang wide, to the right.

Juniper Morgan halted and turned, pointing up the hill at Bush. "Don't think I don't know you, whore-son! You've took two of my brothers from me now, and for that you'll pay!"

Bush was already reloading his rifle. Juniper continued railing and cursing, moving steadily away, but not fast enough. Bush swung the rifle up as soon as it was loaded and leveled it on Morgan.

A dive to the right saved the Morgan family from one more bereavement that day. Juniper Morgan, stung by the grit flung up by Bush's shot, scrambled away, flinging a final curse Bush's way.

Bush went down the hill after him, losing his footing in about the same spot Morgan had. But he deftly came up on his feet at the bottom, rifle in reloading position. He was ramming the ball in place, ready to set out after Morgan, when he heard Israel call to him in a pain-filled voice.

Bush looked at Morgan, disappearing now over a small ridge, then over at Israel, and knew the chase was, for now, ended.

Israel had been hit again. This time the ball had clipped through the side of his neck, not lodging but going fairly deep, and he was bleeding profusely.

Bush ran to the dead body of Milliard, ripped off Milliard's shirt, wadded it, and with it applied pressure to the wound, which over time began to staunch the flow of blood. "I'm sorry, Bush, I'm sorry," Israel said. "You leave me . . . go on after him."

"I'll not leave you here to bleed to death."

"Then stuff the wounds full of rifle patching, wrap something around it, put me on a horse, and I'll go back."

"You'll never make it."

"Bush, one time I crawled ten miles through a blizzard with a broke leg and no shoes, and lost nothing but half a toe. I'll make it. I saw Juniper Morgan running off afoot. You think he's got a horse hid out?"

"I suspect so. They probably hid them in the woods before they went up the knoll to set the ambush."

"Then take Milliard's horse—it's faster than mine or yours. Go after him."

"He knows me, Beck. By sight at least. He remembered me from the flatboat, and they apparently count me as killing the young one even though it was really the river that got him."

"I heard."

"The blood's slowing, Beck. You sure you can make it back?"

"Want me to tell my blizzard story again?"

"No. Come on, then. We'll get you up on your horse. You go straight on back, and let Lorry Squire patch you. I'll be back quick as I can."

"The Morgan up on the hill . . ."

"Trey. He's dead."

"Only three of them left alive now."

"That's right. God speed to you, Beck."

"And even more to you. Don't let him get away, Bush."

Indeed Juniper Morgan had retrieved a hidden horse. Bush found the tracks on the trail and followed them. Juniper didn't make any obvious effort to hide them. Maybe he thought he'd shaken Bush off at the knoll.

Bush sensed an advantage. If he could advance quickly enough, keeping to the trail while it was fresh but not alerting Juniper Morgan that he was followed, he might find where Morgan was bound, and maybe the remaining Morgans, and maybe even *her*.

Keep your mind clear, Bushrod. Don't let yourself get over-run with thoughts about what, about who *you might find. You get careless, you'll end up like Jim Lusk, like Milliard. Just keep going, and keep your mind clear.*

He kept riding, following the track of Juniper Morgan.

Bush slid out of the saddle and tied his weary horse in a thicket. Keeping low and his rifle ready, he trotted into the trees, then to the edge of the brush that extended to the bank of the river.

He hid there behind a thick patch of saplings, looked across the water, and watched Juniper Morgan poling a small raft across toward an island in the middle of the river. The horse, tethered to the raft, swam behind him.

On the near bank of the island a man watched Juniper Morgan's raft approaching. Bush squinted, trying to see him across the distance. Blast it! Too far away.

But wait . . .

He rose and went back to the horse. Milliard's horse, actually; Bush had taken Israel's advice and chosen the swiftest mount. He'd noticed Milliard tucking something into the bag on his saddle earlier.

Bush found it. A folding spyglass, nautical variety. He ran back to where he'd been, reaching the spot just in time to see Juniper Morgan reaching the bank of the island. Bush extended the spyglass and through it watched Juniper exiting the raft, talking to the man—the eldest Morgan, Zachary—gesturing and exclaiming, telling Zachary that he'd lost yet another brother, and that the fault belonged to the same man who'd fought Coley atop the flatboat shelter. Through the spyglass Bush could see Zachary's expression changing, darkening, as he listened to the message.

Someone came out of the trees toward the center of the island. Bush swung the glass and watched the remaining Morgan brother, Rafe, join the others and receive the same news. Whereas Zachary had reacted with stiff, cold anger, Rafe displayed a wild physical response, kicking the gravel at his feet, flinging his arms like he was throwing punches, gesticulating angrily. Juniper threw his hands up helplessly, said something, then saw to his dripping, exhausted horse.

Bush lowered the glass. He'd been hunting the Morgans; how long now until the Morgans began to hunt him? He'd killed Trey today, and, in their interpretation of the facts, Coley on the flatboat.

They didn't know his name, but they did know his face, and that he was here along the Missouri.

Let them come, he thought. *I'd welcome the opportunity to give to them the same treatment they gave to Cephas.*

* * *

And then, she was there.

Bush turned his head and saw her, standing on the island, well away from the men. Her hair was dark and flowing, her arms crossed in front of her; her long skirt moved in the wind as she stared across the water, seemingly just looking for its own sake. Even without the glass he could see a pensive quality in her pose.

The glass. He closed his eyes a moment; then, trembling, raised the glass to his eye.

He adjusted it, bringing the view of her into focus.

Even before he saw the dark mark on the side of her neck he knew it was Marie. The face, though matured by the years, was the same beautiful countenance he'd known in Coldwater. She was the same girl he'd defended while she was still in her crib in a cabin where their parents lay dead.

Bush watched her until his eyes became blurred and wet, and he could see her no more.

He stood, not thinking of the Morgans now. She was there, before his eyes, after all these years of wondering and searching. He'd not turn and walk away, leaving her with *them*.

Bush rose, looked around, and found a log section that had broken away from a deadfall, slightly rotted, but strong enough to hold him, light enough to float. He carried it to the bank and put it in the water. Then, laying his rifle atop it and holding it there as he clung to the log, he pushed out into the water and began kicking toward the island.

He heard their voices, shouting. They'd seen him.

I'm doing it again, he thought. *Just like at the flatboat . . . heading right for them, across the water.*

But this time they knew more of him, and were more ready. He saw Rafe running back into the trees and returning with rifles, while Juniper pushed the raft into the water again.

Bush, clinging to the log, looked at Marie. She watched him, unnerved, and ran away.

"Marie!" he called. "No! No! Come back!"

She turned to look at him, puzzled and afraid, then vanished into the trees.

When she was gone, Bush mentally pulled back, and examined what he was doing. He realized he'd been overwhelmed by the shock of seeing Marie again. If he kept up this approach, he'd be dead before he reached the island, or if not, dead as soon as he did.

They were on the raft now, pushing off and poling his way.

Bush began to turn, a terribly slow process. He kicked toward the shore.

On the raft, Zachary had taken position in the middle of the craft, raising his rifle, aiming.

Bush let go of the log, and his own rifle, and slid beneath the surface. His clothing, water-logged, seemed to be sucking him down, trying to hold him there. He swam in the direction of the bank.

He heard a muffled crack; something passed fast through the water, leaving a spiraled trail that broke up instantly into miniature bubbles shooting upward.

He dived deeper and swam harder.

Bush went as far as he could, then headed for the surface, desperate for air. He broke the top of the water.

"There he is!"

Another shot, the bullet passing just over his head. He sucked in air and went under again.

When he came up next, he was almost at the bank. The raft had veered off in a different direction, the Morgans apparently having lost sight of him.

Bush swam to the bank and climbed up. Another shot almost hit him. He pulled himself over the crest of the bank, came to his feet, and ran for his horse.

In that, at least, he had an advantage. Their horses were on the island; his was here.

He mounted and rode hard, hearing them shouting and crashing through the brush, looking for him.

Bush bent low over the horse's neck, riding hard. For now, he'd lost them.

And he'd seen her. With his own eyes, he'd seen Marie.

CHAPTER THIRTY-ONE

They'd buried the dead near Bush and Israel's little cabin. Coming out the door with a bit of bread in his hand, Bush saw Lorry standing beside the grave of Willie Squire, her back to Bush, her hands clasped in front of her and her head bowed. Bush finished the bread, dusted the crumbs from his face, newly clean-shaven, and went to her.

"I'm mighty sorry about your husband, Lorry," he said. "Though Willie and I didn't meet in the best of ways, I know he was a good man, and all he did he did because he cared so much for you."

"He was a good man," she said softly. "I'll miss him."

"It's a sad thing to see any woman made a widow, and especially one so young as you."

"I'm not a widow," she said.

"I don't understand."

Lorry looked at Bushrod. "Willie wasn't my husband. He was my brother."

Bush said nothing, but his face showed his confusion.

"Bushrod, Sariah was conceived in a rape. Her father, in the physical sense, is Zachary Morgan."

"Lord, Lorry . . ."

"Perhaps I shouldn't have told you that, because it might affect the way you look at my daughter. Please don't let it. She's still my child, and I love her dearly. She isn't to blame for who fathered her or how it happened."

"Yes. I know."

"It happened in Kentucky. The Morgans had come back off

the river for a while, probably running from trouble. Zachary Morgan caught me alone, doing washing at a stream.''

"I'm sorry."

"Sariah was born the next year. By then Willie and I had lost our parents. We decided, finally, to leave Kentucky, where so much bad had happened. We came here to start over. Along the way here, Willie and I found people assumed he was my husband because of the baby and because our last names were the same. It came to us that we should just let people go on thinking that way.''

"And Willie lived in fear that the Morgans would turn up again . . . and that's why he attacked me that day.''

"Yes. He had nightmares about them. So do I, to this day.''

Playing on intuition, Bush asked, "Lorry, how did your parents die?''

"In a fire. The family cabin. Willie tried hard to save them, but he couldn't.''

"A fire started by accident?''

"We never knew. Willie always believed the Morgans did it, trying to get rid of me and the baby Zachary Morgan had fathered.''

Bush could find nothing proper to say in the face of such a dreadful matter. He pondered it, hating the Morgans all the more deeply by the moment.

They looked at Willie's grave a few moments more, saying nothing. Bush spoke at last. "I found Marie.''

"Your sister?''

"Yes. I saw her, with the Morgans. It was her . . . her face the same, and the birthmark.''

"Oh, Bush! What will you do?''

"I have to find a way to get her back. I even tried to reach her on the island, but that was a foolish thing. I should have waited, but I was so overwhelmed to see her that I lost my good sense for a few minutes. And the Morgans heard me call her name, so now they know that I know her, though they can't know she's my sister.''

"Will you go back? Take men and look for her?''

"I will. But they won't be there. After all this, they'll leave that island and go somewhere else."

"Oh, Bush, you must find her. You must. I can't imagine what she's surely suffered, being with those foul men, being sold by them like meat—"

"Please, Lorry."

"I'm sorry."

Bush looked at her. "I love you, you know."

She smiled. "Yes. I know."

"I want you to marry me, Lorry. I want to be your husband, and Sariah's father. I don't care about how her birth happened. She's a lovely child, and I love her dear."

Lorry looked at Willie's grave, and a tear slid down her face.

"Will you marry me, Lorry Squire?"

She nodded. "Yes. I'll marry you."

Bush pulled her to him and kissed her. "I love you, Lorry."

"And I love you, Bush."

When Israel had returned from the Morgan pursuit, Lorry had patched up his wounds. But now, as Bush examined them, he was concerned. A dark line was beginning to form above the bullet wound on Israel's leg, extending up his leg and growing longer by the hour.

"It ain't good, Bush," Israel said. "I saw the same thing happen to my own father when he cut an arm. When that dark line reached all the way up into his head, he grew sick and feverish. And then he died."

"We can't let that happen to you, Becker."

"What can we do beyond cutting off the leg?"

"We may have to, but there's something I want to try first. Something Granny Tork gave me as she died."

"One of them remedies of hers?"

"Yes, I know it's probably nothing but rubbish, but it surely helped me when I was down. It can't hurt."

When Beck Israel saw the Eden box, he shook his head. "Dirt. You're going to stuff dirt into a wound that's already putrefying, and expect it to help me."

"No, not in the wound. I'm going to have you eat a bite of it. I did when I was laid up at her place, and that trap bruise healed up twice as fast as I thought it would. Granny told me this dirt was—well, never mind. It sounds a little hard to believe. But worth a try, anyway."

"I'm willing. I don't want to lose my leg. But if I get bad, turn madman from fever and such, you take it off for me."

"I will."

Israel got the spoonful of dirt down with the help of a cup of water. Wincing at the gritty texture, he lay back while Bush rebandaged his leg. "I suppose we'll see what happens now."

With a sizeable band of armed men, Bush rode back to the island. They found the Morgans' raft at the riverside and took it across. As Bush expected, the Morgans were gone.

In the interior of the island, however, they found a rough cabin that apparently had been the Morgan dwelling for whatever time they'd been hidden here. Bush explored it, thinking of Marie, and wondering where she was now.

They attempted to find a sign to indicate which direction the Morgans had traveled, but the tracks had been covered. They might have gone anywhere, one of the men with Bush said.

Bush agreed, but kept a private thought: The Morgans, wherever they had gone, had probably not gone overly far away. He'd seen the intensity with which they'd come after him while he was in the river.

They wouldn't go far. Because now they wanted the hide of Bushrod Underhill far too badly.

He'd find them again. Or they'd find him.

The dark line was already almost entirely gone from Beck Israel's leg the day that Bush and Lorry stood side-by-side and took their vows before a traveling preacher. Israel was strong enough to stand up through the ceremony, and to enjoy greatly the shivaree that followed.

That night, as Bush lay at Lorry's side in the cabin she and her brother had built, she stroked his chest gently. "This is as things ought to be, Bush. The way a man and woman ought to be with one another. Not like what your sister is probably having to live with.''

''I know. I've thought the same thing this very night.''

''You've got to find her and bring her back, Bush. She'll be welcome here. She'll be my sister, too, and I'll understand the things she feels. Because I've suffered at the same hands she has.''

''I will find her. No matter what it takes, or costs.''

Lorry pulled away. ''Don't say that.''

''What?''

''About what it might cost. Because as much as I want to see her free of the Morgans, I'm not willing to lose you for it.''

''I don't intend you shall.''

''Willie didn't intend to die, either.''

''Hush, Lorry. This isn't a thing to talk about tonight.'' He kissed her.

Sometime before dawn, he heard Lorry moaning in her sleep, then she cried out. ''No! No . . .''

Bush didn't sleep the rest of the night. He knew what terrible thing she was dreaming about, and who.

He made a vow, to himself. He'd not give up the quest until Marie was safe, and Zachary Morgan, who haunted his wife's dreams even on the night of her marriage, was dead.

Beck Israel, thoroughly recovered from his wounds, traveled down the river to St. Louis a month later to explore the opportunity of buying interest in a boat and planning a major pelt-gathering expedition up the river the next winter. Though he could sell the pelts in St. Louis, he had in mind the possibility of carrying them all the way to Natchez or New Orleans. With his partner now married and no longer the footloose fellow he'd been, Israel was growing restless for a journey.

He returned from St. Louis ahead of schedule, and with his hand wrapped in cloth. Before Lorry and the other locals, he joked about having cut himself with his own hatchet, while building a sleep shelter one recent night. But he called Bush aside at first opportunity and told him the truth.

"This cut was give to me by a knife, Bush. Zachary Morgan's knife."

"You saw them?"

"I did. They're in St. Louis. Don't know where they're living there, but they were in a tavern, Zachary, Rafe, and Juniper. And Bush . . . I saw Marie."

"She's alive? Well?"

"Alive. But I've never seen a sadder woman. And she was bruised. They've been hurting her, Bushrod."

Bush closed his eyes a moment, a wave of hatred and fury passing through him.

"Tell me what happened."

Israel outlined the story. He'd entered a tavern one night after haggling over the boat all that afternoon, and in the corner, he'd seen them. She was nearby, at a table, alone, and the Morgans were talking to another man. What they were bargaining for was obvious, because the man kept casting hungry glances in Marie's direction.

Israel had gone to her and even tried to snatch her away, but she'd misunderstood his intention, and screamed. There had been no time to explain the truth before the Morgans were upon Israel. He'd bested both Juniper and Rafe with a couple of well-aimed blows with the flat of his hatchet, but Zachary had come after him with a knife. The fight had spilled from the tavern into an alley, and there Israel received the cut on his hand. Then a local constable showed up, called by the tavern keeper, and ended the fight. Israel and Zachary Morgan managed to evade the constable, and when Israel returned to search for Marie, she and the Morgans had vanished. Israel had been forced to flee, and had rushed as quickly as possible back up the river to tell Bush what he'd found.

"I've got to go there, Beck," Bush said. "This time I'm going to find her, and bring her home."

"I'm going with you."

"Figured you'd want to."

"You'll tell Lorry?"

Bush thought about it. "We'll tell her it's business. That I'm thinking of going in with you on that boat, and need to look it over."

"Think she'll believe you?"

"No."

And she didn't. But she didn't argue. She watched her husband gathering weapons and food and supplies, and Bush knew that she knew.

"Come back safe, husband," she said, kissing him.

"I will," he promised.

"Do you think you'll get all your business settled?"

"Yes. I don't think I'll be coming back until I do."

She kissed him. As he and Israel departed, Bush looked back and lifted his hand. She lifted hers as she stood before their home, Sariah at her side. Bush saw the tears on Lorry's face and felt an urge to return to her—but he rode on.

It was time to bring his sister home at last.

CHAPTER
THIRTY-TWO

It was nearly dusk the day they reached St. Louis, the great city of trade and travel that linked the more civilized nation on one side and the dark frontier on the other.

Weary from travel, Bush and Israel did nothing that first night but find a good inn with warm and clean beds and a well-laden table. They dined well, but Bush tasted little of what he ate. His mind was already on the confrontation that would come.

Bush anticipated poor rest that night, considering the turning of his mind. In fact he slept well, a hard and dreamless rest. Yet when he awakened he still felt tired, and the day's looming search for the Morgans, and Marie, hung heavy above him, like rain clouds.

Having nothing else to go on, they began the search by going back to the inn where Israel had first seen the brothers. Bush went in alone to inquire, fearing the innkeeper might remember Israel from the earlier brawl and be uncooperative. Fortunately, the innkeeper proved willing to answer Bush's questions, though he unfortunately knew very little. Yes, he did know the Morgans, good customers, prone to drink too heavily and get lewd with his tavern maid, but he put up with them because they always put their money down before asking for a drink, never even asking to run up a bill on credit like so many others. But no, he had no idea where they could be found—wait a moment, maybe he did at that. It seemed that once he heard one of the brothers, a fellow named Rafe, he thought, talking of work he was doing on a damaged boat. He might be a boat's carpenter, and if so, he could probably be found somewhere along the riverfront.

So to the landing they went, and Israel looked about, trying to spot any face that looked familiar. He saw no one. Inquiring casually, they found that Rafe Morgan did indeed work some at the landing as a repairer of damaged craft, but he hadn't been about in two or three days and no one could or would say where he might be located.

They pursued meager clues all around the city for the full day, achieving little. By sunset, Bush was frustrated and concerned. Such intensive searching and questioning couldn't fail to rouse some curiosity and perhaps news would get back to the Morgans themselves. It might even make the Morgans do some searching of their own. He dreaded badly enough the idea of finding them; to be found by them first would be worse.

But if it happened, let it happen. When he thought of Lorry while she was still a Kentucky mountain girl, being raped by Zachary Morgan, he felt a strength rooted in pure anger. He'd fight all three of the brothers to the very gates of hell if he had to.

Weary and dispirited by their lack of progress, Bush and Israel made for a quiet-looking inn to have a meal and a tankard or two. Perhaps they'd make the rounds of all the taverns they could find tonight in hopes that the Morgans, like bats, might be more easily found by night than day.

Israel was especially weary, and his color was bad. Bush noticed him favoring that injured hand more than he should, and asked him if it was going bad on him like those prior wounds had.

"No, no. Already starting to heal," he said, a little too fast, and unconvincingly.

"Beck, if that wound's bad, then you leave. Go back home as quick as you can, and get Lorry to treat you like we treated you before. I didn't bring Granny's box with me."

"Don't fret over me," Israel said. "I'm fine."

Bush could look at him and see that he wasn't. "A Morgan gave you that wound, Beck. If you let it go bad and kill you, that means you died at a Morgan's hand. Don't let that happen.''

"I ain't going to die. Now just shut up about it.''

"Let me see that hand?''

"No.''

Bush wasn't quite sure what sparked the problem between Israel and the drunkard who came wandering into the inn halfway through the meal. Bush had taken a moment to step out back to empty his bladder, and on his return saw Israel and a loud stranger shoving one another. The table was overturned already, their half-eaten meals dumped across the floor.

As misfortune would have it, a constable happened to be outside on the street, and entered when he heard the sounds of the fray. Bush had been heading up to help Israel out, but stopped short when the constable got there first.

"You!" he said into Israel's face. "I've dealt with you for fighting once already, I do believe!"

Oh, no, Bush thought. This is the same constable who'd intervened in the fight between Beck and Zachary Morgan.

The constable obviously saw Israel as a troublemaker—and Bush couldn't blame him, after having found the same man in two separate brawls—and hauled him off as a peace-breaker. Bush followed, arguing with the constable, pleading for his partner to be given a second chance, but the constable was angry and obstinate. He informed Bush that he'd have his partner back the next day, after a good night in jail to give him time to calm down and sober up.

Alone now, Bush headed back to the inn where he would sleep tonight. There would be no further search for the Morgan brothers tonight.

Because he had gotten turned about while following the constable and Israel, it took him some time to find the inn. When he did, there was a man in the shadows near the door, who stepped toward him as he approached.

Bush came close enough to see the man's face, and stopped. They'd found him.

*   *   *

"My name's Rafe Morgan," the man said. "They tell me you been asking around after me and my brothers today."

"So I have."

"Who are you?"

"My name's Underhill," Bush replied.

"I know you. You killed my brother Trey on up the river. And my brother Coley before that."

"Two things. First, your brother Trey was trying to ambush me and my companions. And I didn't kill Coley. A sharp sawyer took care of that bit of business."

"All the same, it wouldn't have happened but for you."

"I don't expect you're looking for me to tell you I'm sorry he died. Because I ain't."

"Didn't figure you were. Tell me: are you really chasing us just because of that nigger Coley and Trey killed?"

"That's reason enough. But there's other reasons."

"When you was splashing across toward the island, you'd called the name of Marie. How you know her?"

Bush now wished he hadn't called Marie's name that day. He didn't want the Morgans to realize that she was the central object of his quest, because they might spirit her off to someplace where he'd never hope to find her.

All he could do was try to evade, and play an imperfect hand the best he could. "I'll talk no more to you. It's Zachary Morgan I want to see."

"What do you want with Zack?"

"That'll be between me and him."

"You know Zack?"

"Never met the man. But he's been the cause of a lot of hurt for some people I care a lot about."

"What are you talking about?"

"I'll talk about it to Zack Morgan and no other. Does he always hide behind you?"

Rafe chuckled coldly; there was a threat in the mere sound of it. "Zack don't behind nothing. I come here myself because I was told it was me you asked after at the boat landing this morning."

"So we did, but only because we thought you might lead us to Zack."

The man's eyes flicked about. "Where's your partner?"

"Maybe he's watching from the dark. Maybe he's got a gun trained on your heart right now."

"Maybe he got hauled off by the constable, too. Maybe I seen it happening."

"Where's Zack?"

"You want to see Zack, do you? You ain't going to see him alone."

"I'll see him no other way. This is between me and him."

"There's something you'll learn if you muck about with the Morgan brothers. We stay close, and we fight each other's battles. You've killed two of us, and your life is over, my friend."

"Maybe I'll be killing some other Morgans before I'm through."

That one made Rafe mad, and Bush was glad of it. "I'll take you to Zack," Rafe said. "We'll see who kills who."

"I ain't going."

"What? You said you want to see him, I said I'd take you to him. You turning coward all at once?"

"No, and neither am I turning fool. Three men against one ain't the best of chances. You go to your brother, Rafe. Tell him that unless he's a dung-eating, coward dog, he'll come here tonight and meet me, man to man, one to one. And if he don't, Bush Underhill knows that he's worse than a rake, that he's a trembling coward too."

Rafe shot out a finger and aimed it at Bush's nose. "Them's words you'll live to regret."

"You tell him. Him and me, that's all." He paused, then spoke further. "Tell him it's for a Kentucky girl named Lorry Squire."

The narrow eyes narrowed a little more. "So this is about that little trollop, is it?"

Bush barely restrained himself. His body lunged forward of its own accord, his hands rising to reach for the offender's throat. But somehow in the explosion of white anger that cast a flash of light across his vision, he held back. He needed Rafe Morgan unhurt, to deliver the message to where it truly belonged. Struggling against his own fury, he pulled back, breathing hard.

"You tell him to come, alone. Tell him to come, or the world will know that he's a coward!"

Rafe nodded. "He'll be here. And you'll wish he wasn't."

Bush had no more to say. He walked past the man into the inn, jostling him hard and deliberately. Rafe Morgan muttered obscene words after him, then turned and was gone in the St. Louis darkness.

As Bush waited in his darkened room, seated on a stool, looking out the window onto the street, he wondered if he'd erred in telling Rafe Morgan his name, and mentioning Lorry. Knowledge could give a man an edge, and he'd just given the Morgans a bit more knowledge.

What if Marie heard the name of Bush Underhill called? How might she react? If she revealed their kinship, the Morgans might make use of her as a hostage to manipulate him and protect themselves. For that matter, they might do the same anyway, simply because he'd made the mistake of calling out her name that day at the river island.

Blast it all—he'd not handled this matter as he should.

Something was out there. No. Someone. Bush realized that he'd been seeing the unmoving form for nearly a minute now, a figure that had slipped in so carefully and subtly that he hadn't detected it at first.

He stood and looked down, wondering if the dark room fully hid him or if he, like the man below, was a phantom shape to other eyes. Bush stepped back, checked the pistol beneath his coat and the knife sheathed in his boot, and left the room. Down the ladder to the lower level of the inn he went, then out the door, walking toward the dark figure outside. He stopped ten paces away.

"Zack Morgan?"

"That's right, Mr. Underhill. Tell me, how's the little Squire gal faring?"

Bush stared at him.

Zack Morgan laughed. Bush burned to hear it. "Bet she dreams about me. I gave her a fine gift one time back in Kentucky. Oh, that was a day! She's a pretty thing, she is. Quite the little trollop."

Bush knew what he was doing. Trying to anger him. Make him lose his control.

"I hear her brother died right tragic the other day."

"I hear two of yours did. I had a bit of a hand in it, you may recall."

"Go to hell."

"No. That's what you'll be doing, very soon."

"What'd you come here for?"

"To kill you."

"You want a chance to try?"

"Where and how?"

"A big storehouse down by the landing. Empty just now, and locked, but I know of a loose shutter and a busted glass. You and me. Knives."

"Where's your brothers?"

"Nowhere near. I told them to stay away. You, I can handle by myself."

Bush wondered if it were true, or if even now they lingered out in the dark, watching, making sure that their brother took no disadvantage. But Bush saw no option but to accept Morgan's terms.

"Let's go," he said. "Show me the place where you want to die."

Bush and Zack Morgan walked side by side through the dark city, down to the broad Missouri river and the boat landing with its docks and wharfs. All the way Bush kept his hand on his pistol, just waiting for Morgan to make some treacherous move, but it never happened.

The warehouse seemed vast once they had gone inside, and when Morgan built a fire from scraps on a slab of metal lying on the wooden floor, the empty space seemed to grow even larger.

Morgan grinned. Unendingly. His face was handsome and ugly at the same time. He would not drop his gaze from Bush. No sense of guilt in this man. No fear. This was fun for him.

"Strip down," he said. "I'll not fight a man with a shirt that can snag my blade."

They bared themselves from the waist up. Morgan provided the knives—keen blades, made for both slicing and stabbing. "I'll give you the sharpest. I can kill you as easy with a dull blade," he said.

By firelight they stood facing one another. Bush staring. Morgan grinning.

"I could tell you how I'm the toughest gator ever swum, the meanest babe ever to drink hot whiskey, but I doubt you much care to hear it."

"Never was keen on fighting banter," Bush said. "Just gets in the way of doing business."

"Then let's get at it."

They moved together, blades glinting in the light of the fire.

CHAPTER THIRTY-THREE

Sweat mixed with blood and stung Bush's eyes. His breath was coming hard, his legs weary and trembling. But still he fought.

He'd lost track of how long they'd been at it, knives slashing in the air, often missing, but sometimes cutting flesh. Zack Morgan, like his youngest brother on that flatboat, was a grinner—his smile glinted in the light of the fire, making him seem something not fully human. Bush did not smile. He was a man driven by fury. He lacked experience in knife-fighting, but his will compensated for much.

In time, Zachary Morgan's smile faded. Sweat pouring off him, he stood in a crouched fighter's stance, the knife in his right hand like a deadly sting, his left hand curved and held out for balance.

"You're . . . determined . . . I'll say that . . . for you," Zachary said, waving the knife in Bush's direction.

"I'm going to kill you, Morgan," Bush replied. "Even if you kill me, the moment that blade cuts my heart, my knife will be in yours."

"The hell—" Morgan lunged and probed. Bush felt the sting of another cut, but a glance showed it to be minor. He summoned up his will and forced out a contemptuous laugh.

Around the dark perimeter where the light of the fire faded away in the blackness of the huge and empty building, Bush saw movement. The other Morgan brothers. He should have known that Zachary Morgan wouldn't fight him without treachery.

"What is it, Morgan? You afraid to face me alone?"

"I ain't . . . afraid of nobody."

"You're gasping for air, Morgan. What's wrong? Getting weary?" Bush slashed and nipped some flesh off Morgan's arm. "You know what happens to fighters who get weary? They die. Like you're going to die."

"I die . . . and my brothers . . . will kill you anyway."

"Let them try."

Talk ceased for another five minutes as the fight intensified. More slashes, more cuts, but neither man went down. The floor became slick with blood and they slid about as they grappled.

Juniper Morgan stepped in closer, a knife in his own hand. "Let me spell you, Zack," he said. "Let me finish him for you."

"No . . . no . . . he's mine . . ."

"He's wearing you down, Zack." Juniper pushed his panting brother aside and took his place.

"Come on, you piece of dung, see if you can get a bit of *me*!"

"Another grinner, I see," Bush said. "You may have noticed that Zachary ain't grinning no more."

"Shut up and fight."

Juniper, rested and full of energy, advanced upon Bush. Bush grunted in pain as the knife cut a slit across his belly. More blood gushed, running down his front, his legs, slickening the floor even more.

Juniper laughed. "A thumb's width deeper, and you'd be collecting your innards off the floor!" He came on hard at Bush . . . and slipped in the blood. His feet flew up and he came down on his back.

Bush descended upon him and rammed his knife into Juniper's heart once, twice, three times. Bush pulled the blade free the final time and backed off. Juniper's face was frozen in an expression of horror that slowly faded out, softened in death.

Bush shoved the corpse aside with his foot, plucked the knife from the dead hand, and tossed it toward Zachary.

"Come on, Zachary. Or have you lost your courage?"

Zachary shouted, "Rafe! Come in here—kill him for me!"

Rafe backed away. "It's your fight, Zack. You finish it."

Zachary Morgan cursed his brother bitterly, took up the knife, and moved slowly in. Bush stared into his eyes, letting Morgan see the hatred and determination there.

"Why?" Morgan asked. "What do you care . . . about that little Squire gal?"

"Because she's my wife," he said. "Because I hear her groaning and crying in the night, going through what you did to her again and again, in her dreams."

Zachary actually managed another grin, feebly. "I told you she probably still dreamed about me!"

Bush closed in. It was time to finish this. Zachary managed to cut him, but without much effect. Bringing up his left fist, Bush struck Morgan unexpectedly on the jaw. He shook and slumped back, waving his knife wildly. Bush slashed Morgan's arm. Morgan fell to his knees and Bush moved in, driving the blade deep into Morgan's chest and pulling it out again.

Bush withdrew, watching Zachary Morgan stare at the blood spurting from his own chest, a disbelieving look on his face. He lifted his head slowly and stared at Bush, silent.

"That was for Lorry . . . for Cephas Frank . . . for Willie Squire . . . for all the people you and your brothers have hurt through the years. But mostly that was for Marie."

Zachary Morgan looked bewildered. "Marie?"

"That's right. My sister."

Morgan's eyes glazed. He pitched straight forward, face down in the blood smearing the floor. His handed tightened around the grip of his knife, twice, then relaxed.

Bush looked around for Rafe Morgan, but did not see him. Then something hard and very hot struck the back of his head and he fell.

Twisting, he saw Rafe Morgan behind him. He'd just struck Bush with a heavy piece of burning wood pulled from the fire that had lighted the battle.

Bush tried to get up, but the brand descended again, striking his head, sending hot sparks down his body.

Rafe Morgan, cursing, brought it up again. Bush twisted one more time and thrust the knife into Rafe's belly, one quick, deep jab.

Morgan screamed and backed away, still holding the burning brand. He cursed at Bush and staggered off into the darkness.

Bush tried to rise, but his vision went white, and he passed out, senseless, on the bloody floor, looking like the two corpses that already lay there.

He awoke in smoke and heat. Weak, head throbbing and spinning, body numb and bloody, he tried to rise but fell. Coughing, choking, he tried again, and this time succeeded.

The warehouse was aflame. Hot, dancing light filled it, but it was lost in a thick and boiling smoke that made the air hardly breathable, robbing its oxygen, filling it with acrid and hot fumes.

Bush staggered away from the worst of the flames, realizing that the fire seemed to be heaviest not around the bonfire on the floor, but off in the direction in which Rafe Morgan had staggered away.

He must have dropped that hot brand he'd been carrying. It had caught something ablaze, and the fire was spreading through the entire structure.

Bush tried to regain his orientation. Where was the door? He couldn't remember, and in the thickening smoke, could not see. He sucked in the best air he could find, and plunged off into the smoke, away from the flames.

It was like being lost in some nightmare of hell. He could see nothing, and he could not breathe. His body, already weak, threatened to fail him and drop him to the floor again. He refused to let it. If he fell he wouldn't get up again.

He ran bodily into a solid wall. Laying his hands flat against it, he let it hold some of his weight, and began edging along it, hoping to find a door.

He heard a scream. A woman. Muffled and faint, but full of terror.

"Marie . . ."

He tried to ascertain from which direction the scream had come. To the right, he believed. He edged along the wall, and found a door.

Another scream. On the other side of the door.

"Marie!"

Bush tried to open the door and found it locked. Yelling in frustration, he withdrew into the smoke, then rammed forward, driving his shoulder into the thin, nearly rotten timbers. The door shattered into splinters, his shoulder poking through. He went back, rammed again, breaking away more of it, then a third time, and then the opening was big enough for him to get through.

It was a small room, empty of furniture. But she was inside, huddled against the far wall, terrified of the smoke, the heat—and of him.

He staggered toward her and fell at her side, on his knees. She screamed and pulled away, burying her face.

"Marie . . . Marie . . . it's me . . ."

She was crying hard, not looking at him.

"It's me, Marie . . . Bushrod . . . your brother."

She raised her head, slowly, and looked at him. Somehow, in the midst of all this hell, he managed to smile at her. "It's your brother, Marie. I've come to take you away."

"Bushrod?" She whispered it. Looked closely at him. "Bushrod!" She threw her arms around him and wept.

He wept, too. But there was no time to linger.

"We have to get out of here, Marie. Come on."

"Zack . . ."

"He's dead. So is Juniper. Rafe . . . I don't know."

"Zack . . . dead . . ."

"Yes. He can't hurt you anymore."

She wept harder, and despite the danger of the moment, Bush felt her body relax as the deepest of relief swept through her.

He picked her up and carried her out the door, into the smoke and heat.

*   *   *

Bush wasn't sure how he found his way out, but he did. A door, partly ajar, let the fresh air in, sucked in by the inferno. He shoved it farther open with his foot and carried Marie out. For a long time he simply walked, the direction unimportant, as long as it was away from the fire.

He laid her down in an alley near the river, then sat down wearily, leaning back against the wall, panting, closing his eyes. She sat up and scooted back against the wall opposite him, and stared at him.

Bush opened his eyes and looked back at her. From somewhere inside, a small laugh rose, then built. She heard it, smiled, and in a moment she laughed, too. They sat there, looking at one another, laughing in the joy of deliverance and reunion.

"It really is you," she said.

"It really is."

"Things have been hard for you these past years, I think."

"Yes, very hard."

"Not anymore. All is going to be well now. You're safe. You're with me. You're free."

She bowed her head, and the laughter mixed with tears.

Israel was in the room at the inn when they arrived, lying on the bed, looking very weak. He stared at Bush, who was shirtless, bloodied, blackened by smoke, then at Marie.

"I'll be," he said, weakly. "I'll be. You found her."

"I did."

"The Morgans?"

"Gone. All dead but one, and maybe he is, too. But I don't know."

"Thank God."

"How'd you get out of that constable's hands so fast, Beck?"

"Because I'm sick . . . he didn't want me around, afraid I'd die on him . . . let me go."

"The hand?"

"Yes."

Bush went to Israel and removed the bandage. He stared in

shock at the putrid, infected thing it revealed. Bush looked at
Marie.

"We've got to get him home, and quickly."

Bush washed off as best he could in a bucket of water that
served as the room's basin. Marie curled onto Bush's bed and
slept. He couldn't stop staring at her, hardly able to believe
she was really with him at last.

Israel had him worried. He seemed to have gotten worse
even since Bush had reentered the room.

Dressing, Bush left and headed down to rouse the landlord
and have the horses brought out of the livery. He'd not wait
until morning to leave. Israel was in a bad way. Furthermore,
Bush didn't want to remain in St. Louis and face possible
delays if the local authorities somehow linked him with that
warehouse fire. Glancing out his window, Bush could see the
dancing light of the fire against the clouds, even though it was
far from where he was.

One good thing about it: a fire that hot would thoroughly
consume the corpses. It was likely that no one would ever find
any trace of the Morgans.

He wondered again about Rafe. Had he survived? If so,
would he bring trouble in the future? No way to know now.
He'd think about that another day.

Bush managed to dig up a couple of long poles, and with
a blanket taken from the inn, rigged a travois to carry Israel.
Marie, when stirred awake again, was at first fearful, then quietly joyous as she saw Bush and remembered that her situation
was utterly different now.

She was even more eager to leave this city than Bush was.

They set out before dawn, Bush so weary he could hardly
stay awake in the saddle. Marie rode the horse to which Israel's litter was tied. They traveled along the river, heading
upstream, toward home.

When morning came, Bush knew it was too late for Becker
Israel. The infection had thoroughly taken him. Bush consid-

ered amputation of the bad arm, but an examination showed that it was too late even for that.

They camped near the river for a day as Israel's condition worsened. He suffered much at first, but in the end he was mercifully unconscious. Bush sat by his side as he breathed his last.

Another partner, gone. Perhaps the best friend he'd ever had.

It was bitterly ironic to Bush that in death Zachary Morgan had managed to claim one last victim.

CHAPTER
THIRTY-FOUR

Lorry Underhill was at her spinning wheel when she heard the approach of riders. Rising, she looked out the cabin window.

"Oh, no . . ."

She saw a man on a horse, and a woman with him, also mounted. Dragging behind the woman's horse was a litter bearing the form of a man. Completely covered, as a corpse was covered.

"Oh, Lord, let it not be Bush, let it not be Bush . . ."

She ran outside, and was overwhelmed with joy as the riders drew closer and she saw that Bush was the man in the saddle. She ran to him as he slid down and opened his arms. Their embrace was long and emotional.

Lorry pulled back and studied his face, then glanced at the woman in the saddle, and the litter dragging behind.

"Beck?"

"I'm afraid so."

"Bush . . . how?"

"We'll talk about it later. There's somebody I want you to meet first."

Lorry went to the woman, who seemed afraid to dismount, looking back at Lorry warily. "Marie?"

The woman nodded, saying nothing.

Bush slipped his arm around Lorry's waist. "Marie, this is my wife, Lorry. She's a fine woman, and you two are going to get on quite well."

Marie smiled, fleeting and small, and looked away. Bush led Lorry to one side.

"She doesn't talk much. She's like someone who's been through a torture. It's going to take a long time, I think, before she's really the same again."

"I would have expected nothing different. We'll help her, Bush. We'll bring her back."

"Lorry, Zachary Morgan is dead. And Juniper. The other one may yet be living, but I don't know it for a fact. He was hurt and might have died, too."

"How did it happen?"

"It's a long story, and I'll get around to telling it soon enough. For now I'm just glad to see you again . . . and to let you know that you needn't fear Zachary Morgan anymore. You needn't dream about him. From now on, your dreams can be good ones."

Lorry closed her eyes and drew in a long, deep breath. "I love you, husband."

"I love you, too."

Lorry went back to Marie, who was still in the saddle, looking about in a way that reminded Lorry of a small animal in a cage. Lorry smiled at her. "You can come in now, Marie. This is where you belong, with us. You'll be safe here."

Marie looked at her, and slowly dismounted. Lorry slipped her arm around her and gave her a quick hug.

"You're home now, Marie. And it's all going to be different from now on."

Marie looked at the cabin, then at Lorry, and smiled.

"Thank you," she said.

"Come on inside," Lorry said. "I want you to meet Sariah, our daughter."

They walked to the cabin together. Bush watched them, and lifted his face briefly to the sky, giving a small, silent prayer of thanks. He walked after them into the cabin, and closed the door behind him.

TERRY C. JOHNSTON

THE PLAINSMEN

THE BOLD WESTERN SERIES FROM ST. MARTIN'S PAPERBACKS

COLLECT THE ENTIRE SERIES!

SIOUX DAWN (Book 1)
92732-0 _____$5.99 U.S. _____$7.99 CAN.

RED CLOUD'S REVENGE (Book 2)
92733-9 _____$5.99 U.S. _____$6.99 CAN.

THE STALKERS (Book 3)
92963-3 _____$5.99 U.S. _____$7.99 CAN.

BLACK SUN (Book 4)
92465-8 _____$5.99 U.S. _____$6.99 CAN.

DEVIL'S BACKBONE (Book 5)
92574-3 _____$5.99 U.S. _____$6.99 CAN.

SHADOW RIDERS (Book 6)
92597-2 _____$5.99 U.S. _____$6.99 CAN.

DYING THUNDER (Book 7)
92834-3 _____$5.99 U.S. _____$6.99 CAN.

BLOOD SONG (Book 8)
92921-8 _____$5.99 U.S. _____$6.99 CAN.